Lynne Francis grew up in Yorkshire but studied, lived and worked in London for many years. She draws inspiration for her novels from a fascination with family history, landscapes and the countryside.

Her first saga series was set in west Yorkshire but a move to east Kent, and the discovery of previously unknown family links to the area, gave her the idea for a Georgian-era trilogy. Lynne's exploration of her new surroundings provided the historical background for the novels, as well as allowing her to indulge another key interest: checking out the local teashops and judging the cake.

When she's not at her desk, writing, Lynne can be found in the garden, walking through the countryside or beside the sea.

By Lynne Francis

THE MARGATE MAID
A Maid's Ruin

THE MILL VALLEY GIRLS
Ella's Journey
Alice's Secret
Sarah's Story

Lynne FRANCIS

A Maid's Ruin

PIATKUS

PIATKUS

First published as *The Margate Maid* in Great Britain in 2020 by Piatkus
This paperback edition published in 2021 by Piatkus

1 3 5 7 9 10 8 6 4 2

Copyright © 2020 by Lynne Francis

The moral right of the author has been asserted.

A CIP catalogue record for this book
is available from the British Library.

ISBN 978-0-349-42459-0

Typeset in Caslon by M Rules
Printed and bound in Great Britain by Clays Ltd, Elcograf S.p.A.

Papers used by Piatkus are from well-managed forests
and other responsible sources.

Piatkus
An imprint of
Little, Brown Book Group
Carmelite House
50 Victoria Embankment
London EC4Y 0DZ

An Hachette UK Company
www.hachette.co.uk

www.littlebrown.co.uk

PART ONE

SPRING–SUMMER 1786

CHAPTER ONE

'What are you looking at?' Molly's tone sounded sharp, even to her ears.

The boy looked confused, as if trying to work out what he had done wrong. 'I'm drawing,' he said. 'Do you want to see?'

She glowered at him, but really it was her uncle William she was angry with, not this boy, whom she'd never seen before. His blond hair, wavy and long, was loosely pulled back into the collar of his brown wool jacket, a heavy lock falling over his forehead. He looked a little younger than she was and small for his age, perching on a tumbledown part of the wall with a book of paper on his knee. Truly, Molly thought, he hadn't done anything to deserve her anger. She moved a little closer and peered at what he was doing.

'Why, you've captured it well!' she exclaimed. She walked round him to stand at his shoulder and squinted at the church he was drawing.

'Where did you learn to do that?' she asked, unable to disguise her admiration.

The boy shrugged. 'I don't know. At school, I suppose. I've always been able to draw.'

'You go to school?' Molly felt cross again. She had wanted to learn but her father and uncle had said it was a waste of time. What need would she have of book learning? they asked. They already had a life mapped out for her: a milk-maid for her uncle and a dairymaid for her father, selling the milk to those who came by the stable-yard in Church Street. Married before she was twenty, no doubt, and a houseful of children to follow. It wasn't at all what she had in mind.

She was making her way to Church Street now from her uncle's barn, where she'd had a falling-out with him. He had said her bad temper at milking time was making the cows yield less, and accused her of spiteful squeezing of their teats. She could have told him that the poor yield was because they needed fresh pasture: the grass had been over-grazed and was no longer rich enough. But she was barely fourteen years old and he wasn't going to listen to her.

Molly had cut through the churchyard, hoping that the peace as she walked between the yew hedge and the grave-stones would calm her before she set to work in the Church Street dairy. Ahead of her was a morning of ladling out the milk from a great churn to whoever had the farthings to pay for it, while her father took the other churns on his rounds in the horse and cart.

She knew she was going to be late, but her admiration for what the boy was creating on the page had made her curious.

'I must go,' she said eventually, as the church clock struck eight. 'My father will wonder where I am.' She turned to leave, then stopped. 'What's your name?' she asked.

'Will. Will Turner.'

'Molly Goodchild,' she said, although he hadn't asked. 'Perhaps I'll see you again.'

Molly's day had begun before dawn, when she'd risen from her bed in the room she shared with her younger sisters, Lizzie and Mary, and crept down the stairs, boots clutched in her hand. The cows would be plodding towards her uncle's barn from the fields, and by the time she arrived they would be jostling for space, filling the air with their warmth and ripe smell. A mix of fresh grass, milk and muck, Molly thought wryly, as she sat on the bottom stair to lace up her boots. She hadn't even bothered to wash her face – she'd fallen into the habit of washing after her return from her morning's work, seeing little point in doing the job twice.

She closed the back door of the cottage behind her, then hurried through the yard and out into the alley that led into Charlotte Place. From there she could cut through the grounds of St John's Church and be at the field edge in no time. Molly pulled her shawl around her, glad of its warmth – even though it was spring it was still chilly so early in the morning. As she started to cross the field, fingers of light crept across the sky, released by the sun rising over the sea. She felt the damp strike through the thin soles of her boots and picked up her pace, welcoming the thought of the warmth of the cow barn.

The lowing of impatient cattle, waiting for their milkmaid, carried over the final stretch of field. Thomas, her uncle's cowman, shook his head as she all but ran the final stretch across the yard.

'He's not best pleased with ye,' he said as she passed, untying her bonnet and pulling off her shawl. Molly turned her head and stuck out her tongue, hearing Old Tom splutter with laughter just as she came face to face with Uncle William.

'Late again,' he said grimly. 'I told that feckless brother of mine I'd give him a hand when Sally died, Lord rest her soul, so I'd expect you to be grateful enough to get yourself here of a morning in good time.'

Molly had been about to offer an apology until her uncle had mentioned the death of her mother. She drew her brows into a frown, convinced that her long, wavy chestnut hair, now released from her bonnet, had fallen far enough across her face to disguise her scowl. But her uncle added, 'You'll be frightening the cows with that face on you. It looks set to freeze the blood.'

She ignored him, taking her smock down from the peg and hanging her bonnet and shawl in its place. Then she went to fetch the milking stool and the metal pail, settling herself in the nearest stall where a cow already waited. The bucket grated on the stone floor as she pulled it into position and the animal shifted uneasily. Molly rested her forehead against its warm flanks and tried to still the hammering of her heart. She was out of breath from hurrying and also furious at her uncle's words. She didn't want her feelings to transfer themselves to the cow, and to the rest of the herd. They were sensitive to mood and to the way they were treated. Molly forced her fingers to work rhythmically, uttering soothing words as accompaniment.

'I'm a bit late but we'll soon sort you out. Hmm? Hmm? No need to get into a bother, is there now?' The words were directed at the cow – but aimed at her uncle. Molly thought she'd kept her voice low, but he was hovering, watching her. His sharp ears caught her words.

'I'll not speak to you about it again, Molly. There's plenty of other girls around here who'd be glad of regular work. They'll be on time and work hard, without giving me and Old Tom any cheek.'

Molly made a face at the cow's flank. As the milk eased to a trickle, then ceased, she stood up, patted the animal's neck and emptied the milk into the churn before she took

6

her stool and milking pail to the next stall. It would be easier if there was more than one milkmaid, she was sure, but her uncle maintained his herd was too small to require it, so Molly worked her way along the five stalls, milking each cow in turn. Old Tom sent them back into the fields with a slap on the rump, then led in another to wait patiently in a stall.

Molly tried to calm herself and clear her mind. She didn't want to make the animals uneasy, and her own job harder. But the unfairness of her uncle's words stung.

CHAPTER TWO

I t was hardly her father John's fault that his wife had died, Molly thought. Her mother, Sally, had faded away after the birth of the youngest, christened Alfred but known to the family as Boy, and she'd died six months later. Boy had followed shortly after. Molly, aged nine, found herself mother to Lizzie and Mary and to her own father. He'd lost his job as a carpenter when her mother had died, grief and despair rendering him helpless and unable to concentrate.

His brother, Uncle William, had found him work at a corn merchant's, in a much lowlier post. William, who had been very fond of his sister-in-law, viewing her as the sensible one of the family, saw it as his duty to help his brother's family. He'd been furious when, three months into the new job, John had met Ann, a young woman barely ten years older than Molly, a farmer's daughter who delivered his sacks of grain to the corn merchant. John and Ann were married within the year and a baby was born not six months after.

Molly had heard her uncle shouting at her father when he'd told him of the marriage plans.

'So you couldn't wait, eh, John? Sally barely cold in her grave and you're having Ann up against the corn sacks?' Her father had shut the kitchen door after that so she didn't hear his reply, and Molly had pushed the little ones up the stairs to their bedroom so that they weren't upset by the quarrel.

Molly had mixed feelings about her new stepmother. She was grateful to have an extra pair of hands about the house but disliked the way that Ann hung on her father's every word. She monopolised his attention and seemed to want to sit on his knee just as much as Lizzie and Mary did. Of an evening, after they'd eaten their supper, she'd follow him around, draping her arm about his waist and whispering in his ear until Molly could bear the sight of it no more and took herself away. In summer, she'd go out to the fields and wander across them as the sun set, watching the rabbits at play, or she'd sit by the shallow pools of the Brooks, where dragonflies hovered and water voles plopped into the water at her approach. She returned as late as she dared, steeling herself for a scolding from her father for going off without a word. In winter, she'd turn her back on the pair of them, taking a basket of mending and going to sit by the fire. Or she'd take a candle up to her room with the one book that the house possessed, the Bible, trying to spell out the words there that she recognised.

It was hard to escape the influence that Uncle William had over Molly's family and their lives. He was their neighbour in Princes Crescent, along with his wife Jane and their three children. Although her uncle's house was next door, it was much grander than theirs. It sat in a terrace of five houses that stood high above their neighbours' much smaller and rather down-at-heel cottages. Each of those houses was set over three floors, with an additional basement – a sign to one and all that they could afford servants – and their drawing rooms were elevated above the street, giving them an airy outlook. Uncle William's house had a proper garden at the back, rather than a yard, with a lawn and flowerbeds. Aunt

Jane grew roses there and sometimes sat out on a summer's evening with her husband. Before Molly's mother had died, her family would occasionally join them, the children playing while the adults chatted. This hadn't happened since her mother's death, and Molly missed it.

Once John had remarried and Molly was needed less around the house, it had been Uncle William's decision that she must work. The position of milkmaid was less an offer, more of a command, and Molly was pretty sure that it suited her uncle's purpose very well and wasn't simply a charitable move on behalf of his brother's family. He'd also suggested to John that he should give up the job at the corn merchant's and work for him, distributing the milk produced by his cows. Demand had grown and he had increased his herd accordingly, shrewdly seeing a future business in the making.

Uncle William's proximity meant that she had no chance of escaping his eagle eye. Even though Molly had started to leave her home by the kitchen door and the yard, rather than the overlooked street entrance, it felt to her that her uncle kept an eye on her every move. He himself worked hard to keep his own family well provided for, having fingers in many pies around the town. He not only kept a herd of cows but had an interest in a corn business and a bakery. In keeping with his determination to be seen as someone of note, he was a trustee of Prospect House, the poorhouse nearby, taking his role seriously, visiting regularly and always keen to find gainful employment for the inhabitants.

Molly's day – which had not begun well after the argument with her uncle – had improved following her encounter with Will. She wondered about him as she made her way to the Church Street yard, where her uncle's milk churns would be delivered, ready for distribution around town. The fact that

Will was at liberty to sit with a sketchbook in the churchyard on a weekday morning signified he wasn't in employment, while his accent and clothing set him apart from anyone she knew. She resolved to find out more, for surely he would be back in the churchyard sketching again at some point. But, for now, she had arrived in Church Street and her father was standing at the yard gate, on the lookout both for her and the cart carrying the churns.

'A lovely morning, Molly,' he observed, as she approached. The sun picked out the silver threads running through his once-dark hair, and his habitual worried expression was erased by the smile he gave her. She smiled back and reached up to kiss his cheek. Private moments with her father were few and far between and all the more precious since his marriage to Ann. This short period each morning, before he set off on his rounds, was all that Molly had left to remind her of how their life used to be.

Stopping only to wash her hands at the pump, with the block of harsh soap that always made her skin feel as though it had been flayed, she went into her father's cubbyhole of an office. It was at the back of the stable, empty now because the horse was standing in the yard, stamping his feet and jingling his harness, impatient to be off. The office was barely deserving of the name, being just big enough for a chair and a small table covered with an untidy pile of papers. It smelt strongly of horse, as always. Molly put on the white apron that she always left hanging on the hook behind the door, noting as she did so that it would need to be taken home for washing at the day's end. Tying the strings behind her she picked her way back through the stable, wrinkling her nose.

'Has the boy not been yet?' she asked her father, who was now leaning on the gate, ear cocked, as he listened for the arrival of the milk.

'Not yet. I'm sure he'll be here soon.'

Molly sighed. The stable lad came from the poorhouse each morning, employed to do menial jobs. The cleaning of the stable looked beyond him, though, for he was small and undernourished and looked hardly able to lift the pitchfork, although he stoutly maintained that he could manage. He'd been with them barely a month, and in the last week he'd been late every morning. Molly's father, a gentle man, refused to say anything about this to her uncle who had arranged the boy's employment.

'Let's give him a chance, poor thing,' her father had said. 'I daresay he's barely seven years old and he's got a cough that will see him into the ground at St John's if he doesn't shake it off. If he's late a few days it does no harm.'

Molly privately thought that for the customers who came to the stable-yard to buy their milk it was nicer to be greeted by the aroma of freshly laid straw than by the stink of horse manure, but she kept her counsel. Her father was right to worry about the boy. She had taken the pitchfork from him on more than one occasion and bade him rest to ease his cough, while she finished the job.

Chapter Three

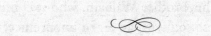

The metallic ring of a horse's hoofs on the cobbles announced the arrival of her uncle's milk churns just as a boy arrived at the gate.

'Customer, Molly,' her father called, busy helping the cart back up so the churns could be unloaded. 'Can you bid him wait?'

Molly looked the boy up and down. She had at first thought him to be the stable-boy, grown in stature by at least a foot overnight. He wore the same sort of garb – a loose working jacket and trousers that were too short, as well as ill-fitting boots with snapped laces, much worn around the toes and heels. But as he approached she saw that he was a good deal older, closer to her own age perhaps. He had a shock of brown hair that looked as though he had slicked it down at the pump that morning when he set off but, dry now, it had half sprung back to its usual boisterous state. He looked nothing like her usual customers, for the most part local women or their small children, all of whom she recognised. Before she could ask him who he was, he introduced himself.

'I'm Charlie. I'll get going with the jobs, shall I?' Before she could reply he'd turned on his heel and leapt onto the back of their cart, causing the horse, Nell, to start and look around in astonishment. Charlie beckoned to her father to hand the churns up to him. Molly could see that her father was bemused, but he wasn't about to decline the offer of help. Manhandling the full churns onto the cart was a difficult job for him – he wasn't a great deal taller than Molly herself.

In contrast to his brother William, who was broad and tall, and carried himself with an air of importance, Molly's father always looked a little apologetic about his existence. As a result, her uncle's delivery men never seemed to feel they should offer to assist. Once the churns were unloaded from their cart they would doff their caps to Molly and her father, then give the reins a shake to encourage the horse to set off at a brisk trot down the road. Molly's father was left to manage his own affairs.

Charlie made short work of the loading, then rolled the last churn over to the corner of the yard as directed by John. The churn left behind was always placed in the shadiest spot, beneath the branches of an overhanging tree from the orchard next door, Church Street being at the limit of the town, with countryside stretching out to south and west. Shade wasn't necessary now, but as the sun crossed the yard during the morning it would help to keep the milk cool until most of it had been sold, usually by midday.

'Thank you, lad,' her father called from his seat on the cart. Then he shook the reins and off they went, to visit the three big squares closer to the centre of town. Here the kitchen-maids would be waiting to hear the particular rumble of their cart and her father crying, 'Whoa,' to encourage Nell to stop. They seemed to be able to distinguish his cart from that of the coal merchant or the various pedlars, and would soon be lining up, jugs in hand, for supplies to see the households through the day.

Molly had marvelled that their wealthier customers could

get through such a quantity of milk until Aunt Jane had told her they were in the habit of making junket and all manner of milky desserts that were served at dinner. Uncle William and Aunt Jane were sometimes invited to dine at the grand houses in Hawley Square, in view of William's position as a trustee at the poorhouse, and so were well qualified to comment. The poorhouse, at William's behest, had become a customer of the Goodchild Brothers milk business, following his assertion that milk would be good for undernourished children's bones.

Molly had to admit to a grudging admiration for her uncle's business sense. If he hadn't seen an opportunity to grow his milk business, her job would have involved more than just milking the cows. She would have been expected to carry full pails up the hill, suspended from a great wooden yoke across her shoulders, then to hawk the milk around town. She was lucky to have the relatively respectable role of selling milk from the churn kept in the yard for those who couldn't afford to pay for the convenience of the deliveries.

Molly had gone to fetch her book and pencil to keep account of those who preferred to settle their bill at the end of the week, when she saw that Charlie had seized the pitch-fork and was setting about mucking out the stable.

'Have you come from …' She let the question hang in the air. Everyone locally called it the poorhouse although its name, Prospect House, suggested that those who entered its doors would receive the basic help required to set them on the path to a more secure future. The destitute were offered a dormitory bed, a uniform and a diet consisting mainly of soup, stew and potatoes, with meat on a Sunday after church, which all except the very sick must attend. Children who grew up in the poorhouse were expected to be apprenticed at seven or eight years old, the boys to a farmer or maltster, or as a sailor, the girls to the bakers, laundries and milliners of the town. Charlie, if he was a poorhouse boy, should surely be apprenticed to a trade at his age and not available to work in their yard.

Molly realised that Charlie had paused, hands folded over the top of the pitchfork handle, and was regarding her with deep brown eyes that held the hint of a smile.

'Am I a Prospect boy, d'you mean? Aye,' he said cheerfully. 'Did your uncle not tell you? My brother Samuel is too poorly to come.' Here Charlie's face took on a sombre expression. 'So I'm here in his stead. Just until he's well again.' Molly had a feeling that his words were more to convince himself than her. A cough such as his brother had could spread quickly through the poorhouse, carrying off the weak, the young and the old.

'Nature's way of limiting things,' her uncle said briskly, whenever Sunday service at St John's ended with prayers for a list of names from Prospect House, all of whom had succumbed to ailments that week.

'Samuel,' Molly repeated, aware that neither she nor her father had troubled to enquire about his name. Now that he had one, his health seemed more of a concern. 'I hope he makes a quick recovery.'

Further conversation was prevented by the arrival of the first of a regular stream of local customers, and it was only when this had dwindled that Molly was able to question Charlie a little more. He'd finished and was scrubbing his hands at the pump. Realising how hungry she was, and how long she had been up and working, with just a mug of milk to sustain her, she unwrapped the hunk of bread and cheese her father had brought in and left for her in his office as usual.

16

'Would you like some?' she asked Charlie. Without being asked, he'd not only mucked out the stable but had somehow restored order to the yard. He'd stacked boxes and hung up various implements that Molly and her father had left out, intending to deal with them at some point.

Charlie hesitated, as if wondering whether she really meant it.

'Go on,' she urged. Within the hour she would be going home, with whatever milk was left in the churn, and she could be sure of a hot dinner shortly after that. Charlie looked as though he barely saw enough food to keep his bones covered with flesh, although there was no doubting that he was strong.

Molly halved the bread and cheese as well as she could and handed his portion to him. 'What do you do?' she asked. 'Usually, I mean.'

'I work in the poorhouse gardens,' Charlie said, speaking through a mouthful of bread. He swallowed hard. 'I'm apprenticed to the head gardener there, although I've barely another month to go.' He bit into the bread again and chewed thoughtfully. 'I'm one of the lucky ones. I love what I do and Mr Fleming has said that if he can't keep me there he'll find a garden to take me on his recommendation.'

Molly noticed that he'd pocketed all but a fragment of the cheese, which he now ate with the last morsel of bread.

'Mr Fleming is good to me. He let me come here today so that Samuel could rest. Samuel will take over my apprenticeship when I'm done.'

Another customer arrived and Molly hurried to serve her, asking how her son fared, newly away to sea. When she turned back to Charlie, he was already on the other side of the gate.

17

'Will we see you tomorrow?' she called.

'Aye, if Samuel's no better,' he replied. He waved and was gone before she could thank him. As Molly tipped the churn to empty the dregs into a metal can to take home, she thought about the two boys she had met that day, both strangers to her. It was unusual in a town where so much was routine, day after day and season after season.

CHAPTER FOUR

An hour after Molly had arrived home, her father returned from his rounds. He came straight up to her in the kitchen as she stirred the stew for dinner.

'I must thank you for the job you did on the yard,' he said, clasping her shoulders and giving them a squeeze. 'It hasn't looked so clean and tidy in a long time. Your uncle stopped by as I was stabling the horse and he was most impressed.'

Molly blushed. 'Oh, it wasn't me. I can claim no credit. It was Charlie.'

'Charlie?' Her father paused in washing his hands and turned to her, puzzled.

'The boy who helped load the churns this morning,' Molly said. 'He wasn't a customer at all.' She started to explain about Charlie's younger brother Samuel to her father, until Ann called them to the table and her father's attention was diverted by Lizzie and Mary.

Molly was to see Charlie each day over the next week, even on Sunday, when she could pick him out among the congregation in the pews at the back reserved for the poorhouse inmates. There was no sign of Samuel at his side, and he'd had little good news to report each morning. Samuel struggled to eat or sleep, being plagued by coughing fits, and Charlie, who had no family in the poorhouse other than his brother, was clearly very worried.

Molly had learnt a little more about Charlie in snatched conversations while they both worked in the stable-yard. He'd arrived at the poorhouse with his mother, when he was six. His father had been lost at sea and his mother, expecting Samuel, had had no means of taking care of herself and her family. Charlie had been separated from his mother on arrival and put into a dormitory with the other boys. Having lived until then with mostly just his mother for company, Charlie had found Prospect House hard to bear. His mother had survived Samuel's birth by less than a twelvemonth and Charlie had become his little brother's protector. He stated these facts with very little emotion, but his words created a vivid picture for Molly. He went on to describe how he had started to hide in the poorhouse garden whenever he could as an escape from the place he now had to call home.

It hadn't taken long for Mr Fleming, the head gardener, to notice Charlie lurking among the currant bushes but he'd chosen to ignore him. He'd worked in the walled garden as though Charlie wasn't there, but after a couple of days, during which Charlie always slipped away to his dormitory at night but crept back at the first opportunity each morning, Mr Fleming had begun to talk to him as he worked. He'd told him what he was doing and why, as he'd staked up straggling plants or raked over the soil in the borders ready to sow seeds. He'd taken care not to catch Charlie's eye or to address him directly, but Charlie had watched and listened.

After a week, his curiosity had got the better of him. He edged out from under the bushes to ask Mr Fleming why the trees had grown flowers. The head gardener's answer was followed by a whole stream of questions that Charlie had obviously been storing up. Mr Fleming must have spoken to the authorities, for no one queried Charlie's absences each day, and soon he and Charlie had become inseparable around the garden. On Charlie's seventh birthday he found himself summoned to the overseer's office.

'Now, Charlie,' Mr Dalton said, 'I have something for you.' Mr Fleming was also there, hands and face scrubbed and looking a little cleaner and tidier than usual. He nodded encouragingly at Charlie as Mr Dalton said, 'I want you to make your mark on these papers here, to signify that you are apprenticed to Mr Fleming for the next seven years. Do you understand what this means, Charlie?'

Charlie nodded, for Mr Fleming had spoken to him about this. He was a little overawed by the seriousness of the occasion but made his cross on the page as asked, then went about the rest of his day in the garden as usual. He had been working with Mr Fleming ever since.

A week and a day after she had first met him, when Molly was checking the stable-yard gate every few minutes for signs of Charlie, another figure appeared. He was smaller than Charlie but taller than Samuel, and dressed in the Prospect House uniform. The boy introduced himself as Mark, but Molly was barely listening.

'Charlie isn't coming today?' she asked him.

'No, miss.'

'Why not?' Even as she said the words, Molly knew the answer.

'He's back in the gardens, miss. I'm your new stable-boy.'

'And Samuel?' When the boy merely looked at her blankly, she added, 'Charlie's brother.'

'Dead, miss.'

An image of Samuel as she had last seen him, his clothes hanging off his frame and his nose running as he coughed and coughed over his work, came into Molly's mind. She'd been irritated by his cough, she remembered now with shame.

There was nothing more to be said, so she gave Mark the pitchfork and his instructions, and took up her post by the milk churn. The morning seemed to drag without Charlie to talk to and, by the time she was walking home for dinner, Molly had decided she would go to the poorhouse gardens that afternoon and seek Charlie out. She needed to thank him for his help, she reasoned, and Mr Fleming, too, for allowing Charlie to come to them in his brother's place.

But after dinner Ann needed her to go into town to deliver a box of ribbon decorations to the milliner. This was another of Uncle William's fortuitous connections: the milliner's business had grown to such an extent that she was forced to seek the assistance of nimble-fingered outworkers to create adornments for her hats. William had suggested to his brother that Ann could be doing this while she was at home with the children, to add a few pennies to the family's budget whenever she could. Ann had proved adept at the job but all efforts to train Molly in the art had failed. Her attempts looked as though the horse had chewed them, according to Ann, so Molly was demoted to messenger, for which she was thankful.

Usually, she was glad to get away from the house and walk down the hill towards the sea, not least to escape the household chores. Today, with sunlight sparkling on the water and the sails of the ships waiting to enter the harbour billowing in the brisk breeze, it should have been a particularly delightful stroll. Molly would normally have dawdled, taking in the view and the smell of the sea on the air, keen to linger at the shop windows, admiring the trinkets set out to tempt residents and visitors alike. She was in a hurry, though, wishing to complete her errand so that she could visit the poorhouse gardens on the way home, in search of Charlie.

Molly burst through the door of the milliner's shop, a little out of breath from hurrying. Mrs Hughes looked reprovingly at her over the top of her spectacles and continued to devote herself to the customers in the shop. Molly was forced to stand back respectfully while Mrs Hughes dealt with them, which allowed her to catch her breath and gave her flushed cheeks a chance to cool.

While she waited, Molly observed the customers, two well-dressed young ladies: one younger and the other a little older than herself. Sisters or cousins, perhaps. Mrs Hughes clearly knew the older of the two for, although she was treating her with deference she was also asking questions, which implied a degree of knowledge about her and her family.

'How is Lady Bridges?' Mrs Hughes asked, as she deftly placed the bonnet that one of the young ladies had purchased in a box. 'Is she in town today? Might I have the pleasure of her custom later?'

'Mother is indisposed,' the young woman replied. 'We have her carriage all to ourselves. In fact, it will be calling here shortly, expecting to find us. Would you mind giving the footman this parcel?' She indicated the box with the bonnet in it. 'And could you tell him that I have decided to take tea at the Assembly Rooms? Our visitor, Miss Austen, has been very patient while I've attended to all Mother's errands, and I think she deserves a treat.'

'Very well, Miss Bridges.'

The young lady so addressed picked up her parasol from where it rested against the counter and linked arms with Miss Austen. They nodded at Molly as they left the shop. She fancied that the younger girl swept her from top to toe with a curious glance and felt herself blushing furiously. Molly was only too aware of the contrast she presented to the two elegant figures: Miss Bridges was attired in a rose-coloured summer gown while her companion was wearing white muslin, sprigged with tiny pink flowers. Molly looked down at herself. Her own plain cotton dress was clean but faded and had been let down many times as she grew, now barely covering the tops of her boots. The two young women appeared to glide as they moved, their gowns practically sweeping the floor. The boots peeping from beneath their hems were dainty, made in the softest glossy leather, while Molly's own were practical rather than pretty and worn within an inch of their life.

'Ann's done a lovely job as usual,' Mrs Hughes said, as she lifted the lid from the box that Molly presented to her. 'Tell her I'll have more for her to do later this week. Now that the boats from London have started their extra services into the harbour, we're getting more visitors by the day. They seem to like treating themselves to a new bonnet while they're here. I'll be run off my feet again.' Mrs Hughes looked up from making a note of Molly's delivery in her ledger. 'I'm not complaining, mind. All good for business.'

'Were those ladies from London?' Molly asked, finally finding her voice.

'Bless you, no. That's Miss Elizabeth Bridges and one of their family visitors. The Bridges live in the country, a few miles from here, and they've come in her mother's carriage. Lady Bridges is a very good customer of mine and her daughters like to come here for their bonnets, rather than go to Canterbury, as they say I keep up with the London fashions.'

The doorbell rang to herald another customer and Mrs

Hughes turned aside from Molly, a ready smile on her lips. Molly slipped out, eyes cast down, and breathed a sigh of relief as she stood outside the shop. She could go back up the high street towards home, but call in first to the poorhouse garden in search of Charlie.

'Pssst!'

Molly looked around. Was someone trying to attract her attention?

'Over here.' She became aware of a figure waving from the other side of the road and, with a start, she recognised Will. She hadn't given him a thought over the past week but now he was before her, sketchbook in hand, leaning against the wall of the King's Head inn.

She crossed the road to him, as he clearly had no intention of coming to her.

'Are you drawing again?' Molly asked on reaching his side, for she saw that his book was open.

'I am,' he said, 'And I was hoping that you could help me, perhaps.'

'Me?' Molly was astonished. 'What can I do?'

'Well, I'm drawing this view down the hill to the harbour.' Will held out the sketchbook for her to see. 'But although the harbour is busy, I realised that the street in front looks a bit dull, with no one in it. People come and go so quickly I haven't been able to capture them.'

Molly frowned. It was true – all the interest was at the back of the sketch, although she would have been hard-pressed to realise that without Will pointing it out.

'I still don't see how I can help,' she said.

'Two ladies came out of the shop just before you,' Will said. 'They loitered for a moment or two while one of them tried to put up a parasol but was defeated by the breeze. I was struck by the colours of their outfits and how much they added to the scene.'

Molly looked at Will. Did he expect her to go after Miss Bridges and her visitor, for it was surely them, and to fetch them back to pose for him?

She was about to tell him that the ladies he had referred to were too fine to be his models when he spoke again. 'I thought perhaps you might pose for me.'

Molly stared at him, incredulous. She looked down at her clothing, then at him in some bewilderment.

'I just need you to stand in front of the shop, as they did,' Will added hastily. 'I struggle to draw people, you see. I can't just make them up.'

'But my clothes?' Molly asked.

'I can remember what they were wearing,' Will said. 'I just need someone to stand there, to get the proportions right. Will you do it?' He looked hopeful.

Molly was not a little embarrassed at being asked, but also intrigued: an artist's model – who would have thought it? She returned to the shop front and allowed Will to direct her from over the road. She stepped forwards and backwards and turned towards the harbour until she was standing at an angle that Will found pleasing. She steadfastly ignored Mrs Hughes within the shop, although she was aware of her out of the corner of her eye. She still had customers, luckily, or she would have come out and scolded her before sending her on her way.

She prayed that Will would get the bare bones of his sketching done quickly, but he wanted her to pretend to raise a parasol, something that proved problematic as she had never done such a thing in her life. By the time he professed himself happy, Molly was quite red in the face from embarrassment. She had also attracted a small and giggling crowd of street

26

urchins and she was sure that Mrs Hughes would have something to say about it when she next took a delivery to the shop on Ann's behalf.

She crossed back over the street to Will and asked to see what he had produced. He had already closed and bound up his sketchbook, however, and declared himself keen to get home to work on it while it was still fresh in his mind.

Molly was annoyed but, sensing he was unwilling to share the unfinished work, she instead asked him in which direction his route home lay.

'I'm staying with my aunt in St John's Street,' Will replied.

'Why, that's just around the corner from me,' Molly said. 'We can go back together.'

As they walked, Molly managed to coax him into revealing that his mother was ill so he had been sent from home in London to stay with his aunt in Margate and to be schooled in the town. 'Although I'm probably spending more time drawing than I am on any of my other subjects,' Will confessed.

'I could show you where to get good views of the town, if you like,' Molly offered. 'Places you might not find by yourself.'

They'd reached the point where their paths divided so they parted, Molly promising to meet Will the following afternoon to show him some vantage points. It was only when she reached the kitchen door that she realised she had forgotten all about going to visit Charlie.

Tomorrow, she thought, before remembering her arrangement with Will. Well, then, it would just have to be the day after.

CHAPTER FIVE

The following day, Molly walked with Will along the cliffs to Margate Mills, the row of corn mills set high at the field edge to make the most of the wind that blew in off the sea. The day after that, she took him out along the medieval pilgrim route from St John's Church towards St Peter's, which had views over the countryside. On the way back, they made a detour through the fields so Molly could show him the cow barn where she did the milking each morning. When Will saw the cows in the fields he became more animated than she had seen him all afternoon, pulling out his sketchbook and resting it on the fence while he quickly sketched a group of cattle, huddled together and observing them suspiciously.

'I'll be back to do more of these,' Will said. 'I can imagine how well they will look in a painting.'

Molly, viewing them through the eyes of a milkmaid rather than an artist, was sceptical. She saw only the muck halfway up the cows' legs and around their tails, which they swished constantly to drive away the flies. But she was happy to have pleased Will.

'If you are prepared for a long walk tomorrow, I can take you to see Dandelion,' she said.

'Dandelion? The flower?' It was Will's turn to be puzzled.

'Well, I think its proper name is something French but everyone around here calls it Dandelion,' Molly said.

She smiled and shook her head when Will tried to quiz her, telling him it was to be a surprise. She discovered she rather liked teasing him: he might be younger than she was, but his obvious talent and his schooling often made her feel at a disadvantage. When he grew tired of her game and threatened not to come the next day it was her turn to cajole, and she told him to meet her at the Church Street yard in the morning.

'If you liked the cows as a subject, you might well like our horse and cart. Or the milk churns,' she added, as an after-thought. She struggled to see why he found these subjects more appealing than the views around Margate but she was determined to prove herself useful to him. It was a challenge to please him but trying to do so was a novelty. It made an exciting break from the monotony of her days.

'Father will like to meet you, too,' she added. This was true – her father was less than pleased that Ann had com-plained about Molly 'traipsing off everywhere with some boy' instead of helping her with the chores around the house in the afternoons. She hoped that if her father met Will he might approve and allow their expeditions to continue. If not, their trip to the Dandelion would have to be abandoned.

The next day Will was at the Church Street yard by mid-morning, as Molly had arranged. She gave him a quick tour of the yard and thought he was quite taken with some of the farm implements, and the comings and goings of the cus-tomers to buy milk. She smiled as she observed him settle in various corners as the morning wore on, sketching furiously and frowning over his work.

It was going to make them late starting on their

expedition, but she would have to wait until her father returned from his rounds, for she would need his blessing. She had been watching the weather anxiously but the grey clouds of the morning had peeled back to reveal a bright blue sky, with enough of a breeze to make the walk to come a pleasant one.

Finally, Molly heard the clip-clop of Nell's hoofs and the jangling of her harness as her father drove the cart down Church Street. He turned into the yard, then jumped down from the seat as Molly moved to hold the horse's head.

'And who might this be?' he asked, looking at Will, who was seated in the corner of the yard with his sketchbook open on his lap, seemingly oblivious to anything going on around him.

'This is Will,' Molly said, speaking loudly to attract his attention. 'I came across him sketching in St John's church-yard and I've been helping him find places to draw. I'd like to show him Dandelion this afternoon. I think it would make a good subject for him.'

Her father was frowning. 'You know what Ann has said about you neglecting your work around the house, Molly.'

'I know, and I promise that after today I will help. Come and look at Will's work,' Molly said, seizing her father's hand and drawing him over to where Will was seated on an upturned bucket. Will, finally aware of their presence, scrambled to his feet and extended his hand to Molly's father.

'How d'ye do, Mr …' He stopped, looking agonised, having forgotten Molly's surname.

Molly's father, amused at the formality of his greeting, shook his hand saying 'Goodchild – John Goodchild. Molly tells me you're quite the artist.'

Will flushed, whether from pleasure or embarrassment

Molly couldn't tell, and clutched his sketchbook to his chest.

'May I look?' John Goodchild held out his hand and Will reluctantly handed it over.

'I hear Molly has plans for a special expedition today.' Her father was flipping through the pages but paused when he came to the sketch of cattle.

'Are these William's cows?' John looked enquiringly at them both. Molly nodded. He chuckled. 'I think you might find a buyer for something such as this with my brother. How old are you, lad?'

When Will revealed that he was eleven, John looked suitably impressed. 'Well, I foresee a great future for you, my boy. And if Molly can help you in some way, I'm sure we can spare her for the day.' He turned to Molly. 'I'll make it right with Ann for today, Molly. Get off with the pair of you, and be back before dark. But tomorrow you must expect to make up for your holiday.'

He spoke sternly, but there was a twinkle in his eye. Feeling proud, as though she was in some way responsible for Will's talent, Molly hustled him out of the yard before her father could change his mind. She'd miss dinner today but she could share her bread and cheese with Will. If they were still hungry they could forage in the hedgerows along the way and perhaps one of the farms would sell them further supplies. Molly jingled the coins in her apron pocket, taken from the few she had managed to squirrel away from the deliveries she had made to Mrs Hughes. All her other earnings went straight into the family's housekeeping pot.

The journey to Dandelion took them across the marshy ground of Margate Brooks before they could strike out over the meadows. It wasn't a straightforward route but Molly was confident, having explored the surrounding area many times.

The countryside was at its best, she thought as they walked, fresh and green and new. It hadn't yet had the chance to grow tired under the heat of a summer sun so the grass in the fields was long and lush, and the hedgerows were bursting with flowers.

Will seemed preoccupied as they went along, and Molly grew weary of pointing things out to him, for he answered in monosyllables and didn't appear to take the same interest that she did in a particular view. Neither did he show any interest in poking sticks into rabbit holes, throwing stones after a vanishing stoat or letting fly at the birds in the trees with a catapult, as other boys would have done. Discouraged, she ceased to talk and fell to wondering whether Dandelion would be a disappointment to him after all.

As they walked across the final meadow, Molly saw that Will was looking ahead and had quickened his pace.

'What's that building?' he asked, pointing. 'It looks like some sort of gatehouse.'

'It is,' Molly said, feeling her spirits start to lift. 'That's Dandelion. That's where we're going.'

But Will was already striking out over the meadow, no doubt intent on finding the best place to sit and start sketching. Molly sighed. Will would be lost to her for a good hour or more, absorbed in his work. She might as well visit the farmhouse that lay behind the gatehouse to see whether she could buy anything there for them to eat.

Returning shortly after with rolls, ham and freshly baked seedcake, she found Will hard at work.

Molly tried to appraise the building with Will's eyes, seeing afresh the banded colours of the brickwork and the ornate designs on the arches. The grand medieval house to which it belonged was long gone, just a farm and its yard remaining. Only farm carts passed beneath the grand arch-way now, and the battlements and the arrow slits were no longer in use. She had seen the building many times since her first introduction to it and had ceased to be amazed by its incongruity in the countryside but it looked as though Will was very taken with it, as she had hoped.

Molly shared out the food, then settled down in the shade cast by the spreading branches of the great elm tree, chosen by Will to provide a frame for his sketch. She drifted into sleep, tired from her early start and the walk, only to be roused by an exclamation from Will.

'I was almost done and then this fellow arrived. He would be perfect to include in front of the gate.' Molly looked up to see a rider on his horse, two hounds squabbling beside him. Will was staring at her with a speculative gleam in his eye. 'I wonder ...'

'No!' Molly protested. 'You're going to ask me to delay him, aren't you? While you sketch him.'

'It's my only chance. Please,' Will begged.

Not for the first time, Molly questioned what drove her to try to help Will. Didn't he just take advantage of her, per-suading her into awkward situations? Why did she feel she couldn't deny him? She sighed and struggled to her feet. 'I'll do what I can. But then we must go home. I'll be in trouble if I'm late.'

As she made her way over to the rider she had no clear idea as to what she might say to detain him. The dogs, which had been tussling over some scraps on the ground, looked up warily as she approached, and then, deciding she wasn't a threat, they bounded up to her. Molly stooped, patting them and fussing over them, grateful for their attention because it would buy her some time.

'Could you tell me, is this the Dent-de-lion?' The man's voice was cultured and Molly marvelled at his pronunciation of Dandelion – but before she could question it he continued, 'Am I on the right road for Woodchurch Manor?'

Molly straightened, causing the dogs to bound joyously around her in an attempt to regain her attention.

'Castor! Pollux! Behave yourselves.' The gentleman on the horse sounded exasperated. Molly had a chance to take a good look at him now. His cream breeches had been made dusty by the road, as had his riding boots, once smartly polished. His jacket was deep red and smartly cut, and his silver curls were almost covered by a shiny black top hat. Her uncle would have described him as 'well-to-do'.

'You are on the right road, sir. Woodchurch Manor is just a few miles further along this road.' Molly gestured up the broad track that continued past the gatehouse. 'But I wonder whether I might beg a favour first.'

The man frowned and Molly almost lost courage.

'My friend over there,' she gestured to Will, sitting beneath the tree, 'he's sketching the gatehouse and when you arrived, sir, he saw that you added the perfect detail to the picture. He begged me to detain you for a little while so that he might capture your likeness.'

'Did he indeed?' Now the man appeared amused. 'And how old might this budding artist be?'

'He's eleven, sir,' Molly replied.

'Well, I do believe I'll have a look.' The man began to dismount. 'Take hold of this nag for me.' He tossed the reins to Molly. The horse side-stepped, flaring his nostrils and stamping his hoofs, and Molly, a little taken aback, had to utter soothing noises and attempt to stroke his nose, even as the animal baulked and pulled away from her. Then, seeing that

34

his master had no intention of going more than a few paces, the horse dropped his head and began to crop the grass.

No sooner was he calmed than his rider was back by Molly's side, taking the reins from her and patting the neck of his mount.

'That's quite a talent your friend has,' he remarked to Molly, as he swung himself back into the saddle. 'I'll be looking out for his work in the future and I'll be telling my friends the Powells at Woodchurch to do the same. What did you say his name was?'

Molly hadn't said, but obligingly filled him in, all the while anxious that he shouldn't leave until Will was done.

Observing her stricken look, the gentleman said, 'Don't worry. Master Turner has declared himself happy with what he has. Now I'll be off. It has been most instructive.' And the rider went on his way, with a nod and a click of his fingers to his dogs, which immediately bounded ahead of him along the track.

CHAPTER SIX

That night, Molly's stomach was rumbling as she took her candle and went yawning up the stairs to bed. She'd muddied her skirt on the way home, losing her footing as she picked a path through the Brooks in the fading light, and Ann had been less than pleased with her.

'You're late,' she'd snapped, as Molly opened the kitchen door to the sound of wailing and fractious children. 'You can put young John to bed, then see to Lizzie and Mary. Your father and I will be at the Spread Eagle.'

Molly had been puzzled, since neither her father nor Ann cared for spending time at the inn around the corner. She wondered whether Ann had arranged it just to spite her. As she left, Ann caught sight of Molly's clothes and aimed a cuff at her head, catching her unawares. She'd stumbled back, tears starting to her eyes, wishing her father was there. He would never have allowed her to be treated in such a way.

'Look at the state of you! You can get that skirt washed out and hung in the yard overnight to dry. And don't be expecting any supper. There's none saved. If you think you can go gallivanting off around the countryside when there's work to be done here, you can think again.'

Molly stuck out her tongue at Ann's back, which made Lizzie and Mary, who'd fallen silent after their older sister had been struck, break into a fit of giggles.

Ann, suspecting insolence, spun around in a fury. 'I'll have none of your cheek in this house. Your father's too soft on you.' And with that she slammed the door behind her.

Molly was too tired to pay any heed to Ann's words when she went to bed that night and she'd forgotten all about them the next day. But when she arrived at the Church Street yard, milking done and in good spirits because it looked set to be a lovely day, her father was waiting for her, grim-faced.

'We need to have a talk, Molly.'

Molly's heart sank. Suddenly her stepmother's words of the previous evening came back to her.

'I can't be trying to keep the peace between you and Ann. You must set your mind to being a helpful daughter around the house. If you can't, then we must look to getting you some live-in work elsewhere.'

Molly stared at her father in horror. Surely her behaviour hadn't been so very bad. 'Live-in work?' she stammered. 'What do you mean?'

'Ann tells me that her father could do with help around the farm and you're an able girl. I'm not sure what your uncle would say about the loss of his milkmaid but still ...'

Molly experienced a sudden flash of rage. 'Is this why you were at the Spread Eagle last night? Ann has been plotting this, hasn't she? I've done nothing to deserve it!'

Molly's raised voice had brought the stable-boy away from his duties to stare, and she saw that her father was looking uncomfortable. She took a deep breath and tried to get her feelings under control. 'I won't see Will any more this week. He has plenty of sketches for his paintings. I'll work at home every afternoon and do as Ann tells me.'

Even as she spoke, Molly could feel her temper rising

again. How dare the woman imagine she could take over from Molly's mother? How could she think of trying to turn Molly's father against his daughter? And plot to drive her out of her home into the bargain.

'Now, now, Molly. There's no need to get into such a state. I'm sure if you do as you say then all will be well in a day or two.' It was clear that her father didn't want to pursue the matter, and the arrival of the milk churns gave him an excuse to busy himself preparing for his rounds.

Molly took up her position by the milk churn with such a fierce expression on her face that her father was forced to say placatingly, 'We'll let no more be said. I'll see you at the dinner table, but in the meantime, you've a face on you that looks set to curdle the milk. Our customers have done nothing to you, Molly. Remember that and try to mend your looks.'

Feeling as though the whole world was against her, Molly did her best to serve her customers in the manner they deserved, but they were puzzled by her pinched expression and short answers and didn't linger in the yard that day. She wished Will might appear so that she could share the injustice of it all with him, but there was no sign of him.

When Mark was done with his chores he came up to Molly and said, 'Begging your pardon, miss, but Charlie asked me to remember him to you and to say he hoped you might drop by the garden one day.'

Molly bit her lip. Charlie! She had intended to go and see him to thank him for his work in the stable-yard and to tell him how sorry she was about his little brother, Samuel. And now more than a week had gone by and he had sent her a message, which made her feel very contrite.

Had he been at church on Sunday? She tried to remember.

Surely Samuel's name would have been read out in the list of deaths at the end of the service? To her shame, she couldn't recall. She had been preoccupied with planning where she might take Will on their sketching expeditions and had merely gone through the motions at church.

Mark looked as though he expected an answer.

'You must tell him that I'm sorry I haven't been able to visit – I meant to. I will come …' Molly paused. She had been on the point of saying 'this afternoon' when she remembered that she must stay at home and work for the next few days at least.

'I will come as soon as I can,' she finished. Perhaps Ann would need to send her to Mrs Hughes and she could make a detour then, as she had planned to do a week ago.

The boy nodded, touched his cap and left. Within the hour Molly was at home, resolving to hold her tongue no matter what Ann said to her, to work hard and to earn the right to some free time as soon as she could.

It was clear that Ann had other ideas. She said very little when she came in but, as Molly washed and peeled the carrots for dinner, she said, 'I've sorted out some sewing for you to do this afternoon. Both Lizzie and Mary have grown since last summer and their dresses must be let down. I don't know what your father does to his shirts but there's more buttons off than on. And there's stockings to be darned as well.'

Molly glared at the carrots as she peeled them. Ann knew perfectly well that her sewing skills were limited. She would inspect the work and no doubt insist that it was redone until it met her approval. But, if she was to earn any free time, she must do as Ann asked and, besides, she had promised her father. So, while Ann took the three younger children out for a walk and some fresh air, Molly stayed at home and gazed longingly out at the sunshine. She fumed as she struggled to stop the thread knotting in the needle and clenched her teeth in concentration as she tried to keep her hemming stitches neat and even.

The children returned full of how they had watched men at work on a great park they might go to one day, with trees and flowers and paths already laid out for walking. Molly listened to their excited chatter and felt envious, but she supervised their hand-washing with good grace, although her heart sank as she saw Ann pick up her afternoon's handiwork and scrutinise it. Ann's mood, however, seemed to have been favourably affected by their outing.

'Thank you, Molly. It's a shame that you're a little slow but your sewing has improved. The stockings must wait until tomorrow, I see.'

Molly attempted a smile in response but she was aware that it barely lifted the corners of her mouth. She hated darning with all her heart. Every attempt produced lumpy results guaranteed to cause blistered heels in the unlucky owners of the stockings. Her darning would never win Ann's approval, but that problem could be set aside for the future. For now, Ann wanted a pie prepared and cooked for the next day.

'We'll have a cold lunch tomorrow so we can make a good start on the journey to my father's,' she said. 'John will join us and you can take advantage of the empty house, Molly, to wash the floors throughout. While they dry, you can be getting on with the darning.'

Molly wanted to ask why they were going to visit Ann's father. Mindful of the words of her own father that morning, she wondered whether it was to discuss her employment there. But wouldn't Mr Dixon have wanted to see her, too, if that was the case? Ann could not be questioned, however, having taken herself up the road to visit a neighbour, leaving Molly to manage the children and make the pie.

Molly's life was to continue in this way over the next fortnight. Ann had apparently decided she would live a life of leisure, making Molly do all the work around the house that a servant would do. Molly would have been glad to lend a hand to her mother, had she still been alive. But after a day that began before dawn with the milking, followed by working in the Church Street yard, she felt it deeply unfair that she was expected to take on the role of an unpaid servant for the hours that remained, until she fell into bed.

By the end of the fortnight, she was beginning to wonder whether she might, in fact, profit by taking a position elsewhere, for in that way she would surely have earnings in her pocket and a little free time for herself.

CHAPTER SEVEN

Being tied to the house in the afternoons and evenings meant that Molly saw nothing of Will. She hoped he might call at the Church Street yard when she was at work there, but each morning she looked for him in vain. The rest of her day kept her too busy and confined to the house to go in search of him, so she was left to wonder whether he had found a new companion for his sketching expeditions.

Two weeks into her enforced routine, Molly heard some surprising news from her father over dinner.

'That artist lad you know, Molly – it looks as though he might have a business head on his shoulders.'

Molly glanced up from helping little John with his dinner as her father continued, 'Aye, he's gone and sold your uncle a picture of his own cows, the ones he can see standing in his fields whenever it takes his fancy.' Her father chuckled and shook his head in wonder at his brother's folly. 'He said you'd never guess it was the work of such a young lad, he's captured such a good likeness. He reckons he'll be famous before long.' John chuckled and shook his head again. 'Famous for drawing cows, eh?'

Molly was staring at her father, eyes wide and mouth open.

'Shut your mouth, Molly. You look like a fish.' Ann spoke sharply and John glanced between his wife and his eldest daughter, a worried frown creasing his brow.

'Will was here? Next door, I mean?' Molly found her voice.

'I suppose so,' John said. 'William didn't say where he came across him, just that he'd made a purchase.'

Molly resolved to find out more as soon as she could. She imagined that she would have to wait and quiz her uncle the following morning, at the cow barn, but her stepmother unwittingly gave her an earlier opportunity.

'I want you to sweep and wash the front step. My father is calling this afternoon and the house must look as smart as possible.'

Although she felt the insult of being asked to clean the front step, always the job of the lowliest maid in a house, Molly dutifully took the broom, scrubbing brush and bucket from the scullery. It was a job best done first thing in the morning, when fewer people were about, but she must do as she was told. The soap for the step, though, was nowhere to be found.

Ann was cross. 'How can this be? There's no time now to go to the high street to buy more. You must go next door and ask whether we might borrow a bit of theirs and replace it tomorrow.'

Ann was tying on her bonnet as she spoke, expressing her intention to take the younger ones out for a walk, so Molly undertook her errand with a glad heart. If her aunt was at home, it would give her enough time to quiz her about Will's visit and still complete her task before Ann's return.

'Molly!' Aunt Jane answered the basement kitchen door to Molly's knock. 'Why didn't you come to the main door?' She thought a moment, then laughed. 'Mind you, I would only have had to run upstairs myself to answer it.'

'Where is Elsa?' Molly asked, glancing around the kitchen.

'I came to ask her a favour. But, of course, it is lovely to see you, Aunt,' she added hastily, realising that she must have sounded rude.

'Oh, Molly,' her aunt said. 'Why do we never see anything of you these days? And you only live next door. It's such a shame.'

Molly thought she could see the glimmer of tears in her aunt's eyes. Aunt Jane knew well enough why they saw so little of each other, with Uncle William having taken against John's marriage to Ann.

Her aunt remembered Molly's question. 'Elsa? Why, Elsa has left us. Her sister has died, leaving three little ones under the age of five, and Elsa has done her duty and gone to help her brother-in-law.' Aunt Jane looked pensive. 'I fear she may also feel it is her duty to marry him and look after those children for ever more so we won't be seeing her again. I must find someone else to help.' She sighed at the prospect.

'I came to borrow some soap for the front step,' Molly said, and explained that she would return it the next day.

Aunt Jane went to rummage in the scullery and emerged triumphant, clutching the soap. 'Have it and welcome, although to get the full whitening effect it needs to dry properly.' She frowned. 'But why are you undertaking such work? Can your father not take on a girl, since you are already working as a milkmaid and dairymaid too?'

Molly hesitated, then blurted out her story: how she was in trouble because of her sketching trips with her friend, Will, and how Ann made her work all afternoon and evening at home. 'She's threatened that I must go and work for her father, in his house and on his farm,' Molly said. 'He's coming to visit this very afternoon and I'm worried in case the decision is already made.'

44

'This makes no sense at all,' her aunt said robustly. 'You are far too valuable to your father and your uncle to be sent off in this fashion. Whatever can your father be thinking of? I will speak to your uncle this evening.'

Molly was seized with fear that her unguarded words would cause further trouble between her father and her uncle, and for herself. 'Oh, please don't say anything,' she begged. 'It's hateful but at least for the moment I am at home with my sisters. I just miss being able to go out of the house as I please.'

As she was about to leave, she remembered her reason for calling, other than to borrow soap. 'I heard from my father that Uncle William has purchased a picture from Will, the friend I mentioned. I wondered whether I might see it.'

'Ah, the cows.' Her aunt had a wry smile on her face. 'Your uncle is mightily taken with them. But I'm afraid the picture is at the framer's.' Observing her niece's crestfallen expression, she quickly added, 'I do believe it will be back by Friday, though.' She hesitated for a moment, then said firmly, 'You must all come to view it.'

Molly was startled by the invitation, unsure of how her uncle would take it, but grateful nonetheless. 'I will tell Pa and Ann and I will look forward to it. But now I must go and finish my tasks before Ann's return.'

She kissed her aunt's cheek and hurried out, unaware of Jane's thoughtful gaze following her out of the door and up the basement steps.

CHAPTER EIGHT

The warm afternoon sunshine worked in Molly's favour and dried the steps in time for Ann's return from her walk with the children. No sooner was she indoors than Mr Dixon arrived. Molly showed him into the parlour and fetched him a glass of ale without being asked; he was mopping his brow and seemed quite overcome, exclaiming about the heat in town.

Molly was as unobtrusive as possible throughout Mr Dixon's visit. A big man, his presence filled the tiny parlour and his bulk threatened to break the spindly ladder-back chairs that Ann had insisted on for this room, despite their lack of comfort. It was clear that the visit was all about showing her father how well she had done in marrying John Goodchild.

Molly folded laundry in the kitchen and set about baking bread, so that there might be a fresh loaf to be had with supper. Absorbed in the rhythmic kneading of the dough, her thoughts taking her out over the meadows to retrace the steps of her last outing with Will, she wasn't aware of Ann calling her from the parlour. She was dragged back to the present by the appearance of her stepmother, clearly irritated, in the kitchen doorway.

'Molly, I've been calling you. Were you ignoring me? What sort of impression do you think you are making on my father?

Now come through. There is something we would like to talk to you about.'

Hastily, Molly wiped the dough from her fingers with a cloth, smoothed her apron and followed Ann through to the parlour. Lizzie and Mary were entertaining little John in the middle of the floor with a painted wooden spinning top, which Molly recognised at once to be new. A gift from a doting grandfather, no doubt.

'Molly, sit down. I've just been telling Father what a great help you have been to me around the house. How you can cook, clean and manage the laundry, and how your sewing skills are much improved under my tuition, too.'

Molly tried not to let her irritation show at the way in which Ann was taking credit for Molly's own efforts.

'Father is in need of help around the farm and in the house, and since you have skills as a milkmaid, I think you would be very well suited to life at Eastlands Farm.'

Molly looked from father to daughter. Mr Dixon had the look of a man who had spent much of his life out in the fields, his face tanned and deeply etched with lines that made it impossible to hazard a guess at his age. He could have been anything from forty to seventy. His daughter, who was rather plain although blessed with a very fine figure, had made every effort to appear at her best for her father's visit. Curls peeped out from beneath her cap and she was wearing what Molly recognised as her Sunday-best dress.

Molly knew that politeness required an answer of her, along with fulsome thanks at the kindness of Mr Dixon's offer. But the prospect of living at Eastlands Farm, away from her sisters and everything she knew, was just too much.

'What does my father think about this?'

Ann flushed. 'Don't be impertinent, Molly.'

47

She didn't answer the question, Molly noticed so, emboldened, she continued, 'I cannot accept your offer until I have discussed it with my father. If you will excuse me, I have bread to make.'

She got up and marched out of the room, head high, to a 'Well, really,' from Ann and what sounded suspiciously like a chuckle from Mr Dixon.

'I think you've met your match, Ann,' Molly heard him say, as she closed the door behind her.

Her behaviour in the parlour left Molly feeling decidedly shaky as she finished preparing the dough. She hoped her father would be home soon – she didn't relish spending time alone with Ann after Mr Dixon had left. Surely, with his father-in-law visiting, he would be here at any minute.

The unwelcome thought that perhaps her father didn't know about the visit had just occurred to Molly when she heard his voice in the yard, exchanging cheerful greetings with their neighbour. She flew to the door to open it.

'Pa, thank goodness you're home!' She flung her arms around his neck as he came in, showering flour down his jacket.

'Why, Molly, whatever is the matter?' John appeared bemused by his daughter's greeting.

'Mr Dixon is here with Ann in the parlour and—' Molly's hurried explanation was interrupted by Ann, who had appeared in the kitchen doorway.

'John, you're just in time to see my father. He dropped in unexpectedly while he was in town. He was just about to leave.'

The smoothness of Ann's lie took Molly by surprise. Earlier, she had described this to Molly as a planned visit. Why had she given her husband a different impression?

Her father was drawn into the parlour, protesting that he was hardly dressed to receive guests as he was still in his work clothes, and the door was shut firmly behind him. Were they going to tell him about Mr Dixon's offer of employment?

Mr Dixon left shortly afterwards and Molly was on tenterhooks, wondering when the subject would be raised again. She had already decided that she would run away rather than go and work for Mr Dixon. His farm, which she had never visited, was a good ten miles away to the south-east of Margate. It was too far to consider making regular visits home. Molly knew she would be stuck there, living among strangers and deprived of her family. A tear plopped into the soup she was stirring, swiftly followed by another.

But not a word on the subject was said over supper. Molly saw her father cast one or two glances her way while Ann ignored her, focusing all her attention on her husband, as usual. Molly went to bed none the wiser as to what decision might have been reached about her future. She spent a restless night, waking more than once to watch her sisters as they slept peacefully beside her, untroubled by the thoughts and fears that beset Molly.

The next morning, once the milking was done, Molly waited eagerly for her father to arrive at the Church Street yard. The weather had changed overnight and a light drizzle was falling, bringing with it a coolness to the air that made Molly shiver. She noticed Mark, the stable-boy, casting one or two glances in her direction as he swept the yard. She was abruptly and unpleasantly reminded of her failure to visit Charlie, as she had promised. Confined to home as she was, there had been no chance to do so but she felt no less guilty about it.

Her father came upon her in the office, where she was trying to make sense of the bills in an effort to distract herself.

'Well, Molly, what a to-do!'

Molly swung around to face him, noticing how tired and sad he looked. 'What's wrong, Pa? Is it something to do with me?'

'Aye, it is. I don't want to let you go, Molly, but I'm persuaded it's for the best.'

'Oh, no, Pa.' Molly threw herself onto his chest. 'Please don't make me. I'll never get to see you all, except if I can get leave to come on a Sunday now and then.' She stopped, her sobs making it hard to speak.

John grasped her shoulders and held her away from him. 'But why wouldn't you be able to see us when you'll be just next door? Your aunt won't have you locked up, silly child!' He shook his head. 'I don't know what your mother would have to say about all of this. But William is right …' He was speaking half to himself and didn't notice Molly's confusion.

'But, Pa – Eastlands Farm? Mr Dixon, Ann's father. Am I not to be sent there?'

'Good heavens, no, child.'

Molly, aware that her mouth had fallen open, closed it quickly and tried hard to concentrate on what her father was saying.

'Your aunt Jane needs help around the house until Elsa returns, or she finds someone to step into Elsa's shoes. There's a room spare in the attic that you can have all to yourself. In return, William has offered to pay for someone to help Ann with the house and the children. With a new baby on the way, we'll be needing more than one pair of hands, mind you.'

John frowned. He had been forced to submit to his brother's stern words at his fecklessness in creating new life when he could barely afford to support the family he already had.

Molly hardly took in the news about the new baby, for her mind was whirring. She had a good head for numbers even though her reading and writing skills were basic. Her aunt must have spoken to her uncle and persuaded him to offer board and lodging to Molly in return for her services, which he would pay for by funding a servant in his brother's house.

Molly's delight in escaping the prospect of employment against her will at Eastlands Farm, far away from home, eclipsed any worries that she might have had over the new arrangement at her aunt and uncle's house. Anyone else might have thought it odd that, with another baby on the way, the family would see fit to loan their capable eldest daughter to relatives next door, but Molly put that thought aside. The arrangement served the additional purpose of keeping Molly and her stepmother apart. She would still be next door to her beloved father and sisters, in an area that had been her home for the last fourteen years, and that was good enough for now.

She went about the rest of her day with a smile on her face and all but forgot that her father had been mystified by her mention of Mr Dixon and Eastlands Farm. Her thoughts raced ahead – her very own room in the attic and, perhaps, the possibility of bettering herself in her uncle's house. Her life, which only that morning had seemed frightening and uncertain, had now taken on a much rosier hue. What a difference a few hours had made to her future.

After their dinner that day, John took the unusual step of saying that he would accompany his wife on her excursion to the gardens in Hawley Square with the children.

'I know they've done much work there, for I've seen it when I've been delivering the milk, but never had time to take a walk around. I've a mind to see them for myself today,' he said, firmly setting aside Ann's objections that he would be bored. Ann was forced to confess that they were unable to gain access to the pleasure gardens that lay at the heart of the square as they were still being laid out, but she enjoyed walking around the square and seeing the fine ladies and gentlemen coming and going between their houses and carriages.

'I hope one day we will be able to walk in the park,' she said, somewhat forlornly, as they set out, John looking uncharacteristically grim. On their return an hour later, Ann went straight up to her and John's bedroom, slamming the door. Furious weeping could be heard but John sat at the kitchen table, stony-faced, before turning his attention to playing with his younger children while Molly set about preparing supper.

Ann was tight-lipped at the supper table and Molly went to bed none the wiser as to what had passed between her father and his wife that afternoon. The next morning, she planned to probe him for answers but she had no need.

John was barely through the yard gate before he burst out, 'Molly, your uncle was quite right. I have allowed my wife to behave in a foolish manner through my own lack of attention. I didn't see what was going on under my very nose. I wish that you had spoken to me rather than your aunt about your treatment under my roof but what's done is done and now I am to lose you.' John shook his head sorrowfully and Molly hurried over to put her arms around him and soothe him. He submitted to her murmured words of comfort for a moment or two, then held her away from him. 'No, it was not right and I have told her so. You are my daughter, not some skivvy. As to what she was thinking in pursuing arrangements behind my back to send you to her father's farm, I can't begin to think. I was foolish to go along with her idea to use that threat to bring you into line when you were too fond of gallivanting off every afternoon.'

John sighed. 'I can only think that her move into town from that godforsaken farm has given her ideas above her station. Our walk yesterday went some way to confirming that. I will not have her parading our children around Hawley Square to be the laughing-stock of the gentry there. Those gardens are for the use of the residents, or by a subscription that is sure to be beyond my means. If Ann aspires to such a life then she has married the wrong man.'

Molly had rarely seen her father so animated since her mother was alive, but his speech seemed to have drained him of energy and he sat down suddenly on the wooden chair at the little makeshift desk and ran his hands through his hair.

'If only my wife and daughter could be made to see eye to eye.' He was talking to himself again, but Molly felt a surge of indignation. The fault lay with Ann, surely. For her part, she had tried her best to be on good terms with her stepmother. She pushed aside all thoughts of her 'gallivanting' with Will as her father spoke again.

'No matter. Tonight, we are to visit your aunt and uncle, to see the picture your young friend Will has done. And to discuss how our new arrangement will work. I confess I shall be glad if it will ease relations between our two families.' John's face was troubled once more. 'Things have been difficult with your uncle since your mother died.'

Since you took up with Ann, you mean – it was a thought to which Molly didn't give voice. Instead, she asked, 'Do you expect Will to join us this evening?'

Her father, now flicking through the bills on the table, was distracted. 'No, no, I do believe your uncle mentioned he has returned to London. To attend school there, I think he said.'

CHAPTER NINE

C harlie was on watering duty in the garden, taking several trips to the tap with the metal watering can. It was so big it needed two hands to lift it when it was full, making it hard to control the flow of water. Charlie had learnt how important this was: newly planted seedlings would lift out of the ground if not watered gently, to lie languishing in a sea of mud. If the flow was too fierce, the water would just run off the sun-baked earth. With the bed thoroughly watered, Charlie carefully wound nets around and over the bamboo canes, just as Mr Fleming had taught him, double-checking that there were no gaps where a rabbit might get through.

He was concentrating hard on the task in hand, but he couldn't help a tear rolling down his face and splashing onto the mud of the vegetable bed. Samuel had loved the tomatoes that came from the garden later in the year. Little memories like that would creep up on him, no matter how hard he tried to stay strong. He stole a look around from under the brim of his cap to make sure that no one had noticed, although Mr Fleming was the only person likely to be around, and he wouldn't mind.

But, to Charlie's surprise, someone else was in the garden, walking purposefully down the path towards him. The sun was so strong today that even the peak of his cap wasn't proof against its brightness and Charlie had to shield his eyes to make out the details of the figure approaching him. It was female, of that he was sure, and not one of the residents or staff of Prospect House, because this person wasn't wearing either the poorhouse uniform or the garb of a servant. It was only when she was within a few feet of him, as the sun picked out a red glint in her chestnut hair, that he realised it was Molly, and his heart gave a little leap.

When he had returned to the poorhouse garden, after his spell at the Church Street yard and Samuel's death, Charlie had been confused by how things in his world had shifted. He had been content until then, working every day with Mr Fleming and settled in his mind that Samuel was as well cared for as it was possible to be within the poorhouse. Samuel had his bed in the dormitory, his three meals a day – none of which could be called substantial, but still ... He had a bit of schooling and the promise of taking over as the new apprentice in the garden when Charlie's own apprenticeship was over. In the autumn, Mr Fleming let Charlie have the pick of the windfall apples to give to his brother, and in summer there were squashed raspberries, which he cradled in his palms to preserve them on their journey from garden to dormitory. Once, there had been a scoop of honey from the hives that Mr Fleming was experimenting with, spread on bread that Charlie had saved from lunch under instruction from the gardener. He could still remember the sticky sweetness, how it had stayed on his lips and tongue rather than dissolving away, like the shaved curls of sugar his mother used to cut from a sugar loaf, long ago when they still had a home to call their own.

Working at the Church Street yard and meeting Molly had disrupted his contentment. At Prospect House, men and women, girls and boys were all segregated. Charlie spent his time in exclusively male company, apart from the briefest of interactions with the cook or other female staff at the poorhouse. It came as a shock to him to discover that girls were very different from him. They behaved and thought in a different way, asked questions that a boy would never think to ask. After he had got over how it unnerved him, he discovered that he rather liked it, and he looked forward to seeing Molly. Having her frank gaze rest upon him and seeing how her brown eyes widened in sympathy when he mentioned that Samuel had grown worse made it more easy to bear.

And then it was all over for Samuel and he had gone, another under-sized boy already sleeping in his bed. Charlie, now alone in the world, had returned to his work in the garden, where all was the same but somehow different. The work had helped distract him and take his mind off Samuel and how he had failed in his responsibilities, but he realised that he missed having Molly to talk to. He had not wanted to do so but had found himself asking Mark, who had taken his place as stable-boy for the Goodchilds, whether he could ask Molly to visit the garden one day. He wanted to show her around, so that she might see what he did with his days. But she hadn't come and he hated himself for asking Mark whether he had delivered the message.

'Aye, I did,' Mark had replied. 'She said ...' he frowned in concentration, trying to remember '... she said she would come one day.'

So, each day for quite some time Charlie had expected her to appear, saving up little things to tell her. He paid extra heed to the vegetables and flowers in season in the garden so that when she came he might ask Mr Fleming if she could take something home with her. And now here she was, when Charlie had given up expecting her and had become used once more to being closeted within the walls of the garden, with no need to venture further, except to church on a Sunday. He had seen her at St John's, it was true, but just a tantalising glimpse of the back of her head and her distinctive chestnut hair, or her profile as she turned to hush a child. One week she was missing, and his heart lurched, his mind taken up with imagining that she had succumbed to a cough, like Samuel, only to notice her a half-hour later, seated in a different pew, alongside the family of William Goodchild, one of the trustees of Prospect House.

The residents of the poorhouse took their places last, at the back of the church, and they left first – to avoid any contact with the people of the town, Charlie supposed. The great and the good, whose donations helped to support the poorhouse, would graciously listen to carols sung by the residents of Prospect House at Christmas. They would come on visits, led around by Mr Dalton, to observe what their money had achieved. But for Charlie, working every day within the garden walls, there was no interaction with the townsfolk. His spell in the Church Street yard had been quite a novelty.

Now Molly was standing before him and Charlie barely knew what to say other than 'Hello.'

'Charlie, I'm very sorry that I haven't been to see you before. As soon as I heard about Samuel I meant to come but something prevented me.' Molly paused, apparently thinking back. 'And then I got into such trouble with Ann – my stepmother – that I could not leave the house after dinner but must work all afternoon and evening. But now I am living in my uncle's house and my duties there give me much more free time.'

Molly ceased her explanation and took a good look around. 'This is a lovely place, Charlie.'

Charlie, tongue-tied since her arrival, finally found his voice. 'Aye, it is on a summer's day like today when the sun is shining, but less so in the cold of the winter, with work to be done every day to keep it in order.'

He couldn't think why he had chosen to speak as though he had found fault with her observation. He loved his work, and in any case Molly was no stranger to the winter cold, working as she did in the Church Street yard. Before he could seek to redeem himself, he saw Mr Fleming approaching.

'I'd best introduce you to Mr Fleming,' Charlie said.

'Oh, we've met,' Molly said. 'He saw me coming in at the gate and I introduced myself. I wanted to say thank you to him for allowing you to work for us.' She turned to Charlie. 'And I had quite forgotten my reason for coming. I wanted to thank you, too, for helping us in the yard. But mainly I wanted to say how sorry I was to hear about Samuel.'

Mr Fleming had arrived by their side but he stepped respectfully away as Molly continued to speak.

'I was upset to hear that Samuel's cough had carried him off. Poor child, he wasn't well when he came to us. And now you have no one.'

Charlie sensed that Molly was looking directly at him but he was unable to meet her eyes. He feared her sympathy would cause him to cry, so he bit his lip and stared fiercely at his boots, scuffing them on the ground.

Mr Fleming stepped in to rescue him. 'He'll not be alone, miss, while I'm alive.' He spoke firmly, clapping Charlie on the shoulder. 'He's a good lad and like family to me. And, Charlie, I have some news for you.'

Charlie peered hopefully from under the brim of his cap.

His apprenticeship was almost finished and he knew that Mr Fleming had approached the trustees about keeping him on as an under-gardener.

'They've agreed, Charlie. You can stay for another two years and then we must apply again.'

Charlie, who had been longing to see Molly, now found himself wishing that she hadn't chosen this particular day to visit. Already made tearful by memories of Samuel, he found himself affected again. He had been dreading having to leave the security of everything he knew – the garden, Mr Fleming and even his narrow bed in the shared dormitory. Now he could set himself right in the world again and feel secure for two more years in this place he had had to learn to call home. And then, perhaps, he would feel ready to join the world outside the garden walls.

Charlie swallowed hard and looked up. Mr Fleming had tactfully drawn Molly away to show her his prized roses, now in full bloom, so he had more time to collect himself. He could thank Mr Fleming later, although it would hardly be necessary. They understood each other so well. For now, he must try to make the most of Molly's visit and show her around in the hope that she would return one day, when he was fully in command of himself.

Molly, though, had other plans. She was coming back up the path with Mr Fleming, carrying a bunch of roses, and as Charlie bent at the pump to wash the mud from his hands she said, 'Charlie, I must go. I have errands to run for my aunt. But I know where to find you now and I won't leave it so long next time.'

Mr Fleming looked after her approvingly as they watched her walk away along the lavender-lined path, towards the gate.

'She's a nice young lass, Charlie. A good friend for you

to have, with her uncle being one of the trustees here.' He looked at Charlie with something of a twinkle in his eye.

'Perhaps she might be more than a friend, with time?'

Charlie blushed and protested, 'She can't be more than thirteen or fourteen!'

He was quite shocked by Mr Fleming's reply.

'Aye, well, you're fourteen now and you'll be sixteen by the time you've had experience as an under-gardener here. It won't be long after that before you're in a position to think about setting up home. She'll be catching the eye of many a young man by then. You'd do well to think on it.'

Mr Fleming took himself off, a hard-to-read expression on his face, leaving Charlie to work his way through the rest of the day's tasks with an unsettled mind. There was the news that he could stay on in the garden, then Molly had been to visit at long last although he had been wrong-footed by her appearance. He hardly knew what to think about Mr Fleming's startling parting words. Charlie found himself pink-cheeked and with a headache by the end of the day – and he knew it wasn't due to the sun because he had taken care to work in the shade and keep his hat on.

As he lay that night in his bed in the long dormitory, which was stifling despite the open windows, he listened to the regular breathing of the other boys and their occasional mutterings as they slept, and he remembered Molly's words as she left.

I know where to find you now and I won't leave it so long next time.

Chapter Ten

By the time Molly had been living at her aunt's house for a few weeks she felt quite settled there. Life was better than it had been next door, she had to admit, although she missed seeing Lizzie and Mary each morning when she awoke. At night, tucked up in solitude at the top of the house, she thought of the others asleep in such close proximity to her: her aunt and uncle at the front of the house; Clara and Louisa sleeping below; her sisters abed in the little house next door, arms wrapped around one another. In fact, it was hard to believe that the two households were truly next door to each other, for the way of life in each was quite different. Her cousins were older than Molly's family – Nicholas, at sixteen years old, was the eldest son, away at school much of the time, his father having high hopes of a naval career for him. Clara, his older sister, was still at home but Molly had the feeling that she would be married before long.

Louisa, the youngest, was two years younger than Molly and much occupied with the sort of pursuits that it was impossible to imagine taking place in John and Ann Goodchild's household. Louisa's father had decided, as his prosperity increased, that he would be in a position to make a good marriage for his younger daughter. He had instructed his wife that Louisa was to be taught the skills to make her 'as accomplished as the daughters of the gentlefolk in Hawley Square'.

Louisa had already laboured for a short while under a drawing master, before persuading her father that her talents could be put to better use elsewhere. Her mother, who had reservations about her husband's sometimes over-inflated ideas, backed her and persuaded him that sewing skills would be of more use and were just as genteel. So embroidery was added to the plain sewing that Louisa had learnt from an early age and music was substituted for art. Louisa went out to a singing master for her lessons, which Molly privately considered to be a good thing, having dutifully listened to her practise at home. Aunt Jane supervised the sewing, to ensure that she learnt useful skills as well as decorative ones. Molly noticed, with some envy, that darning wasn't considered necessary for her. Louisa would marry well enough not to need to undertake that in the future.

As Molly dusted the drawing room she could admire the framed samplers that Louisa had produced, and marvel that her cousin had had the time to sit for hours on end to create such things. Her uncle and aunt's house had many decorative items on display – the walls were hung with pictures as well as Louisa's samplers, and plants were placed in fine china pots in the drawing room. In Molly's own house, every item was useful; nothing was there just for ornament. Molly traced the scrolls of the acanthus foliage on the plant pot after she had dusted it. How could someone be clever enough to think of such a design, let alone draw it? Her eye moved to Will's sketch of her uncle's cows, now framed and hung near the door so that it caught her eye every time she left the room. Will had that skill: he could capture the shape of something with just a few strokes of his pencil and he could wash in the colour so that it suddenly came alive.

Will hadn't been at the great unveiling of his picture, that awkward evening when her uncle had invited them in to see his new acquisition. By then Molly knew that Will had gone back to London, but her uncle proclaimed with some pride that he'd promised to create a proper painting of the cows when he next returned to Margate, which would be within the year. Molly's heart had leapt at the news: she'd been sad to hear of his sudden departure, without a word of goodbye to her. She often paused as she went about her aunt's business in town and thought how a particular view would make a good sketch for Will, mentally squirrelling away the idea for the future.

The evening of the unveiling had been difficult on many levels. Ann had glowered at Molly and been barely civil to Aunt Jane, so that Molly burnt with shame and rage. Her poor father had looked uncomfortable, torn between trying to be grateful for his brother's hospitality while being sensible to his wife's displeasure. John and Ann had departed after less than an hour, leaving Lizzie and Mary to stay a little longer at Aunt Jane's insistence. As Molly chased them up the stairs to show them the room where she would be sleeping, she thought she heard her aunt say, 'What a dreadful, odious woman. Whatever was your brother thinking?' before her uncle firmly closed the drawing-room door.

Within a fortnight of her arrival in her aunt and uncle's house, Molly had established a new routine. She milked the cows each morning and worked in the Church Street yard, as before, then returned to eat with her aunt, who would list her duties for the afternoon. Uncle William dined out most days, but never on a Sunday when all the family ate together

64

after church. Molly felt awkward sitting in her uncle's pew, instead of with her own family, but Aunt Jane and Uncle William made a point of being there early – her uncle maintained it was so that they would be quiet and composed at the start of the service, but Molly suspected it was because he liked to be seen by the townsfolk. More often than not, Molly's own family barely made it through the door before the poorhouse children entered, so sitting with her relatives seemed the most sensible thing to do.

Molly's daily duties were generally light – her aunt had decided to employ a cook, Hannah, to replace Elsa and she already had a maid, so Molly helped to wash the dishes, performed light household duties and was sent into town on errands. It was on one such expedition on a hot day in late June that she had paid her first visit to the garden at Prospect House. It hadn't been a success: Charlie had appeared ill at ease. He was quite short with her when she apologised for failing to visit earlier and tried to express how sorry she had been to hear of Samuel's death. She'd promised to come again, although she'd only half meant it.

Mr Fleming the head gardener, whom she'd met that day for the first time, had been charming but she'd found it hard to meet his piercing gaze. It made her uncomfortable, as though he could look right through her and read her mind. As she'd left, he'd insisted on her taking roses as a gift for her aunt. His face was turned away from Molly as he leant into the rose bush to cut several long stems for her to take home. 'Charlie's still very sad over Samuel's death,' he said. 'Pay him no mind if he seems a little odd. Try to come back – he's in need of a friend of his own age.'

Molly was still musing on his words when she returned to the Princes Crescent house to find all in chaos and confusion.

'Molly, wherever have you been? You've been gone for hours,' her aunt said, sounding cross as she hurried past her niece in the hallway.

'I've brought these for you.' Molly held out the bunch but her aunt was already halfway down the stairs to the kitchen so, gathering up the packages, she followed her, to find the new cook, Hannah, looking flustered as her aunt reeled off a list of instructions.

'Aunt, whatever has happened?' Molly couldn't understand what might have precipitated such a panic: all had been calm when she had left. Clearly, important news must have arrived.

'Nicholas is coming home tomorrow,' her aunt flung over her shoulder, as she climbed back up the stairs again.

Molly followed her, frowning. 'Nicholas? But he isn't due until next week, surely.'

'He is being allowed home a week early. And nothing ready for him!'

CHAPTER ELEVEN

Molly became caught up in her aunt's frenzy of preparation for Nicholas's homecoming. He'd been away at school for two years now and Molly hadn't seen him in all that time, but as she swept the dust from beneath his bed, shook out the rag rugs in the garden and placed sprigs of lavender in the clothes press, she thought back to when they'd last spent time together. If her memory served her well, it had been in the garden of this very house, when Nicholas was intent on using his catapult to knock the sparrows from next door's garden wall.

Molly was scouring pans in the kitchen when she heard the commotion that announced his arrival. By the time she'd made her way up to the drawing room her aunt, pink-cheeked with excitement, was seated beside him, gazing up at him. Molly checked herself in the doorway. Was this really Nicholas? Her one-time playmate had been replaced by a tall young man who was holding forth in a confident voice, his mother hanging on his every word. Nicholas turned at Molly's entrance and she wished, in a moment, that she'd seen fit to wear a better frock that morning and had thought to check her appearance in the glass that stood in the hall.

Her uncle, a difficult man to impress, was clearly pleased

and proud at the transformation his schooling had effected on his son. Molly had heard him only recently telling her father that the fees at the Naval Academy had been a struggle to manage but that he felt sure it was the best course for the future. The Navy would always be in need of officers, Uncle William had said, for no sooner was one war over than another began. It looked as though he was to be proved right: Nicholas gave every appearance of being a fine, upstanding young man. He looked set to be a credit to the Navy and the career that his father had planned for him.

By the end of the afternoon, though, the atmosphere had taken a very different turn. Molly, at work in the kitchen helping Hannah to prepare a special dinner for Nicholas's homecoming, became aware of raised voices upstairs and a slamming of doors. Hannah glanced at her and Molly was about to ask what she thought might be amiss when they heard footsteps on the kitchen staircase. Molly went on chopping potatoes, and Hannah became intent on basting the fowl, which she had just removed from the oven. A glance at Aunt Jane's face as she entered the kitchen was enough to tell her niece that all was most decidedly not well.

'Why, Aunt Jane, whatever is the matter?' Molly dropped her knife, wiped her hands on her apron and quickly pulled out a chair for her at the table. Aunt Jane's pink cheeks of earlier had faded to a startling pallor and her eyes, red-rimmed, were evidence that she had been weeping. Molly noticed that her aunt's hands were shaking at the same instant that Hannah hurried to the dresser and extracted a bottle and glass.

'Here you are, ma'am. It's what I use for cooking and not

as good as what you have upstairs, but a drop or two should see you right.'

Hannah poured a generous measure of brandy into the glass and put it in front of Aunt Jane, who stared at it, then took a tentative sip, then another, before draining half the glass.

She sat in silence for a moment or two and Molly, unsure of what to do for the best, picked up her knife and prepared to tackle the potatoes again. Hannah gave her a barely perceptible nod of encouragement, so Molly carried on peeling and chopping, waiting to see whether her aunt would speak without being questioned.

After five minutes had elapsed, Aunt Jane let out a great sigh. 'You may as well stop your preparations now. There'll be no celebratory dinner tonight.'

Hannah raised her eyes to the heavens as she regarded the quantity of meat already roasted, and the fowl she had just basted. She glanced at Molly, grim-faced, and shook her head in despair.

'It seems Nicholas is not home a week early by chance.' Aunt Jane's lip trembled. 'He has not behaved as the Academy would have wished so he is not to return there.'

Neither Molly nor Hannah knew how to respond to this but there was no need for, once started on her tale of woe, Aunt Jane could not keep it in.

'Yes, a letter has just arrived from the Academy by the afternoon post. It would appear that Nicholas was hoping to keep the news from us. Your uncle ...' here she looked at Molly who, aware that her mouth was half open in surprise, attempted to compose her features '... your uncle is very angry. He has had words with Nicholas and left the house. And Nicholas has gone up to his room.'

Her aunt's shoulders heaved with sobs and Molly put down her knife and hurried to her side. She had a painful image of Aunt Jane, left alone in the drawing room after the quarrel, dismayed and distraught by the news and mindful of her husband's anger, with no one to confide in and a celebratory dinner about to be ruined.

'Oh, Aunt, is it really that bad? Perhaps they just wish to teach Nicholas a lesson. If he writes an apology for whatever he is thought to have done, surely all will be well.'

Molly, who had no knowledge of the workings of academies and the like, was basing her judgement on her observations. Money seemed to take care of most things. Surely the Academy would wish to hold onto Nicholas for the sake of his fees. Whatever he had done could hardly warrant more than the threat of harsh discipline.

Her aunt's sobs redoubled. She tried to speak but was unable to do so for crying.

'Sssh … sssh …' Molly soothed, uneasy at the turn of events. Hannah shrugged and returned the fowl to the range – it would have to be eaten cold during the week if there was to be no big family dinner that evening.

Aunt Jane reached for her glass, drank the rest of the brandy and finally managed to force out some words. 'Nicholas has formed a …' she struggled to find a way to express it '… a *friendship* with the daughter of the Master of the Naval Academy.'

Molly was puzzled. 'Is that such a bad thing?' she asked. Her aunt's handkerchief was a sodden mess on the table and Molly handed over her own as the sobbing continued. 'Wouldn't that be a good match?'

Nicholas was a bit young for marriage, it was true, Molly thought, but an alliance with the daughter of the Master of the Academy was surely to be welcomed. And presumably Nicholas could pursue his naval career before they needed to marry, which would satisfy Uncle William.

'It seems they have strayed beyond the bounds of propriety.' Aunt Jane forced out the words and Molly wasn't entirely sure of her meaning but she saw Hannah turn away to hide a smile.

'Your uncle is to leave for Portsmouth this evening and we will dine quietly, alone. Molly, would you go next door and tell your father that the invitation to dinner has been cancelled?'

Her aunt had managed to pull herself together. Years spent doing her duty and organising the smooth-running of the lives of others meant that it was easier to deal with practical matters than confront emotions. Her husband would decide what to do about Nicholas.

'What shall I say, Aunt?' Molly had enough sense to know that she shouldn't share with her own family what Aunt Jane had just told her. It felt wrong, but it would be disloyal to her aunt and uncle. Ann would be the likely recipient of the news – her father would no doubt be out – and she could not be relied upon to be kind or discreet.

Aunt Jane took a deep breath, trying to prevent her distress breaking out afresh. 'You must say …' she paused, thinking '… you must say that Nicholas is back but feverish and unwell. It may be contagious so we will dine alone tonight.'

It made good sense, Molly thought. Ann was not yet halfway through her pregnancy and would not want to risk catching anything. And the excuse would give her aunt and uncle's household a good enough reason to lie low and refuse visitors for a few days.

Her aunt stood up, visibly composing herself to return

upstairs, and thanked Hannah for the brandy. As she climbed the stairs from the kitchen, Molly hastily left via the basement steps to deliver her message, glad to avoid Hannah's inevitable explosion of wrath over the time wasted in the preparation of the homecoming dinner.

CHAPTER TWELVE

With William Goodchild on his way to Portsmouth and not expected back before the week was out, the household settled into a new routine. For the first day or so, Molly found mealtimes uneasy. Her aunt was quiet and seemed on the verge of tears most of the time, while Nicholas was mostly sulky and sullen. Both of them took to their rooms as soon as they had eaten, and Molly was glad to be able to help clear up and escape to the kitchen. One afternoon, finding herself at a loose end and with no errands to be run, she took herself off to see Charlie again, hoping to find him in a better humour than on her first visit.

This time, he was hard at work in the corner of the walled garden. Mr Fleming had led her to him, for he was quite hidden from view by the foliage rambling across the canes where he worked.

'You can give him a hand,' Mr Fleming said. 'Charlie will show you how. Two of you will get the job done quicker than one. Then you can both take a break with me.'

Charlie showed her how he had been loosely tying in the stems of abundant foliage along the length of each cane, gently untangling the tendrils where the neighbouring plants were trying to cling to each other for support.

'What are these plants?' Molly asked. She soon found

her smaller, nimble fingers better suited to the untangling, so she concentrated on that while Charlie cut short lengths of rough twine and loosely knotted the stems to the canes. The red flowers were particularly attractive to the bees, she noticed. She'd already given a few cause to buzz angrily as her work made the flowers wave about, unsettling them.

'Runner beans,' Charlie said. 'They grow so quickly that it won't be long before the flowers have gone and the pods will be forming. Then we'll be eating beans every day for weeks. They make a nice change when they first appear but after that …' He shrugged and sighed. 'I remember Samuel complaining about how we ate nothing but beans last summer.'

'I don't think I've ever tried them,' Molly said, as she concentrated on untangling a mass of stems that seemed determined to form a knot.

'Then you certainly must this year,' Charlie declared. 'If you're here a couple of weeks from now you'll be able to try the youngest and freshest ones.'

They concentrated on finishing the job so that they could escape the heat of the sun to sit in the shade by the gardeners' hut. Mr Fleming had made rhubarb cordial earlier in the year and he produced a bottle, bidding Charlie to fill a jug at the pump to dilute it for drinking.

'We're lucky to have the sweetest water you ever did taste, here in the garden,' Mr Fleming said to Molly, as he poured some of the pink syrupy cordial into a cup for her. 'I dread the day it dries up.'

'Is that likely?' Molly asked, as Charlie topped up their cups from his water jug.

'Well, legend has it that if the spring that feeds it ever runs dry, a great plague will fall upon the town.' Mr Fleming looked grave. Molly, who could see Charlie attempting to keep a straight face, tried hard not to catch his eye in case he made her laugh.

'Mmm, this is delicious,' she said, as she tasted the cordial. 'Did you really make it yourself? If you have the recipe I'd like to pass it on to Hannah, our cook. She could make some for us, perhaps.'

'Hannah, you say?' Mr Fleming said. 'Why, if that's who I'm thinking of, she's from the kitchens here. She'll know the recipe – she's the one who gave it to me!'

Molly's description of Hannah – small in stature, yet big-boned with greying hair, rosy cheeks and a seemingly permanent dusting of flour across her ample bosom, despite her apron – confirmed her as the assistant cook from Prospect House, on loan to Uncle William.

The next twenty minutes passed in talk of gardening matters until Mr Fleming told Charlie it was time to get back to work and Molly reluctantly forsook the shade of the hut to make the short, but hot, walk home.

Mr Fleming stooped to pick some sprigs of lavender, tying them into a loose bunch for Molly. 'Come again soon,' he said, handing it to her as he opened the gate for her to leave.

As she made her way back to Princes Crescent, Molly felt lighter of heart than she had done over the last couple of days. She gave the lavender to Hannah, who set it in a white enamel jug on the kitchen windowsill and exclaimed over the lovely scent. 'Is this from the garden?' she asked.

'From the one at the poorhouse,' Molly said. 'I've been visiting. I drank some rhubarb cordial – Mr Fleming said the recipe was yours. It was the most delicious drink I've ever tasted. Will you make some here for us?'

Hannah turned pink with pleasure. 'If I can get the

rhubarb, I certainly will. Mr Fleming is a magician. He can grow anything in that garden. We were spoilt for fruit and vegetables.'

'Charlie's promised me some runner beans,' Molly said. 'I don't think I've tasted them before.'

Hannah chuckled. 'We must have eaten them every day for weeks last year. We were all sick of the sight of them.' She paused. 'Who's Charlie?'

It was Molly's turn to blush. 'A friend. He worked for my father for a short time as a stable-boy but he's really Mr Fleming's assistant.'

Hannah gave Molly a knowing look. 'Ah, I know the lad you mean. The good-looking boy with the dark eyes, yes?' She cocked her head enquiringly at Molly who, her colour having subsided, found herself blushing furiously again.

Aunt Jane's arrival in the kitchen put paid to Hannah's teasing. Nicholas had apparently shaken off his gloom and had a fancy for some anchovy toast, and Aunt Jane had decided that they would take tea together while he ate it.

At the table that evening, Molly discovered quite a different side to Nicholas. He could be entertaining, witty and solicitous when he put his mind to it. He teased his sisters gently, sat after supper on a footstool at his mother's feet, and insisted on handing her things from her workbox as she needed them. Then he asked Molly whether she had ever visited the secret caves in the town, for he planned to take his sisters there the following evening. He wondered whether she might care to join them.

'Secret caves?' Molly hadn't heard of them. 'Somewhere along the shore, do you mean? Won't it be dangerous in the evening, with the tides?'

She was already thinking of the damage to dresses and

petticoats, not to mention shoes and boots, that a trip to the beach would entail, with the washerwoman not due until next week at the earliest.

'No, no, these caves are in town.' Nicholas was laughing at her expression. 'They're hidden in a garden, but Robert has the key and a party of us are going tomorrow.

'It's quite safe,' he continued, as his mother looked set to protest. 'They aren't at all deep or extensive, just a single chamber, I think. But I believe they are decorated in quite a spectacular way.'

He refused to say more, saying it would spoil the surprise, and instead Clara was prevailed upon to play the piano so that Louisa could sing. Molly made the excuse of needing to help Hannah in the kitchen and slipped away. But later that evening, as she was making her way upstairs to bed by candlelight, she was startled by Nicholas stepping from the darkened doorway of his room as she passed. She gasped and almost dropped the candle as he put his fingers to her lips, gripped her arm and drew her close to him, whispering in her ear, 'Do come tomorrow. It will be fun, I promise you.'

Then he stepped silently back into his room, leaving Molly wondering whether she had imagined his presence. Hot wax dripping onto her hand from the candle she was holding brought her to her senses and she hastened up the last flight of narrow attic stairs just as the guttering flame gave out and died. She undressed in the dark and that night she tossed and turned in her bed, disturbed by the memory of Nicholas's grip on her arm and his hot breath in her ear.

CHAPTER THIRTEEN

The next day Molly had some difficulty getting through her duties patiently. The thought of the trip to the caves was uppermost in her mind. She had never heard of such a place in Margate and she half wondered whether Nicholas was telling the truth. Had he, in fact, some other escapade in mind? Molly felt sure that her uncle would have quizzed Nicholas much more vigorously than Aunt Jane had seen fit to do. She suspected that the expedition would have been banned, had he been at home.

As it was, it was a beautiful July evening when Molly joined Clara, Louisa and Nicholas, already assembled in the hall.

'You must take a shawl,' Aunt Jane was saying firmly to her daughters. 'I'm sure that caves are nasty damp places. It may be warm outside now but I don't want either of you taking a chill.'

Molly, not being included in these strictures, took her chance and slipped outside to wait on the front steps. The sky was a beautiful pearly blue with barely a cloud to be seen as the sun dropped slowly towards the horizon. Molly gave a little shiver of excitement, quickly suppressed for fear her aunt might see it: she was now standing anxiously in the doorway as she watched the little party set out. 'Don't be late back. I will be waiting up,' she said.

Molly turned at the end of the crescent to see her still standing there, looking a little forlorn.

As soon as they had left their road behind, Nicholas said, 'Now, Robert will meet us at Dane Hill with his party. We are going to blindfold you all before we take you any further.'

Louisa and Clara began to express doubts but Nicholas was firm.

'The caves truly are a secret and Robert has the key to their entrance by chance. We must be very quiet until we are inside and then we'll give you candles. Prepare to be amazed.'

He refused to answer any more questions, despite the excited entreaties of his sisters, who were hanging off each of his arms, leaving Molly to walk behind. She didn't much mind – it allowed her to think about his words. How would they find their way blindfold? They would surely stumble and fall. There would be trouble in Princes Crescent if either Clara or Louisa took a tumble.

Then a wave of excitement swept away her doubts. She'd never had such an adventure. Nor had she ever visited this part of town. The narrow streets of cottages and squares of grand terraces had given way to something quite different. Molly thought they might have been in the countryside, except that every now and then an imposing wrought-iron gate would appear beside their path, set across the entrance to a grand carriage drive that led to what was no doubt a very large house, hidden behind trees. Once Molly thought she glimpsed a roof and chimneys, and the glint of a window as it caught the rays of the sun, before a large wall obscured whatever lay behind. She was driven to wonder who could be living in such a place before her musing was disturbed as Nicholas called a halt on reaching a junction in the road.

'Robert should be here at any moment,' he said confidently

and, sure enough, the sound of voices carried to them on the still evening air before they sighted the remainder of the party, Robert and his two sisters, Sarah and Catherine. They were a little younger than Nicholas and very pretty, Molly noticed. The four girls obviously knew each other already and Nicholas didn't see fit to introduce Molly to them, so she hung back while the girls exchanged greetings. She felt hot and cross all at once but no one paid her any heed.

'Now, hush,' Nicholas said, after a moment or two. 'We don't want anyone to wonder about our presence here. Robert is going to hand out the blindfolds. You must each put one on, then join hands and we'll lead you to the caves.'

As more excited chatter broke out, Nicholas held up his hand. 'I really must impress on you the need for quiet. In fact, we must be silent once we are under way, or we will abandon the whole thing.'

The tying on of the blindfolds took place amid much giggling and shushing. Nicholas and Robert proved useless at securing them, managing either to catch the girls' hair and pull it as they tied the knots, provoking squeals of protest, or to knot the bands so loosely that they slid down over their noses. Molly looked on before silently taking over, releasing trapped hair and securing the bands so that they were comfortably in place. She wondered where Robert had come by the blindfolds, which were made of dark-coloured velvet and held traces of perfume, but she observed the rule of silence and didn't ask.

Nicholas smiled gratefully as she completed Louisa's knot, then held out the remaining blindfold to her. Molly tried hard not to meet his eyes as she took it from him and wrapped it around her head, thankful that she could hide in its dark folds as yet another blush threatened to cover her cheeks. She started as she felt a warm hand on hers as she tied the knot. Then a voice whispered in her ear, 'Just making sure. We don't want you peeping, do we?'

She wasn't sure whether it was her imagination but she felt the fingers had lingered a moment too long, and the lips remained by her ear even when he had finished speaking; she could feel his breath on her cheek.

Then Nicholas and Robert were issuing instructions in low voices. The girls were to join hands in single file with Robert at the front and Nicholas bringing up the rear. They were to remain quiet.

'It's not far,' Nicholas reassured them. Molly could sense that he was walking along the line, making sure that blind-folds were secure and hands firmly joined. She had stood a little apart, unsure what to do, then felt Nicholas take her left hand and pull her forward. 'Now, Louisa, you hold onto Molly. Take care to keep in step with each other.'

She felt Louisa's warm fingers reach out for her own, then Nicholas took her right hand in his grasp and called to Robert in a low voice that they were ready to move. Molly's first few steps were tentative, prompted by Louisa moving forward and pulling her along after her. She was fearful of falling, as were the other girls, judging by their cries of dis-tress, quickly hushed. The sensation of walking while being unable to see anything, no matter how hard she strained against the material covering her eyes, made Molly shake a little with anxiety. But, as the strange crocodile of blind-folded girls progressed and she lost her fear of falling, she felt a thrill of enjoyment, enhanced by Nicholas's firm grip on her right hand.

He said very little, other than once or twice to tell Robert, 'A little slower,' but the consciousness of his presence burnt into Molly's being. Louisa became of little importance, other than as a guide to set Molly's pace. Her own quickened heartbeat, Molly came to realise, was not caused by fear of falling but by contact with her cousin. Her focus on him was so strong that she couldn't have said how far they had walked or whether they turned left or right, walked on the flat or went up or down an incline. She walked as if in a dream.

Mutterings of discontent from elsewhere in the crocodile brought her back to the present.

'Are we there yet?' The plaintive voice, straying above a whisper, had to be Louisa's, while one of Robert's sisters was heard to complain, 'You've walked us in a circle, surely.'

Just as it seemed mutiny might break out among the blind-folded walkers, the crocodile came to a halt. Molly heard the sound of metal on metal, then faint squeaking and grating sounds. Her ears straining, she took this to be a gate or door opening. The crocodile shuffled forward and Molly sensed a change in the atmosphere – a damp coldness that told her they must have reached the entrance to the cave.

'You can all let go of each other now,' Robert said. As Molly released Louisa's hand she realised how tightly they had been holding onto each other. She had to flex her fingers to return feeling to them. Nicholas, she noticed, held onto her right hand for a moment or two longer so that she had to wriggle her fingers to signal a wish for release. She needed both hands to untie her blindfold but even as it fell away, she felt as though it were still in place, such was the level of blackness. Then, as her eyes adjusted, Molly began to make out the pale faces of her companions in the gloom. Robert had opened his tinder box, and she could hear him striking the flint and see the sparks. A moment later, Nicholas had lit a candle and their faces were bathed in a yellow glow.

The appearance of light caused a release of nervous tension and chatter threatened to break out between the sisters, but a stern 'Sssh' from Robert and Nicholas returned the party to silence. Robert lit candles one by one and handed them out, while Nicholas collected the blindfolds. He laid them on a stone bench running along one wall of the narrow entrance chamber where they were now standing. Molly caught a glimpse of an iron gate behind her, which seemingly led out into a mass of foliage, before she found herself pushed in the other direction, towards the caves, with Nicholas's hand in the small of her back.

'Look around you as you go,' he breathed in her ear.

Dutifully, Molly raised her candle as she walked but so far there was nothing to see, except the chalky whiteness of the passage walls, stained here and there with streaks of green where water must have penetrated from the rocks above. The passageway sloped slightly downwards and Molly tried hard to concentrate on watching her footing in the dim light and on keeping up with the other members of the party, their silhouettes ahead of her lit by the wavering flames of their candles. Yet she found all her attention was focused on Nicholas. He walked a pace or two behind her and she was aware of his every movement: she could hear his breathing and the sound of his shoes striking the hard floor of the passageway; she could feel the heat from his candle close to her back and smell the wax as it burnt. The only thing she could not do was to turn her head to check his expression and she wasn't even sure that she wanted to.

CHAPTER FOURTEEN

Molly, aware that the rest of the party had descended rapidly, very soon found herself at the top of a set of steps cut into the rock.

'Steady now.' Nicholas's voice again, breathed into her ear, his hand on her waist as she reached out to the wall to check her balance as she descended.

The steps delivered her into a much wider space, a rectangular chamber, where she found the sisters clustered in front of one of the walls, candles raised, while Robert looked on with every appearance of satisfaction.

Louisa turned her head and called over to her: 'Molly, come and look.' No one hushed her, so they were clearly far enough underground to talk in safety, Molly thought. She found herself a little reluctant to leave Nicholas's side, but she knew it would look odd if she didn't, so she went to join Louisa.

The light of the candles revealed hundreds of shells set into the walls so that they formed patterns. Molly recognised whelks, limpets, mussels and oysters, all shells that she had seen on the beach or laid out on the stalls of the fish market, their contents still within them. Here, empty, they were set into the walls in intricate designs, the candlelight picking out the mother-of-pearl interiors of the oyster and mussel shells, while the raised surfaces of the whelks and limpets cast strange shadows.

'Stand away a little.' It was Nicholas again, encouraging them to move away from the wall and spread themselves out so that their candles illuminated a larger area. 'What can you see?'

'I think that's a star.' Clara was pointing.

'And another here,' Louisa said, in excitement. 'Or is it a flower?'

Molly saw the great curve of an arch, created in shells, along the wall, but didn't say anything. She felt it was her place to help where needed and to observe, but not to make her thoughts known. Robert was now set on chivvying them into a passage that led away from the chamber.

'We'll be coming back here but there's much more to be seen this way,' he said, holding his candle aloft to encourage them into the dark passageway. The sisters followed him closely, laughing and chattering in excitement. Molly made to follow but Nicholas held her back.

'I want to show you something over here,' he said, drawing her to the corner of the chamber. Molly opened her mouth to protest but no sound came out. She looked over her shoulder as the backs of the sisters faded into the gloom of the passage, then turned to look at the wall. Nicholas held up his candle, revealing a whole wall of geometric patterns, floor to ceiling. It was spectacular, Molly had to admit, but there was nothing to set it apart from the wall that they had already examined. He must be expecting a response that shows how impressed I am, Molly thought, and searched for something suitable to say. In the event, all she could come up with were the questions that had been uppermost in her mind throughout their journey.

'Why is this place so secret?' she asked. 'Who created it and why?'

'Ah, it's a secret because we aren't supposed to know about it, let alone be here,' Nicholas said. 'It's in the garden of a great house owned by some gentleman from London, who lets it be known that he likes to live as a recluse when he's here. Although Robert said that the parties he has down in these caves suggest something quite different.' Nicholas grinned and Molly wasn't sure that she liked the strange shadows the candlelight was casting on his face. He no longer looked like the Nicholas she knew.

'So how has Robert managed to come by a key?' she asked.

'The gardener at his father's house also works here. And he owed Robert a favour.' Nicholas sounded impatient. 'But that isn't why I wanted you to come over here. We must join the others before they notice our absence. But first …'

Before Molly understood his intention, he had pulled her to him and, as her lips parted in surprise, he was kissing her. Startled, she tried to pull away but he held her close and she found herself kissing him back. Even as she did so, she was half aware that this was not right, that she should not be doing this. She was holding one arm rigidly away from herself, to prevent the flame of the candle she held burning either Nicholas or herself. She hoped he was doing the same, for she feared her hair or clothing might be set alight. As if conscious that he did not have her full attention, Nicholas leant back and looked at her.

'These damn candles,' he said. Molly looked away in embarrassment and, as she did so, she caught a glimpse of their figures, locked in an embrace, casting a giant shadow across the wall before Nicholas let her go and stepped back.

'We must catch up with the others,' he said, pulling her

into the passageway. Then he paused. 'Later, tonight, come to my room,' he said, before striding ahead so that Molly had almost to run to keep up with him. The candle flame revealed more shell patterns heavily encrusting the walls as she hurried by, but there was no time to examine them. And, in any case, Molly was too caught up in her thoughts to pay them any heed, marvellous though the designs were. She was seized with a kind of terror that had nothing to do with the dark passageway but was focused instead on Nicholas's words.

What did he mean? She couldn't visit him in his room at night. But how was she to deny him? Would he lie in wait for her on the landing as he had the night before? Her aunt and uncle would throw her out and Ann would never have her back in the house next door. All this ran through Molly's mind in the short time that it took them to travel along the curving passageway and rejoin the others.

Their absence hadn't been noticed – as they arrived, Robert was explaining to the sisters that they were in a circular chamber, lined with many panels of decoration. He pointed up at the centre of the ceiling. 'In the daytime, the opening at the top allows light into the space,' he said. 'And on a clear night, if you are lucky, you can see the stars.'

The fact that it was so dark up above told Molly that the sun must have set. How long had they been away? Would Aunt Jane be starting to worry?

The same idea must have occurred to Nicholas, for he suggested that they shouldn't spend too long in the chamber, making just one circuit before returning to the first chamber by the curved passageway.

'Then we must be on our way back,' he said.

Molly made a point of standing close to Louisa and Clara,

to look at the same things they were looking at and, in this way, she managed to progress a good way around the circular chamber, exclaiming with her cousins over the way the shells glittered in the light and the strangeness of the designs.

'That one is meant to represent a serpent,' Molly heard Robert say to Sarah and Catherine. They were a few panels ahead of her and she had found herself once again at the back of the line, beside a dark passageway that led off to the right and which the others had passed, unremarked. But Nicholas saw his chance and caught her hand, pulling her back into the shadows and whispering, 'Sssh!' into her ear as she stifled a cry of surprise. His warm mouth was on hers again and despite her worried jumble of thoughts Molly found herself enjoying this more than his first surprising kiss. She was almost sorry when he pulled away and gently propelled her back into the chamber.

'Hurry up, Molly. Don't dawdle,' he said loudly, striding past her and winking.

Molly, heart beating fast from their encounter, found that she didn't like being last in line at all. She glanced nervously behind her, where the darkness seemed bent on swallowing her. Then she hurried as fast as she could after Nicholas, sparing a glance neither left nor right and so missing the remainder of the decorations in the circular chamber and along the curving passageway. She caught up with the others grouped in front of a panel that Robert was describing as depicting a tree. He pointed out the branches, which Molly viewed with some scepticism. She was thankful, though, that no one had noticed she hadn't been with them the whole time.

Molly was starting to feel hot and light-headed. Was it something to do with the air in the caves? Or was it the number of candles burning at the same time and somehow overwhelming the atmosphere? She felt as though all the air was being sucked out of her lungs and she wasn't sorry when Robert and Nicholas chivvied them towards the exit. Once they had climbed the steps hewn into the rock and left the caves behind, Molly began to feel a little better. Perhaps it was the hint of fresh air coming along the passageway towards them. Or maybe it was because she had somehow managed to slip between the two sets of sisters so that she was no longer last, no longer next to Nicholas.

She was determined to maintain that position once they were away from the caves and blindfolded again but, on reaching the surface, Robert looked out at the night and said in a low voice, 'It's so dark now I think we might dispense with the blindfolds. What do you think, Nicholas?'

Nicholas joined him at the gate and peered out. 'I think you're right. It's damned dark.' He turned back to address the sisters and Molly. 'Ladies, blow out your candles and give them to me. Keep your eyes on your feet and don't utter a word until we say so.'

The sisters and Molly gathered outside the gate while Robert collected the blindfolds, then closed and locked the gate, making barely a sound. Molly glanced up – clouds must have blown in for there was no sign of the moon or stars and the night truly was as black as pitch. She wasn't used to being out so late and in such darkness. She wasn't sure whether it was the coolness of the evening, fear of falling or anxiety over what lay ahead when they got home that made her shiver so. This time Nicholas took the lead, for which she was grateful, while Robert brought up the rear. Even so, she had steadfastly maintained her position between the two sets of sisters on their single-file walk back to Dane Hill. She didn't want to find out whether Robert might have the same disposition as Nicholas.

The group split into two at the corner of Dane Hill, exchanging muttered farewells. Everyone was keeping quiet, Molly noticed, even though now there was presumably less need. An air of anxiety seemed to have overtaken them all. How long had they been away? Molly strained her ears to catch the chiming of a church clock but could hear nothing. Darkness had brought silence to the town.

Yet once they were back on streets they recognised, it was if noise also returned to their world. Dogs barked, people could be heard within their houses through the open windows, and Molly felt calmer. Perhaps it wasn't so late after all.

As they climbed the steps to the front door in Princes Crescent, Molly noticed the dusting of chalk on the hems of Clara and Louisa's gowns as they ascended in front of her. She registered the striking of the St John's Church clock just as the front door opened. There stood Uncle William, candle in hand.

'It's eleven o'clock,' he said. 'Who is going to tell me the meaning of this?'

CHAPTER FIFTEEN

Aunt Jane was hovering anxiously in the hall behind her husband. As the party entered, any vestiges of high spirits over their outing crushed, she shepherded Clara and Louisa up the stairs. Molly hung back in the shadows of the hallway, unsure what to do, while Nicholas stood his ground in front of his father. They faced each other across the hall as Uncle William closed the front door firmly, the draught threatening to extinguish his candle.

'You're back early from Portsmouth, Father.' To Molly's amazement, Nicholas was calm. He was already in trouble – how could he sound so unconcerned when it was clear that his father's anger had been further fuelled by discovery of their outing?

'Nicholas, what were you thinking of? Your mother tells me that you saw fit to conduct your sisters, and your cousin' – Uncle William cast a glance in Molly's direction, causing her to step back: he was aware of her presence so she could scarcely escape to the basement now, although she had been edging in that direction as he spoke – 'to some caves,' he continued. 'What nonsense is this? Where are these caves? I'm not aware of any such thing in the town. And how do you explain the lateness of the hour? Even without the folly of taking your sisters and your cousin into danger, it is certainly not acceptable to be walking the streets at this time.'

Uncle William's voice had risen gradually throughout his speech and the last few words were uttered in a bellow of rage. Molly, alarmed, shrank back against the wall but Nicholas's features didn't betray any anxiety.

'I am very sorry, Father, to have caused any distress to you and Mother. I can assure you that my sisters and Molly were in no danger at any point during our outing and I can only apologise for the lateness of our return. We had simply failed to notice the time and I hope Molly will confirm that this is because everyone was enjoying themselves.'

Nicholas looked to Molly as he spoke and his father said, gruffly, 'Well, Molly, what have you to say for yourself? Is there any truth in the tale Nicholas is telling me?'

Molly swallowed hard to control her nervousness. Nicholas had managed to avoid giving any details of where they had been and she hoped she wouldn't be called upon to do so, for she feared it would make her cousin angry if she divulged their secret destination.

'Indeed, it is true,' she said. 'We had a very happy evening in each other's company, and Robert and Nicholas took very good care of us.'

'Robert?' William said sharply. 'Who is this?' His question was directed to Nicholas and Molly held her breath, hoping that she had not caused him yet more trouble.

'Robert Anderson, Father.'

'Ah.' The answer seemed to mollify William a little. 'The Andersons. A fine family.'

To Molly's alarm, he swung back towards her, holding the candle up so that its light sought her out as she shrank back in the shadows.

'Go to bed, girl. Not many hours remain until you must be up to attend to the milking.'

Molly nodded vigorously, then scuttled past him up the stairs, heading for the attic floor. As she took the first flight she heard her uncle say, 'Come into the drawing room, Nicholas. We shall discuss this matter further.'

Molly stumbled up the final flight of stairs to the attic, having made the ascent without the benefit of a candle. She had been far too anxious to escape the scene downstairs to light one. She undressed quickly in the dark, then slipped into bed, shivering. It wasn't so much that the night was cold but, rather, fear of the outcome of her uncle's interview with Nicholas. She felt guilty, for reasons that she couldn't at first identify but gradually, as she ran over the events of the evening in her mind, she realised it had to do with Nicholas's actions. She knew he wouldn't reveal to her uncle anything that had passed, but she fell into a sleep clouded with dreams in which she was being ejected from the house, her aunt and uncle standing on the doorstep with their arms folded. Next door, her father and Ann were standing in the same posture outside the cottage.

Molly woke more than once during the night but all was quiet in the house below, as it was when she crept from her bed and dressed in the light of an early dawn. She splashed her face with cold water to wake herself up but her eyes still felt gritty with tiredness as she picked her way through the dew-laden fields on her way to the cow barn.

Last night's adventure looked different in the light of day and she had to force herself to be calm and serene around the cows as she milked them, for she did not want her whirling thoughts to transmit themselves and make the animals skittish. She rested her hot forehead against their flanks and made her hands move rhythmically, trying to remember to utter the usual 'Well done, good girl,' as she worked. The cows expected it of her and, when her thoughts strayed and stilled her lips, they turned their heads and regarded her enquiringly.

Molly was dreading an appearance by her uncle at the cow barn, but he didn't come. He wasn't a daily visitor so his absence went unremarked by Old Tom and she was grateful: she didn't know how things stood between Uncle William and Nicholas.

She was glad when milking was over and she could set off for the stable-yard. Once there, though, she was restless, worrying as to what might await her back at the house in Princes Crescent. Her father, luckily, did not appear to notice anything different about her, and when at last he departed on his rounds she was left alone with her thoughts.

Nicholas was already in disgrace over whatever had led to him being sent home before the school year had finished. Molly wasn't sure just how much more trouble he could be in. And would any of this reflect on her? She felt sure that Clara and Louisa would be considered to have played an innocent part in their outing. But had either of them noticed her absences, and the way Nicholas was behaving towards her? And if they had, would they tell their father?

Molly had thought herself hungry as she made her way from the cow barn to the stable-yard. Her father had continued the tradition of bringing breakfast for her but now the bread tasted like sawdust in her mouth, her uneasy stomach rebelled and she could take only a bite or two before casting it aside.

The morning passed at a snail's pace. She could see Mark, the stable-boy, giving her odd looks as she sighed repeatedly, and he looked as though he might be about to speak, but she was quick to turn away and discourage him. She tried to be her usual self with their customers and thought she had succeeded, although it was an effort to appear light-hearted. When there was no more milk to sell and the time came to go home, Molly didn't know whether to feel glad or worried that she could at last turn her steps to Princes Crescent.

CHAPTER SIXTEEN

Molly hesitated outside once she reached the house. Should she mount the steps and enter by the front door, or go in by the basement kitchen entrance? Thinking that Hannah would be able to enlighten her as to what had happened that morning, she went down the steps and entered by the kitchen door. To her surprise and disappointment, the room was empty, with no sign of Hannah. Molly cast around for clues as to what might have happened but, finding none, she climbed the internal stairway to the hall. The first thing she saw was Nicholas's wooden school trunk.

Her heart skipped a beat. Was he returning to school? A second later, she realised how unlikely that was since he'd been sent home in disgrace. Molly stood at the foot of the stairs and listened. The house seemed eerily quiet. There was no sound of Clara playing scales on the piano, or Louisa calling down the stairs, in search of hair ribbons to match the frock she wished to wear that day. Uncle William was certainly not at home. He was heavy-footed and loud-spoken: had he been there, Molly would have known in an instant. As she listened, though, she thought she heard sniffing coming from the drawing room. Cautiously, she pushed open the door and peered around it.

Aunt Jane was sitting in a chair by the window, gazing out,

handkerchief in hand.

'Aunt Jane! Is everything all right?'

Her aunt started and turned at the sound of Molly's voice, displaying eyes puffy from weeping. 'There you are, Molly. I saw you come in and hoped you would come upstairs.'

'I didn't find Hannah in the kitchen. Is something amiss?'

It was quite clear to Molly that something was very much amiss but she didn't want to question her aunt too directly.

'I've sent Hannah to market to buy a few things. For Nicholas.'

'Is – is he going somewhere? I saw his trunk in the hall.' Molly, on the verge of discovering exactly what was happening, felt very anxious indeed.

Aunt Jane clutched her handkerchief tightly, as though hoping to draw strength from it. 'He's going to sea. Your uncle arranged it all while he was in Portsmouth and came back in great haste so that all could be prepared.'

'So this has nothing to do with the – the outing last night?' Molly enquired.

Aunt Jane sighed. 'I'm afraid that Nicholas and I are both in a great deal of trouble over that. Nicholas should never have suggested it but, of course, I should never have allowed it. I think your uncle was so angered by the folly of it that he brought Nicholas's departure forward by a day or two.' Tears began to roll down Aunt Jane's cheeks. 'But it was all decided, in any case.'

'Is he to go into the Navy?' Molly asked.

'Yes,' her aunt replied. 'William has found him a position as a midshipman on the *Valiant*. She's at anchor now just outside the harbour, in the Downs.'

She seemed disinclined to answer any further questions and continued to stare out of the window. Molly took herself back to the kitchen, resolving to busy herself until her uncle and Nicholas returned.

She found Hannah there, back from her errands, but she had few insights to offer. All she could say was that conversations had taken place behind closed doors during the morning between different combinations of Uncle William, Aunt Jane and Nicholas, after which Molly's uncle and cousin had departed for the harbour in the late morning. Nicholas's trunk had made its appearance in the hallway before they left.

Molly knew of no one who had spent time in the Navy but Hannah was happy to impart the knowledge she had. Several boys from the poorhouse had taken up positions on the ships over the years.

'Bless 'im, the youngest was but nine years old,' Hannah said. 'And not particularly tall for his age, neither.' She brightened. 'But it can offer good prospects. For those that start as cabin-boys, there's a chance their officer will take them under his wing and bring them on. The nimble ones with a head for heights get to work on the rigging, or as powder monkeys.'

She laughed at Molly's puzzled expression and took pity on her. 'A powder monkey brings the gunpowder up from the ship's hold to the cannons on the other decks. It's a job for short boys who are quick on their feet, for when the cannons are being reloaded there's a need for speed.' She pursed her lips. 'It's true that they get to see places all over the world, the likes of which you and I could never imagine, but for myself I wouldn't like to be spending months on end at sea.'

Molly frowned. 'And is this the sort of thing that Nicholas will do?' She struggled to imagine her cousin undertaking such menial work.

'Bless you, no.' Hannah was amused by Molly's ignorance. 'He'll be going as a midshipman, I don't doubt. Your uncle will have seen to that. He'll have pulled a few strings to get him a position where he can move up to be an officer within a few years.' She shook her head. 'Mind you, there's tight discipline on board ship and no room for those who see fit to break the rules. Nicholas is going to have to knuckle down or he'll not last.'

Molly thought this was exactly why her uncle had determined that Nicholas should go to sea, but she kept her counsel.

'My cousin is in the Navy,' Hannah volunteered, as she methodically rolled pastry to fit an oval pie dish. 'He's done well for himself, too. He's a lieutenant now.' She looked very proud as she spoke. 'To think that he was a real tearaway when he was younger, and didn't even know how to read and write when he enlisted. He was lucky with his ship, the *Kent*. The crew was like a family, he said. There was no chance they were going to let him step out of line. One day he might even be a captain.'

Molly wondered whether this could be Nicholas's future, too. She had occasionally seen naval captains down by the harbour, guessing at their rank by the splendour of their dress – the tight-fitting navy-blue frock coats with gold piping and frogging and the smart cream breeches. Nicholas would make a very handsome captain, she thought, and a little thrill ran through her. Hadn't he made it plain that she was special to him? Last night's thwarted assignation suddenly took on a different light. Could her cousin be her way out of the rut she had become stuck in, her route to a new life? Before her thoughts could draw her too far along this path, though, she heard the front door slam and the loud rumble of her uncle's voice in the hallway.

Hannah and Molly looked at each other.

'You go up,' Hannah said. 'It won't seem odd. Then you can tell me what's afoot.'

Molly nodded, but she had barely set foot on the bottom

tread of the staircase before she heard Aunt Jane let out a great wail.

Molly and Hannah exchanged glances, then Molly set off up the staircase in great haste, with Hannah in hot pursuit. As Molly reached the hallway she became aware of Clara and Louisa hovering anxiously on the upstairs landing.

Aunt Jane was beating her fists against Uncle William's chest, while he attempted to hold her away from him, a bemused expression on his face.

'Jane, Jane, calm yourself,' Molly heard him say.

'I will not.' She was defiant and Molly was astonished by the change in her usually pliant aunt. 'How could you do this to me? Nicholas gone to sea! You didn't even give me a chance to say goodbye.'

Molly cast an inadvertent glance at her cousin's trunk, which still sat in the hallway. How could he have gone to sea without his belongings?

'It's better this way.' Her uncle's voice was firm. 'The boy needs discipline. He can spend his first two nights getting to know the ship and the crew before they set sail.'

Aunt Jane let out another wail. 'And when will he be back? When will I next see him?'

'A few months, perhaps.' William's tone was evasive. 'It depends on their orders.' He looked pensive, then said, 'What I wouldn't give for his chances! The places he'll see—' He was interrupted by a rapping at the door, which turned out to be a boy come to collect the trunk.

This precipitated another fit of wailing by Aunt Jane and, since she looked fit to collapse, Molly supported her into the drawing room and onto a sofa. Hannah hastened to fetch the last-minute items she had been dispatched to buy that morning and, with them safely packed away and the trunk carried off, an uneasy silence settled on the house.

PART TWO

SUMMER 1786

CHAPTER SEVENTEEN

H ot summer days saw the walled garden at its best and Charlie at his worst. He could only really appreciate the beauty of his surroundings at the end of the day as the sun began to sink in the west and heat started to radiate from the walls all around. The garden delighted him, too, when he arrived in it before 7 a.m., but the knowledge that Mr Fleming was waiting for him, ready to impart the list of the day's tasks before the dew had even begun to lift from the grass, meant that he paid it scant attention at that time. Watering filled at least the first two hours of the day, leaving Charlie with sore shoulders from the constant filling, carrying and emptying of the heavy metal cans, one for each hand.

Mr Fleming was insistent that the watering must be done before the sun rose too high in the sky. 'I don't want to see water droplets sitting on the leaves, remember.' He repeated this instruction every morning before Charlie began work, having drummed it into him that any droplets would magnify the sun's rays and cause the leaves to scorch. Charlie had to keep a close eye on where the water fell, stopping frequently to set down the watering cans and shake off any splashes from the foliage. The reason for such particular care just now was the annual opening of the garden, which took place at the end of July when the trustees of Prospect House were entertained to a tour of the gardens and tea, before the public were allowed in from four o'clock.

The approach to the open day was an anxious time. With the watering completed, Charlie's next job was to concentrate on a single area of the borders or kitchen garden, as instructed by Mr Fleming, deadheading, staking, trimming, weeding and tidying so that every single plant looked its best. This process would take place at least twice for every section of the garden before the date of the open day. Tasks reserved for the rest of the day included sweeping and weeding the associated paths, taking ripe produce from the kitchen garden to the poorhouse kitchen (returning with some bread and cheese or cold ham) and checking the climbers around the walls. The end of the afternoon was reserved for more watering, to replenish the moisture lost from the ground during the hours of sunshine. Mr Fleming always helped with this final chore, for which Charlie was grateful. He was wiry and strong and his daily physical labour had afforded him muscular arms and shoulders, but by then his energy was flagging. Watering done, he was always glad to sit with Mr Fleming on their bench by the garden hut. They sat in silence, although Charlie knew that Mr Fleming would be busy planning what needed to be done the next day. For his part, he was happy to empty his mind and enjoy the serenity.

The evenings were peaceful, but not quiet. The birds would be in fine voice again, after resting during the hottest part of the day, and the swifts would be swooping and calling above, feasting on the insects visible only to them. The scent of the garden was at its best – not only the perfume of the flowers but also the warm richness of the freshly watered sun-baked earth. Charlie breathed deeply and savoured these moments. It would soon be time to line up for his dinner, and although his rumbling stomach told him food would be welcome, the noise and bustle that went with the serving of it would jangle his nerves.

First, though, he must wash away the dust and grime of the day's labour. He sighed and stood up, knowing he could not prolong his stay on the bench any longer, bidding Mr Fleming goodnight before making his way to the pump. Here he pumped a little water into a wooden bucket and splashed it over himself, gasping at the chill on his sun-flushed face and neck. Next, he concentrated on scrubbing his hands, where the dirt from the garden had settled under his nails and in the fissures of his roughened skin. He'd have to submit himself for inspection before he could take his place in the dining hall. He was lucky in that he was usually treated with some leniency because his efforts in the garden were appreciated by the overseer and the kitchen staff.

'All set for the open day?' Mr Dalton, the overseer, was checking for cleanliness today.

'Yes, sir.' No other answer was acceptable, Charlie knew. But he also knew that the garden truly did look its best and, provided the weather held, all would be well. Mr Fleming had been indulging his love of growing flowers, as well as the essential fruit and vegetables, for just such an occasion as the prestigious open day. Perhaps, Charlie thought – as he did at intervals through the day – perhaps Molly would come. Her uncle and aunt would certainly be invited to tea, but would Molly join them afterwards when the gates were thrown open to the public? He had wondered whether he might send a message to her somehow, to invite her, but he didn't know how. He had heard that there had been some trouble at her house and that her cousin Nicholas had been sent to sea. It was hard for news of that nature not to become public knowledge very quickly in a town the size of Margate. Mr Fleming had spoken of it during the week but was quite sure that William Goodchild would put in an appearance on the day.

'He's not the sort of man to hide away,' Mr Fleming had said. 'He'll face down any gossip and put a brave face on it. After all, he's always said he wanted his son to go into the Navy, so no matter if he's there a year or so before it was planned. He'll learn as much doing the job as he could in any school.'

The head gardener was more than a little scornful of those who resorted to books and lessons for their knowledge, being of the firm opinion that anything that needed to be learnt was best mastered in the doing of it.

Charlie slid into a space at the long table in the dining hall, settled himself on the wooden bench and began to spoon up his dinner. He was so hungry that he ate it without any notion of what it was, although that signified little. It was always some form of stew, with more vegetables than meat, the latter identifiable mainly by its stringy nature and grey-brown colour. He cleaned his plate with a piece of bread, making sure to savour that at least, then contemplated what lay ahead. Bed, very soon, for he would sleep the moment his head touched the pillow, waking before six in the morning, ready to start all over again.

CHAPTER EIGHTEEN

July's weather had been hotter and sunnier than usual, and as the open day drew close, Mr Fleming was on the lookout for signs of change.

'It can't last,' he told Charlie. 'We'll get rain – we need it after all. But when it comes it might be heavy. All our work could be ruined.'

Charlie knew only too well the havoc that even a sharp shower would wreak on the garden. The roses would shed their petals, delicate flower heads snap from their stems, overburdened by the weight of water, and pathways become impassable to the ladies in their best gowns due to the mud underfoot and the dampness of the foliage bordering them.

Each day, Mr Fleming anxiously examined the strip of seaweed hung in the shed to see if it showed signs of becoming plump with humidity, suggesting approaching rain, rather than dry and desiccated as it had been throughout the month. He checked the sky at sunrise every morning, looking for angry redness in the east, which might herald a storm. He muttered gloomily over a flurry of ladybirds that descended one day, fearing they might be harbingers of rain, yet the next day they had vanished after feasting on any aphids they had found.

In this fashion, they arrived at the eve of the open day, the weather having held out. Charlie had caught Mr Fleming's anxiety: that evening he had sat on the bench and admired the perfection before him, while worrying that the unbroken spell of fine weather would choose to spoil itself the next day. But he said nothing of this to Mr Fleming, wishing him goodnight as usual before washing, eating and retiring to bed.

There, for once, he did not fall straight to sleep but instead tossed and turned. Was the night hotter and stiller than usual? Was that a distant rumble of thunder? What would they do if all their efforts were spoilt? He willed the night to be over so that he could get up and face the day, dealing with whatever it brought. Of course, the more fiercely he wished for time to pass, the further he drove sleep from his tired mind, and he endured several hours of others' snores before he fell finally into a fitful sleep.

He woke with jangled nerves, convinced that he had over-slept, but the clock on the dormitory wall showed that he had woken even earlier than usual. He rose and peered out of the window, relieved to see the early light was much as it had been on any other morning that month. No rain had fallen overnight and the sky was clear of clouds. Charlie dressed hastily before going downstairs, pausing only for a hurried bowl of porridge before joining Mr Fleming in the garden.

'Just the watering this morning, Charlie, and some last-minute tidying. I'm going to suggest to the trustees that the garden tour takes place before their tea, for I fear the weather won't last.'

Mr Fleming was scanning the sky anxiously as he spoke and Charlie raised his eyes, too, hoping to pick up on the signals that the gardener was seeing. All looked as usual, other than a faint whitish haze round the sun, but Charlie bowed to Mr Fleming's greater knowledge of weather lore

110

and set to work with the watering can.

He wouldn't be sad if the rains came later that day or the next, he thought, to save him from this task. He hoped more than anything, though, that the weather would hold long enough for the visitors to appreciate the gardens at their glorious best.

By two o'clock that afternoon the haze was more apparent, muting the sunshine, but it meant that the trustees could walk the gardens in comfort, without feeling overheated. Charlie felt the tension that had been building in him since the previous day start to dissipate. The important guests had arrived and he watched as couples strolled along the paths arm-in-arm, many of the ladies now using their silk parasols more as a fashion accessory than a necessity. Their finery added to the already brilliant colour palette of the garden.

He was gratified to hear exclamations of delight over the colour and profusion of the roses and the scent of the jasmine and honeysuckle. Other visitors were examining the vegetable garden, where Mr Fleming was in great demand to explain how he had achieved such fine results. Charlie knew that he should mingle and answer questions but he felt shy, content to watch the scene from his station near their hut, and before he could rouse himself to make himself useful, the guests had begun to drift inside to take tea.

Mr Fleming appeared at his side, all signs of worry erased and replaced by a cheerful expression. 'Mr Dalton is very pleased. He said it's the best showing we've ever had and the trustees are delighted.' He glanced up at the sky. 'And, with a bit of luck, the weather will hold long enough for the townsfolk to have a look. Now, get yourself inside and find something to eat before they start to arrive.'

Charlie, who hadn't stopped to eat at midday, wasn't sorry to hurry inside. He stopped short when he caught sight of Molly standing behind one of the long dining tables, now set back close to the wall. She was pouring ale for the gentlemen, while the ladies would take tea served on Prospect House's finest china, usually packed away in straw-filled chests until it was brought out for special occasions such as today. Unobserved, Charlie watched Molly for a moment. Her hair was inexpertly pinned beneath a cap and strands were beginning to escape, while her cheeks were flushed. He could see that she was doing her best to serve the gentlemen, filling their glasses from a jug that required both her hands to lift it, while maintaining polite conversation.

Mr Fleming appeared at Charlie's elbow and followed his gaze.

'Go on, then,' he said. 'Go and have a word and I'll find us something to eat.'

Charlie waited until all the trustees had been served before he at last found himself face to face with Molly.

'Charlie!' She set down the jug, flexing her fingers, then swiped sweat from her forehead with the back of her hand. 'I hoped I would see you. I want to look around the garden and hoped you would be my guide.' She looked a little despairing. 'If I ever get away from here, that is.'

Mr Fleming was back at Charlie's elbow, his plate piled with pastries and tarts from the kitchen, and caught her last words.

He glanced around. 'It looks as though the guests are all seated and served. Why don't you come and join us in the garden? Just leave the jug there and they can help themselves if they want more. We've only got twenty minutes before the gates are open to the public.' And with that, he hurried outside.

Molly took a quick look around, then slipped off her apron and unpinned her cap before joining Charlie on the

112

other side of the table. 'Quick, before my uncle stops me,' she hissed, propelling Charlie ahead of her into the garden.

It was quiet out there, after the chatter in the dining hall, and noticeably cooler. Charlie wasn't sure whether that was because the throng of visitors had heated the dining hall or whether it was a sign of an imminent change in the weather.

They found Mr Fleming on the bench by the hut, already tucking into a pastry.

'Help yourselves,' he said, pushing the plate along the bench. 'The kitchen was very generous.'

He bent down and pulled a stone flagon from beneath the bench, pulling the cork from it as he did so. 'I think we deserve a toast,' he said.

'Thank you for all your hard work, Charlie. It's safe to say it was a success.' He took several gulps of beer and sighed with satisfaction before a distant rumble of thunder made him look up sharply.

'Hello! Looks like a storm's on its way after all.' He stood up and handed the flagon to Charlie. 'I'm going to open the gates. It's a little early but I'd rather everyone got a chance to enjoy the gardens before the rain ruins them.'

Charlie was torn. He wanted to stay with Molly, enjoy his ale and talk to her, but he also felt that he should be on hand to talk to their new visitors. They would be less daunting than the trustees, he felt.

But Molly stood up. 'I'd better go back in, help tidy up and you can show people around. Then I'll come out again and you can give me a tour when they've gone.'

Charlie stood up and watched as Molly headed back to Prospect House. He noticed that she was dressed more smartly than he had ever seen her, in a blue-striped gown with a matching ribbon in her hair, although the bow had become untied and was starting to slip down. Then she was lost to sight as the crowds came into the garden and he was kept busy answering their questions as best he could for the next hour.

Ever-increasing rumbles of thunder gradually thinned the throng, who were casting anxious glances at the darkening sky. Charlie was conscious of how still the air had become, and how powerful the scent of the roses, when Molly was suddenly at his side again.

'Have you still got those pastries somewhere? Then show me round – quickly, before the rain comes,' she commanded. 'Uncle William and Aunt Jane are sitting with Mr Dalton and I'm sure they won't notice I'm missing for a while yet.'

Charlie chose two pastries, studded with plump raisins, and left another for Mr Fleming on the plate in the hut. Handing Molly hers, he said, 'What would you like to see?'

She shrugged, picking out the raisins one by one from the pastry and popping them into her mouth. 'I don't know. Show me your favourite plants.'

So Charlie showed her the grapevine and its tight bunches of hard green fruit, the medlar and the quince, laden with its greenish-yellow fruits. He was proud of the amount of fruit on the fig tree, growing against the warm brick of the garden wall.

'They're lovely,' Molly said, after admiring them. 'But now show me some flowers.'

Charlie laughed. 'You need Mr Fleming for that. The flowers are his pride and joy.' But he showed her the roses and encouraged her to bury her nose in them, to appreciate the scent. When she exclaimed in delight he led her to the jasmine and honeysuckle, tumbling over the wall.

He had just noticed the absence of the bees and butterflies

that normally sought out those flowers when there was a huge clap of thunder followed by a splattering of raindrops.

'Oh!' Molly had jumped. Charlie realised how dark the sky had grown and how few people were left in the garden. He and Molly stood and looked at each other for a moment but before either of them could speak a great torrent of rain fell from the sky and they both ran as fast as they could for the hut. It was empty, but Mr Fleming must have been there for Charlie noticed that the pastry plate was empty.

Molly stood and laughed, holding her arms away from her body as the water ran down and dripped off her fingertips. Just a few seconds of rain had been enough to drench her gown and turn her hair a shade darker. Raindrops ran down her forehead and off the tip of her nose. She caught them with her tongue, then shook herself like a dog.

She went over to the door and peered out. The rain was falling straight and hard, creating a grey mist over the whole of the garden. Charlie joined Molly in the doorway and watched as pink and white rose petals cascaded to the ground and rivulets of water ran along the paths, gathering to form small streams. Although the flowerbeds had been well watered, the ground was still too dry to absorb a great quantity of water in such a short time.

Molly watched, mesmerised by the downpour. Charlie was thinking he should be saddened by the destruction, but he was aware only of the warmth of Molly beside him, the damp smell of her hair. He felt happy, not sad.

Molly turned to him. She was smiling and Charlie could almost feel the excitement bubbling up inside her. Her brown eyes held his and he felt his colour rise. He knew he should say or do something that would make her stay with him for a little longer, but the right words wouldn't come. Then it was too late – she turned away, the spell between them broken.

'Aunt Jane will be looking for me,' Molly said. 'I mustn't shelter here any longer. I'll have to make a run for it.'

Before he could stop her, she laughed with a kind of glee and took off down the path. He could hear her little shrieks as she splashed through the puddles, and then, in a flash, she was gone, back into Prospect House.

Charlie sat inside the hut, his mind in a whirl as he thought over what had just happened. Mr Fleming's words on first meeting Molly came back to him. *Perhaps she might be more than a friend.* At the time, Charlie had dismissed the idea but now he knew he felt differently. He watched the rain falling, cross with himself for letting Molly go without a word. But what could he have said?

CHAPTER NINETEEN

The atmosphere in Princes Crescent had been strained for several days after Nicholas's departure. Aunt Jane had remained upset with her husband, who was adamant that he'd done the right thing. Molly was thankful that her uncle didn't appear in the cow barn over the next few mornings, and she had avoided him when she was in the house. She didn't want to be quizzed any further about the visit to the caves.

By the weekend, though, her uncle and aunt were acting as though Nicholas's surprise return and rapid departure had never happened. Her uncle had been very keen that he and his wife should appear at the Prospect House open day as usual. Aunt Jane prevailed upon Molly to help serve the teas, saying that it would please William if she were seen to be doing so.

Molly hadn't minded too much. And she'd enjoyed seeing Charlie and Mr Fleming again. She'd loved her private tour of the garden – the scent of the flowers on the still air had entranced her. All at once she knew that one day she must have a flower garden – not as grand as the Prospect House garden, of course, but somewhere that could awaken the same feelings that the glorious colours and scents there had done. Before she'd had time to consider whether she should, or could, share the thought with Charlie, an enormous clap of thunder startled her and the heavens had opened. She had made a dash for the hut along with Charlie, but when she got there, she was reluctant to stay inside. She felt unsettled, whether by the garden or the storm, she couldn't say. She'd watched the rain from the doorway, raising steam from the paths where it fell. She was very aware of Charlie beside her, watching the rain … and watching her too. When she remembered that Aunt Jane would probably wonder where she had got to, she turned to Charlie to tell him she must go, but the expression on his face stilled her tongue. He'd looked as though he was about to say something to her, something important.

He hesitated and, in that instant, Molly wasn't sure whether she wanted to hear his words. The urge to run bubbled up inside her and, without giving him a chance to speak, she ran back through the garden, then stopped short when she reached the entrance to the dining hall at Prospect House. Her sisters Lizzie and Mary were huddled under the dripping porch, with her father and a miserable-looking Ann standing behind them. Lizzie and Mary squealed with excitement at the sight of her and she squeezed in to stand beside them, shivering as she realised how wet she was.

'Whatever are you doing?' her father asked, as Ann, at the same time, said, 'You'll catch your death of cold.'

'I was going to ask you the same thing,' Molly said to her father, ignoring Ann's remark. 'Why don't you go inside?'

'It's not our place,' her father said stiffly. 'It's for the invited guests.'

Ann sniffed, whether because of the rain or to make a point, Molly wasn't sure.

She peered into the dining hall. 'There's hardly anyone left.

They've all gone home, apart from Uncle William and Aunt Jane. They're talking to Mr Dalton.' Molly pushed open the door. 'Come in. There's no sense in you standing here.'

Lizzie and Mary didn't need to be asked twice and scurried inside, their eyes immediately fixed on the few remaining pastries.

'Come,' Molly urged her father and Ann. 'I'm sure we can find you a cup of tea.'

Her father started to protest but Ann shushed him. 'Be quiet, John. You've as much right to be here as the next man.'

Molly wasn't sure that it was her place to suggest they come in and take tea but she couldn't leave them standing in the rain. She found a plate for her sisters, who watched, eyes like saucers, as she put two pastries on it. Then she went to beg two teacups from the scullery where a Prospect House kitchen-maid was grimly working her way through the stacks of dirty china.

John and Ann were hovering awkwardly at the edge of the room when she got back. Her Aunt Jane didn't seem to have noticed them but she spotted Molly as she passed through the room and called her over, standing aside from her husband's conversation to scold her for her appearance.

'You're soaked, girl. Whatever where you thinking of, out there in the rain?' She glanced towards the door as she spoke and caught sight of John and Ann. Molly followed her gaze and saw that her stepmother had turned slightly aside to hide how the rain had soaked her dress and made it cling to the swell of her belly.

'I found them outside, caught in the rain too. I told them to come in. I hope that's all right,' Molly said hastily.

'Of course,' Aunt Jane said, moving to her husband and putting her hand on his arm. 'Your brother is here, my dear.'

Then she turned to Mr Dalton. 'John Goodchild. He delivers the milk to Prospect House.'

Molly watched, impressed, as her aunt engineered introductions, poured fresh tea and put John and Ann at their ease. Then Molly went over to sit with Lizzie and Mary, asking them why little John wasn't with them. Lizzie told her he'd refused to put on his shoes and so he'd been left behind with a neighbour. She listened to their prattle with half an ear while she looked out at the garden where the rain still fell. She wondered at the destruction it was causing. Roses that had been standing proud and tall less than an hour before now hung their waterlogged heads or shed their petals into the puddles on the ground. Clumps of other flowers, whose names she didn't know, now looked as though someone had sat on them, their papery blooms wrecked. How would Mr Fleming and Charlie feel, with all their hard work ruined? But she wasn't given long to ponder, for her aunt came over and said they were leaving, the rain now having eased off, and that Molly should walk back with them.

Lizzie and Mary seized her hands and pulled her away before she could give the garden a backward glance. All her efforts on her homeward journey were focused on avoiding the puddles and preventing her sisters stepping in them as they danced around her, still full of excitement at the novelty of such an outing.

CHAPTER TWENTY

Despite outward appearances, Molly was sure that her aunt still grieved over the manner of Nicholas's departure. She must have felt it keenly that his going into the Navy meant she would hardly see him, Molly thought. Aunt Jane wasn't the only one to hold Nicholas in her thoughts, though. Now that he had gone, Molly fell to wondering what might have happened had they returned from their outing to the caves to find her uncle still away. She felt sure that Nicholas would have continued to press her to come to his room. The idea both intrigued and scared her. Molly had a fair idea of what Nicholas was expecting, and an equal certainty that it wouldn't have been right. But the memory of his secret kisses drew her back time and again to thinking about him, until she wondered at herself and grew hot with shame.

The Prospect House open day reminded Molly of how remiss she had been about spending time with her sisters. They lived next door and she had barely seen them over the past six weeks. She resolved to spend less time thinking about things that might have been and concentrate instead on her family.

Ann declared herself only too delighted to have Lizzie and Mary out from under her feet in the afternoons so, when Aunt Jane had no need of her, Molly took her sisters off to spend time in the fields or to walk down to the harbour to watch the comings and goings of the boats.

One late August afternoon the three of them were on the harbour, looking across to the pier as the passengers disembarked from the London boat. Molly thought she spied a familiar face among the crowd. She had to jump to her feet and stand on a fisherman's box to get a proper view over the heads of the passengers as they spilt off the boat into the sunshine, but she was sure she had seen Will Turner among them. She tried calling his name but her voice was blown away by the breeze and soon the knot of passengers had moved on.

Disconsolate, Molly flopped down beside Lizzie and Mary, who were too busy gawping at the crowd to pay her much heed. 'I'm sure that was Will,' she said, half to herself. If she hadn't been with Lizzie and Mary she could have followed the stream of passengers into Margate and no doubt caught up with him soon enough. Then she comforted herself with the thought that it wouldn't be hard to find him out and about in the town.

'Let's go and walk along the sand,' she said to her sisters, feeling guilty at wishing to cast them aside so easily.

When Molly took her sisters home, Ann scolded them. 'Look at the state of you. Sand all over your boots. Take them off at the door and don't go bringing it onto my floors.'

Molly looked at her feet. Sand still clung in patches to the damp leather, despite the length of the walk home. She decided that she had no need to stay and listen to her stepmother's complaints, so she smiled apologetically at Lizzie and Mary and made the excuse that she would be needed next door, then hurried away to her uncle's house. There, she was startled to find her uncle and Will in the drawing room.

Will had been accompanied by his uncle to Margate and was once more staying around the corner. He'd wasted no time in calling to see her uncle to ask whether he would be interested in another study of his cows. Will confided this to Molly the next day as they walked along the pier, this time without Lizzie and Mary.

'I need money for my paints, sketchbooks and other things.' Will was kicking a stone along as they walked. 'And I've applied to study at the Royal Academy but I'm too young yet. They've said I can come in three years' time.'

Molly had to ask Will what he meant by the Royal Academy, thinking it something to do with the King. On hearing his explanation that the Royal Academy was a prestigious London school of art, which held important exhibitions, she felt a stab of envy. It wasn't fair, she thought, yet again. Why was he able to study and travel about the country while she had to do everyone else's bidding? Her cousin Nicholas had gone to sea, and she had no doubt he was seeing lots of new places while learning new skills. Charlie loved his work as an apprentice in the garden, where he learnt something new every day, but all she did, it seemed to Molly, was milk cows, sell milk, help to cook and wash up, and run errands. And it looked like this was what she could expect for the rest of her days. Unless she did some-thing about it.

Overwhelmed by frustration, she stuck out her toe and flipped Will's stone into the harbour.

'What did you do that for?' he protested.

'Oh, I don't know.' Molly shrugged. A black mood threat-ened to descend and spoil her afternoon. She'd gained time off by asking her uncle if she might show Will some sketch-ing spots while he was staying in Margate, appealing to him rather than her aunt because he seemed rather taken with Will. She knew her uncle well: she suspected he was busy calculating how he might profit by association with such a promising young artist from London.

'Of course,' her uncle had said. 'You must help him whenever he needs it. That young man clearly has a bright future ahead of him.'

And so Molly found herself trying to remember all the places that she had earmarked as suitable spots. She'd thought Will might find something of interest in the bathing machines lined up at the water's edge, waiting to be tethered to horses then pulled into the water so that their occupants could take a seawater cure. To her eyes, the ribbed cloth covers on the machines made them look like giant caterpillars squatting on the sand. But Will had dismissed them with barely a glance. Nor had he been particularly interested in the panoramic view of the town afforded by the tip of the pier. He had, however, spotted something for he stopped suddenly, almost causing Molly, who was now walking behind him, to cannon into him.

It was her turn to ask, 'Why did you do that?' but he wasn't listening, just slowly revolving on his heel and gazing out over the water. Molly wasn't sure what had caught his eye, for the only boats to be seen were far distant, but he pulled out his sketchbook and began to scribble furiously. She settled herself against a great coil of rope and closed her eyes.

She must have dozed, tired after her early start, for the next thing she knew Will was saying, 'Come on, then.'

She struggled to her feet as he fastened the binding around his sketchbook. 'Can I see?' she asked.

'There's nothing to see,' Will said.

'It wasn't a good spot?' Molly was downcast.

'Oh, it was! But I just made notes. Look at the colour of the sky,' Will gestured upwards, 'and the light on the water. You can't capture that in a sketch.'

Molly must have looked puzzled for he pressed on. 'I've written down some ideas to try. Colours to experiment with. Different techniques.'

Will was animated and set off at a great pace along the pier back towards town. Molly could only guess that he was happy with whatever he had seen and in a hurry to be home. She threw a glance over her shoulder as she tried to catch up with him. Surely the sky was just blue, with a few fluffy white clouds. And the sea, well, it was blue, too, but with some green in it. As she looked she saw how the sunlight sparkled on the ripples made by the breeze and she wondered for a moment how you could possibly capture that with paint. Then she shrugged. That was for Will to work out.

olly's hopes of having Will to herself were dashed by Will himself. After their outing to the harbour she didn't see him the next day, or the one after. She was cross with herself for not making a proper plan to meet, other than suggesting they might go to look at some new sketching spots. She kept expecting him to come and collect her from the stable-yard at Church Street and then, when he failed to appear, she felt sure he would come to Princes Crescent in the afternoon, but there was no sign of him.

She didn't know why she put up with him. He intrigued her, she supposed. He had talent, she knew – even her uncle had recognised it. And he might be younger than she was, but he travelled around as though he was much older. He had a much more exciting life than she did, and by associating with him she felt a little of it rubbed off on her. Yet he lived inside his head for much of the time; she was often unsure whether he was aware that she was there or not.

After five days had passed without a sighting, she began to think he must have returned to London to prepare for the school term. It was then she remembered, guiltily, that she had forgotten Lizzie and Mary again and, for that matter, Charlie. She resolved to put it to rights that very afternoon. It was the last week of August and the weather was glorious.

She would take Lizzie and Mary to see Charlie, she decided. She was sure Mr Fleming wouldn't mind. They wouldn't stay long and it would be an adventure for her sisters. They'd loved the gardens when they had visited on the open day and they'd taken to calling it Prospect Park, thinking of it as some sort of public space. Her father had told her they'd asked him more than once when they could visit again.

Once Molly had checked that Aunt Jane wouldn't need her that afternoon she went, unannounced, to collect Lizzie and Mary from next door.

'Oh, so you've remembered your sisters again, have you?' Ann said.

Molly ignored the sour comment. 'I've come to take them to Prospect Park.' She smiled as her sisters shrieked with glee.

Ann started to object, then thought better of it. She looked weary, Molly thought, with little John clinging to her leg as she pushed herself up with difficulty from the kitchen chair. She was big with child now and Molly felt briefly sorry for her.

'Why don't you sit down again?' she suggested. 'I'll get the girls ready.' The pair of them were running around, looking like ragamuffins, barefoot, hair uncombed, wearing cast-off dresses that Molly recognised as having once belonged to her.

Ann scowled but didn't argue, sinking back into her chair with a sigh. Molly took her sisters up to their room, noticing the disorder there. The brushing of hair and finding of suitable shoes didn't take long and soon the three sisters were out in the road, Molly having promised Ann they wouldn't be late home.

Lizzie and Mary skipped along, hand in hand, clearly delighted to be out of the house. Molly felt another pang for having been a neglectful sister, and vowed she would speak to her father to see whether there was a way for her to tactfully offer help: it looked as though Ann wasn't coping well. She had little time to dwell on this, though, for they reached the walled garden of Prospect House in no time. As they peeped through the gate to see whether Mr Fleming or Charlie was about, Molly was struck with delight on seeing the garden once more. It had been nearly a month since the open day and her last visit. The day when the storm had struck, and she had seen how Charlie had looked at her. She felt suddenly nervous at the thought of seeing him again.

The garden had been fully restored to glory but of the gardeners there was no sign. Molly pushed open the gate, sure that the squeak of the hinges would alert someone to their presence. Sure enough, she saw a head, crowned with a straw hat, pop up from the vegetable garden at the far end. Mr Fleming, the owner of the hat, straightened and waved, and Molly shepherded her sisters over to him.

'How d'ye do,' Mr Fleming said formally, to Lizzie and Mary, causing them to giggle. He turned to Molly. 'And it's good to see you again, Molly. You've been quite the stranger.'

'Is Charlie about?' Molly looked around, expecting to see him lurking behind the runner beans.

'Aye, he is,' Mr Fleming said. 'He's yonder, with his prized fruit trees. Talking to them, no doubt.'

Molly followed the direction of Mr Fleming's pointing finger and saw Charlie, his back to them, close to the far wall of the garden. He seemed oblivious to their arrival, stooping every now and then as he worked.

'Go and have a word,' Mr Fleming said. 'I reckon these little lasses would like to check whether the raspberries are sweet enough to pick.'

Lizzie and Mary were saucer-eyed when he pointed to

the plump fruit, out of reach of marauding birds behind fine muslin on the other side of the path. Molly smiled and made her way to Charlie. He'd finally become aware of their presence and had turned towards her, his back to the wall and shading his eyes against the sun. He was wearing a faded blue shirt and Molly noticed at once how brown his face was, and also his hands and wrists, exposed by the too-short sleeves. His face broke into a grin as she approached and Molly's nervousness vanished in an instant.

'I was keeping my head down. Thought we had visitors and I could let Mr Fleming deal with 'em. Didn't realise it was you.'

He looked happy at the discovery and Molly bit her lip. How easily she had forgotten about him when Will had appeared. She didn't know why she felt the need to impress Will Turner, who repaid her by ignoring her and vanishing back to London without a word of goodbye, when here before her was a boy who was always genuinely glad to see her.

'What are you doing?' she asked.

'Why, tying in a few loose branches and checking the pears,' Charlie said. 'We grow them against this wall to catch the sun but they ripen quickly. I want to pick them at just the right moment, before they start to ripen, so we can finish them off back in the hut.'

Molly looked at the golden fruit, which looked heavy enough to break away from the branches that lay flat against the wall. 'These aren't normal trees, are they?' she said, doubtfully.

Charlie smiled. 'No, they're called espaliers.' He sounded the syllables carefully. 'It's a good way to grow fruit in a garden like this, flat up against a wall that the sun warms. Apple and pear trees would take up too much space otherwise – they're best off in an orchard. This way, there's no excuse for not making use of every fruit. None of them drops off to rot on the ground.'

It was the longest speech Molly had ever heard Charlie make. But he hadn't finished. He showed her the fruit he had picked already, lying in a basket at his feet, and pointed out the apple trees that were growing in the same fashion. Molly, however, had spotted a couple of trees with pear-like fruit growing in a small plot in the corner of the garden and she pointed them out to Charlie.

'Why aren't these ones flat against the wall like the others?' She couldn't remember the word he had used.

'Espaliered, you mean.' They walked over together to examine the trees. 'These are quince. They wouldn't take well to being treated like that and, in any case, they don't grow too tall. It'll be a little while yet before this fruit is ready.'

Molly's gardening lesson was interrupted by the arrival of Lizzie and Mary.

'You're to come and sit by the hut,' Lizzie said. She looked proud to be entrusted to be the message bearer.

'We're going to have lemonade,' Mary burst out, unable to contain her excitement.

'Anything else?' Charlie enquired.

'I don't know.' Lizzie frowned. 'Mr Fleming said he was going to get it.' She looked hopeful. 'Do you think there will be something else?'

Charlie smiled. 'There might be. I'll be surprised if there isn't.'

Lizzie and Mary raced back up the path, Molly and Charlie following.

'They're having a lovely time,' Molly said. She frowned. 'I don't think they have much fun with my stepmother.'

130

They arrived at the hut where Mr Fleming was already pouring lemonade and telling Lizzie and Mary to take a piece of cake from the plate he had brought out on a tray.

'When we've had this, we'll need to think about going home,' Molly warned her sisters. They pulled faces but settled down in the shade without protest.

'The garden looks lovely,' Molly told Mr Fleming. 'You'd never know there'd been that storm on the open day.' She looked around, marvelling at the profusion in the vegetable patch and the clumps of bright blooms in the borders.

'Aye, we have to make the most of it,' Mr Fleming said. 'In a week or so it'll be on the turn as we go through September.'

'One of our busiest times,' Charlie said, his mouth full of cake.

'It is with your fruit trees,' Mr Fleming said, pretending to scold. 'You're busy cosseting them when all the while we need to start putting the whole garden to bed for the winter.'

'Don't talk of winter yet,' Molly chided. The prospect of her walk to the cow barn on a frosty winter's morning was unwelcome during the heat of such a day. She leant back against the wall of the hut and closed her eyes, and the three sat in companionable silence while Lizzie and Mary chattered quietly to each other.

CHAPTER TWENTY-TWO

Molly was in a buoyant mood as they walked home. She would make a point of going to visit Charlie at least once a week, she decided. The Prospect House garden was so calm and peaceful, it made her happy just to be there. The thought popped into her head that Will might find places there to sketch, but she pushed it firmly away. She'd done enough to help him.

She pushed open the door of the Princes Crescent cottage and ushered in Lizzie and Mary.

'Ann, we're back,' she called.

She could hear little John crying upstairs, but there was no response from Ann. Molly was half inclined to shut the door behind her sisters and make her way next door. Then she thought better of it, remembering the state of Lizzie and Mary, and of their room, when she had arrived. If Ann wasn't managing, perhaps she should stay and make sure that at least they had something to eat before she left them.

She told the girls to wash their hands while she looked through the larder to see what she could find. It struck her that this wasn't her home now and she really ought to ask Ann so, sighing, she went to the foot of the stairs and called again. 'Ann, we're home.' Again, there was no response although John wailed on.

I suppose he'd better eat, too, Molly thought, as she climbed the stairs. She hesitated outside her stepmother and father's bedroom door, where John's cries had now subsided into sobs, before knocking and entering.

Little John was sitting on the floor, his face bright red, wet with tears and streaked with dirt. Ann lay on the bed, eyes closed, hands clutched to her belly. As Molly entered she let out a low groan and half turned on her side, drawing up her legs.

'Ann,' Molly whispered, to avoid startling her.

Ann's eyes opened wide. 'The baby's coming!' She shouted the words, startling John, who had calmed down at the sight of Molly, and provoking a fresh bout of tears.

'Here, John.' Molly took his hand and pulled him to his feet. 'Lizzie and Mary are downstairs. I'll make you all something to eat.' She half pushed him towards the door, then turned back to Ann. 'I'll fetch help,' she said, then hustled John down the stairs, all the time trying to still a sense of rising panic.

She scrubbed at John's face with a damp cloth then sat him at the table and cut hasty, rough slices of bread, smearing them with butter. She found a jar of jam on the larder shelf and quickly spread it over some of the slices, heart beating fast as she worried over what to do next.

Telling the children she would be back shortly and that on no account were they to move from the table, she went out of the back door, closing it carefully behind her, then flew down the path and round to her aunt and uncle's house. She burst through the front door and met her aunt in the hallway.

'Whatever is the matter, girl?' Aunt Jane was taken aback by her hurried entrance.

'It's Ann. She's having the baby. I must get back. Please

send for help,' Molly gabbled, then turned on her heel and ran back to her father's house. She didn't want to leave Lizzie, Mary and John alone for a moment longer than she had to but she was also very scared at the thought of trying to help Ann.

To Molly's relief, she hadn't been back in the cottage for more than ten minutes before her father arrived home. He found her anxiously mopping Ann's brow while the children, quite content, ate their bread and jam in the kitchen. Molly's relief was short-lived, though: after a few reassuring words to his wife, her father left the house to see whether a message had reached the midwife.

Molly was alone once more and began to worry that her sisters would finish their supper and be inclined to come upstairs to see what was happening. Another groan from Ann convinced her that she couldn't leave her post so she sat on, patting her stepmother's hand and murmuring soothing words, while her gaze took in the state of the room. The floorboards looked as though they hadn't been swept in some time and the windowpanes were smeared, as though by little John's sticky hands. Her father's work clothes, in need of a wash, were piled in an untidy heap in the corner. Had Ann been feeling unwell for some time? It looked as though she'd failed to keep up with the most basic housework.

Molly knew that the first girl they had engaged as maid-of-all-work had left after a few weeks, although she didn't know the reason. Perhaps she hadn't liked her difficult employer, Molly thought, then felt guilty when Ann cried out again in pain. Molly's heart began to hammer. Ann's pains were increasing in frequency, which Molly guessed must mean that the baby was close to coming. She had no idea how to set about helping to deliver it, so the sound of voices – her father's and a woman's – on the stairs came as a great relief.

Molly was more than happy to be sent downstairs by the midwife to boil water and to keep an eye on the younger children. Her father was banished, too, and he paced the kitchen floor until Molly sent him out into the yard. 'You're getting in the way and unsettling the children,' she scolded, stepping round him as she ferried jugs of hot water up the steep stairs to the bedroom. She wasn't sorry to be able to call her father back into the kitchen after less than an hour to tell him that he had another daughter. Molly didn't feel it was her place to share what the grim-faced midwife had muttered, too.

'If this bairn ain't their last, it will be the death of the mother.'

It was a piece of news best kept for later.

PART THREE

SPRING 1789

CHAPTER TWENTY-THREE

C harlie leant on the handle of his spade and surveyed the patch of dug earth with some satisfaction. He was tired but he'd achieved a lot that day. Mr Mawson, the head gardener, had been away from the garden, busy talking over plans with Mr Powell most of the afternoon. Charlie reckoned that he'd be pleased with what he'd achieved when he got back.

It was springtime and the garden was bursting into life after its winter sleep. The sun today had some warmth in it and the birds had begun nest-building, although one or two were still singing for a mate. The soil was warming up and Charlie had been digging over the vegetable beds, preparing them for the sowing of seeds. And Molly was due at any minute. Charlie smiled – the day could get no better.

He had been at Woodchurch Manor for nearly nine months now, from late summer through to spring, and he felt quite settled. At first, he'd been unnerved by Mr Mawson, who was a hard taskmaster compared to Mr Fleming. But Charlie, determined to work hard and make Mr Fleming proud of recommending him for the position, gave Mr Mawson little cause to quarrel with his work. Charlie had been well taught, and he'd told Mr Fleming so the first time he saw him after he'd left Prospect House.

'That's as may be,' Mr Fleming said. 'But you were a good and eager learner. That's more than can be said for the lads they've seen fit to give me since.'

Charlie, having no family of his own now, had spent Christmas Day with Mr Fleming and had heard, over a Christmas dinner cooked by Mrs Fleming, just how difficult his old head gardener was finding life without him at Prospect House.

'I've had two boys already. One couldn't abide being out in all weathers and the other couldn't keep a thing I taught him in his head for longer than five minutes.' Mr Fleming sighed. 'Heaven alone knows whether the latest one will still be there when I go back after Christmas.'

Charlie was dismayed. He'd struggled at first to get used to his new position at Woodchurch Manor but after the first couple of weeks, absorbed in his work, he'd barely given Mr Fleming and the garden at Prospect House a second thought. And it was Mr Fleming he had to thank for finding him the post at Woodchurch Manor and for giving such a glowing report of him. He'd said it would be wrong to keep Charlie on at Prospect House once his time as under-gardener was up, telling him that he needed to start working towards being in charge of his own garden.

'They can't give you just any lad to work with,' Charlie said, thinking back to his own beginnings at Prospect House. 'He needs to have a mind to want to do it, to want to work outside and to want to learn how things grow. Otherwise it's just hard labour.'

'Aye, well, if Mr Dalton can't find me a boy like that at Prospect House, then he'll just have to employ one from outside, won't he?' Mr Fleming brightened at the thought. 'I can't manage the place all on my own, and as they have need of the food I grow then a way must be found. Now, let's talk no more about work. Have you seen young Molly of late?'

The abrupt change of subject caught Charlie by surprise and brought a blush to his cheeks. Molly had become a regular visitor to the Prospect House garden and Charlie knew that she thought of him as a good friend. She'd shared tales of her family woes on her visits, her stepmother proving an unwilling mother to her newborn daughter while Lizzie and Molly were neglected, too. Only little John appeared to benefit from his mother's undivided attention, and Molly was constantly worried at the state of affairs. She used the garden as a refuge, Charlie knew, and often turned up with her sisters and baby half-sister in tow.

'It gets them all away from Ann,' Molly confided. 'I can see how Lizzie and Mary are doing and someone has to look out for Harriet, poor little mite.'

Molly had discussed with Aunt Jane whether or not she should move back to her family home to help, but her aunt wouldn't hear of it.

'Molly, you'll be a slave to that woman if you do,' Aunt Jane had said. 'Your father needs to take matters in hand and see to it that his children are properly cared for. I'll not have you skivvying for Ann. You're welcome to bring your sisters here whenever you need to but you can just as well keep an eye on them while you live here.'

Molly had been upset when she told Charlie of her aunt's words. 'It's not the same being next door as being with them in my father's house. At night, we'd have a chance to talk in bed and I could make things right.' She sighed. 'They've got each other, I suppose. And they're older now. Old enough to keep an eye on Harriet. But still …'

They'd been sitting talking on a bench in the Prospect

House garden and she'd managed to shred a rose, tearing off the petals one by one until she had a pile of pale pink teardrops at her feet.

'Oh! Look what I've done!' Molly gazed at Charlie in consternation. 'It was such a lovely rose, too.'

Charlie had laughed. 'There are plenty more in the garden. Don't worry. I just wish I could make things better for you.'

More than anything, he had wanted to take her in his arms and give her a hug, and to have her bury her face in his shoulder and hug him back. But he had no idea how to go about doing such a thing and he feared that if he did she would pull away, horrified. And then he would have lost a friend for ever.

He didn't know whether Mr Fleming was responsible for causing him to think differently about Molly – after all, he had been the one to suggest they would make a good match for each other the first time she had visited the Prospect House garden. But he knew the old head gardener had enjoyed and encouraged her visits. Whether she would be able to continue coming had worried him when he'd agreed to take on the job at Woodchurch Manor. Over their Christmas dinner, he'd been able to tell Mr Fleming that he had seen Molly, and that she'd visited him every fortnight when her duties allowed it, but always on her own and always for a short time. The distance from Margate curtailed the time they could spend together, but he was never less than grateful for it.

Today was one of the days she had arranged to see him and he was expecting her to arrive here, in the walled garden at Woodchurch Manor, at any moment. He'd promised her a surprise that day, refusing to be drawn on what it was, or even to give her a clue, despite her entreaties.

CHAPTER TWENTY-FOUR

I n Margate, Molly was trying hard to contain her excitement at the news that her cousin Nicholas was expected
home, nearly three years after he'd left under a cloud. Aunt
Jane, Clara and Louisa were overjoyed, and even Uncle
William was looking rather more pleased with himself than
usual. Molly suspected that Clara and Louisa's excitement
had more to do with the prospect of visitors than with any
pleasure at the thought of their brother's company. Aunt
Jane, she knew, was just overwhelmed at the thought of
seeing her son again.

What changes would his time at sea have wrought in
Nicholas? Would he be civil and polite to her, as befitted a
cousin? Or would he attempt to resume the acquaintance
broken off so abruptly nearly three years before? It gave
Molly a little thrill of anticipation to ponder on this, and
she revisited these thoughts again as she lay in her bed that
night. She found the contemplation led her to become too
excited to fall easily asleep and when she did so at last, it was
to slip into colourful dreams in which Nicholas demanded
to marry her forthwith and take her away from Margate
without further ado.

It was a good thing that they had had only two days' notice
before Nicholas's arrival, or Molly's fevered speculation

would have left her exhausted from lack of sleep. What had started out as a dream had now taken firm hold of her imagination, lodging itself in her mind as a solution to how she might better herself. The months spent in her aunt and uncle's house had taught her that making a good marriage was the most obvious way for a young girl to improve her situation in life. But Molly had few male acquaintances. Will Turner was talented, but young and too much inclined to live in his own world, she had decided. In addition, she rarely saw him these days: he was so caught up with his London life and his travels. Charlie was more promising, as he was hard-working, dependable and his new position at Woodchurch Manor proved he had ambition. Yet, Molly thought, the fact that she was so comfortable in his company, combined with the way in which they understood each other so well, had to rule him out. Where was the thrill in that? It was clear to her that Nicholas – who appeared to offer excitement as well as prospects – was returning at just the right time. It was less fortunate that a planned visit to see Charlie coincided with his return.

Over the years, Molly had come to look forward to seeing Charlie as much as she had enjoyed being in the garden at Prospect House. She valued his quiet passion for everything that grew and they spent a lot of time in companionable silence, while Charlie went about his tasks and Molly simply sat and watched, relishing the time away from Princes Crescent. She had become increasingly concerned about Lizzie, Mary and Harriet, spending as many afternoons as possible in activities that involved them, to get them out of the house and away from Ann's bad humour. She was glad now that Aunt Jane had been insistent that she shouldn't move back into her family home; even living next door she found herself worrying over her sisters as a mother might. Lizzie and Mary were growing up fast and Ann was doing little to set them a good example or hold them in check. Molly felt she should do what she could to guide them, and although she often took them with her to Prospect House, she was happiest when she went alone.

When Charlie had informed Molly that his two years as an under-gardener were up, and that Mr Fleming had told him he should seek employment elsewhere, for the sake of his own future, Molly had been taken aback. What if he found a position at one of the grand estates Mr Fleming sometimes spoke about, the ones he had visited in the north of the country? She had been pleased when he'd quickly found a place at Woodchurch Manor, on Mr Fleming's recommendation. Molly's only knowledge of it was as the destination of the horse rider that Will had sketched at the Dandelion – she had never travelled that far herself.

The first time she had set out to walk there to visit Charlie it had felt like a great adventure. She'd been impressed and not a little overawed by the size and grandeur of the manor, but had had the sense to approach it around the back and seek out the walled garden where she knew she would be most likely to find Charlie.

She'd found Charlie's new employer, Mr Mawson, severe and unwelcoming, quite unlike Mr Fleming, but Charlie said to take no notice. The gardens covered many acres at the front and back, not just the walled kitchen garden, making Mr Mawson's role an important one. He was as likely to be found making plans for the future with Mr Powell, the owner of Woodchurch Manor, as he was in the garden.

Visits to Charlie were harder to manage now that he was so much further away, but once Molly had hit on the idea of arranging lifts with wagons heading in that direction, she and Charlie settled into a new pattern. They saw each other about once a fortnight and she no longer took Lizzie, Mary and Harriet with her. She didn't enjoy the garden as much as she had at Prospect House, for it was primarily used to produce food, and Mr Mawson grew just a few rows of flowers for cutting to supply the floral displays for the house. Charlie, though, was as good company as ever.

He had promised Molly a surprise on her next visit to Woodchurch Manor. Surprises had barely featured in Molly's life and she had been filled with excitement, while failing to imagine what might be involved. By the day of her arranged visit, though, she had become impatient with the idea. Nicholas's visit home – a surprise in itself – was imminent, and she would have preferred to be in Princes Crescent, helping Hannah and her aunt to prepare.

CHAPTER TWENTY-FIVE

It had taken Mr Mawson several weeks to get around to asking Charlie where he was living. On learning that he was walking from Margate every day, he had raised his eyebrows but said nothing. Charlie had taken a shared room in the town after the end of his apprenticeship and his right to a bed at Prospect House. The walk was at least four miles in each direction, which had proved hard in the winter months. Snow had meant that Charlie couldn't take his usual short-cut over the fields and had to stick to the road, although sometimes this was to his advantage as passing carts would occasionally offer him a lift. Having no one to complain to he had simply endured it, wondering every now and then whether he might seek rooms closer to Woodchurch Manor but at a loss as to where to look: he passed through only hamlets, with very few cottages, along the way.

A couple of days after posing his question, Mr Mawson bade Charlie to follow him from the walled garden to the stable block at the side of the manor. He'd climbed a ladder to the loft above the stables and, after a moment's hesitation, Charlie had followed him. He'd assumed they were going to collect tools for the garden, stored up there over the winter, but to his surprise he found himself not in the open loft space he was expecting, but a narrow corridor with four doors leading off it.

Mr Mawson threw open the one at the end of the corridor and said to Charlie, 'It's yours, lad, if you want it.'

Uncomprehending, Charlie stepped into a small room, with panelled lime-washed walls and a small window overlooking the stable-yard. It held a narrow single bed with a couple of blankets flung over it, a small table and, unexpectedly, it had a low ceiling rather than the rafters Charlie had expected to see.

'It'll save you the walk – aye, and the rent.'

Only then did it dawn on Charlie that he was being offered accommodation at Woodchurch Manor, and for free.

'There's only the stable lad living up here at present,' Mr Mawson continued, 'so you'll be quiet enough.' He paused. 'I'll be expecting you in the garden not far beyond dawn in the summer, mind.' He clearly didn't want Charlie to think he was going to have it too easy.

Charlie had never had a room that he hadn't shared with someone else – usually with several others. If Mr Mawson had offered him a room in Woodchurch Manor itself he couldn't have been happier. He could barely stammer out his thanks without his eyes filling with tears. Mr Mawson, to help Charlie cover his confusion, suggested they get back to the garden and get on with some work. Charlie had transported his belongings to his new room over the next couple of mornings and now, with everything set up to his satisfaction, he wanted to show it to Molly.

As he packed away his tools in the hut, all the mud wiped off as he'd been taught, he heard the hinges creak as the gate to the garden opened. Stepping back onto the path from the hut he saw Molly coming towards him, her cheeks flushed from exposure to the strengthening March wind.

Charlie feared that his grin on seeing her was too broad and would make him look foolish but he couldn't help himself – seeing Molly always filled him with such delight.

'I hope this surprise of yours is going to be worth the journey.'

Charlie wasn't sure from her tone whether Molly was teasing or cross.

'I can't stay too long. I'll be needing to get home before darkness sets in and it looks as though rain is on its way.'

'Then I'll show you at once,' Charlie said, closing the tool-shed door and pocketing the key. If Mr Mawson came back and had need of it, he would know where to find him.

'Follow me,' he said to Molly, much as Mr Mawson had done. He led her around the back of the house to the stable block, then on into the yard. The lad was attending to a visitor's horse, rubbing it down after its journey, and he nodded to Charlie and Molly as they passed.

Charlie climbed the ladder to the loft, then turned at the top and beckoned Molly to follow. Once she was standing beside him, he opened the door at the end of the corridor, stepping back so that she could enter.

'This is yours?' Molly took in the small pile of folded clothes on a chair in the corner, the rag rug beside the bed, the blankets neatly tucked in. Charlie had made sure to leave the place as tidy as possible that morning. She crossed to look out of the window, then turned back towards him.

'Yes, it's my room. Just for me.' Charlie could still barely believe his luck. 'And, if all goes well here, I'll get the chance of a cottage in the grounds in a few years' time.' He hesitated, remembering Mr Mawson's recent words to him: *Mr Powell likes to look after his workers. If you do well, and if you marry, you'll be able to apply for tenancy of one of the cottages here. You couldn't ask for a better place to bring up a family.*

Yet again, Charlie was reminded of Mr Fleming's advice, over two years earlier, that Molly would catch the eye of the young men of the town and he would do well to make her his own without delay. Now he wanted to ask her something, but he feared she saw him only as a friend. Would she be horrified by what he was about to suggest?

Charlie swallowed hard, then began, 'Molly, I was wondering whether you might agree …' He stopped, his cheeks flaming. He hadn't thought to rehearse what he wanted to ask her and now he didn't know how to phrase it. He didn't think '… agree to be my wife,' was quite right. He wasn't even sure he meant that quite yet. 'Agree to walk out with me'? Was that better? But he didn't see how they would walk anywhere, now that he lived at Woodchurch Manor and not in Margate. He couldn't read Molly's face, cast into shadow by the bright light from the window behind her, so he stumbled on.

'What I mean to say is, in the years to come, we could have a future here together if you'd agree to …' He was stuck again.

Molly stepped towards him and laid her hand on his arm. His hopes rose – her face looked clear and untroubled – but then she spoke.

'Oh Charlie, I've got my own plans for the future. I don't intend to stay around here all my life.'

His face must have shown how her words hurt him for her hand flew to her lips. 'I'm sorry, Charlie. It was thoughtless of me to speak to you like that … I hope we can still be friends?'

Charlie swallowed hard again. The life that he had imagined for himself here with Molly at Woodchurch Manor, which had seemed full of colour and promise just moments before, was crumbling into dust. He was embarrassed but tried to hide it.

'Ah, well, I'm glad of having a space to call my own.' Even as he said it, he didn't feel quite so glad. His room would feel lonely now, without the future to daydream about. 'I'm sorry, Molly – your surprise was hardly worth the wait. Come – I've got some things to show you in the garden.'

Suddenly he couldn't wait to get Molly out of his room and away. There was little worth showing in the garden – it was still too early in the year – but this was turning out so differently from how he had planned it that he could hardly bear it. He had imagined himself taking Molly in his arms and holding her close. He wanted to be her protector, to look after her. He had thought she might take up a position as a servant at Woodchurch Manor and that they would live out their lives here, bringing up children in the sort of warm, cosy family setting that they had been denied as children. He had never known she had her own plans since she had never spoken of them before.

The rest of Molly's visit was a little strained. They had walked in the grounds and she had told him how naughty little John had become and how Ann still favoured him over Harriet. She said how happy her aunt Jane was to hear that Nicholas would be home in a day or two, on shore leave for the first time in nearly three years while his ship was in Chatham for repair. Big celebrations were planned for his homecoming and Hannah required Molly's help in the kitchen that evening.

For the first time, Charlie wasn't sad to see her go. She had arranged to be picked up by the corn merchant's wagon as it made its way back to Margate and Charlie had waited with her in the lane, handing her up, then giving her a perfunctory wave as he turned away in the gathering dusk to go to his room. That night, as he lay in bed, he wondered whether he would ever see her again. Had his clumsy attempt to woo her spoilt their friendship? He hadn't even asked her about the mysterious plans she had alluded to. She had mentioned that she didn't want to stay in the area. But where did she intend to go? She knew no one away from Margate that he was aware of. His sleep that night was troubled by strange dreams and his work over the following days was so badly affected that Mr Mawson began to wonder whether his faith in Charlie had been misplaced.

Within the fortnight, though, Charlie had mastered his disappointment. Since Molly wouldn't have him, he would put all his efforts into the garden. He would ask Mr Mawson whether he could devote a neglected corner of the kitchen garden to growing fruit trees that weren't to be found in the orchard. They already had a mulberry but he wanted to try a couple of different varieties of quince and he also had his heart set on a pomegranate. Mr Fleming had told him about this strange fruit, which had a hard outer skin surrounding juicy, ruby-red jewel-like seeds, with a sweet, yet dry, taste. He had also described pineapples to Charlie, fleshy green-yellow ground-growing fruits that required brick-built miniature glasshouses, heated by running hot-water pipes through them, to give them a chance of surviving in England, so far away from their hot overseas home.

Mr Powell would be keen to grow such things in his garden, Charlie thought. It would be something to boast of to his visitors, who came quite frequently from London. Perhaps Charlie himself might have the chance to travel to London, in years to come, to visit some of the great gardens there, and elsewhere in the country, that Mr Fleming had told him about. Charlie set his sights on a new future. He would turn the walled garden at Woodchurch Manor into one that was admired far and wide. And he would turn himself into the greatest gardener he could possibly be, and forget all about Molly in the process.

CHAPTER TWENTY-SIX

M olly knew she hadn't, perhaps, treated Charlie as well as she might have done. His suggestion, which he had failed to utter but which was quite clear all the same, had indeed come as a surprise, but not a welcome one. After that moment in the rain at the Prospect House open day, when Molly, sensing he was about to say something important, had run off before he could give voice to it, nothing more of that nature had passed between them. Molly had all but forgotten about it and she had long viewed Charlie as a good friend – perhaps her only friend, it's true – but nothing more.

It was unfortunate indeed that Charlie had chosen that day to ask her to be ... what? His sweetheart? His wife? Either way, Molly knew in her heart that she was destined for greater things than to be the wife of a gardener.

As the wagon bumped its way from Woodchurch Manor towards Margate, Molly had felt a little frisson of excitement. She could hardly wait to get back to Princes Crescent and the preparations for Nicholas's homecoming. Her thoughts ran on: judging by what had happened on their outing to the caves when he was last at home, Nicholas must harbour feelings for her. He would, without a doubt, want to pursue them, which would surely lead to their marriage. Perhaps he would want them to take a house in Margate or, more likely,

Chatham or the immediate area. She might even travel with him – she knew that some Navy wives did just that, living on board ship.

Her mind leapt ahead: when she was married to Nicholas, she could use his influence with her uncle to make things right for Lizzie and Mary. Arranging suitable marriages for Clara and Louisa would be her uncle's first priority, of course, but there was no reason why, when Lizzie and Mary were a little older, he couldn't find suitable matches for them, too. It came to her that of course she might do this herself, finding husbands for them among Nicholas's fellow officers. The idea made her smile.

If Ned, the wagon driver, was struck by what a very lovely young woman William Goodchild's niece was and how he'd do well to keep an eye on her and stop her gallivanting off around the countryside, he kept his thoughts to himself.

Back at home, as the hour approached for Nicholas's return to Princes Crescent, Molly was glad she'd had the foresight to make preparations. She'd brushed her chestnut hair the night before until it shone, then spent some moments wondering whether to tie it up so that it wouldn't tangle in the night. She feared it would be uncomfortable, though, and since her sleep was likely to be disturbed by nervous apprehension she'd left it loose, as normal. Even so, she'd half woken every time she'd turned over in the night, and dawn found her with tired eyes. There was no respite from her normal routine: she still had to milk the cows for her uncle, then sell the milk for her father.

As she trudged across the fields, shivering in the chill March wind and eyeing the dark clouds, hoping they didn't hold rain that would soak her before she could reach shelter, Molly reflected that this wouldn't always be her lot. She hadn't given it much thought before, accepting that this was simply the way things were. Now that her eyes were opened to the possibility of change, though, a great surge of joy filled her heart. How wonderful it would be not to have to make this journey each morning, in what this year had felt like endless winter. Molly glanced down at her hands, reddened by her work and the wind, and thrust them hastily into the pockets of her apron. She would be a captain's wife before long, she was sure, and she would need to take more care of herself.

That morning, the working hours dragged for Molly, even though she was as busy as ever. She was impatient to be back at her aunt and uncle's house, wanting to wash away the toil of the morning and put on the dress she had already laid out on her bed. It was one that had previously belonged to Clara and was barely worn, in a colour that she knew enhanced her dark eyes and pale complexion. It wasn't smart enough to invite comment from her aunt, but Molly knew that it showed her to advantage.

As it was, she arrived home to find her aunt in a terrible flap, having come up with several jobs that she felt needed attending to before Nicholas's arrival. She would have the rosewood table in his bedroom polished so that the room might smell of beeswax, then she wanted the pictures in the drawing room dusted. The silver cutlery must be cleaned, too, ready for dinner later that day. Molly, who couldn't see how this could be achieved in the time, persuaded her that Nicholas was highly unlikely to notice dust on a picture frame. Then she took herself upstairs with the tub of beeswax and a cloth, allowing herself ten minutes to climb the staircase to her room and effect a quick wash and change before she set to work to polish the table. Molly glanced around

Nicholas's room as she worked – all had been cleaned and prepared, the bed neatly made. After such a long spell at sea, Molly felt sure her cousin would be more than happy with his accommodation. Leaving the table gleaming and the air filled with the warm scent of beeswax, she hurried down the two flights of stairs to the kitchen, where she found Hannah looking pink and cross because Aunt Jane kept trying to interfere.

'There's no point in her changing her mind about what they're to eat and when they're going to eat it,' Hannah said, clattering the pans in frustration. 'It's all cooking now and there's nothing I can do about it. But if she comes down here one more time I doubt anything will ever make its way onto the table.'

'I'll try to keep Aunt Jane away,' Molly soothed. 'Once Nicholas arrives, she's sure to calm down.'

Molly took the cloth and the whiting to clean the silver to the dining room, rather than bringing the cutlery to the kitchen. There, she would be able to waylay her aunt and prevent her from heading downstairs to issue yet more instructions to Hannah. She'd barely started to clean the silver, which in any case was sparkling and untarnished, before she heard the clatter of hoofs outside that could surely indicate only one thing – the arrival of a carriage. Molly, her heart starting to race, quickly bundled up the cloth and the whiting and hurried down to the kitchen.

'I think he's here,' she said to Hannah.

'Then you'd best get back upstairs to greet him, you being part of the family,' Hannah said. She looked Molly up and down. 'You're looking remarkably well, Molly Goodchild. You'd do well not to catch the young master's eye.'

Before Molly could ask her what she meant, Hannah

pushed her towards the staircase and nodded at her to go up. Molly could hear excited voices in the hallway and all at once she felt a little sick with apprehension. She took a deep breath and climbed the stairs, entering the hallway as though this was nothing other than an ordinary day and Nicholas was no more important to her than any other visitor to the house.

Nicholas had changed in his time away, in visible and more mysterious ways. He was taller – at least as tall now as his father – broader, and his hair had grown while he was at sea, so that he was wearing it tied back in the manner fashionable among seafarers. He greeted his father, mother and sisters with a quiet gravity that made the excited chatter of the female family members sound overly hysterical. Molly hung back, nervous in his presence, but she caught a glimpse of his easy charm when he spotted her.

'Is that Cousin Molly I spy, hanging back in the shadows? I do declare, you've changed so that I would barely have recognised you.'

Molly blushed hotly but was spared a reply, for Nicholas was swept into the drawing room on a tide of questions from his mother and sisters, leaving Uncle William to follow them, shaking his head and smiling wryly.

Molly turned to go back to the kitchen to help Hannah, her heart beating fast and her colour still heightened. Had she really changed so much since she'd last seen him? She supposed she must have, for Nicholas certainly had. Yet it felt to her, since she had stayed in the same place, that she had not been subject to the passage of time in the same way.

Hannah wanted to know how Nicholas looked and what had been said, while all the time focusing on whisking and stirring to be sure to have dinner ready on time. Molly answered her questions as best she could, protesting that she'd barely caught a glimpse of him but that he looked, not unnaturally, older.

'And wiser, it's to be hoped,' Hannah said. She straightened up from tasting the gravy and looked at Molly. 'And did he have a greeting for you?'

Molly could feel the colour rising to her cheeks once more as she repeated his words.

'Hmm. Well, you're a young woman now and one likely to catch the eye of any young man. You'd do well to keep out of his way. Don't let him turn your head – we don't want the sort of trouble coming to this house that he brought on himself at school. Now, help me to start getting the dinner up to the table before we have your aunt down here giving me the benefit of her good advice.'

Molly helped to carry the plates and dishes up to the table while the family took their places, still busy questioning Nicholas about his adventures. Once she was sure that everything was ready she took her seat next to Louisa and waited her turn to lift slices of meat from the platter and vegetables from the tureens.

She listened to Aunt Jane prattle on, asking questions of Nicholas but barely waiting for an answer before she recounted a piece of local news that she felt sure would interest him. Nicholas gave his full attention to his immediate family and didn't, as far as Molly was aware, look in her direction once other than to address Louisa.

When she was sure that the family were done with their dinner she rose and quietly removed the tureens and platters to the sideboard, then gathered up the dirty plates and cutlery. As she took Nicholas's plate her wrist brushed against his hand and she started a little. She would have dropped the plate if he hadn't reached up to steady it with 'There,' and a smile, looking straight into her eyes.

Molly moved on swiftly, hoping no one had noticed, but they were too busy laughing and talking among themselves, full of good humour. She took the stack of plates down to the kitchen and returned to collect the tureens and platters. She thought she felt Nicholas's eyes on her back as she did so but the conversation continued, uninterrupted.

As Molly brought the last dishes into the kitchen, Hannah observed, 'You're looking flustered.'

'It's a special dinner,' Molly protested. 'Those dishes are heavy. I didn't want to drop anything, especially after all the effort you've put in.'

She looked with some dismay at the tray of syllabubs Hannah had set out for her to take up for dessert. The glass dishes containing the pale frothy mixture were closely packed and would, Molly felt, betray the shakiness that had seized her. She steeled herself, then set off up the steep staircase, bearing the tray before her and praying that she didn't stumble or catch her foot in her hem.

In the dining room, she was relieved to be greeted by a wave of chatter that would effectively drown any nervous chinking of the glassware. Molly set the tray on the sideboard then handed out the syllabub, starting with Aunt Jane, then Uncle William, then Nicholas as guest of honour, before delivering dishes to Clara and Louisa. She slipped silently into her seat and took up her spoon, raising her eyes to find Nicholas's gaze full on her.

CHAPTER TWENTY-SEVEN

I t was late before Molly could make her way up to bed. The washing-up and setting the kitchen to rights took longer than usual. Then Aunt Jane, flushed with excitement, came down and wanted to talk about plans for entertaining during the coming week.

Hannah looked pleased at the chance to show off her skills but not a little daunted by how all the work might be managed. Molly's heart sank, for she could see that she would find herself confined to the kitchen after her milking and dairy duties. When would she have the opportunity to see Nicholas again?

That night, despite feeling desperately tired, she struggled to fall asleep. Nicholas's homecoming was not at all how she had imagined it. It looked to Molly as though her role over the next few days would be very much that of a servant: she would be unlikely to see anything of her cousin, except in passing.

She awoke the next morning in a panic lest she had overslept but the grey half-light told her it was still early. The house was quiet and as she crept down the stairs, boots in hand, she glanced at Nicholas's bedroom door. It was firmly closed but she couldn't help picturing him lying in his bed, fast asleep. How would he feel at having his own bed to sleep in, in a proper room in a proper house, after the confines of life aboard ship? Would he be sprawled in abandon, she wondered, luxuriating in the space? Or would he be neatly asleep on his side, face turned away from the window? The thought suddenly seemed too intimate and she blushed and hurried past, suddenly glad to be out of the house and in the cool morning air.

That day in the cow barn, Molly was distracted and monosyllabic. She was thankful that her uncle didn't appear: she had no wish to be drawn into a conversation about Nicholas's return. As she walked back through the fields towards the Church Street yard, she tried to formulate a plan that would give her some precious time in Nicholas's company.

'Why the frown?' her father asked, as she swung open the heavy gate.

Molly opened her mouth to reply but thought better of it and shrugged. 'It's nothing,' she said, and busied herself preparing for the arrival of the day's customers. She did her best to be cheerful but the thought of an afternoon of hard work in the kitchen weighed her down, and her walk back to Princes Crescent that day was punctuated by heavy sighs.

Tantalising aromas drifted up through the kitchen window as Molly descended the steps to the basement. As she opened the door she was surprised to hear a voice that was out of place in the kitchen, but one that she recognised.

'Lizzie!' she exclaimed, taking in the sight of her sister standing at the scrubbed table, knife in hand and a pile of vegetable peelings before her.

Her sister beamed at her. 'I've come to help!'

Molly looked from Lizzie to Hannah for confirmation.

'Yes, it's true,' Hannah said. 'Your aunt didn't think it was fair for you to spend the morning working for your uncle and father, then to come home and spend the afternoon preparing for dinner. She said she would rather you were helping, and sitting, at the table this evening.'

Having been quite worked up about the unfairness of it all, Molly now had the wind taken out of her sails. She didn't know what to say, or quite what to do with herself. Lizzie, who was clearly excited to be considered old enough to be employed in this way, was busy chattering to Hannah and looked more than capable of getting on with whatever menial task was sent her way.

Molly found her spirits much revived, the elaborate schemes she had formulated on her walk home having now been rendered unnecessary. 'Is there anything I can do?' she asked, hoping the answer would be no.

'I've set some food aside for you,' Hannah said, nodding to indicate a covered plate on the dresser, being up to her elbows in flour. 'Then, unless your aunt has any tasks for you around the house, I'd say you were at liberty to do what you want.'

Molly settled herself on a chair in the corner of the kitchen, to be out of the way of Hannah and Lizzie, while she ate the bread, ham and pickles. She observed Lizzie at work and was struck all at once by how her sister had grown and was starting to fill out. She would soon be in need of regular work, Molly thought. It flashed through her mind that when she married Nicholas, Lizzie would make the perfect replacement for her here in Princes Crescent, maybe even in the cow barn and the Church Street yard. Molly tried hard to quell her imagination but to no avail. Her day had suddenly taken on a much rosier hue.

She brushed away a few crumbs, smoothed her dress in sudden nervous anticipation of seeing Nicholas, then made her way upstairs in search of her aunt. She found her sitting with Clara and Louisa, all three of them poring over a copy of the ladies' journal to which they subscribed, in search of news of the latest fashions.

'Aunt Jane, thank you for bringing Lizzie in to help,' Molly said. 'I'm very grateful. Is there anything I can do for you this afternoon?'

'It felt unfair to give you the burden of preparing for another big dinner when you've already worked all morning,' Aunt Jane said. 'The Andersons are coming and I know you've already met the son and daughters. I'd like you to help serve and be at the table, and it suddenly came to me that Lizzie was of an age where she could be of use.' Aunt Jane looked very pleased with herself for having managed things so well.

Molly, however, having had her hopes raised with regard to the evening, found them dashed once more. The Anderson sisters, Sarah and Catherine, had been charming and attractive girls when she'd last seen them, nearly three years ago on their trip to the caves. She had no reason to think that anything would have changed. Nicholas's eye would surely be caught. Before her thoughts could take her any further down that path her aunt was speaking again.

'I would like flowers for the dining room this evening. It's a little early in the year but your uncle assures me he has seen some blooms in the garden at Prospect House. I wonder whether you might prevail upon the gardener there to spare us something.'

'Of course.' Molly nodded to confirm her reply. She would be glad to have a task to occupy her that afternoon, to prevent her dwelling too much on the dinner that lay ahead. And she hadn't seen Mr Fleming for some time, she realised, not since Charlie had left the garden. It would be good to see how he was.

CHAPTER TWENTY-EIGHT

As Molly pushed open the gate to the Prospect House garden, she was surprised by how sparse it was. Bare earth was showing in all the beds and borders, while leaves had yet to appear on the trees. Her uncle was right, though. There were splashes of colour here and there. She hoped Mr Fleming wouldn't find her errand too much of an imposition. She spotted him at the far end of the garden, raking over the soil in the vegetable beds, a small figure working beside him.

Mr Fleming looked up as she stepped into the garden and even at that distance she could see a smile break out on his face. He spoke to the boy at his side, then came towards her along the path.

'Molly! How lovely to see you. You've been a stranger here since Charlie left.'

Molly coloured faintly at the mention of Charlie's name. Had he been in touch with Mr Fleming since her visit to Woodchurch Manor? She didn't think there had been enough time, but the memory of how she had turned Charlie down came back to her in a most unwelcome fashion. Hoping to divert Mr Fleming from asking questions about Charlie, she blurted out the reason for her errand. 'My aunt wondered whether it might be possible to have some flowers from the garden. She has a dinner tonight in honour of her son Nicholas and she has a fancy to use flowers to decorate the room.'

Mr Fleming raised his eyebrows a fraction, whether in displeasure at her request or at her bluntness, Molly couldn't say. She hurried to make amends. 'How are you, Mr Fleming? I'm sorry not to have been to see you. I so loved it here, and I've missed it.' She took another look around. 'I don't remember it so much at this time of year, only in the summer when it was full of colour.'

As she spoke, Molly was taken back to the garden as it had been on her previous visits, the beds full to overflowing and bees buzzing everywhere.

Mr Fleming sighed. 'I've had to take out a good proportion of the flowers. Mr Dalton would have me grow more vegetables, to supply Prospect House but also to sell to the new hotel in town. It seems the garden must generate an income these days.'

'Oh, that's such a shame!' Molly looked around with new eyes. 'But you have managed to keep *some* flowers.'

'Aye, some for the great and the good, and some for Mr Dalton's lady wife at home. And some for myself, although I tell him I'm testing new varieties for a friend of mine in London who will pay me for my work. It's partly true, I suppose.' Mr Fleming indicated a bed that was filled with broad, firm, upright leaves, pointed at the tip, without a flower to be seen. 'These are tulips but it's too early for them to be in flower. I'm to see what colours the bulbs produce. There's still a market for the more unusual ones among the wealthy in London.'

Frowning, Mr Fleming surveyed the borders. 'I can give you a few primroses, which can be used as posies, and I think

I can spare you a few daffodils. If we add some colourful foliage they should make a bit of a display.' He was clipping away as he spoke and Molly, distracted by the ease with which he was assembling a beautiful assortment of flowers and leaves, was taken unawares when he suddenly asked, 'How is Charlie?'

'Well, I think,' she stammered, feeling the colour rush to her cheeks.

'When did you last see him?' Mr Fleming asked.

'Ah ... um ... just a few days ago,' Molly said.

Mr Fleming looked at her quizzically. 'I had high hopes of you and Charlie, you know,' he said. 'You haven't quarrelled, have you?'

'No, no,' Molly protested. 'I've been to see him regularly at Woodchurch Manor.'

She wanted Mr Fleming to think well of her, and his words were making her feel guilty. In a rush she continued, 'We haven't quarrelled, exactly, but I think I have disappointed him.'

'I see,' Mr Fleming said, continuing to clip. At last he stopped and turned to Molly, presenting her with an armful of foliage and flowers. 'You'd better get these home, and into water. And don't be a stranger here, Molly. You're always welcome to come and spend time with us.'

No more was said about Charlie, but as Molly headed home she felt as chastened as if she had received a thorough scolding from Mr Fleming. Not for the first time she felt as though his eyes could pierce her very soul and see exactly what she was thinking.

Molly was glad to relinquish the flowers to Aunt Jane back at Princes Crescent. Her aunt exclaimed with delight over the selection and went off in search of vases while

Molly slipped away to her room. They would dine early and she wanted some time to herself. She didn't think anyone would bother coming to the top of the house to find her so she took off her work dress, washed her hands and face with water from the jug and settled herself by the window, wearing just her shift as she brushed her hair. She gazed out as she did so, watching the birds swoop around the rooftops, and allowed her mind to wander.

It felt as though barely five minutes had passed before there was a timid knock on the door.

'Wait a moment.' Molly, startled, leapt up and pulled the quilt from her bed, clutching it to her chest.

The door opened slowly and Lizzie peeped cautiously around it. 'Hannah said, if you're ready, could you come to the kitchen?'

'Well, as you can see, I'm not.' Molly spoke crossly. As usual, she would have to throw on her clothes and hurry to do someone else's bidding. She wouldn't have a moment to try to make herself look nice.

Then she saw Lizzie's expression and sighed. 'Don't worry, go down and tell Hannah I'm just getting changed. I'll be there in a few minutes.'

It wasn't as if she needed to spend time deciding what to wear, she reflected, as she took her only half-decent dress out of the cupboard. Clara, the dress's previous owner, thankfully never remarked on it when Molly wore it. As Molly pulled the pale blue garment over her head, she wondered whether it was because Clara knew the dress suited her cousin's figure and colouring far better than it had ever suited her.

She wound her chestnut hair up on top of her head, stabbed in a few pins to hold it at bay, barely glancing in the mirror as she did so. She'd have no need of pinching her cheeks to bring up the colour. By the time she'd carried all the plates and serving dishes up from the kitchen, she suspected she'd be rosy-cheeked enough.

CHAPTER TWENTY-NINE

I t was only a few hours later that Molly, weary in body and spirit, climbed the stairs back up to her bedroom. She flung herself onto the bed, face down and fully clothed, and cried bitter tears of frustration into her pillow.

The evening had been a success, there was no doubt about it. Aunt Jane, a little giddy from excitement and the wine she had drunk, had come down to the kitchen afterwards to congratulate Hannah on the quality of the dinner.

'I think I can safely say that the Andersons were very impressed. Mrs Anderson wondered whether she might have the recipe for the syllabub and I promised to ask you. I don't think I need to hurry to send it over – I feel sure that the Andersons will return our invitation to dinner very soon. I don't doubt that Sarah and Catherine will prevail on their father to do so.' Here, Aunt Jane permitted herself a small smile of triumph. 'It's clear that Nicholas has made a very good impression on them.'

Hannah glanced sharply at Molly, who kept her head down and lips pursed as she concentrated on piling up dessert dishes for Lizzie to wash in the scullery. Her sister was drooping with exhaustion, she noted, and she felt much the same herself. It had been a very long day.

Aunt Jane sighed, recollecting a less pleasing aspect of the evening. 'If only I could say the same about Clara. She was so quiet at dinner. I don't think Robert Anderson even noticed she existed. I rather think his eyes were fixed on Molly for a good part of the evening.'

Molly started and almost dropped the tureen, freshly washed and dried and retrieved from Lizzie, as she was about to return it to the dresser shelf. She turned to find Aunt Jane looking her up and down.

'I do believe, Molly, that you have grown into a fine young woman right under our very noses and we hadn't even noticed.' She frowned. 'I will speak to your uncle. Perhaps he knows of a suitable young man, in trade in town perhaps, whom he could introduce to you. You're nearly eighteen now, Molly. It's time to start thinking about your future.'

Aunt Jane looked around and, seeing that all was in hand in the kitchen, she thanked them all again and bade them goodnight.

Few words were spoken after her departure. Molly told Lizzie to hurry home to bed: she would see to it that the last dishes were dried and put away. Hannah, yawning, saw that everything was in place for the morning, then took herself home. It wasn't until Molly was alone in her room, lying on her bed, that she was finally able to revisit her impressions of the evening.

It had left her feeling cross and prickly. She had watched as Sarah and Catherine had given Nicholas the full benefit of their attention, flirting with him as blatantly as they could with their parents at the table. They had had a good deal of liberty in that respect, since Mr Anderson's attention was engaged by Uncle William, while Aunt Jane monopolised Mrs Anderson, and Robert had attempted to gain Molly's undivided attention. Molly, while appearing to be listening to Robert and responding to his questions – which were few, luckily, as he talked mainly about himself – had tried to give half an ear to the three-way conversation between Nicholas and the Anderson sisters. This had involved a good deal of giggling and shushing and had also drawn in Louisa – never one to hold back – and, to a lesser extent, Clara. Molly had noticed how quiet Clara had been that evening and it was only now that her aunt's observations on the subject came back to her. Oh, heavens, was Clara interested in Robert, who all the while had been ignoring her in favour of Molly?

Molly groaned into her pillow. The evening had not gone at all as she had imagined. Conscious of how late it was, she struggled into a seated position, unpinned her hair and rubbed the tears from her damp cheeks. She was about to step out of her dress when she heard a creak on the staircase. Puzzled, she listened. Lizzie had gone home – she'd seen her safely off, and had bolted the kitchen door behind Hannah. Who else would be coming up to her room at this time of night? Surely the whole house was asleep.

Molly never locked or bolted her door. There was no need: she was the only one to come up here. Now she looked around for something to use as protection. Her hairbrush was the only thing to present itself so, seizing it, she stood by the bed, heart thumping and ears straining for further sounds.

The silence was so complete that Molly began to think she had imagined it when there was a quiet tapping at the door.

'Who is it?' Molly's voice shook slightly, even as she reassured herself that anyone meaning ill wouldn't bother to knock.

'Molly. Can I come in?' The low voice was unmistakably that of Nicholas.

Molly gasped and took a couple of quick steps to the door,

standing close up against it. Thoughts flew through her mind.

'What's wrong? Is Aunt Jane ill? Are you ill?'

Nicholas laughed softly. 'No. At least, not in the way you imagine. There's something you might cure, though.' He laughed again.

Molly, facing the door, had her whole body pressed up against it now. Her torment over the evening suddenly vanished. Nicholas, who had paid her not the slightest bit of attention all evening, was here now, outside her door.

'Nicholas, it's very late.' Molly thought quickly. 'I can't let you in. Go back to bed.'

'I can't sleep, Molly, for thinking about you. Take pity on me.' Nicholas had adopted a cajoling tone.

A wave of heat swept over her. The turnabout from her earlier unhappiness was overwhelming. Although she wanted nothing more than to open the door and to have Nicholas take her in his arms, she held back. It was too soon. He must woo her first. Molly tried to make her voice sound firm.

'Nicholas, this isn't right. You must go back to bed.'

Would he try the door? She knew she had very little hope of keeping him out if he did.

Her feelings when she heard Nicholas sigh were confused. Had he given her up so easily? With her face still pressed to the door, she heard him speak again, so close.

'Molly, you have quite bewitched me.' Then she heard the creak of the stair again and she knew he was returning to his room.

Despite Molly's exhaustion, a troubled night lay ahead. Her thoughts were too taken up with what had just occurred to allow sleep to come easily.

CHAPTER THIRTY

Hhe next day Molly's thoughts were still in turmoil. She barely noticed her walk to the cow barn, her feet automatically following the path they had trodden so many times before. The cows were restless and she was impatient with them. Old Tom frowned and said that her uncle wouldn't be pleased: the milk yield was lower than usual that day.

Molly couldn't even be bothered to reply. She just sighed, took her bonnet from the peg by the door and walked back into the town. At the stable-yard, she tried her best to respond to her father's queries as to how the dinner had gone. No doubt Lizzie had told him something of it over breakfast that morning.

As she described the courses that were served and how his brother and Mr Anderson had been in conversation for virtually the whole evening, she reflected on how different her mother's questions would have been. She would surely have wanted to know who had sat next to whom, what the ladies had worn, what the Anderson sisters were like. She would have picked up on Molly's slightest hesitation or evasion and drawn her own conclusions. What advice might she have offered Molly if she were still alive? Molly hastily shut out that thought.

She was glad when the cart was loaded and her father set off on his rounds, for it gave her chance to dwell on the events of the night before. Whatever was to happen next, it would be Molly's decision alone. She felt a shiver of anticipation at the thought of seeing Nicholas again. The memory of his voice on the other side of her bedroom door just a few hours before came back to her and she smiled to herself when it was time to go home.

Down in the basement kitchen all was calm, with just Hannah there, sitting and eating at the scrubbed table. She patted the chair beside her, inviting Molly to sit, while she cut a slice from the loaf she had baked earlier that day.

'Has everyone gone out?' Molly asked, puzzled by Hannah's unusual behaviour. She was normally too busy preparing dinner to consider stopping to eat at this time of the day.

Hannah pushed the butter across the table towards her. 'Your uncle has gone with Nicholas to Chatham – something to do with checking on the progress of the repairs to his ship – and your aunt and cousins have gone visiting.' She chuckled. 'They're quite in demand now Nicholas is home.'

Molly spread butter on her bread and frowned. 'Why would Nicholas being home make a difference?'

Hannah shook her head. 'Because they will have to return the invitations. All the good mothers of Margate will be keen to visit here with their daughters in the hope of a glimpse of him.' She glanced sideways at Molly. 'He's quite the most eligible bachelor in town, you know. Young, good-looking and with excellent prospects.'

Molly found it hard to swallow, her earlier hunger fast ebbing away. She was half tempted to confide in Hannah, to tell her about Nicholas's visit to her bedroom the previous night, but she held back.

'There's no point in thinking that you and Nicholas might make a match,' Hannah said abruptly. 'The family would never consider it. Your uncle will be looking for a wife with good connections for his only son. Don't waste your time sighing over him. Remember what your aunt said last night. There's many a boy in Margate who'll make a fine match for you. Sooner rather than later, I'd say.' Hannah stood up and took her plate into the scullery. Her last words floated back to Molly. 'You're looking rather too much like a fruit that's ripe for plucking. Your aunt would do well to keep an eye on you.'

Hannah's words decided Molly. As she saw it, it was Nicholas who was the fruit that was ripe for the picking. It was as if she'd been set a challenge. She would need to act fast. The decision calmed her and she quickly finished her bread and butter, downed a glass of milk, then set to work helping Hannah prepare a light meal for the return of the ladies of the house.

'We must make the most of today,' Hannah said. 'I dare say there'll be more entertaining to be done over the next few days.'

And so it proved. Ladies paid morning and afternoon calls, and whole families arrived for dinner. The ones who were most prompt in paying their respects were sadly disappointed when they discovered that Nicholas was absent. News of his subsequent return from Chatham was quick to spread through the town and, more often than not, Molly would arrive back from the stable-yard to find Lizzie already hard at work, assisting Hannah.

Even Aunt Jane began to tire of the endless round of

visitors, while Clara and Louisa complained bitterly to their father that they didn't have enough frocks to maintain appearances. Grudgingly, he agreed to fund them two summer dresses apiece, which had a side benefit for Molly, who inherited another cast-off from Clara. While the dressmaker was in the house, Aunt Jane had her let out the side seams on all of Molly's acquisitions.

'You fill them out rather better than Clara did,' she mused. 'It's unseemly for you to have such close-fitting dresses, I feel.'

Molly didn't dwell too much on her meaning – why should she be denied a flattering dress while others might have them? – for she was nursing a secret. One that occupied her thoughts for the greater part of each day.

On the night of Nicholas's return from Chatham there had been a quiet family dinner, much to everyone's relief. Molly had brought the dishes up as usual and set them on the table, then slipped into her seat. Her uncle was busy telling everyone about their trip and how highly Nicholas's captain had spoken of him.

'But it seems there may be a delay in setting sail again, as several of the crew have gone down with the smallpox and must be replaced.'

Aunt Jane was horrified but Nicholas was at pains to reassure her, saying most likely they had contracted the disease while on shore leave.

Molly was delighted to hear that he would be with them a little longer, although she tried hard not to let the thrill that Nicholas's presence caused her become apparent to anyone, least of all to her cousin himself. She kept her eyes fixed on her plate, listened politely but didn't speak, and cleared the plates away as soon as her aunt signalled to her.

Her uncle was disposed to sit on at the table after they had finished eating and Molly found herself plucking anxiously at the narrow lace trim on the cuffs of the dress she had most recently inherited from Clara. Her heart was beating rapidly and she wanted the evening to be over so that she could set her plan in motion. But as they all rose and Molly began to clear the final dishes from the table, her uncle told Nicholas to join him in his study.

'There are matters I wish to discuss with you,' he said.

Molly looked up at his words, which she feared could be the ruin of her plan, to find Nicholas gazing directly at her. His eyes locked on hers and, for a moment, it was as though no one else existed in the room. She looked away quickly and began to gather up unused cutlery. Had she imagined it or had he mouthed, 'Later,' at her?

Molly was preoccupied and monosyllabic as she helped Hannah in the kitchen. When the cook enquired as to whether she was all right, she replied hastily, 'Yes, yes. Just tired.' She didn't want to arouse her suspicions. Since Hannah had done most of the work before Molly joined her, it was only a short while later that she found herself on the way upstairs to her room. The study door was firmly shut and she could hear voices within.

Reaching her own room, she closed the door and stood with her back against it for a moment or two. Then she blew out the candle and set it down beside her bed, letting her eyes become accustomed to the gloom.

Molly moved towards the un-curtained window and looked out, then turned around again, feeling restless. She released her hair from its pins and began to undo the buttons on her cuffs. She didn't hear the creak on the stairs but she heard the door open and just as quickly close again as

Nicholas stepped into the room. He came towards her as she stood at the window and she noticed that he needed to stoop slightly because of the slope of the ceiling. Then all rational thought ceased as Nicholas cupped her face and bent to kiss her, deep and long. His hands moved from her face to her shoulders, then skimmed across her breasts. Molly shivered and made to move back but there was nowhere to go.

Now Nicholas was plucking urgently at the fastenings on her dress and Molly surfaced from the spell he had cast, fearing he would tear the fabric. A damaged dress would be hard to explain away. She quickly slipped out of it and stood before him in her shift. Nicholas exhaled slowly then took her by the hand and drew her towards the bed. Molly's legs threatened to buckle beneath her. Now that she found herself in the situation she had longed for, without any benefit of experience, she began to feel a kind of terror. But Nicholas had begun to kiss her again, the imprint of his lips running down her body as they lay on the bed. Molly obediently moved her limbs to suit his wordless, ardent actions and found herself wondering at his urgency. She was only half caught up in what was happening, and when it seemed as though it was over, she felt a kind of triumph. She hugged the thought to herself and smiled and Nicholas, turning his head to look at her, caught the smile.

'Well, Molly, it was worth the wait, was it not?'

She wasn't entirely sure that she took his meaning but she nodded, as he appeared to expect it. Then Nicholas was on his feet by the bed, gathering up scattered items of clothing and hastily shrugging them on. Molly watched him, a question forming on her lips, but Nicholas bent over, kissed her and, as swiftly as he had entered the room, he was gone. Molly lay on her bed and thought over what had just happened, exhaustion tipping her into a shallow sleep not long before dawn broke.

CHAPTER THIRTY-ONE

Throughout the weeks that followed, Molly lived a double life. By day, she continued to milk the cows and sell the milk from the stable-yard, returning to Princes Crescent to help with preparations for visitors and dinners. At night, more often than not, Nicholas found his way to her bed. Once he knew how early she had to get up in the morning he took to staying until dawn, creeping down the stairs with her, then kissing the tips of her fingers as he silently parted from her on the threshold of his room.

Molly, who had that first night been disappointed by his abrupt departure from her bed, discovered that this new arrangement was not to her taste, either. Nicholas tossed and turned in his sleep, mumbled and snored. If she shook him awake to silence his snores or to gain herself a fraction more space in the narrow bed, she was in danger of rekindling his ardour and disrupting her own sleep even further. Within the fortnight, Hannah was commenting on Molly's hollow-eyed appearance and frequent yawns. And one evening at dinner, Aunt Jane exclaimed, 'Good heavens, Molly. Are you unwell? You look exhausted and I declare there was no need to have had Clara's dresses altered to fit you. You are fading away before our eyes.'

All eyes turned to Molly and she blushed scarlet. She was

glad that Nicholas wasn't at the table. That evening, as on an increasing number of evenings, he had been invited to dine at the Andersons'. On the first couple of occasions, Molly had found this distressing. She feared that the sisters would be wheedling their way into Nicholas's affections. But when he continued to appear in her room at night after such visits she felt reassured. She wouldn't have liked him to hear his mother's concerns over her health, though. She didn't want him to think she was anything other than blooming.

Aunt Jane came down to the kitchen that evening, a stoppered glass medicine bottle in her hand. 'Molly, I think you are in need of a tonic. I want you to take a spoonful of this, morning and evening.'

She poured out a large dose of the dark, treacly liquid, then stood over Molly as she took it. Molly gagged at the vile taste.

'She looks unwell, don't you think, Hannah?' Aunt Jane applied to the cook for confirmation.

'She does,' Hannah said. 'And tired with it.'

'Hmm.' Aunt Jane gave Molly a sharp glance and, for one heart-stopping moment, she wondered whether her aunt had suspicions of her nocturnal activity. 'I will speak to your uncle. Perhaps someone else can be found to milk the cows for a short while, to allow you time to recover your strength.'

As Molly suspected he would, her uncle prevaricated and said that no one had a way with cows quite like Molly did. His wife was impatient with him but Molly was, in any case, granted some unbroken nights. Nicholas returned to Chatham for a week to spend time with his captain in making sure that the *Valiant* was well set up for their next voyage.

And when, halfway through that week, Molly was looking

and feeling far less exhausted, Aunt Jane exclaimed in triumph over the success of her tonic. 'I will fetch another bottle from the apothecary,' she said, administering Molly's usual evening dose. 'And I will speak to William again about finding a suitable young man for you to walk out with. I know he has been slow to act on this, because he prefers to keep you bound to his cows, but I won't have it. You've grown into a fine young woman, Molly, and you have a look of your mother about you. She would be proud of you. You're a credit to her.'

That night, Molly tossed and turned in her bed. She didn't want her uncle to come up with suggestions of suitors for her. She'd been half tempted to explain to her aunt that it was unnecessary as she already a suitor: Nicholas. Now as she lay in bed, the covers thrown back – the day had been warm and her attic room was stifling – she pondered her aunt's words. *Would* her mother have been proud of her? Molly could remember little about her now, for she had been just nine years old at the time of her death. Perhaps her mother would have been proud that her daughter was going to make a good marriage, but she might well have had something to say about the secrecy of her arrangement with Nicholas.

Molly resolved to discuss the situation with Nicholas as soon as she could. He would be off to sea again before long and it would be best not to delay their marriage. She knew with certainty that she was not prepared to carry on living in this way for much longer. The early-morning milking duty would not be suitable for the wife of a naval officer, and although she would be sad to give up helping her father, Lizzie was more than capable of taking over from her. She and Nicholas would look for a little house in Margate, she decided. Not too close to the harbour area, of course, for that had an unsavoury reputation, but somewhere between there and Princes Crescent, where the streets were more genteel. Above all, it would need to have a little garden, for Molly had resolved to ask Mr Fleming's advice on how to go about establishing one. She would have fruit and vegetables, to prove how practical she was in managing the house, and scented flowers to bring her joy. On such happy thoughts, Molly finally drifted into sleep.

CHAPTER THIRTY-TWO

A few days later, her aunt had come into the kitchen, cheeks pink with excitement, to find Hannah and Molly preparing the vegetables for the planned dinner with the Andersons that evening. Aunt Jane had clapped her hands and all but squealed as she broke the news.

'I just had to tell someone! Clara and Louisa are both out at the Andersons and William has lost all patience with me. Nicholas has just told us that he has spoken to Mr Anderson and that he has asked for Sarah's hand in marriage, and been accepted! Can you imagine? And they're to be wed as soon as possible, at the naval chapel in Chatham, for Nicholas has learnt that he sails within the week.'

Aunt Jane looked as though she might burst with excitement and Hannah hurried to pull out a chair for her, then to fetch a glass and the brandy. As she poured a measure, she shot a worried glance at Molly. Only the day before, Molly had confided in Hannah the news that had filled her with joy and fear. No longer able to hide the nausea that afflicted her as Hannah boiled a joint of ham for dinner, Molly had blurted out, 'I'm to have a baby, Hannah.'

Hannah almost dropped the pan she had just lifted from the range to drain off the cooking water. 'A baby! Why,

Molly …' She was lost for words, but only temporarily. 'And whose baby might this be?'

'Why, Nicholas's, of course.' The answer was so obvious to Molly that it hadn't occurred to her that Hannah might not have realised.

'Oh, Molly.' Hannah, distracted, set the hot pan on the kitchen table, causing Molly to wince. The burn marks in the wood would take some effort on her part to remove.

'Whatever were you thinking?' There was such a world of reproach in Hannah's voice that Molly was immediately defensive.

'It doesn't matter. We'll get married and all will be well.' Even as she spoke, she felt less confident than she sounded. Hannah's reply voiced her own secret worry.

'And has Nicholas agreed to this?'

'Well …' Molly hesitated. 'Well, no.' He hadn't agreed to it because they hadn't discussed it. She hadn't even told him about the baby yet. It had never felt like quite the right moment, even though a part of her had known that it wouldn't be long before he was at sea again.

Hannah had shaken her head. 'Molly, your aunt and uncle will never agree to it. They have plans for Nicholas. A good marriage, with connections, and captain of his own ship before too long. It will raise the standing of the whole family in the town.'

Hannah glanced down at the table, then looked up at Molly. 'How do you imagine marrying his cousin, who works as his father's milkmaid and his mother's servant, fits into those plans? Molly, you have let yourself be taken for a fool.'

Molly had flung down the knife she was using to peel the potatoes and shouted, 'I'll prove you wrong,' before fleeing the kitchen. She'd stayed in her room for the rest of the day, refusing to come down to eat and sending word with Louisa, who'd come to enquire after her, that she felt unwell. She'd hoped that Nicholas would come to visit her that night after dinner but he hadn't appeared. She'd manage to convince herself it was because she'd said she was ill.

After milking the next day, she'd resolved to tell her father. Perhaps he could help her and suggest how best to approach her uncle and aunt, she'd thought.

His response had been no less horrified than Hannah's. 'Molly, whatever can you have been thinking of?' His face changed, from consternation to anger. 'Did he force you? He's not without a reputation. That's why he was sent to sea in the first place. I'll speak to your uncle.'

He looked set to leave the stable-yard at once to go in search of his brother, while Nell stood placidly in the yard, the cart already loaded with milk churns. Molly grasped her father's arm to stop him. 'No, no, it wasn't like that. We love each other. He'll marry me. I'm sure of it.' Even as she said the words, Molly felt a tiny prickling of doubt.

For the past few weeks, she *had* been sure. Why else was he coming to her room each night, even when he'd spent the evening out visiting? It was to Molly he always returned. She'd felt secure in her great plan, convinced that she would make a fine wife for Nicholas. Seeing Hannah's, and now her father's, reaction had shaken her. Was she so wide of the mark? Others seemed to view her prospects so differently.

Her father's expression registered disbelief. He still looked angry, but now – as Molly soon realised – his anger was all directed at her.

'You *stupid* girl. Has all sense deserted you? Nicholas will never marry you. Your aunt and uncle will throw you out and then …' Her father paused, and in a flash Molly could already

188

envisage how the events he was describing would unfold. 'And then you will have to come back and live with us and there will be another mouth to feed.' Her father turned away from her. 'William won't want a reminder of such disgrace living next door to him. We'll have to move. He won't want me doing his milk round for him, either.'

Her father swung back to face her. 'Molly, what have you done?'

Although Molly was appalled by the picture his words had painted, she was determined to prove him wrong. 'It won't be like that. I'll show you,' she said, defiant. 'You wait and see.'

Her father pursed his lips and climbed up on the cart behind Nell. He shook the reins and left without uttering another word. He failed to give her his usual cheery wave as he left the yard.

Molly didn't wait for his return but went back to Princes Crescent earlier than usual. She was troubled by her father's words and determined to seek out Nicholas. Back at the house, Hannah had told her that only her aunt and uncle were at home but, since a family dinner was planned for the evening, no doubt everyone would be there later.

Molly had to curb her nervous impatience and get on with dinner preparations. She and Hannah worked in silence, Molly deep in thought as she contemplated how best to approach Nicholas.

Her aunt had burst in on this scene, delivering the news of Nicholas's engagement. While Hannah was administering a calming measure of brandy, Molly had clutched the table for support, feeling all the colour drain from her face.

Aunt Jane, revived rather than calmed by the alcohol, had chattered on. 'Nicholas and Sarah will be at the dinner tonight so we can all celebrate. He will be away to Chatham before midnight. We shall follow him there before the weekend so that the wedding can take place. Such marvellous news!' She stood up as quickly as she had sat down. 'But I must get on. There are so many plans to be made.'

Hannah had barely uttered a word and Molly had said nothing, but Aunt Jane was satisfied. She had stunned her audience into silence.

After Aunt Jane had left the kitchen, Hannah looked at Molly but didn't speak. She opened her mouth more than once, but no words came. Instead she pushed the brandy bottle across the table and raised an enquiring eyebrow at Molly.

Molly shook her head. She had a pounding headache. If only that would go, perhaps she might be able to get her thoughts in order and work out what to do for the best.

Hannah had eventually come around the table to where Molly was still standing, rooted to the spot, and pushed her gently into a chair.

'Are you going to say, "I told you so"?' Molly asked. Her tone was bitter, but even as she said it, she knew it was wrong to take out her distress on Hannah.

The cook, though, was unperturbed. 'It's a sad state of affairs, Molly. But now you've seen how things are, maybe it's time to work out what to do for the best.'

Molly stared at the table before her, as though the grain of the wood and the scars from the kitchen knives wielded there might hold the answer. 'And what will that be? It seems I've brought trouble on everyone, including myself.' She described her father's reaction to Hannah, who tutted.

'It's a shame. But that's men for you. If only you hadn't lost your mother. Your stepmother will be no help. We must find another way.'

Hannah refused to be drawn on what that might be but told Molly to let her think about it. In the meantime, there was that evening's dinner to be prepared. As Molly chopped and peeled and scraped she changed her mind a hundred times about what she would do that evening. First, she decided she would be at the dinner table to watch Nicholas and Sarah receive everyone's congratulations and to see whether he cast even one glance her way. Then, reflecting on the role she would be obliged to play, getting the dishes to the table, she felt she couldn't do it. How could she play the servant, then sit and listen to Nicholas toast his wife-to-be, a role she had imagined herself playing? And all the while she would be there, his baby in her belly and unable to say a word about it.

Molly shuddered at the thought and had to lay down the paring knife. Only one thought was making itself increasingly clear through the jumble in her head. She must get away.

PART FOUR

JULY 1789–JANUARY 1790

CHAPTER THIRTY-THREE

awn was breaking as Molly crept down the stairs. It looked as though it would be a glorious day, but she would have preferred dark clouds and driving rain, in keeping with her mood. She had tied what few clothes she had into a bundle, taking her plain work dresses and Clara's cast-offs. She left the house in her usual quiet, early-morning fashion, then cut through Charlotte Place, turning right towards the centre of town instead of left towards the fields and her uncle's barn.

She felt a momentary pang over the cows, which would not be milked unless Old Tom's creaking bones would allow him to sit and take up her task, once it was apparent she wouldn't be there that day. Then she turned her thoughts to her onward journey and hurried towards the Duke's Head at the western edge of the town, where all the coaches and wagons travelling in and out of Margate gathered at the start or end of their journeys. This was where she had found a wagon to drop her at Woodchurch Manor on her visits to see Charlie, but now she was keen to avoid any driver who might know her uncle. To this end, she had taken a straw bonnet from the house, one her aunt wore, with a large brim to shade her from the sun when she was in the garden. Molly was ashamed to have taken it, but it allowed her to hide her distinctive hair, and cast her face into shadow.

The wagon drivers were congregating in the yard, yawning and stretching after their night asleep in the barn. Only the passengers of the stagecoaches that passed through could afford to take rooms at the inn, but that morning the landlady was doing a brisk trade in ale, bread and ham among the drivers.

Keeping her head lowered, Molly loitered at the edge of the yard, trying to appear inconspicuous while peering out from beneath her bonnet to see whether she could work out whom to approach. An insistent nudging at her skirt distracted her and she looked down to see a long-haired black-and-white hound beside her. She recognised him as the constant companion of a driver who had dropped her at Woodchurch Manor on several occasions and, before she could stop herself, she bent down to make a fuss of him with her free hand, the other clutching her bundle to her chest.

'Well, if it isn't Mistress Molly.'

She straightened with a start to find the dog's owner, Ned, standing before her.

He must have registered her expression for he said, 'Is something wrong?' His eyes slid across the bundle, then back to her face.

Molly had no choice but to offer a partial confidence. 'I need to get away, to Chatham. But I don't wish my uncle to know. At least, not for a little while,' she added hastily, as Ned frowned. She knew it was unfair to expect him to lie and risk her uncle's displeasure if he should have enquiries made.

'I doubt you'll find a wagon here going that far,' Ned said. 'And I can't take you even a portion of the way as I'm going in the other direction today.' He scanned the yard, where drivers were now climbing onto their wagons and the landlady's daughter was scurrying around, collecting the empty tankards to take back to the inn.

'There's a lad over there who's set to make a delivery over Canterbury way. That's your best bet, then see whether you can find another wagon to take you on from there.'

Ned didn't wait for Molly's reply but strode over to the boy he had indicated, who looked to be about Molly's own age. He spoke briefly to the boy, who glanced at Molly several times before he nodded. Ned beckoned her over and, as she left the safety of the edge of the yard with the hound by her side, she suddenly felt conspicuous as the only woman among all those men.

'Nathaniel will see you right as far as Canterbury. You're on your own from there,' Ned said. Molly stammered out her thanks as he handed her up onto the wagon, where she tucked herself in beside Nathaniel, head still down.

'I hope we'll see you back in Margate before too long, Molly,' Ned said, then took himself off, dog at his heels, to his own wagon.

Molly had been in her seat barely five minutes before the wagon was lurching out of the gate, the wheels catching and bumping in the heavily rutted road. Nathaniel concentrated on negotiating his way around the other wagons to get the short distance out of town and onto the open road, saying nothing to Molly. She felt as though everyone must be looking at her, sitting up beside the driver, and would have preferred to be in the back of the wagon – impossible, since it was fully loaded. Even in her distracted state she recognised the road they were taking: it led out past Woodchurch Manor and beyond. She'd never been further than that and had very little idea in which direction Canterbury lay, or how long it would take to get there. Her only thought since she had learnt the truth about Nicholas had been flight.

Now she was being jolted around on the wagon as it passed

through the countryside. Her thoughts had consumed her for a fair stretch of time and, as she looked up, she saw that they were passing the turning to Woodchurch Manor. Molly gazed down the lane that led to the manor house. She was struck by a sudden wish to see Charlie and to confide in him, telling him everything that had happened, but the horse plodded on and she didn't ask the boy to let her get down. What good would it do? She thought back to the last time she had seen Charlie. He wouldn't want to hear about the mess she had got herself into.

Nathaniel looked curiously at her, his attention having been caught by her movement as she craned her head for a last look down the lane.

'Know someone there, do 'ee?' he asked.

Molly nodded. 'Yes. Or, rather, I did once.'

They travelled on in silence, each pace the horse took along the road carrying her further and further away from everything that she knew.

'How long will it take us to get to Canterbury?' she asked, at last.

'I reckon near enough four hours in all,' the boy said. 'We must rest the horse halfway or he won't be fit to get us there.'

'I have to travel on to Chatham from Canterbury,' Molly said.

'Ned did make mention of it,' Nathaniel replied. 'I doubt you'll get there in the day. Must be another six hours or more. An' all the wagons will have set off at first light.'

'But I must get there today,' Molly, having set off at dawn, could face no further delay. She had decided, almost as soon as Nicholas had left the house the previous night, that she must follow him to Chatham and let him know about their baby.

She had stayed hidden in her room during the evening,

refusing to come down to dinner because she knew she would find it impossible to congratulate Nicholas and Sarah with even the slightest appearance of good grace. She was lucky that Aunt Jane was too caught up in the excitement to think about her, other than to be irritated that someone else must be found to fetch and carry, which was easily addressed by sending for Lizzie from next door. If she had been less distracted, Aunt Jane might have toiled up the stairs with her bottle of tonic, but Molly was sure that under the circumstances her presence wouldn't be missed until lunchtime that day, when word of her absence from the cow barn might have reached her uncle. Her father would have been aware that she was missing but was unlikely to discuss possible reasons for that with her uncle. And it would be next morning at the earliest before anyone would think to ask at the inns as to whether she had been seen trying to leave the town.

Molly had convinced herself that once Nicholas found out why she was in Chatham – and realised that a baby was on the way – why, he would break off his engagement to Sarah immediately. But she needed to reach Chatham before the family arrived for his expected wedding. They wouldn't be travelling in a wagon, as she was, but in one of the fine coaches that occasionally overtook them on the road, travelling a good deal faster than their stately pace and churning up great clouds of dust.

'You might have done better to take a boat from the harbour,' Nathaniel commented.

'A boat?' Molly was startled from her thoughts.

'Aye, for London. Some of them stop along the way. Takes around eight hours to London, I'm told, so less to Chatham, I suppose.'

Molly was silent. The idea of a boat hadn't occurred to her

since she had never been on the water and had only a hazy idea of the direction in which Chatham lay. But of course it must be accessible by boat, for wasn't Nicholas going there to board a ship, ready to sail away to sea? She worried briefly whether the family might choose to travel by boat, then discounted it. Her uncle and Nicholas had travelled by carriage when they had visited Chatham before and she doubted her aunt would agree to travel by sea. She had no alternative but to continue with the plan she was pursuing.

Chapter Thirty-Four

Sitting up beside Nathaniel, there was no escape from the sun and Molly was glad of her bonnet. She was relieved when at last they pulled into an inn along the road to allow the horse to rest and drink. The glare of the sun and the swaying of the wagon made her feel nauseous and it was good to step inside the inn where it was dark and cool. She was thirsty and needed refreshment, although she knew she must conserve the money she had. The price of a cordial was within her reach, though, and she took it to a corner table and sat with her back to the door. There was a regular flow of travellers and she felt less conspicuous than she had in Margate, but even so there were few women on the road. The landlady, serving her, had been curious and asked where she was bound.

'To Canterbury, to meet my betrothed,' Molly replied, which appeared to satisfy the woman's curiosity for she turned away to serve the latest arrivals.

Although Molly was eager to reach Chatham, it seemed all too soon when Nathaniel declared his horses rested, watered and ready to be off. She climbed back up onto the wagon and took her seat beside him once more. As the wagon rolled on, her thoughts drew her back to Margate and her sisters. What would they make of her departure, without a message or a word left for them? She would contact them as soon as all was made right with Nicholas, Molly decided. She had vowed to set a good example to her sisters and it was important that they should have no idea of her predicament.

She thought she should make some effort at conversing with the boy who had been good enough to carry her as far as Canterbury but he was either shy or surly, for she could get barely a word beyond 'yes' or 'no' out of him. So, Molly continued with her thoughts as the road took them along past field after field until it was clear that they were approaching a town somewhat bigger than Margate, with the tower of a great church at its heart.

Nathaniel let Molly down at an inn on the edge of the town, for his journey onwards would take him farther from her destination. She was hungry now, but also eager to find someone to help her complete her journey. The boy had been doubtful that she would succeed, telling her that she would do better to wait until morning and the departure of the first wagons from the inn. But it seemed that luck was on Molly's side.

The inn's landlady was another curious soul who also asked about Molly's destination and the purpose of her journey. When she learnt that Molly was trying to reach Chatham, where her betrothed was waiting to join his ship, she said, 'Why, there's a wagoner just been in here, bound for the dockyard there with a load of timber. He must still be in the yard. You can't miss his wagon.'

Molly, who had just put down a shilling for her drink and her dinner, ran from the bar and was just in time to see a thickset man swing himself up onto the driving seat of a wagon loaded with timber. A pair of the biggest horses

Molly had ever seen was harnessed to the wagon, each held by a stable-boy.

She gasped out her request for a lift along the road to Chatham, while the boys struggled to hold onto the horses, which were now keen to be off through the open gates.

'Aye, why not? Up you get,' the man said. 'You'll have to get down outside the dockyard, though. They'll not let me through with a woman on board.'

Molly, unable to believe her luck, hurried round the wagon to climb on before he changed his mind. Just as the driver was about to give the nod to the boys, and Molly had settled herself on the hard bench seat, the landlady appeared, clutching a package. 'Here,' she said, handing it up to Molly. 'You paid for a hot dinner but this is the best I can do, seeing as you're away already.'

She stepped back as the wagon driver gave the signal to the stable-boys and shook the reins, so that the great load rolled slowly over the cobbles and out of the yard. Molly unwrapped the paper parcel that the landlady had thrust at her and was very grateful for the bread, ham and cheese tucked within it.

She began to tear into it, then remembered her manners.

'Have you eaten, Mr ... ?' She hoped he would supply his name.

The man laughed. 'Aye, I have. And a good deal more than you've got there. You get on with it. We've a way to go before we stop again, if we're to make Chatham this side of midnight.'

He was busy negotiating his way through quite a crowd of wagons, all seemingly bent on taking different routes out of the town, so Molly kept quiet and concentrated on her food. This wagon was altogether bigger and heavier than the one she had travelled on before. She could see that it required some skill to manoeuvre it, with the horses so fresh and eager to be off.

From what Molly could see as the wagon rolled on, the town was mainly set behind high grey stone walls, but she caught glimpses of narrow streets through the town gates as they passed. The inn where she had been set down lay outside the walls, and although Molly was curious about what lay within, and half regretful that she had had no chance to explore, it wasn't long before they were on the turnpike, surrounded by farmland. Turning in her seat to look back, Molly caught a glimpse of the great church once more. Then it was lost to view behind a stand of trees.

'So, what takes you to Chatham, then?' The wagoner was ready to make conversation now that the busy town streets were left behind.

'I must visit my betrothed before he sets sail,' Molly said. The white lie felt natural to her now that it had tripped off her tongue more than once that day.

'Oh, aye?' Out of the corner of her eye she saw the man's brows knit together in a frown. 'And what's he doing, letting you travel across the countryside on your own?'

'I was supposed to be with my family,' Molly improvised hastily, 'but they were unable to start out just yet and I feared I would miss him if I delayed. So I came on ahead.'

'Hmm.'

Molly wasn't sure whether his reply was a sign of disbelief or disapproval. 'Do you travel this road often?' she asked, hoping to divert him from the topic.

'Aye, backwards and forwards all week. They can't seem to get enough timber for the shipyard. They use it up as fast as I can get it there, from what I can tell.'

As the journey progressed, Joseph (for she learnt that was the driver's name) told Molly more about the place she was making for, of the great naval dockyard there and all the ships being built, of how the town, at the water's edge, so grand and full of gentry, had begun to spread up the hill behind it to accommodate the workers. Still the town continued to grow and Joseph said he could barely recognise it any more.

'You'll be heading for his ship, I suppose?' Joseph asked.

'Yes,' Molly said firmly, hoping she was managing to keep her growing anxiety well hidden. How would she find Nicholas in a town the size of the one Joseph had just described? She hadn't thought through the practical aspects of her quest until just now.

It was late evening before Chatham came into view on the horizon. The sun had dipped below the horizon, leaving the sky in a blaze of red, and Molly was wearied to the bone after her long day. Her nose and mouth were clogged with dust from the road, her throat was parched and her skin burnt from the day-long exposure to the sun's heat. Her eyes were sore – from the dust and the glare, she supposed. Looking down at her clothes, she saw that they were coated with dust too. A fine sight I must look, she thought.

Joseph must have read her mind for he glanced at her, then said, 'I'm thinking you'll want to look your best for your young man. I'll let you down at an inn this side of town. There's a well in the yard where you can wash away some of the road dust, and you can get a drink and some food.'

Molly began to fall prey to rising panic. She wished she could stay by Joseph's side. He was a big, strong presence and she would feel safe in his company. The idea that had seemed such a good one in Margate – to seek out Nicholas, on her own in an unknown town – now had the feel of something foolhardy and dangerous. But she must keep up the pretence of knowing what she was doing.

The road from Canterbury had been long and straight and Molly had dozed a couple of times, but the jerking of the wagon had shaken her awake. Now, though, with the town ahead of them and the scent of the sea on a rapidly cooling breeze, the wagon began to vibrate alarmingly. Joseph cursed as he pulled back on the reins and shouted to the horses.

Molly shrank in her seat at his sudden anger and was too scared to question him when he jumped down and vanished round the back of the now stationary wagon. When he came back after a minute or two he was grim-faced.

'There's a crack in the axle. We'll be going no further tonight.'

Molly felt a mixture of emotions: relief that she wouldn't have to hunt through the streets of Chatham in the dark for Nicholas; fear at the thought of spending the night in the open with a stranger; and worry that the delay in finding Nicholas would mean that Sarah reached him before her.

There was nothing to be done, though. She must put a good face on it and do what she could to help Joseph.

CHAPTER THIRTY-FIVE

The night felt endless to Molly. It was completely dark by the time she found herself lying exhausted, but sleepless, beside a hedge in a field close to the wagon. Joseph had unharnessed the horses and hobbled them at the side of the road so that they could crop the grass. He took a couple of blankets from beneath the wagon seat and handed one to Molly.

'I use these to keep the horses warm in winter. They won't smell the best. But if you find a spot in the field and wrap yourself up you might get some sleep. You're safer here than setting off on your own on the road to Chatham.'

Molly knew he spoke sense and she was grateful to Joseph. He apologised for having nothing to offer her by way of food, then settled himself a little distance away. It wasn't long before Molly heard his deep snores.

She had never slept in the open before and was unnerved by every little rustle. Clouds that until now had obscured the moon drifted away and she found she could make out more of her surroundings. There was little to be seen other than the dim outline of hedges and trees, with no sign of lights burning in any dwellings, for Chatham lay a few miles onwards yet. Molly shivered as she was struck by the coolness of the night air under the clear skies. She drifted into an uneasy sleep, thinking of what lay ahead in the new day, and woke with a start more than once, wondering where on earth she was.

When Molly woke again, to the sound of voices, it was already dawn and she was stiff from lying huddled on the hard ground. She lay for a few moments trying to work out who was talking, and then, realising that her blanket was soaked with dew, she threw it off and stood up, stamping her feet and rubbing her arms to try to get some feeling back into them. She now recognised one of the voices as Joseph's and, going over to the gate, she found him in conversation with another driver, the pair of them at work on the axle of Joseph's wagon.

Joseph straightened up and saw Molly watching them. 'Good news,' he said. 'It looks as though we've managed to patch it up. It should see us as far as the town.' He turned to the other driver, thanked him, then set about walking the horses round to get them into harness.

Molly would have liked to help him, not least to get her circulation working properly again, but she was wary of the huge animals. In any case, Joseph had manoeuvred the horses into harness in no time at all and before long they were on the road once more. After enquiring whether she had managed to get any sleep, Joseph lapsed into silence. Molly sensed that he was listening for any unusual sounds from his wagon and her nervousness at the thought of what lay ahead in Chatham was now exacerbated by the thought that they might be further delayed. The glorious early morning was wasted on her as she chewed her lip and willed the wagon on its way.

Within the hour, though, they had reached the outskirts of the town and Joseph let her down at an inn, as he had promised the previous evening. He pointed out the road she must take to reach the wharves where the ships were moored, then she watched the great wagon roll away. The courtyard of the inn was already very busy with comings and goings, and Molly made her way to the pump without feeling too conspicuous. She pumped a little water to splash on her face and gave her hands a cursory wash before pumping a little more, which she gulped down.

She was very aware of what a sight she must look, having slept overnight in the open air, and she did her best to smooth her creased garments, then used her fingers to comb through her hair before tying her bonnet back into place. She didn't look out of place in the inn yard, where most of the wagon drivers had slept that night in the barn and looked as crumpled as Molly felt. She feared it would be a different matter on the streets.

The smell of cooking wafted from the inn kitchen and filled her nostrils, making her feel faint. It was such a long time since she had eaten properly, but she didn't want to subject herself to public scrutiny by going to sit at a table inside. Molly stood for a moment, indecisive, before she spotted a hatch-like window giving onto the courtyard, in front of which a short line had formed. As Molly watched, she saw coins being slid through the hatch and pies handed out in return.

Molly wasted no time in joining the line and ten minutes later, with a steaming hot pie wrapped in paper, she left the courtyard and headed towards the gleam of water across the road, glimpsed earlier from her vantage point on the wagon. She picked her way through a collection of wooden shacks, where men were already at work hammering and banging. No one paid her any heed and she arrived at the water's edge unchallenged. Before her stretched an expanse of river, which, even at this early hour, was alive with activity. Small craft moved at speed up, down and across, while ships far larger than anything Molly had ever seen at such close quarters were anchored along the bank.

She sat down on a flat stone and watched the activity, trying to make sense of something that was entirely foreign to her. She saw that some of the smaller boats were laden with barrels and sacks that were being ferried to the larger ships. These were too far distant for her to see what happened next, but Molly noticed that the boats returned empty and travelled past her upriver, presumably to reload with supplies. The air was filled with noise, the banging and hammering overlying the calls and greetings of those on the river. The smoke drifting up from numerous small fires along the shore made her cough. She would have liked to stay and watch the activity for longer but consciousness of the passage of time spurred her into action. She needed to set off in search of Nicholas and she must start by finding his ship.

She scrambled to her feet and turned back towards the collection of wooden shacks. She would need to ask for directions: Joseph had said she should walk along this road but she didn't know how far. Molly looked at the scene before her. The men were all hard at work, each concentrating on their separate tasks and not paying her, or each other, any attention. She selected the oldest of the workers, a grizzled, white-haired man in a loose blue jacket, and approached him. 'Could you tell me, are the Navy's moorings far from here?'

The man squinted against the morning sun. 'What would you be wanting with the moorings?' he asked.

One of the others, overhearing her question, sniggered. 'It's more usual for the likes of you to be seeking them out at night, ain't it?'

'You watch your mouth,' the older man said sharply.

Molly, while trying to ignore the implication, felt herself

colour. 'I'm looking for my betrothed. I want to see him before he sets sail on the *Valiant*.'

'Well, ain't he the lucky one?' the younger man said, refusing to be put off by the other's glare.

'You'd best try Admiralty Wharf. It's along this road, just a short distance. There's a sentry at the gate and you'll have to convince him of your right to be there.' The old man looked her up and down. 'I doubt he'll let you through. Not unless you can persuade him you have business there. Have you something to collect or deliver, perhaps?'

Molly thanked him and hurried away, eager to avoid inviting any further comment. The old man's words had given her an idea, though, of how she might gain entrance to the wharf. She turned back towards the inn courtyard where she'd noticed a basket by the hatch in the wall. One of the servants at the inn presumably used it to collect the empty tankards left around the yard by the wagon drivers. Molly removed a shawl from her bundle and walked towards the hatch, dropping her bundle by the basket as she did so. She bent to pick it up, then swiftly placed her bundle in the basket and tucked the shawl over the top. She grasped the basket and walked purposefully from the yard, expressionless but heart thumping as she waited to be challenged.

No one called after her and Molly slowed her pace a little as she walked in the direction of Admiralty Wharf. Now that she had the basket, no plan suggested itself to her, other than presenting herself at the gate and saying that she had been asked to make a delivery to Nicholas Goodchild. She hoped he would be there.

Chapter Thirty-Six

The road that led to the wharf was thronged with carts and wagons travelling in both directions, all seemingly on shipyard or naval business. Molly didn't feel so conspicuous now: there were plenty of people on foot along this stretch. She had little time to feel anxious about her mission, for within a few minutes she found herself beside an imposing set of gates, guarded by a man in what she took to be naval uniform. The anchor in the coat of arms above the gates persuaded her that she was in the right place so, before she could change her mind about her plan, she strode up to the guard, hoping she looked more confident than she felt.

'I'm here to see Nicholas Goodchild,' she said.

'Are you, indeed?' said the guard. 'And on what business, may I ask?'

'I have a delivery for him.' Molly indicated the basket. 'From his hometown, Margate.'

'Margate.' The guard's eyebrows rose fractionally. 'And are all the girls in Margate as pretty as you?'

Molly held his gaze. 'Well, they say that Kent lasses are bonny but that the ones from Margate are the bonniest of all.'

The guard chuckled. 'I've only got the London lasses to compare you with, but you fair outdo them all.' He stepped aside. 'Go up to the office in the building on the left and ask for your man there.'

As Molly smiled her thanks and hastened past, before he could ask to see the contents of her basket, he called after her, 'And be sure to stop and see me on your way back.'

Molly dipped her head in acknowledgement but didn't turn. Heart thumping, she went to the office he had pointed out where she found a bespectacled man seated behind a tall desk. Her progress was halted there, but only for a short while so that a small boy could be dispatched to fetch Nicholas. Molly could scarcely believe her luck that she had actually found him.

When the boy returned, it was with an irritable Nicholas in tow. Molly, whose heart had been gladdened at the sight of the familiar figure striding across the courtyard, so handsome in his blue jacket and cream breeches, felt a stir of foreboding at his expression.

Nicholas visibly started at the sight of her, then collected himself. 'I believe you have something for me?' he said. As he beckoned her to follow him into the courtyard, Molly tried to comfort herself: his manner was surely so cold because he was playing along with the illusion of messenger that she had created for herself.

She had barely enough time to absorb the impression of a great space, surrounded on three sides by a two-storey building, the fourth open to the river beyond, bordered only by a low wall, before Nicholas swung round to face her.

'What are you doing here, Molly?' he demanded. His brows were drawn together in a frown and Molly hesitated before she spoke. She hadn't thought through what she would say to him when she found him, imagining only that he might be glad to hear her news.

'I needed to speak with you. Before you got married and sailed away.' She heard her voice falter on the word 'married'.

Nicholas stared at her in silence, his expression unchanged. A small group of men marched past, led by a man in uniform whom Nicholas acknowledged with a nod.

'I'm having your baby,' Molly blurted out. 'You can't marry Sarah.'

Nicholas seized her wrist. 'Hush, not so loud,' he hissed, although as far as Molly could see there was no one nearby to overhear them.

'You are quite sure?' he asked.

Molly nodded.

'And it is mine?'

It was Molly's turn to frown. She nodded again. Nicholas began to pace up and down and, as Molly watched him, wondering at his manner, she was overwhelmed by a great wave of fatigue. She could barely remember leaving Margate, or the manner of it. Her journeying, with the lack of sleep and the worry, threatened her with collapse, and she began to sway where she stood.

Nicholas noticed and stopped pacing at once. 'You've gone quite pale, Molly. Here, let's find you a seat.' He took her arm and drew her back to the cool of the office where the man sat at his desk.

'Could you find Miss Goodchild a chair and something to drink while I attend to some business?' Nicholas said briskly, to the man. Then he tipped his cap to Molly and left.

Molly sat on for ten or fifteen minutes. She drank the cordial she was given and felt better. She was relieved that Nicholas seemed to have relented towards her and hoped he would return quickly. Perhaps he would be able to find her some accommodation, for she would dearly love to sleep.

The memory of their nights together in Margate stirred a fondness in her that she hadn't felt at the time, disturbed as she was by being cramped with him in a single bed. Now that he knew of her condition, he would surely take charge and manage the situation.

The small boy who had fetched Nicholas came back into the room and spoke to the man at the desk. The boy reached up on tiptoe to hand over what looked like a small cloth bag, then left again. Molly noticed how patched his breeches were and wondered briefly about him. She guessed him to be the youngest of a family of boys, doomed to wear his siblings' cast-offs.

The man at the desk glanced at Molly but didn't speak. He wrote something in his ledger, then beckoned Molly over to him. 'Mr Goodchild has asked me to say there is no reply and to give you this,' he said. He handed a cloth bag to Molly, the one she had observed the small boy give to him. She heard a chink and felt the outlines of the coins contained within.

Bewildered, Molly looked up at him. 'But there must be some mistake. Nicholas is coming back to fetch me.'

'Mr Goodchild has made it quite plain that you are to take what he has kindly sent for you and leave. Now,' the man added firmly.

Molly stood before the man and opened her mouth as if to appeal to him again, then thought better of it. Comprehension slowly dawned. Nicholas had no intention of coming back. He was buying her off.

Molly turned away, conscious all at once of the shabbiness of her clothes and how like the messenger boy she must look, poor and unkempt. Tears started to her eyes as she stumbled out of the office, back towards the main gate with no clear idea of what to do next.

'Hello again. Found what you were looking for?'

The sentry's voice changed from cheery to concerned as he registered her tears. 'Who's been upsetting you?' he demanded. 'Not that old man in the office? His bark's a sight worse than his bite, you know.'

Molly, blinded by tears, could only shake her head. She wanted to get away from this place, the scene of her humiliation, as quickly as possible but the sentry barred her way.

'Now, we can't have you stepping out onto the street with a face like a wet week, can we?' he said. 'Where are you going?'

Molly, who hadn't yet given this a thought, burst into sobs. The impossibility of her situation struck her, like a physical blow. She couldn't return to Margate. Her father's reaction to her news of a baby had made it clear that she would be unwelcome, and she was quite certain that Aunt Jane and Uncle William would want nothing to do with her. So where was she to go?

CHAPTER THIRTY-SEVEN

T he hour that followed was one that Molly would always look back on with the greatest gratitude, on account of the sentry's actions. Her knees had buckled and given way and she would have fallen to the ground if he hadn't caught her and supported her into the little hut by the gate. There he had let her cry herself out, then asked gently whether she could explain what ailed her. Feeling as though she didn't have a friend in the world, Molly had told him her sorry tale of a love spurned, although she couldn't bring herself to mention the baby. She did say, though, that it was impossible for her to return home. Afterwards, she wondered what had made her confide in a total stranger.

He had looked grave, then excused himself to attend to business at the gate. When he returned, he looked a bit more cheerful and Molly had composed herself a little.

'I have a plan,' he said, checking himself before he went on to outline it to add, 'But you don't even know my name!' He introduced himself to Molly as Stephen Watson, and told her he had a sister called Martha living in London. 'I'm sure she would give you a bed for a few nights and she might even be able to help you find work. There'll be plenty of openings for a bright young girl like you in a big city.' He spoke with confidence.

London. Molly hadn't considered that. It would be taking her even farther away from everything that was familiar to her but, even as she thought of the alternatives, she could see she had few options. She couldn't return to Margate. Neither could she stay in Chatham. She'd already experienced the difficulties she was likely to face as a single girl in a naval town.

With only the bleakest of prospects before her, it didn't seem odd to Molly to take up Stephen's proposal. While she rested, at his insistence, he made enquiries of a wagon coming into the yard and came back triumphant, saying he had found her passage all the way to London. Twenty minutes later, he helped Molly onto the empty bed of the wagon as it passed through the gate. She barely had time to stammer her thanks before it was on its way.

Molly had no wish to see anything further of Chatham. She curled up on the sacks in the back of the wagon and shut her eyes to everything, although she could not shut out her distress. Heartsick and weary, she dozed fitfully as the wagon rattled onwards through the afternoon.

When the driver roused her, telling her that they had passed the Deptford Turnpike and were now close to where he had been instructed to drop her, dusk was falling. Molly peered over the side of the wagon, expecting busy city streets, and was surprised to find fields surrounding the wagon on both sides.

'Are you sure this is right?' she asked the wagon driver.

'Aye. Bermondsey, I was told. Not far now.'

As Molly watched, a few dwellings appeared along the side of the road, and then a few more, but she thought it had the feel of the outskirts of Margate, rather than of a great city.

'Now then.' The driver slowed the horses to a walk. 'Five Foot Lane, I was told, but not down the docks end. Just off Bermondsey Street, then next to the Tanner's Arms.' He drew the horses to a halt. 'I'll have to let you off here. My way lies straight ahead but it looks as though I've brought you almost to the door. There's the Tanner's Arms.' And he pointed along a road, lined with small cottages, leading off to the right.

As Molly prepared to climb down, she was struck by a smell on the breeze, the like of which she'd never come across before. She wrinkled her nose. 'What's that smell?' she asked.

The man laughed. 'It's the tanneries. Bermondsey's full of them.'

'Tanneries?' Molly was none the wiser.

'It's where they treat animal skins to make leather. Filthy places. They soak the skins in piss and treat them with dung, so I'm told. They have to set the tanneries on the edge of town because no one can stand the smell.'

Molly, trying hard not to retch, thanked the man for bringing her all the way to London, and then, as the wagon rolled away, she forced her stiff legs to carry her along the road towards the Tanner's Arms. Stephen had told her to ask there for his sister by her married name, Martha Brookes, although her heart failed her at the thought of entering yet another inn. And she hoped that the work Stephen had spoken of would not involve a tannery.

Luck was with Molly, for she didn't need to enter the inn after all. She found the doorway barred by a woman standing there, arms folded, and looking quite formidable. She addressed Molly before she could speak.

'Are you all right, love? You look done in.' Her tone was quite friendly.

Molly nodded, but the concern in the woman's voice threatened to undo her and it was in shaky tones that she said, 'I was told to ask here for Martha Brookes.'

'Martha?' the woman repeated. She peered at Molly. 'Who

sent you?'

'Her brother, Stephen,' Molly said. She feared she made a dejected figure, travel-weary and doubtless filthy, and now faced with nowhere to stay in a strange city if she couldn't find Martha. Whatever had made her listen to Stephen and go along with his scheme?

'Don't mind me,' the woman said. It was clear that Molly's forlorn expression wasn't lost on her. 'I'm only asking because I didn't want to send you along to Martha's without getting an idea of how you know her. I'm just standing here to bar entry to some of the tannery lads who haven't settled their bills.' She half turned and looked beyond the inn. 'Martha lives along here, not two doors down. That house, there, with the blue door.' She pointed to a flat-fronted cottage, with a scrap of a garden before it, and nothing to distinguish it from its neighbours, apart from the door's colour.

'Thank you.' Molly felt the effort involved in producing a smile of gratitude might crack her face but she did her best, then clutched her bundle to her as she walked the last few yards to Martha's gate. She turned to see whether the landlady of the inn was watching her, but her attention had been caught by a group of men, no doubt from the tannery, trudging up the road towards her.

Molly pushed open the gate and knocked at the blue door, fervently hoping that Martha would be at home. There was a lengthy pause, during which Molly took in the fact that the cottage appeared to be a good deal smaller than her family home in Margate, then the door opened.

A slight, fair-haired woman stood on the doorstep. 'Can I help you?' she asked.

'Are you Martha?' Molly asked. The woman nodded, so Molly pressed on. 'Your brother, Stephen, sent me. From

Chatham. He thought you might be able to help me. I'm a stranger to the city but need to find a bed and some work.'

As she spoke, she realised for the first time that her request was a strange one. Why had Stephen thought she might impose on his sister in this way?

Martha frowned, then laughed. 'That's Stephen, through and through. Always wanting to help someone. You'd better come in.' She stood aside and beckoned Molly in, then closed the door.

'This way,' she said, and led Molly into a small kitchen at the back of the house. 'I was just making some dinner. It looks as though you could do with some.'

She gestured to Molly to sit at the table, then carried on with her preparations. Molly offered to help but Martha waved her away.

'I'm all but done,' she said. 'Just the two of us tonight, and now you, of course.' As Martha talked on, telling her about Stephen and her family, it became apparent to Molly that they were sitting in the kitchen of the house that belonged to the parents of her husband, Daniel.

'Don't worry.' Martha had registered Molly's discomfort. 'Daniel's parents have gone to stay in the country with his aunt. His father had to give up his work at the tannery because of ill health and now they try to get away from Bermondsey whenever they can.'

Molly heard the front door open and looked at Martha, who wiped her hands on her apron. 'That'll be Daniel. He works at the tannery, too.'

CHAPTER THIRTY-EIGHT

Daniel Brookes was a man of few words and spoke little over their meal that night, only asking Molly about her journey once Martha had explained her brother's role in Molly's arrival at their home. Once they had eaten and Molly had helped clear the table and wash up, she asked whether there was somewhere she might sleep that night, feeling more than a little awkward as she did so. 'I'm very tired after two days of travelling,' she said, by way of explanation. In truth, her mind was so full of worry that she felt in great need of a quiet space where she might think over the events of the last few days. And she couldn't expect to stay with Martha and Daniel for more than a night, but when she put this to Martha as they made up a bed for her, her hostess dismissed the notion.

'Nonsense. You're more than welcome here and I'm sure I'll be able to find you work. You can give me a little by way of rent and it will be very helpful to us.' Martha bustled about, being far more effective than Molly in preparing the room, then withdrew, leaving Molly to her thoughts.

Molly had thought she was bone tired, despite sleeping all the way to London from Chatham, but as soon as she lay down, the full horror of her interview with Nicholas returned to her. She saw now how misguided and foolish she had been. How could she have believed that he loved her? He had been less than pleased to see her at the wharf and couldn't wait to be rid of her. She supposed he thought that the money he had given her would be sufficient to support her and his baby. Her cheeks burnt with anger and she clenched her fists, burying her face in the pillow to stop herself crying out. What a fool she had been!

Yet even as she railed against him, a tiny voice inside was asking her whether she had *truly* believed he loved her. Hadn't she just chosen to convince herself that his coming to her bed every night meant that he did, and that they would be married? The reaction of her father and of Hannah, when she had told them about the baby, came back to her, cast in a different light. She had been indignant with them, so sure that she was right and they were wrong.

Earlier, sitting with strangers in their kitchen, eating their food, she had felt desperately homesick and she had thought that would occupy her mind once she was in bed. But now her anger wouldn't let her think of the sisters she had been missing so much a little earlier that evening. Now, as she lay awake, listening to the noises of an unfamiliar house as it creaked and settled for the night, she could focus only on her determination to put Nicholas and her own folly out of her mind. All her energy now must be put into making sure that she had enough money for herself and the baby, and to do this she must take on whatever work Martha could find for her. Even if that work was in the tanneries, Molly thought, although it seemed to her that the air in the room where she was trying to sleep was tainted by that foetid odour.

Daniel Brookes worked long hours and was little in evidence around the house, but he always had a smile for Molly if she was there when he came home from the tannery. This happened less frequently once Molly started work, for within days of her arrival Martha introduced her to the manageress of the tea room where she herself had taken up a new position. The tea room was set in pleasure gardens on the outskirts of Bermondsey and the presence of a mineral water spa in its grounds made it a favourite with the wealthy on the south side of the River Thames, or so Martha said with some pride. Molly had little sense of the geography of London, but she was delighted with her work surroundings.

She could hardly have asked for a setting any more like the fields of Kent that she was accustomed to. The pleasure gardens were set around what appeared to Molly to be a very grand mansion – although not quite on the scale of Woodchurch Manor – with open countryside beyond. Visitors arrived by carriage, rolling up the driveway then stepping down to walk in the grounds or to visit the spring to take the waters, returning to the house for tea.

At Martha's insistence, Molly had dutifully tasted the water when she first arrived and had spat it straight out. 'It's like …' she struggled for words '… like drinking an iron bar. With the smell of rotten eggs. Why on earth would anyone want to drink this? Surely they're more likely to make themselves ill than improve their health.'

Martha struggled to stop laughing at Molly's disgust. 'The waters are very popular with the gentry. Supposed to cure all manner of ills, I'm told. Colic, melancholy, dyspepsia, worms …' Molly's expression sent her into fits of laughter again. 'You'll have to do better than that when you're on duty down here.'

But Molly found it hard to have to stand by the spring, extolling the virtues of the noxious stuff that Thomas Keyse, who owned the house and gardens, saw as the key to making his establishment a great one. She found it far easier to work in the tea room, where she could sneak glances at the ladies and gentlemen, posing in their finery for all to admire. Molly marvelled that such well-dressed customers were free to come and go, spending their days as they pleased. No matter how many times Martha tried to explain it to her, she struggled to understand the nature of their freedom.

'So, they don't work? At all?' She and Martha were standing side by side, alert and watchful for a signal from the tables that more hot water was required or an additional cup and saucer.

'No, they have an income.' Martha was poised to start clearing a table where the occupants were showing signs of leaving.

'But where does their money come from?' Molly asked.

'From their income,' Martha said.

'And where does the income come from?' Molly persisted. But Martha had darted away and Molly was left none the wiser.

The tea-room building also housed an art gallery where Thomas Keyse, who had some talent as an artist, exhibited his own work and that of friends and associates. Molly liked to steal into the gallery when the tea room was quiet, so that she could look at the work hung on the walls.

One day she was standing before a painting of a basket from which all manner of fruit tumbled – pears, plums, grapes and several fruits with which she was unfamiliar. Head tilted to one side, she took in the bird with grey plumage and a hooked beak that sat atop the basket, looking as though it was about to steal one of the soft fruits.

A voice close behind her made her jump. 'Is there anything here that you would hang on your wall?'

Molly, who always had the presence of mind to take a feather duster with her into the gallery, in case she was caught there, tried to pretend she had been surprised in the middle of dusting. A chuckle suggested that her ruse wasn't working, so she turned slowly to find herself facing a ruddy-complexioned gentleman wearing a snow-white wig.

'My dear, the question still stands. Is there anything here that appeals to you?'

Scarlet with embarrassment, Molly nodded. She knew that this was Thomas Keyse, for Martha had pointed him out to her as he walked around the grounds, greeting his visitors. She also knew that some of these paintings must be his work, but here her lack of learning let her down. She couldn't decipher the labels on the paintings so she had no idea which ones he had painted. She must simply be bold.

'This one,' she said, indicating the painting she had been standing before, 'and this one,' pointing to an adjacent work.

'A wise choice.'

The twinkle in Thomas Keyse's eye suggested that these were indeed his creations so, made bold, she asked, 'Could you tell me please, sir, the nature of this fruit? I have never seen such a thing before.'

She pointed at a fruit split open in the foreground, ruby-red jelly-like seeds filling its creamy white interior.

'Ah, a pomegranate,' Thomas Keyse said. 'One of those fruits that, like the pineapple, has become popular to display on dining tables in London, these days. But tell me,' he continued, as Molly considered the vision this conjured up, so far removed from anything in her experience, 'do you like to look at the paintings in the gallery?'

'Yes … I mean …' Molly floundered, unsure of the correct answer and afraid she might be in trouble. She liked the space, the light flooding in through the roof, which had windows set along one side so that it always appeared cool and bright whatever the weather outside. It was a large space, always peaceful, even when filled with visitors. She had watched them from the doorway on occasion and heard how their tones modulated from the noisy chatter of the tea room to a respectful hush that the space seemed to demand.

'I am happy that it gives you pleasure,' Thomas Keyse said. 'It shouldn't be for the delight of the spa patrons alone.' With that, he nodded to her and moved away to pause in front of a painting nearby. Molly bobbed a curtsy, flicked her duster at some imaginary dust and hastened from the room.

After a week, with no word of chastisement from the tea-room manageress, Molly stopped worrying that she had done something wrong. And the following Monday she was asked to split the week between working in the tea room by day and working in the evening when the spa was open as a proper pleasure garden.

Molly was entranced by how different the gardens looked after dark. Lanterns were strung from the trees all along the driveway and throughout the grounds, and the evening visitors came to walk, gossip, listen to music, watch entertainment and to drink. Tea wasn't served: instead Molly found herself dispensing wine, champagne, beer and measures of Thomas Keyse's famous home-made cherry brandy.

The picture gallery was open under Mr Keyse's watchful eye. He hovered anxiously in the doorway as though concerned that boisterous revellers might make off with the art. Molly thought this unlikely – the majority appeared intent on enjoying the gardens and she heard a good deal of scuffling and giggling in the shrubbery as she went around collecting the glasses that were casually discarded as the night progressed.

Molly thought she would never tire of watching the crowds as they paraded for others to see. She had been taken aback at first by the smartness of the men's clothes – tight-fitting frock coats in the sort of bright pastel colours rarely seen in Margate, worn over cream breeches and silk stockings. And the shoes – both men and women strolled in silk shoes decorated with jewelled buckles, the ladies' shoes less visible under their long skirts but glimpsed as they climbed the steps, when she could see that they had heels to make them appear taller than they were. Molly felt sure such delicate footwear must be ruined after one outing in the gardens.

Mrs Hughes, the milliner in Margate, would have been amazed by the adornments that the ladies wore on their heads, while Molly marvelled at the beautiful dress fabrics. Silks and satins shimmered under the garden lights and the dresses swished as the ladies promenaded past. Molly had never had anything grander than her cousin Clara's cast-offs, and she could see that any one of those dresses would have looked dowdy here.

And now, she reflected ruefully, even those dresses – let out at her aunt's insistence – did not fit. Her waist had thickened, and although she was thankful that her condition was not yet too apparent, as summer turned to autumn the evening events would cease. How much longer after that would she be able to continue with her job?

She had been – more or less – honest with Martha and Daniel not long after she had arrived in their home, just tweaking her story a little to represent herself as actually betrothed to her cousin, who had cruelly jilted her. So intent had she been on finding work and earning money that she hadn't thought too much about her plans beyond that, but in September Martha mentioned that Daniel's parents would soon be returning from the country. They seemed to believe that she would return to Margate and reconcile with her family, having the baby there, and Molly didn't seek to dissuade them. She recognised that her summer idyll was all but over and it would soon be time to face up to the next stage in her life.

Chapter Thirty-Nine

It was a chance conversation with Mr Keyse that eventually gave Molly the idea for what to do next. New paintings had been hung in the gallery to welcome the autumn season and Molly crept in one day once work was over and all the clearing up had been done. She was anxious not to be locked in, but also curious to see what had replaced the pictures she had come to view as old friends.

'Are you here to choose something new for your wall?'

Thomas Keyse's tone was teasing. Molly had come across him many times since their first encounter and had ceased to feel quite so much in awe of him.

'This picture reminds me of a sketch that a friend of mine was doing the first time I met him,' Molly said, indicating a painting of a church and churchyard, with the snows of winter on the ground. 'I believe he is studying at the Royal Academy in London now. I would very much like to see him. Can you tell me where that is?'

'Your young friend must have talent.' Mr Keyse sounded impressed. 'The Royal Academy is right in town, set back from the river on the Strand. Some distance from here.'

He didn't speak as though he found town somewhere he cared to be and, if truth be told, Molly was hard pressed to think of a time when he wasn't to be found either in the house or the grounds of the Bermondsey Spa. But his reply sowed a seed in her mind. When October came and the manageress told her that she was very sorry but she would have to let her go since the autumn season was quiet – averting her eyes from the bump that Molly's work apron only seemed to enhance – Molly knew the time had come.

She told Martha and Daniel that she must leave to have the baby. She thought she read relief in their eyes, for the return of Daniel's parents was imminent and Molly suspected they would not welcome the presence of an unmarried lodger who was clearly with child. She made Martha write down Stephen's name and where she might find him in Chatham, hoping one day to be in a position to repay his kindness to her. Then she gathered her belongings together, a bundle that was very little bigger than when she had arrived, and set off one wet and windy late October morning as though she had a clear idea of where she was going.

She had the outline of a plan, it was true: she would make her way to the centre of London, in the area of the Strand, and take a room, biding her time until the baby was due. She had hit on that area because Will Turner might, perhaps, be found there and he was the only other person in London she knew.

Molly was resigned to having to live off her savings, for she knew she was unlikely to find anyone to employ her now. She would also need a midwife to assist at the birth. Beyond that, she had no plan. The memory of Ann giving birth to Harriet stubbornly returned to her again and again: her stepmother's cries and her torment, and the way in which she appeared to be oblivious to the presence of anyone else. It was not an image that reassured Molly about what was to come.

Her first challenge, though, was to find her way to the

centre of town and then to discover where she might live. She had been asking discreet questions of Martha and had worked out that she would need to find her way to London Bridge to cross the Thames, and from there she could perhaps follow the river.

'It's a good four or five miles,' Martha had said. 'It's not a journey I'd want to undertake.'

From this, Molly guessed that Martha had probably never been that far – in fact, had probably never left Bermondsey. Molly wondered at this: she had explored the area all around Margate on foot from an early age. But, then, since most things one might need were to be found in the immediate Bermondsey neighbourhood, she supposed that had she been born there she might well have felt the same.

Thoughts of Margate induced a sense of loss in Molly. What were her sisters doing now? What did they think of her, having vanished from their lives without a word? With the birth of her baby so close she missed them all the more. As she stepped out along Bermondsey Street, walking towards yet another new start in her life, she was glad that the brisk wind allowed her to keep her head bent. She didn't want passers-by to notice the tears trickling down her cheeks.

Bermondsey Street reminded her of Margate High Street. It was full of shops to furnish the everyday needs of the residents in the nearby streets – butchers, bakers, greengrocers – but there the resemblance ended. Instead of a breeze that carried the tang of the sea, the pungent smell from the tanneries overlay everything. None of the shopkeepers greeted Molly, as they would have done in Margate, for she was unacquainted with any of them. Her work had prevented her exploring the area and, in any case, Martha had her favourite suppliers and had dealt with that side of the household management. A stroll along Margate High Street could be undertaken at a leisurely pace, with frequent stops to examine the wares on display and chat to the shopkeepers, but here everyone was in a hurry, not least the carts rolling interminably past, forcing Molly to jump out of the way on more than one occasion.

At the end of Bermondsey Street, she hesitated, her resolve faltering. She knew, from what Martha had said, that her destination lay to the west and then over the water, so she turned left into the busy road that now lay before her. The fields and countryside of Bermondsey Spa felt almost as distant as Margate now, even though they were only a mile or so behind her, so different were her surroundings. These streets were filled with the cries of the men loading and unloading wagons at warehouses that lined one side of the road, and the jingling of horses' harnesses as they stamped their feet and showed their impatience. The other side of the road was lined with workshops and inns, and Molly was glad that she did not need to pass far along this route, for she felt uncomfortable walking there alone.

She was relieved to be able to turn north, to cross the river using the great span of London Bridge. It acted as a funnel, drawing all the carts and wagons in the area towards it before ejecting them at the other side. It was quite the grandest bridge that Molly had ever seen, stone-built and stretching across a river so much wider than she could ever have imagined. But she had little time to pause and wonder: once she had set foot on the bridge she was swept along in the tide of others making the crossing, all caught up with wagons and carts passing in both directions. Some of the wagons were so heavily laden that Molly marvelled there was enough room to pass. Indeed, she had almost reached the far side of the bridge and had, perhaps, dropped her guard a little as she gazed out over the side at the river, which was equally busy with all manner of boats, when she felt herself pulled roughly to the left, banging her elbow hard on the brickwork.

'Ow!' she said, rubbing the sore spot and looking indignantly about to see who was responsible for the action.

'You need to watch yourself on here, love.' An older woman, her face creased and lined, had fallen into step beside Molly. She was carrying a basket covered with a cloth and Molly could have sworn that whatever was beneath it was moving.

She opened her mouth to offer a tart response but the woman continued, 'See that wagon there?' gesturing to one heavily laden with straw that had just passed. 'Almost had you, he did, when the horse took against that dog snapping at his heels.'

She glanced down and registered the bump of Molly's belly. Her sharp tone softened. 'Didn't mean to startle you.'

They walked on a few paces in silence before Molly said, 'Thank you. I'm not used to such a busy place.'

'From out of town, are you?' the woman asked as they drew close to the end of the bridge. 'Where are you going?'

'To the Strand,' Molly said. She thought the woman gave her an odd look but she said nothing, so Molly pressed on. 'Could you point out the right direction? I know to head west …'

Her voice tailed off. Everyone was leaving the bridge, stepping out briskly. Molly feared her nervous indecision might show in her face and make her a target for the footpads Martha had warned her about. Her bag of money was safely stowed away in her pocket looped on a ribbon beneath her skirts, while her bundle held little of value – but she clutched it tightly all the same.

The woman gestured to the road leading north of the bridge. 'Take that road a little way and then, at Great Exchange, you must turn to the west and keep that in your sights.' She indicated a dome on the skyline that had already caught Molly's attention. 'That's St Paul's Cathedral. Go past it and on into Fleet Street. Beyond that you'll find the Strand.' She looked Molly up and down. 'Watch yourself there if you're not used to this city.' Then she turned and walked swiftly away down one of the narrow roads to Molly's left, leaving her feeling very much alone once more.

CHAPTER FORTY

The further Molly progressed on her journey, the more she regretted her decision to ever leave Bermondsey. She hadn't realised until now how the countryside fringing the narrow streets of cottages had sustained her. Her workplace, set right at the edge of those streets, had reminded her of Woodchurch Manor. Even though she was far from home in Bermondsey, she had felt linked to Margate by the nature of her surroundings.

Here, though, as she walked on rapidly tiring feet towards what she had decided would be her destination, she felt out of place and unsettled. The buildings were taller than those in Bermondsey, some of them several storeys high, and they seemed to bear down on her as she walked. She didn't miss the smell of the tanneries but there was a reek to these streets, too – the pungency of piss and of horse dung from the droppings liberally scattered along the way, mixed with woodsmoke and acrid smells from some of the small enterprises hidden away in side alleys. Molly hazarded a guess at candlemakers, soap manufacturers and ironworkers from the trade she saw being plied through open doorways.

Everyone appeared to be in a hurry and she lost count of the number of times passers-by barged into her with neither an apology nor a glance in her direction. She felt conspicuous, even though no one paid her the slightest attention, and it made her nervous and uneasy. As she drew closer to the great dome of the cathedral, she noticed more coaches among the wagons and carts on the cobbled road. Glimpses of their occupants reminded Molly of the finely dressed ladies and gentlemen who had visited the pleasure gardens. The coaches, some with crests painted on their sides, drew to a halt at the cathedral to let their occupants descend, and Molly, who had thought she might go into the cool interior to rest and calm herself, was daunted. She told herself she had as much right to enter as any other person but, looking down at her shabby and now dusty clothes, she feared she would be denied entry.

Hesitant, she stood opposite the cathedral, at the side of a road lined with small shops selling prints and pamphlets. Then, taking a deep breath, she struck out boldly, navigating the horse-drawn carriages to reach the other side. She was hungry and thirsty as well as weary. Perhaps she could find somewhere to sit and eat the food she had brought with her. She'd hoped for something like the pleasure gardens, yet after walking past row upon row of neat graves, many topped with marble statues that surely signified their occupants had been persons of great importance, she found only a small patch of grass with a stone bench. It was in the shelter of some trees, their leaves still clinging on despite the season. She had the area to herself and sank down on the bench, pulling the bread and cheese from her bundle, aware all at once of just how ravenous she was. Now that she was sitting down, her feet and legs aching, she bent down and unlaced her boots, easing her feet out of them. Walking the hard-packed earth and stone flags of the city streets was more tiring than Molly had expected. She hoped she didn't have much further to go.

She thought about lying down on the bench but feared

falling asleep. She could so easily be robbed – and her money must carry her through the next few weeks and beyond, until she was able to work again. She rested a while, chewing her last piece of bread, then bent to lace her boots on and rose to her feet, stretching out her back. She must get on and find somewhere to spend the night before darkness fell.

Molly struck out again, following the road beyond St Paul's. At intervals, she caught glimpses down to the river, from which a cold wind whipped up, making her shiver. For the first time in many weeks she allowed herself to think about Nicholas. Where was he now? she wondered. Somewhere a great distance out at sea, no doubt, married and with Sarah ensconced—Where? In a house in Margate? Or in Chatham? Living the life that Molly had imagined for herself and which she now saw for what it had always been: a dream.

Head down, immersed in her thoughts, Molly walked on, paying little attention to her surroundings until the road brought her to a junction. It appeared to be a place of importance, for the largest statue that Molly had ever seen, of a man astride a horse, was set in the centre of it, while the buildings edging the roads were surely the grandest to be found in London. She had no idea where she was or which route she must take. It was time to ask for help once more.

A young boy, clearly on some sort of errand, judging by his purposeful air and the package tucked under his arm, was the closest person to Molly. She caught him as he hurried by, bringing him to a halt.

'Can you tell me, is this the right way to the Strand?' she asked, gesturing vaguely at the junction.

'It is,' said the boy, 'if you go back that way,' and he jerked his head in the direction that Molly had just travelled. Then he pulled himself free and vanished among the passers-by.

Molly sighed and turned back, this time paying proper attention to where she was. She saw what she had failed to register earlier – the passers-by here were more inclined to be strolling, gazing at posters pasted on boards or the windows of inns and rooms, advertising events or displays to be found within. There were drawings of creatures that Molly didn't recognise, as well as of people who seemed to be freaks of nature, but she moved swiftly on. She could take the time to find out more later – for now, the sky was darkening with the threat of rain and the onset of night, and still she had no bed. Lodgings were to be found in the side streets, she thought, not on such a busy road.

She watched and waited, taking her chance to cross in the company of others who were doing the same, pausing at intervals as a wagon or carriage rumbled by, the driver oblivious to those on foot. She arrived on the other side with a thumping heart but a sense of achievement and the dawning of a nervous excitement. Looking up and down the frontages along the road, she was drawn to an inn sign blowing in the sharp breeze. It showed a half-moon glowing in a dark night sky and, coming to a decision, Molly plunged down the side road that had the inn on its corner. She was halfway along it, without any clear idea of how lodgings might be found, when the boy she had accosted earlier came out of a doorway, now without his package. On impulse, she spoke to him again.

'I'm looking for somewhere to stay the night – well, a few nights. Can you tell me of any place around here I might try?'

The boy looked at her, then surprised her by calling back into the house from which he had emerged, 'Ma, there's someone here wanting a room.'

Molly waited, and within a few minutes a woman came

to the door. She was small and stout, plainly dressed in a black gown and with greying curls visible around the edge of her cap. She looked Molly up and down. 'Can you pay?' she demanded.

Taken aback, Molly said, 'Of course.'

The woman stood aside and inclined her head to indicate Molly must enter. 'I do have one room available. It's right at the top of the house, though, so I'm not sure it will suit.' Her eyes slid to Molly's belly and Molly could feel herself blushing.

She set off up the stairs and Molly followed, taking in what she could of her surroundings. The stairway was tall and narrow, and on each landing a dark corridor led off towards the back of the house, with doors firmly closed on each side. Molly had the sense that people were within: she heard bursts of laughter and at one point a door opened and a girl poked her head out. On seeing the woman, she said, 'Oh, it's just you,' and closed the door again.

The woman was wheezing, and by the time they reached the last flight of stairs Molly was using the banister to haul herself up. Here it was lighter and there was no corridor, just three doors leading off the tiny landing lit by a small skylight. The woman took a key from her pocket and opened one of the doors, stepping aside to allow Molly to enter. The room was small and plainly furnished, with a narrow iron bedstead and a table beside it bearing a jug and bowl. There was a bentwood chair alongside a chest of drawers, with a small cupboard set into the wall above it. The window drew Molly's attention and she stepped over to it, then gasped. She was very high up – far below her people were going about their business on the street, and if she peered to the left the bustle of the Strand was clearly visible, with a glimpse of the river beyond it. The other way, she looked over roofs towards an area she hadn't explored. The room reminded her of her rooms back in Margate, in her father's house and her uncle's, tucked away under the eaves. She felt safe there.

Molly turned to face the woman. 'I'll take it,' she said, then added, 'How much?' She realised, as a small smile crossed the woman's face, that she was now not best placed to bargain, but the amount the woman quoted was less than Molly had expected. Her new landlady introduced herself as Mrs Dobbs. She told Molly that she and her son James had the other rooms at the top of the house, then left her to settle in.

Molly sank onto the bed with a sigh of relief before leaping to her feet again and checking the sheets for any sign of bedbugs. All seemed clean and the room itself was in surprisingly good order, she thought. She had reached her intended destination with no mishaps and had found, quite by chance, the most satisfactory accommodation. For the first time that day she allowed herself to think that everything might turn out well after all.

CHAPTER FORTY-ONE

With relief came a great weariness but, before she gave in to it, Molly looked around for a safe place to hide her money. She discounted the drawers in the chest, for although these had keyholes, there was no sign of a key. The cupboard, which held a plate, a bowl, a knife and a fork, closed with a simple brass latch. Her gaze travelled over the floorboards, which were all level and set tightly together, but when she threw back the rug by the bed there was one board that stood a little proud of the rest. Molly took the knife from the cupboard and used it to lever up the board, thinking as she did so that this had been done before so perhaps it wasn't the best choice of hiding place. But, she reasoned, it was the best she could do for now, so she took her money purse from her pocket, tied beneath her skirt, and extracted a few coins, enough for the rent and some daily provisions, then stowed the purse in the gap below the floor. With the board slotted back into place and the rug laid over it, Molly lay down on the bed and promised herself a few minutes' sleep.

When she woke up the room was in darkness and for a moment or two she couldn't work out where she was. Then the memory of the day came back to her and she eased herself off the bed and went to the window again. The lamplighter had been on his rounds and from above she could see the puddles of light cast by the lamps at each end of the street. If anything, there seemed to be even more people out and about, and Molly watched them awhile, noticing how many people turned off the Strand and came along her street, vanishing out of her view at the other end.

She felt a sharp hunger and realised that, for the baby's sake, she must find food. Pausing only to splash her face with water from the jug and to wrap her shawl around her, she went out of the room onto the landing. It was still quiet below, with just the occasional snatch of chatter or burst of laughter drifting up the stairs. Molly felt grateful to have been offered the last room available in what she supposed to be a boarding house.

Her new landlady must have heard her descending the stairs, for she was waiting to greet Molly in the hallway.

'All settled in?' she asked.

Molly, who had had to do little beyond hanging one or two items of clothing from the pegs on the wall and laying out her hairbrush, nodded. She handed over her rent, then expressed her intention to go out and find something to eat.

'Turn to the right out of the front door and at the end of Half Moon Street you'll find yourself in Covent Garden. There's no shortage there of places happy to serve you a dinner – but keep your wits about you.' Mrs Dobbs looked doubtfully at Molly. 'Are you acquainted with these parts?'

When Molly shook her head, Mrs Dobbs half turned and shouted along the passageway, 'James!'

Her son emerged from the gloom and looked enquiringly at his mother.

'Molly here would like to go out and find herself some dinner. I don't like to think of her getting lost in an area she don't know. You go along and keep an eye on her.' Mrs

Dobbs waved away Molly's protests that she could manage well enough. 'You'll be glad of his company,' she said. 'You'll see. Don't be too long, mind.'

Then she turned and was gone along the passageway and Molly caught a brief glimpse of her in the light that spilt out when she opened a door.

Molly turned to James and smiled. 'Come on, then. You'd better show me the way.'

James opened the door and Molly followed him out, catching her breath in the sharp wind funnelling down Half Moon Street.

'Maiden Lane,' he said, gesturing to a road leading to the right at the end of Half Moon Street, and 'Henrietta Street,' as they reached the next turning. He was walking so fast that Molly barely had time to take it all in, but she couldn't understand why Mrs Dobbs had insisted he accompany her. There were plenty of women on their own in the streets, which were busy with people on foot as well as passing in carriages. She and James appeared to be the only people in a hurry for all the others were strolling, stopping occasionally to chat to other passers-by.

'This is a good place,' James said, halting at the side of a pie stand set up under a streetlamp.

Molly obediently joined those waiting to be served, the aroma of cooked meat and warm pastry making her almost giddy with hunger. She looked around while she waited, taking in the imposing church set at one side of what appeared to be a large square. She turned to ask James about it, then saw two young women had stopped to talk to him. One ruffled his hair as they moved on and the other gave Molly a curious glance. She was about to ask him who they were when James nudged her.

'Your turn,' he said.

Molly hastily turned to the counter, placed her order and paid, then took delivery of her pie, feeling the heat and grease seeping through its paper wrapping.

'Best be getting back,' James said. Molly hesitated, looking back at the square, which she longed to explore. James followed her gaze. 'Covent Garden,' he said. 'It's a market by day. Over there,' he waved vaguely towards the streets leading off the other side of the square, 'that's where all the theatres are.'

'And here?' Molly asked, as they retraced their steps towards Half Moon Street. 'What happens around here? Are all these people going to the theatre?'

'Some of them,' James said over his shoulder, but before Molly could enquire further a sudden squally shower sent them both scurrying back towards the house. As they drew closer, Molly saw the two women she had noticed earlier, now standing by the open door. Light from the interior highlighted their two male companions, who glanced round before stepping inside. James hung back a bit, despite the increasingly heavy rain, until the door shut.

The next minute they were at the door and James opened it, revealing Mrs Dobbs in the hallway, candle in hand.

'Come in quickly out of the rain,' she said, then addressed Molly. 'I do believe James has taken you to his favourite pie stall. Why don't you join us in the kitchen while you eat? James is going to read to me this evening and you might like to listen, too.'

The kitchen was warm after the chill outside and Mrs Dobbs gestured to Molly to take a seat at the table in the centre of the room. She set out a plate, knife and fork for Molly, and poured them both a glass of ale.

'We've already eaten,' she said, at Molly's offer to share her pie. She settled herself in a chair and handed a slim volume to James. 'I hope you've no objection to a ghost story,' she asked. 'It's the newest chapbook and I'm impatient to hear it.'

Mouth already full, Molly could only shake her head. At first, she was taken up with looking around at her surroundings, plainly furnished but clean and tidy and lit by more candles than she would have expected. Then she began to pay attention to the story James was reading, and to admire his fluency and the manner of his delivery.

'He's good enough for the stage, don't you think?' Mrs Dobbs said, with no small amount of pride, after a jangling bell had made James put the book down and leave the room.

'I've never seen a play,' Molly confessed. There had been a theatre in Margate, the Royal House. It had opened only recently on Hawley Square and Aunt Jane and Uncle William had become patrons after some initial resistance from her uncle. He'd been unsure about the suitability of attending something 'where people made a spectacle of themselves for money'.

She pushed away the memories of Margate and her family and tried to concentrate on the conversation. Thinking back to the earlier scene she had glimpsed on the doorstep she had a sudden flash of inspiration.

'Is this a place where actors and actresses live?' She gestured to the building above their heads.

Mrs Dobbs chuckled. 'Lord love you, no, dear,' she said. 'There's only you, me and James living here. The rest of the rooms are rented out by the hour.'

Molly frowned in puzzlement and would have pressed on with her questioning, but at that moment James returned. He picked up the chapbook and Mrs Dobbs held up her hand for silence as he began to read once more.

At the end of the tale, Molly observed that Mrs Dobbs had fallen asleep so she took her plate, glass and cutlery and quietly rinsed them in the scullery. Then, with a smile to James, she let herself out of the kitchen and climbed the stairs to her room.

It took her some time to fall asleep, for her mind was busy with all she had seen that day. One thing was clear to her: the house held some mysteries that were yet to be revealed.

Chapter Forty-Two

Molly had a restless night, the sound of laughter and the low cries that had drifted up the stairwell having blended with her dreams and become ghostly fragments of the story that James had read the night before.

She awoke feeling uncomfortable and lay there for a few moments, gathering her thoughts, until the kicking in her belly reminded her of the baby. Then she was seized with panic. Here she was, having found lodgings in the centre of the city but with no clear plan as to what to do next. One thing was certain: she must find a way to occupy herself. Too much time alone would mean that gloomy, troubled thoughts would overtake her.

So Molly rose, poured water into the bowl and washed herself, then dressed quickly. The room was cold – she would need to ask Mrs Dobbs about obtaining coal so that she could light a fire. First, though, she would walk to Covent Garden and see it by daylight. She would find some breakfast, then work out how to manage her meals, or her savings would dwindle much faster than she had allowed for.

The house was quiet as she made her way downstairs, and there was no sign of James or Mrs Dobbs as she let herself out. It was another bright but blustery day and Molly was glad of the warmth of her shawl as she retraced her steps of the night before. As she turned into Henrietta Street she saw that it was as busy as it had been the previous evening, but this time with a more purposeful crowd. And there were fewer carriages on the street. Instead there were barrows – some empty, some laden – being pushed by young boys.

Molly followed the general direction of the crowd and found herself in the hub of the market that James had mentioned. Stalls were crammed into every available place in the square and some had spilt into the roads leading off it. They were selling all manner of fruit and vegetables, as well as household goods, linen, ironmongery, butter and cheese, meat and fish, the stalls higgledy-piggledy and without any attempt at organisation. Molly supposed that the stallholders set up on a first-come, first-served basis, which would make it difficult for her to find a particular stall, should it become a favourite. She had already decided that this would become a regular haunt. Nibbling a pastry, she walked up and down, planning her purchases, although she soon realised she would need a basket to put them in. Casting around, she found just the thing on a stall at the edge of the market, then devoted the next half an hour to purchasing some winter vegetables, which she hoped Mrs Dobbs would let her cook, as well as apples, which the vendor assured her had only just come out of his apple store. She bought a small piece of cheese, some cooked meat, and finally a crusty loaf.

'Newly baked,' the stallholder declared, as she handed over her money. It still held faint traces of warmth from the oven and Molly sniffed it as she placed it in her basket. It brought back memories of Hannah baking in her uncle's house in Margate and Molly had to turn away quickly to hide a sudden rush of tears.

Were they missing her at home? She hoped so. Only

Hannah and her father had known about the baby when she left Margate – but had they told anyone else? What did her aunt and uncle think? And Charlie? Her heart gave a lurch as she remembered his face when she had turned down his offer in the room he had been so proud of at Woodchurch Manor. Molly had successfully suppressed such thoughts throughout her time in Bermondsey and she fought hard to push them away now as she turned back towards Half Moon Street. There was no point in dwelling on such things, thinking about what might have been. She must shut the door on her past and make a new life for herself.

She paused in front of the church and thought about going in, then turned towards the streets on the opposite side of the square, where James had said that the theatres lay. She hesitated – should she explore the area further now or come out again later? The heaviness of her basket decided her: she would take her purchases back to her room first.

Back in Half Moon Street, all was still quiet. Molly found herself tiptoeing up the stairs, fearful of disturbing the occupants of the rooms, until she remembered what Mrs Dobbs had said. The rooms were rented by the hour, so perhaps no one was there.

As Molly put her purchases away, she thought over her excursion the previous evening, how familiar the women had been with James and how Covent Garden was so different by day and by night. It began to dawn on her what the nature of her new home might be and she had to laugh – both at her situation and her own ignorance. How shocked Aunt Jane would be! And how Hannah would scold!

She went to look out of the window, contemplating the street for some time. She would go out again, she decided, to discover what lay beyond the rooftops in either direction, to walk along towards the Strand and to the river beyond, and to venture the other way to find out where the theatres were.

Molly stood before the looking-glass to check her appearance. Her face was a little fuller than it had been, she decided, and, on the whole, she looked well. Her cheeks were still flushed from the brisk October weather and some of her chestnut hair, scraped back hastily under her bonnet before she went out, had escaped, framing her face rather charmingly. A thought crossed her mind. Why had Mrs Dobbs been so quick to offer her a room, and such a nice room, at that? She frowned, smoothing her dress over the curve of her belly. Her condition was obvious to her, and she was sure Mrs Dobbs had noticed, too.

A sharp rap at the door startled her. She hurried to open it and found Mrs Dobbs, smiling, on the landing.

'Well, my dear, I hope you slept well. I heard you go out bright and early this morning.'

As Molly attempted to apologise for any unintentional disturbance, Mrs Dobbs held up her hand. 'No, no, that wasn't a complaint. I thought we might have a chat. About the house, and about how you might be of help to me.'

CHAPTER FORTY-THREE

M olly followed Mrs Dobbs down the stairs to join her in the kitchen for a pot of coffee.

'My morning indulgence,' Mrs Dobbs said, setting out the cups. Then, when they were both settled at the table, she began: 'I'm guessing that you know the nature of the house that you find yourself in, Molly, and perhaps you are wondering why I let the room to you.' Mrs Dobbs raised an enquiring eyebrow as she looked at Molly, but she pressed on without waiting for an answer.

'To be honest, when James brought you to the door, it gave me quite a shock. You remind me of my own dear daughter, Ellen.' Here Mrs Dobbs paused and an odd expression crossed her countenance. She dabbed at her eyes with the corner of her apron. 'It was obvious to me that you are with child, as dear Ellen was. She took herself off from here after we had words about it and I haven't seen her since.' Mrs Dobbs burst into tears and flung her apron over her face while Molly sat on, feeling awkward, unsure whether she should get up and go around the table to offer some comfort.

Mrs Dobbs pulled herself together, shaking her head in sorrow. 'It was two years ago now and I haven't heard from her since. I heard that she had been seen in Bristol but I don't know whether that's true. I just hope that someone took her in and cared for her.' She brightened, took up her coffee cup and smiled at Molly. 'The moment I saw you, I knew that it was my chance to repair some of the wrong I did to Ellen. You looked done in last night but this morning—' Mrs Dobbs broke off and looked her up and down. 'You are quite healthy?'

Molly nodded in affirmation, a little taken aback by what Mrs Dobbs had revealed and wondering what was to come next.

'Good. Then I think you can be of service to me. I'm not as young as I was and I find keeping this house, and the long hours it demands, are beginning to take a toll. I need someone to help, to run errands in Covent Garden for the girls and me. James does a lot, of course, but he keeps me company until late in the evening and I can't expect him to be up and working from the crack of dawn. So, in return for your room, along with a bit of rent, would you be prepared to help me?'

Molly weighed up Mrs Dobbs's suggestion. She should have known that the rent was too reasonable for the sort of lodgings she'd been given. On the other hand, the type of work that Mrs Dobbs was suggesting didn't sound too arduous and she would be able to keep it up until the baby was due. She wondered whether to agree outright or to push for some additional payment. Or would that risk upsetting her new landlady?

Mrs Dobbs looked expectantly at Molly. 'I'll give you your dinner, too, of course,' she added. Then, as if reading her mind, Mrs Dobbs continued, 'Just until the baby comes. We'll think again after that.'

Molly smiled and nodded. 'Of course. I'll be happy to help.' She wanted to explore the area, she reasoned, and Mrs Dobbs's errands would give her the ideal opportunity to do so. It would also be useful to have something to keep her occupied.

Mrs Dobbs beamed. 'I knew I'd made the right decision. Now, in the mornings there will be one or two things I'll need you to bring in from the market. And I'll need you to supervise Maria, who comes in to do the cleaning. She can't start the rooms until the girls are up so you may have to bang on a few of the doors.'

Molly discovered that although the girls paid for the rooms by the hour, some of them lived there while others went home in the early hours to their children before returning in the evenings. Mrs Dobbs was not the owner of the house, as she'd first thought, but the manager and land-lady, keeping the girls in order and dealing with any unruly customers.

'I've not needed to call on the beadles once,' she said, with some pride. 'The girls here can take care of themselves and I ran the Half Moon Inn on the corner for many a year. There's not much I can't handle.'

The owner of the house was a Mr Percival, Molly learnt, but he never appeared there, sending his manservant once a week to collect what was owed to him.

'He places all his trust in me,' Mrs Dobbs said. 'And I've never let him down. There's not a finer establishment in the whole of Covent Garden.'

The contents of the coffee pot being finished, Mrs Dobbs sighed and rose to her feet, Molly following suit. 'And now, if I might be so bold, there are one or two things I'd like you to get from the market for me.'

So, under Mrs Dobbs's guidance, Molly began to learn the ways of the area. She discovered how to get the best price in the market ('Mention Bridget Dobbs'), which of the costermongers could be trusted and which couldn't, where to go for soap and thread and repairs to shoes ('The girls get through an awful lot of shoe leather'). She learnt that she should stay away from Seven Dials ('Full of filth and disease and the worst sort of slums'), but one day Molly's curiosity took her that way and she was horrified by what she saw. There were children on the streets barefoot and in rags, even though November had come in with a bitter chill. Molly – who was, at times, ashamed of the shabbiness of her own clothes – thought she must have looked wealthy in comparison to the inhabitants of those streets for they pawed at her clothes and begged her for money. Realising how foolish she had been to come here after visiting the market, she clutched her basket and Mrs Dobbs's few coins of change and hurried back to Half Moon Street. For the rest of the day the sights she had seen haunted her – the rubbish in the streets and the rats, nonchalant in broad daylight, the grimy appearance of every building and of all those who lived there, the stench that seeped out of the doorways and alleyways. Some of the inhabitants had seemed cheery, but it hadn't taken Molly long to realise it was a happiness borne of drink, another evil that Mrs Dobbs had warned her against ('It might cost you less than something to eat and bring you a sort of joy, but it will cost you dear in the end').

Mrs Dobbs frowned on any girl being the worse for drink when they brought men back to the rooms, although she didn't appear to mind that the men themselves were frequently drunk. Molly knew, though, that the girls relied on a steady supply of gin to see them through the evenings, for she was frequently asked to purchase it, buying it in stoneware flagons to stow under their beds. They used it to top up the little flasks they always carried with them. Their secret was safe: Mrs Dobbs was now too stout to bend down and sweep beneath the beds and the job fell to the house skivvy, Maria, whom the girls tipped generously for her silence.

Molly came to know the names of all the girls who worked there, but she became friends with none. She sensed that she occupied an awkward position in the household hierarchy – she wasn't quite as lowly as Maria, but neither was she family, as James and Mrs Dobbs were. She supposed that they saw her as a servant and the fact that she was having a baby was an uncomfortable reminder to them of one of their constant fears: that they might fall prey to a considerable inconvenience that would prevent them from working and earning a living.

As the weeks passed, Molly's view of the men that frequented the Half Moon Street establishment underwent several revisions. She went from incredulity to disbelief, then anger, pity and disgust, eventually settling on acceptance tinged with scorn. She knew from idle gossip, overheard when the girls gathered in the kitchen before their evening began, that their clients included the very wealthy, the married, the clergy, writers, merchants, lawyers and politicians. Some visited just once, while others were regulars. Some were keen to try every girl in the place, little knowing that their proclivities were the source of amusement around the kitchen table. Others had favourites on whom they came to dote, believing their sentiments returned – an equal source of amusement.

Molly came to view Nicholas as just such a man as those who visited the house. She remembered how he had been forced to leave school in disgrace, while his behaviour on their trip to the caves took on a new light, predatory in nature. How could she ever have believed that his visits to her bed were proof that he loved her and would marry her?

256

Increasingly, there were nights when Molly lay in bed and clutched her belly in despair, thinking of the baby growing there and worrying for its future, and for hers. How would she be able to love the product of such a flawed union? It would represent the folly of all her youthful dreams but, more than that, how would she find work and get on in life with a child to care for?

CHAPTER FORTY-FOUR

Once December arrived, Molly found herself stepping carefully as she went to market each morning. Frost sparkled on the paving and cobbles and she was nervous of losing her footing. One evening, the girls were gathered around the range in the kitchen and playing cards to while away the time until their work began, when Mrs Dobbs had remarked on the chill.

'I wonder whether the river will freeze as it did last year,' she mused.

'The river froze?' Molly was amazed. The Thames seemed such a broad stretch of water that she couldn't imagine it frozen from bank to bank. The girls looked up from their card game and she saw that one or two were laughing – at her, she supposed.

Emma – always the friendliest towards Molly – spoke up. 'It froze over last year for the first time in about ten years. We hired skates – you can skate right up to boats held fast in the river and touch them. There's all manner of stalls, too. I can still remember the pig, roasting on a spit, and how delicious it was.' She looked wistful. 'But it didn't last long. Perhaps three days, then the ice was too thin, although it still felt bitterly cold to me.'

'Well, I hope it doesn't freeze again.' Mrs Dobbs shook her

head. 'The cost of keeping this place warm. I'll be needing to ask for more money from you girls!'

Her half-threat provoked a heated discussion and all talk of the Frost Fair was forgotten, but it came back to Molly that morning as she watched others slip and slide on the icy streets. It sounded as though it would be a lot of fun, but she wasn't sure she would be able to skate even if it did happen. The risk of falling over would be too great. But she could go and watch, she reasoned.

She was halfway to the market when her attention was caught by a young man who appeared to be in a great hurry, despite the icy conditions. He was striding along, his jacket flapping open and a sketchbook tucked beneath his arm. The sight of it gave her quite a jolt, reminding her of Will Turner back in Margate. As he drew level with her, she gasped. Surely it *was* Will! A little more grown and with a frown on his face – but she was convinced of it.

'Will? Will Turner?' she said.

He had already passed her but stopped and looked back, appearing irritated.

'It is Will, isn't it?' Molly was suddenly anxious. Had she made a mistake?

He stared at her, uncomprehending, and then his face cleared. 'Molly!' he said. His eyes slid to her belly, then back to her face. 'I didn't recognise you. But what are you doing here?'

'I live here,' she said.

'You do?' He looked puzzled. 'As do I. Here, in Maiden Lane.' He pointed back along the road he had been hurrying down.

'And I'm here, in Half Moon Street.' Molly gestured. Their roads lay at right angles to each other and she wondered that their paths hadn't crossed before.

The clock on St Paul's Church in the square struck the hour, causing an expression of anguish to appear on Will's face. 'I'm late. I should be with my tutor at the Royal Academy. I've just had a term's trial and I'm to find out whether they will keep me on.' He began to walk backwards, away from her. 'I have to go. But we must meet again. I want to hear your news.' His eyes slid to her belly once more. 'Meet me in the square, on the steps of the church, at three.' He was already heading away at quite a pace and Molly could only nod.

She fulfilled her errands but she was only half concentrating, taken aback at seeing Will. Once more, her thoughts drew her to Margate and everyone she knew there. Will must be fifteen now – he'd changed a good deal since she'd last seen him. Would Lizzie and Mary have changed, too? She remembered how she used to snuggle up with her sisters in their bed under the eaves in her father's cottage and wished she could see them now. But she had chosen her course and she must stick to it. She had brought shame on her family and she didn't want her sisters to see her like this. But, oh, how happy she would be if they could be there to help her once the baby was born!

'Are you all right, love?'

Molly realised she was standing stock-still at the baker's stall and he was patiently holding out her purchases, waiting for her to take them. Some of the waiting customers were staring at her and she felt her face grow hot. 'I'm sorry,' she stammered. 'I – I just saw someone I hadn't seen in a while.'

'The father, was it?' she heard someone say, to shushes and giggles from the others.

'Take no notice,' the stallholder said. 'You get yourself home now. Looks like you've had a shock.'

Flustered, Molly thrust a few coins into his hand,

thanked him and turned for home. As she walked back to Half Moon Street it occurred to her that Will might have been to Margate since she had been away. Perhaps he would have news of her family. It made her even more impatient to see him again, but first she had to placate Mrs Dobbs, who wasn't pleased that her errands had gone so awry that day.

'Where's the cheese?' she asked, once Molly had removed all her purchases from the basket. 'And why have you bought carrots when it was potatoes I asked for? Did you get the medicine from the apothecary?'

When Molly shook her head in answer to each question, Mrs Dobbs scolded her: 'I think you must have left your wits behind when you went out today.'

Molly explained the cause of her behaviour and promised to make good her mistakes later when she went out to meet Will.

'An artist, you say?' Mrs Dobbs sniffed. 'Not the father, I hope?'

'No!' Molly protested. She had never given her landlady any details of her background, other than that she came from Margate, and Mrs Dobbs hadn't asked. Molly supposed that with some fifteen girls using the house regularly she couldn't hope to remember everyone's history and so had ceased to ask.

Molly kept herself occupied for the next few hours but by half past two she was back in Covent Garden, completing the purchases she should have made that morning and glancing anxiously at the clock on the façade of the church.

By three o'clock she was on the steps, sheltering under the portico from the flurries of sleet now blowing across the square and watching as the stallholders began hurriedly to pack up their wares, recognising that few further purchases would be made that day. Shivering, Molly drew back as close to the walls as she could. She couldn't take refuge inside – not only was she unsure that Will would think to look for her there but, in any case, the building was being renovated. She had peeped in soon after her arrival in Covent Garden and had been startled by the simplicity of the interior. Where she'd expected soaring rafters, there was a flat ceiling, of the sort you might find in a grand house, with relief plasterwork. The exterior promised more than the interior delivered, Molly decided, but before she could explore it further the builders had warned her off, saying that construction work was under way and she must watch herself in case of falling debris. Now, she longed to shelter inside but at last Will bounded up the steps, clearly out of breath, just as the clock struck the quarter-hour.

'Am I late? I'm sorry.' He beamed at Molly. 'The main thing is they like my work and I can study full time now.'

'That's very good news.' Molly sounded as enthusiastic as she was able through chattering teeth.

'I was baptised here,' Will said, looking at the church door. 'It's a shame we can't go in today.' They stood indecisive on the steps.

'Did you say your house was close by?' Molly said.

'Yes, but …' Will's voice trailed off. Molly knew what he meant without him elaborating on it. How would he explain her to his family – a young girl, not much older than himself, clearly with child but unmarried?

She sighed. 'Let's go to Half Moon Street. I'm sure Mrs Dobbs will let us sit in the kitchen.'

She thought it was unlikely that any of the girls would be there yet. They tended to work the evening hours and usually started to gather at five or six o'clock in the afternoon.

By the time they reached the front door the sleet had turned to wet snow that clung to their clothes. Mrs Dobbs hustled them into the kitchen and insisted that they sit close to the range to dry out. 'I'll make you each a cup of chocolate,' she said, 'to ward off the chill.'

While she bustled about heating milk, Molly and Will sat by the range, their clothes gently steaming.

'Have you been to Margate of late?' Molly couldn't hold in the question that had plagued her since that morning.

'No, I spent some time in Oxford with my uncle,' Will replied, 'and I've been working as a draughtsman, for the architect Thomas Hardwick. He's in charge of the work on the church here, in Covent Garden.'

'A draughtsman?' Molly asked.

'Doing drawings,' Will replied, 'so that Mr Hardwick can use them to explain the renovations.'

Not for the first time, Molly felt a stab of envy. Will had a place at what she'd been told was an important art school in the centre of town. He talked casually of working, and of living in Oxford, yet he was so much younger than she was. In the two years since she'd last seen him, he'd become a confident young man.

She suddenly realised he'd been chatting on and she had barely listened to a word he was saying.

'And what of you? Where have you been? How is your uncle? And you are married now ...?' Will faltered to a close.

Molly had little appetite for explaining how she had come to find herself in such a situation but she did her best to come up with an answer that might satisfy his curiosity.

'I've been in London a little while. I was in Bermondsey first but now I'm lodging here until the baby is due.' She was aware that Mrs Dobbs, who was sitting at the kitchen table sipping her chocolate, was paying close attention. 'I haven't seen my uncle since I left Margate in the summer and ...' she hesitated '... the baby's father has gone away.'

She didn't elaborate further, but Will's questions were stirring up memories she had tried to forget. She was glad none of her family could see her here. Will, who lived in Covent Garden, understood the ways of the city. Her relatives would not.

CHAPTER FORTY-FIVE

Laughter and chatter in the passageway heralded the arrival of some of the girls, who burst into the kitchen shaking snow from their clothes.

'We came a bit early,' Emma said, 'although it's snowing so hard, I doubt we'll be busy tonight.' She stopped abruptly when she noticed Will.

He rose to his feet, partly out of courtesy but also to leave. 'My father will be wondering where I am,' he said to Molly. 'He'll be waiting to hear my news.'

'News?' Emma said, her head on one side and a coquettish look on her face. 'Oh, do tell.'

Molly's heart sank. Was Emma going to start behaving badly? What would Will think of her, and the place she was living in?

The girls gathered around him and began to stroke his hair and exclaim over the freshness of his complexion until Will was quite scarlet. Molly felt desperate, but she noticed that Mrs Dobbs was laughing and, after a minute or two, she said, 'Now, now, girls. Stop that. You're embarrassing the poor boy. He isn't here to see you – he's visiting Molly.'

It was Molly's turn to grow hot as the girls turned their attention to her, making all manner of bawdy suggestions so that she stopped Will's ears as she hurried him from the room.

'I'm so sorry, Will.' She was mortified.

'Don't worry, Molly,' he said. She was relieved to see that he was laughing. 'You grow up pretty quickly living around here, you know.'

She opened the door and they were both taken aback by how much snow had fallen while they'd been sitting in the warmth of the kitchen. Will pulled his jacket collar up around his ears and stepped out into the street.

'I've drawn one of them, anyway. The dark-haired one. In life-drawing classes at the Academy.' Then, with a wave, he hurried away, soon lost from view in the swirling snow.

Molly made her way back to the kitchen, musing over his last words. Emma was the only dark-haired girl in the room. It hadn't occurred to Molly that any of the girls earned money elsewhere. London was such a surprising city. If you had your wits about you, there were so many ways to make a living. It gave her a shred of hope for the future.

The talk round the kitchen table had turned to Christmas. Emma was insistent that since today was St Nicholas's Day, the sixth of December, they would find their custom much reduced even without taking the weather into consideration. 'They've all gone to their country estates and they won't be back until the sixth of January. The same thing happened last year,' she declared, seeming rather cheerful at the prospect.

'They haven't all gone.' Mrs Dobbs was inclined to caution. 'Only the gentry. There's plenty of folk who'll be staying in London for the duration.'

A few more of the girls arrived in the kitchen, shaking the snow off their shawls and stamping their feet to warm toes frozen in their wet boots.

'Well, I think we should plan our decorations and festivities. And enjoy having a rest.'

Mrs Dobbs looked less happy at the prospect of a fall in the house's income, Molly thought, as she watched her open her mouth to speak. Then she appeared to think better of it and threw herself into making plans with as much enthusiasm as the girls.

The snow made that evening a quiet one – at least in terms of customers. The girls ventured out in pairs at intervals, but none stayed out long. Each pair returned to report on how much more snow had accumulated and how few people were abroad, either in carriages or on foot. A few callers came to the door but not above ten throughout the whole evening. The girls played cards and drank Mrs Dobbs's chocolate and talked of their Christmas plans until midnight. Then Mrs Dobbs said they might as well call it a night, since the theatre had finished and the snow had deterred nearly all of their customers.

The plans for Christmas Day were settled, though. For those not spending it at home with their families, there was to be roast goose, followed by plum pudding, while the wassail cup would be served all afternoon for the visitors.

Now Molly, who had been sitting listening all evening but with very little to contribute, spoke up. 'What's a wassail cup?' she asked.

Several of the girls stared at her but Kitty, who was originally from Kent and saw this as some sort of bond with Molly, said, 'It's a drink. A spiced punch, served warm. No one makes it better than Mrs Dobbs. Wait and see.'

Mrs Dobbs turned pink with pleasure at the praise and Molly, thinking that her landlady was taken very much for granted by the girls, decided she would look out for some small trinket for her as a Christmas gift.

The next day's bright sunshine and a rise in the

temperature brought a quick thaw of the snow, but the girls were already in festive mood, and each day one or another of them would arrive with an armful of greenery from the market to fashion into swags to decorate the kitchen. Mrs Dobbs asked Molly to buy a bunch of mistletoe but, to Molly's surprise, she didn't hang it just inside the front door, as Molly had expected, or on a landing. Instead, she put it in the kitchen, where the girls squealed with delight when they saw it, then gave each other affectionate hugs and kisses beneath it. When Molly asked whether she should buy more on her next trip to the market, to put in the girls' rooms, Mrs Dobbs told her they preferred not to encourage kissing, seeing it as an intimacy to be preserved for their husbands and children. Molly was surprised, but said nothing.

Molly began to see new items for sale in the market – fruits she didn't recognise, as well as dates and all kinds of nuts. The stallholders competed over who could create the most extravagant display. There was definitely a more relaxed atmosphere around the house in the days leading up to Christmas. Mrs Dobbs had studded oranges with cloves and put them on the overmantel, and their delicious fragrance, mingled with the sharp scent of the evergreen boughs, greeted Molly every time she walked into the kitchen. In the evenings the girls would share something that one of their regulars had brought them as a gift – candied fruits, almond comfits and, one evening, a pomegranate.

Molly came in on the girls howling with laughter over a joke that seemed to be related to the fruit – or perhaps its giver – as it lay split in two on a plate in the centre of the table. Ruby-red seeds spilt from the cut surface, while others clung tightly to their white-lined nest. Molly recognised it from one of the paintings she had seen at Mr Keyse's in Bermondsey. She looked at it with longing.

Emma spotted her fascinated gaze. 'I do believe this is something else that's new to Molly,' she teased.

By now, the girls had decided that Molly must have led a sheltered life. Kitty pushed the plate towards her. 'Go on – help yourself. It's a lot of work to dig out the seeds and I'm not sure it's worth it.'

Molly picked up a seed and marvelled at the translucent pink flesh surrounding it, then popped it into her mouth. The intense burst of flavour was over too quickly for her to fully appreciate it.

'Here, take more than that.' Kitty handed her a spoon and Molly dug into the fruit, meeting resistance but managing to come away with seven or eight seeds. This time, the flavour was more pronounced, and was swiftly followed by a drying of her mouth. She dug in again.

Kitty laughed. 'Next time I'll tell Gideon to give his pomegranate to you. It was wasted on me.'

Embarrassed, Molly put down the spoon and pushed the plate back towards Kitty.

'No, no, you must have it,' Kitty insisted. 'I've eaten them many times before and they've lost all their novelty. Eat it up now.'

Molly obliged as best she could, finding it easier to extract the seeds with her fingernails, until she, too, had had enough. It was a thing of great beauty, she decided. Or, at least, *inside* the fruit – the hard exterior gave no hint of the treasure that lay within. No wonder Mr Keyse had considered it worthy of including in a painting.

Chapter Forty-Six

Christmas Day was a convivial one in Half Moon Street. As promised, the wassail cup was ready for visitors from midday, which was lucky as there was a steady stream of them. Mrs Dobbs prepared it as soon as she returned from the morning service at church, to which she had tried to persuade Molly to accompany her. Molly would have liked to join her, but the local church, St Paul's in Covent Garden, was still closed for building work and the nearest alternative was some distance away. She knew she would find it uncomfortable to walk that far and she was nervous, too, at the thought of slipping on the ice that lay on the streets that morning. Although she felt guilty for not attending on Christmas Day, in truth she hadn't been regularly since her days in Bermondsey. Instead, she promised Mrs Dobbs that she would make a start on preparing the vegetables for their Christmas dinner so Mrs Dobbs left, accompanied by James, who would have preferred to stay at home on such a cold morning, with strict instructions that Molly was not to attempt to assemble the wassail cup.

'It's my family recipe,' she said, as she tied on her best bonnet, 'and one I will not share.'

Molly had a quiet morning, peeling a quantity of potatoes, carrots and swedes. With Mrs Dobbs back home, and the wassail cup gently warming on the range, the visitors began to arrive. Churchgoers, neighbours from Half Moon Street, the tradesmen that Mrs Dobbs frequented, all called in for a drink and stayed for an hour, while Mrs Dobbs served them biscuits topped with anchovy spread and toasted bread with potted meats. Shortly after that, with the wassail cup refreshed, the girls who would be dining in their own homes arrived, bringing with them small children and, in some cases, mothers and husbands. Molly tried not to let her astonishment show at the existence of the husbands, marvelling quietly over their apparent acceptance of their wives' occupation. Instead she busied herself serving drinks and making a fuss of the children, and wondered whether they would manage to fit any more guests into the kitchen.

By mid-afternoon, with the goose set to roast and the kitchen still crowded, Molly felt the need to escape from the heat. As she stepped out into the street she was surprised to see Will approaching the house. Their paths hadn't crossed since the first day she'd seen him in Covent Garden.

'Will!' she exclaimed. 'Are you coming to join the party?'

'Ah, no,' Will said. 'I'm expected at home, with dinner about to go on the table. But I wanted to give you this.' He thrust a square paper-wrapped package into her hand then turned away to go.

'Oh, Will, I don't have anything to give you.' Molly was stricken.

'No matter,' Will said. 'I wasn't expecting it. Happy Christmas!' And with a wave he started back the way he had come.

Mrs Dobbs had told the girls to make clear to any regulars that they would not be received at the house that day. She was equally strict in her observance of Sundays, which had

271

come as a surprise to Molly in her first weeks in Half Moon Street. Mrs Dobbs always attended church and, unusually for the area, the house was not open, although Mrs Dobbs was happy to see any of the girls and would provide them with company and food, if needed. Any male callers who came to the door were politely turned away, and if Mrs Dobbs spotted any of the girls walking the Sunday streets, she always gave them a piece of her mind when they came in on Monday.

'This is a high-class establishment. The girls here do not parade themselves with the idea of entertaining a customer on a Sunday in a dark alley or round the back of an inn.'

Mrs Dobbs made it plain that any further transgressions would result in the girls being asked to find new premises to work from.

Now, as Molly turned her back on Half Moon Street, having watched Will walk off into the distance, she noticed two men hurrying up the street, waving at her to attract her attention. She waited until they arrived in front of her, slightly out of breath, whereupon she recognised them as the best customers of the house.

'Mrs Dobbs said ...' She hesitated, unwilling to offend them but not wanting to upset Mrs Dobbs by inviting them in.

'We're invited.' The taller of the two men swept her an ironic bow.

Molly still hesitated, but as a group of guests leaving the kitchen came along the passageway towards the door, she was forced to stand back in the street. The two men took the opportunity to step inside as the departing guests lingered on the step, turning up collars and pulling on gloves against the cold.

Molly hurried back inside and threw an apologetic glance

at Mrs Dobbs but, in any case, it appeared that all was well. Her landlady was busy serving drinks to the new arrivals. Then she signalled to Molly that it was time to cook the vegetables and make the final preparations for their Christmas dinner.

The few remaining guests began to drift away, the wassail cup being now all but exhausted. Molly had delayed trying it, wanting her wits to be as clear as possible until the food was on the table. Now, with this so nearly achieved, she permitted herself a small glass but spluttered after the first sip, taken aback by its strength.

Mrs Dobbs noticed and laughed. 'You should have tried it when it was first made, Molly. I fear our guests have been adding to it as the fancy took them.'

Molly sniffed the mixture. The spicy aroma of cloves, cinnamon, oranges and roasted apple that filled the kitchen emanated from the punch. She wished she'd tried it earlier but there was no time for regret. Everyone must be organised into chairs around the table. By the time they were all seated, with the goose and roasted potatoes on platters in the centre and dishes piled with vegetables spread around the table, they numbered ten: Mrs Dobbs and James, Molly, five girls and the two male visitors.

Molly looked around the room, where everyone was engaged in happy chatter, helping themselves and each other to food and drink, and thought back to Christmas the previous year, in Margate, before Nicholas's return and all the great changes that had befallen her since. Christmas then had been quiet in comparison, spent with her father and Ann, Lizzie, Mary, little John and Harriet. Her stepmother didn't tolerate much cheer around the table and the portions were on the meagre side. Ann had made much of having an extra mouth to feed – Molly's – on Christmas Day. But Molly had been glad to be there. She wondered how Lizzie and Mary were faring today.

Now, not wanting to be melancholy at such a jolly table, she threw herself into being useful, getting up to replenish the gravy jug and dishing up more vegetables from the big pot on the range.

After the last morsel of pudding had been eaten, Mrs Dobbs opened a cupboard in the dresser and pulled out an array of packages, which she handed around the table. The girls got small trinkets – gaudy jewellery that Molly had seen at the market but over which they exclaimed in delight as if they were fine diamonds. James got a book and the gentlemen visitors received pamphlets of bawdy jokes, while Molly's gift made her weep. It was a baby blanket, knitted in the softest, creamiest wool, which she had seen and coveted on a stall in the market but had been unable to afford to buy.

The conversation had stilled at Molly's reaction and she hastily wiped away her tears and hurried around the table to thank Mrs Dobbs. She slipped a package of her own into Mrs Dobbs's hand, then busied herself replacing one or two of the candles that had burnt low around the room. She'd dipped into her savings to buy a small frame from a silversmith in one of the streets off the Strand, having overheard Mrs Dobbs express a wish to have a miniature painted of James before he got much older.

'I want to remember him as a boy,' she'd declared, sentimental and eyes full of tears late one evening as a couple of the girls kept her company around the table. 'Before he turns into a man, with all their ways.'

She didn't elaborate, but Molly had a suspicion that the Half Moon Street house, and no doubt the inn before, had given Mrs Dobbs decided views on men and their 'ways', which weren't always flattering, despite the welcoming, sociable side she always presented to their clients.

Late that night, as Molly lay in bed unable to sleep due to the discomfort of having eaten too much, she thought over the evening. Her eyes strayed to the small picture she had propped on the mantel over the fireplace. She'd unwrapped Will's gift in private, in her room, after she'd come up to bed. For the second time that day, she'd been moved to tears. It was a watercolour sketch of the Thames, in the soft light of a late winter's afternoon as the sun went down. The boats were captured as blue shadows, moored along the river, and in the distance, there was a suggestion of a bridge across the water.

She had never owned very much in all her life and today she had received two very special gifts – a blanket for her baby and a painting: a celebration of a life to come and of a bond of friendship formed over the last three years. As Molly finally slipped into sleep she felt hopeful about the new year that lay just around the corner.

CHAPTER FORTY-SEVEN

The relaxed atmosphere in the Half Moon Street house continued beyond Christmas Day, with less than half of the usual amount of business conducted. Snow and sleet showers made the girls disinclined to spend long periods on the streets of Covent Garden, and a couple of evenings of freezing fog that rolled in off the river brought them hurrying back, saying they didn't feel safe.

'I can barely see my hand in front of my face out there,' Kitty complained. 'I don't know who I'm talking to. Might be a beadle for all I can tell. I'm not going back out until it's cleared up.'

Molly tried her best to go about her duties as normal but the trips to market – with heavy baskets to carry and the need for frequent stops to rest – seemed to take twice as long. She hoped Mrs Dobbs wasn't too aware of her timekeeping: she wanted to keep on the right side of her, with her time so near. But her landlady had become increasingly short-tempered with the girls and Molly suspected she was worried about meeting Mr Percival's weekly demands for payment.

As the girls who weren't working gathered in the kitchen on Twelfth Night to take down the evergreen boughs, now looking decidedly faded and shrivelled, Mrs Dobbs could barely contain her impatience. 'Right, that's Christmas over and done with,' she said. 'The gentry will be back from the country any day now and no doubt eager to visit their old haunts in Covent Garden. We must make sure we're ready to welcome them with open arms and the promise that 1790 will be a good year for them.'

Only Molly heard her additional words, muttered as she moved away, 'Otherwise we'll all be looking for a new home before the month's out.'

Molly resolved to keep her head down and work as hard as she could. She didn't want to give Mrs Dobbs any excuse to ask her to leave. The thought of being homeless in her condition filled her with such terror that she couldn't sleep that night and she tossed and turned through many strikings of the Covent Garden church clock before falling into troubled dreams.

She awoke again in the early hours – the sky was still dark and she felt as though she had barely slept. She was filled with a sense of panic and couldn't think what to ascribe it to until a sudden pain tore through her, making her cry out. She wanted to get up and off the bed, but she was terrified of provoking another painful attack. She was struck by the memory of finding Ann in agony in the bedroom of the Princes Crescent cottage three years earlier. Was the baby on its way already? Or had she just eaten something that disagreed with her?

The thought of the cold ham she'd had as a snatched supper only a few hours earlier made Molly retch. That at least gave her the impetus to get off her bed and fumble for the chamber pot beneath it but the moment passed and she sat back on her heels, relieved. The respite proved temporary – another wave of pain pushed her onto all fours where she rested a moment, panting. A moan escaped her lips. This was it, she knew. The baby *was* coming. She couldn't manage on her own. She was going to have to wake Mrs Dobbs.

Molly was distressed to find she had to crawl to the door, then haul herself upright to open it, only to drop to her knees again on the landing as the pain besieged her once more. Mrs Dobbs's bedroom door was so close, yet Molly feared that the effort of reaching it would be too much. It was only terror of giving birth on the landing that spurred her on, still on hands and knees, until she could hammer on the door.

When Mrs Dobbs, half asleep, threw the door open she almost stumbled over Molly.

'Good heavens, Molly, whatever is wrong?' The next moment, she answered herself: 'It's the baby, isn't it? James! James!' she called as she bent over Molly. 'Get up, James. I need your help.'

Molly whimpered. She didn't want to involve James. She didn't want him to see her like this.

When James appeared, yawning, Mrs Dobbs sent him downstairs with instructions to put water on to boil and to collect towels from the linen closet on his way back up the stairs. By the time he reappeared on the landing, Mrs Dobbs had got Molly into bed again. She met James at the door and sent him back downstairs with instructions to bring up a jug of the water once it had boiled, and to take care as he did so.

Molly felt better having someone with her, and Mrs Dobbs's assurances that she'd delivered more babies than she cared to remember went a long way to putting Molly at her ease. Until, overtaken by another wave of pain, she heard Mrs Dobbs's instructions as though through a haze and found herself trembling and sweating in turn. She saw James's pale, frightened face as he hovered in the doorway, waiting for further instructions from his mother, and she wished that whoever was screaming would stop it. When she realised that she herself was the culprit, she began to cry, then howled again as another pain seized her. Mrs Dobbs's face, always calm, swam in and out of Molly's vision, uttering soothing words.

Molly could see bright blue sky through the window, with fine white clouds streaked across it, by the time she heard a thin, mewling cry that she realised wasn't her own.

'A fine boy,' Mrs Dobbs said, with some satisfaction. 'A little on the small side but healthy enough all the same.'

She sent James to fetch an extra pillow, then took Molly by her armpits and gently pulled her up. Once she was resting against the propped pillows she handed her a bundle wrapped in a towel.

'There, you admire him for a while,' she said, gathering up bloodied towels from the floor. 'I'm going downstairs to get you some breakfast. James can sit and keep you company.'

Molly sat very still, hardly daring to move. The bundle in her arms was warm against her breast, the little face that was just visible in his swaddling was red, crumpled and, if anything, cross. Molly began to laugh and the baby, as if disturbed by the movement, opened his eyes and looked up at her with an unfocused gaze.

'Look, James. How tiny he is!' The baby had pulled one of his hands free and Molly raised it with her finger, marvelling at its miniature perfection.

'What will you call him?' James had leant over and peered at the infant.

Molly hadn't thought. She hadn't imagined what it would be like to hold her own baby in her arms and she was still a little bemused.

'George?' she ventured, trying out the name. She didn't

know where it had come from – she didn't think she knew anyone named George. There was the King, of course, but she could hardly claim to know him. She looked down at her baby, wondering whether it suited him. Then, as Mrs Dobbs walked into the room bearing a tray with a steaming bowl on it, Molly discovered that she was cold and shivering.

'James, go and fetch some coal and light the fire in the grate,' Mrs Dobbs instructed. 'Now,' she addressed Molly, 'I'll take the baby. You're to drink this broth while it's hot. It's full of goodness and just what you need. Dip the bread in it. And I'll find you something to put round your shoulders.'

She fussed around Molly, making sure that the tray was well settled on her lap before fetching a soft shawl of her own for her.

'How excited the girls will be when they come in today!' she exclaimed.

Molly, feeling a mixture of exhaustion and euphoria, watched as Mrs Dobbs bustled around, telling James how to lay the fire – as though he didn't light fires in all the girls' rooms every day – while she stood and looked on, the baby clasped to her shoulder.

Molly was grateful for the broth. She would have dearly loved to close her eyes and go to sleep when she had finished it, but Mrs Dobbs had other ideas.

'I'm going to help you up to sit in the chair by the fire and then I'll put some fresh linen on the bed and fetch you a clean nightgown. After that, we'll see about feeding the baby.'

The last thing Molly wanted to do was leave the bed – she wasn't even sure that her legs would support her – but she did as she was asked, gingerly lowering herself onto the hard bentwood chair, then holding out her arms for George. She was suddenly impatient to hold him again.

'You're going to need a crib for him to sleep in,' Mrs Dobbs said, half to herself. Her gaze alighted on the chest of drawers. 'We'll have to empty out the bottom drawer.' Mrs Dobbs was too stout to bend down and do it for herself. She swung round to address her son. 'James, take it out for me.'

Molly saw her landlady's surprise on observing that the drawer was already empty. In truth, Molly had so few clothes or possessions that she'd had no need of it.

'We'll have to make do for linen at the moment – I can tear up an old sheet to line it, with a towel beneath for padding. The girls who have babies will come in with all manner of things, I'm sure, once they know what's happened, but it will do for now.'

Molly dozed on and off through the day, attempting to feed George whenever he cried, just as Mrs Dobbs had instructed her. Mrs Dobbs brought up more broth at intervals, before retiring for a nap in the middle of the afternoon. James was all set to sit by Molly but his mother insisted that he nap too. 'We were both up before dawn and neither of us will get through to midnight, let alone beyond, if we don't get some sleep now.'

There was a blissful hour when the whole house was quiet and Molly lay awake against her pillows, George asleep in her arms and the fire shifting in the grate as the embers slowly burnt away. She gazed down at her baby and wondered at his perfection, allowing her thoughts to wander as she imagined what was to come. She saw him growing up to be a loyal son, like James was to his mother, but she had already decided that they wouldn't live in London. Although she had seen how it was possible to scratch a living in the city, if you used your wits, now that she had George to think of she wanted more. She'd like him to have the sort of carefree childhood she'd had, she decided, where he could roam the fields and woods, not one where he walked the city streets on the lookout for farthings and halfpennies in the gutter, or for opportunities to take something from someone else to use to his own advantage. She wasn't sure how her dream could be achieved but she must start striving for it now, she thought.

When the girls came to work that evening, Molly could hear their exclamations from down below, in the hallway, as either James or Mrs Dobbs delivered the news of the baby's arrival. She heard them coming up the stairs in twos or threes. Then they burst into her room, taking it in turns to demand to hold him and talking over each other.

'He's so light!'

'And so small.'

'So perfect.'

'So pretty!'

'I'd forgotten what they were like when they were just born!'

As Mrs Dobbs had predicted, those who had their own children were eager to offer help.

'I have three nightgowns you can have for him, all out-grown now. And some linen.'

'I have a crib. You'll be doing me a favour in taking it – we have no room for it.'

Molly smiled and nodded her grateful thanks to every offer for she had prepared nothing herself. She had only the blanket, given to her at Christmas, and that was almost too beautiful to use. She'd wrap George in it when he was christened, she thought.

'What will you call him?'

'When will he be christened?'

The questions came thick and fast until Mrs Dobbs, who'd

panted her way upstairs and squeezed into the room to join them, held up her hand for quiet.

'Give the poor girl a chance. The baby's barely twelve hours old!'

'It's all right,' Molly said, finding her voice at last. 'He's going to be called George. After the King. And I'm not sure when or even where he'll be christened. I'm thinking we might leave London so it may not even be around here.'

Mrs Dobbs gave her a sharp look, then shooed all the girls down the stairs, telling them to get ready for work. 'You can come up and see him again tomorrow,' she said sternly. Then she turned to Molly. 'I wouldn't go making any plans to leave London, young lady. I've plans of my own for you.'

Molly was startled by Mrs Dobbs's sudden change in tone from solicitous to steely. There was no chance to ask her landlady what she meant, however, for Mrs Dobbs swept down the stairs after the girls, chivvying them along, and Molly was alone once more.

Later that evening, Molly awoke from a doze to find her landlady in her room, bearing more broth along with bread, cheese and ham. The aroma reminded Molly that she was ravenous and, since Mrs Dobbs was as kindly as she had been earlier in the day, Molly felt inclined to believe the memory of her recent unpleasantness was skewed by lack of sleep. But there was something in the direct look that Mrs Dobbs gave her as she left the room, bidding her goodnight, that jolted her and made her think that she had not, after all, been mistaken.

Chapter Forty-Eight

O ver the days that followed, Molly felt as though she was finally a member of the extended Half Moon Street family. Before the baby was born the girls had been tolerant of her, rather than friendly, but now George's presence found them trooping up the stairs whenever there was a lull in their work. He was entirely oblivious to them but they scooped him up all the same, cooing over him and burying their noses in his hair and his neck, absent-mindedly kissing him as they chattered away to each other.

Molly learnt that she wasn't the first girl to have given birth in this room – quiet Cécile, petite and dark-haired, had come to England from France in search of the man she believed to be her fiancé. She had been found lost and alone, huddled in a doorway in Covent Garden, by Mrs Dobbs. Molly didn't like to enquire too deeply into this, assuming from the few scathing words said on the subject that the man had given Cécile a false address or was already married. Cécile, meanwhile, seemed content that her name and her broken English – along with the creation of a history that included a line of French noblemen, now fallen on hard times – made her a great favourite with the patrons of Half Moon Street.

'When there's a new skirmish at sea with the French, Cécile

adopts a new name and becomes Spanish for a few weeks,' Emma teased, while Cécile poked out her tongue at her.

Molly ventured to ask what had become of her baby.

'The 'ospital that Madame Dobbs told me about,' Cécile said. 'They 'ave 'im.' Then she kissed George's head and handed him to Emma, who was growing impatient as she awaited her turn.

'And what of Mrs Dobbs's daughter? Wasn't this her room?' Molly asked.

Cécile and Emma looked blank, then Emma said, 'Maybe so. Perhaps before we were here.'

Molly thought nothing of it but as one week turned to two, then to three, and Mrs Dobbs insisted that she should stay in her room and rest, to get her strength back, she began to piece together a little more of the girls' stories. She learnt that Fanny and Caroline had also had babies in the room, but their infants were now housed with their families out of London and they went to visit them twice a year.

She discovered that Mrs Dobbs had trained some of the girls to satisfy the special preferences of certain patrons and that occasionally the presence of several of these girls would be required at a particular house close to Hyde Park.

Kitty made a face as she told the story. 'Annie always goes, but from what she's told me, I hope I'm never asked. The money's good but sometimes money just isn't enough ...' She tailed off and gazed into the fire.

It was during the third week, when Molly was heartily sick of her room and had taken to gazing longingly out of the window, watching the people going about their business on the street below, that she first had an inkling of what might lie in store for her.

'You're looking well,' Emma remarked, as she walked a

fractious George up and down the room to relieve Molly of him for a while. 'You've got the country-girl freshness back in your complexion that Mrs Dobbs so admires.' She shifted George to her other shoulder, then resumed pacing, patting him rhythmically as she did so. 'She'll be wanting to put you to work soon, and for that you'll need to get your figure back.'

She looked critically at Molly, who was only too conscious of her shape but had convinced herself that the exercise of running up and down the stairs and the daily trips to market and farther afield would soon see her back to normal. She had planned to ask Mrs Dobbs whether it would be all right to bring George's crib down to the kitchen: perhaps she or James would keep an eye on him while Molly went about her duties.

It was only after Emma left, to return to work, that Molly began to wonder about her words. Why would it matter when she got her figure back? It bore no relevance to the work she did. It was only as the week wore on, and Kitty also used the term 'country girl' in reference to Molly, that light began to dawn. She'd learnt from her conversations with the girls that they had a way of referring to themselves – 'the French one', 'the seductress', 'the motherly one', 'the coquette' – that reflected how they presented themselves to the patrons. Was it possible that Mrs Dobbs had this in mind for Molly? Rather than continuing in her previous role as a servant, was she to be established as one of the girls – the fresh-faced country girl?

A chill spread through Molly. It all made perfect sense. A new girl on the premises would no doubt be good for business and Mrs Dobbs must have assumed that since she had been happy – or careless – enough to get herself with child, with no husband in evidence, then she wouldn't mind such a line of work. She would be earning well and she would be able to buy far nicer clothes than she had ever been able to afford and … And what? Molly couldn't think of any other benefits.

The girls at Half Moon Street were, she had discovered, mostly very nice. But she couldn't see herself undertaking the sort of work they did. And, in any case, she had George to care for now. He was her priority and she must make that clear to Mrs Dobbs.

She didn't have long to wait. Mrs Dobbs puffed her way upstairs later that very evening.

'Molly, I'm pleased to see you looking so well. You've recovered very quickly and I'm impatient to get you back downstairs. But if you're to be of use to me, we need to decide what to do about your baby.'

Molly swallowed hard. The time had come to disabuse her landlady of any notions she had conceived.

'Mrs Dobbs, you have been so kind to me. You took me in when I was in a difficult position, no questions asked, and you delivered George. You will always hold a special place in my heart because of that. But I suspect you want me to take up a line of work that I can't consider, although I would be happy to continue to provide the same services to you and the girls as I did before.' Molly threw her landlady a pleading look.

'It really isn't as you imagine,' Mrs Dobbs said, and she laughed pleasantly, to Molly's surprise. 'I have a particular gentleman in mind who, having seen you about the place, has taken a great liking to you. "Such splendid hair," he said to me. "I've never seen a colour quite like it." He's prepared to finance you, buying you clothes and improving your surroundings.' Here Mrs Dobbs cast a look around Molly's room. 'But he grows impatient. And so, my dear, we need to take care of the baby's future, so that you can prepare yourself.

Such an exclusive arrangement is not to be spurned. The other girls would be jealous if they knew.'

Molly was struggling to comprehend what she was being told. Who was this man? Since he was prepared to make such an offer he must be one of the wealthier patrons and, for a moment, she was swayed by the flattery. Then it came to her that no doubt this was exactly what Mrs Dobbs intended.

'I'm sorry,' she said, hoping she sounded firm. 'But I intend to keep George at my side and I hope you will allow me to bring him down to the kitchen as I work, doing exactly what I did before. I do not think that I would be suited to the sort of work you mean.' Then, seeing Mrs Dobbs's frown deepen she added hastily, 'I am, of course, honoured that such an offer has been made.'

If she hoped that would be enough to appease her land-lady, she had sorely misjudged the situation. When Mrs Dobbs spoke again it was with an icy anger that exposed a side of her Molly hadn't witnessed before.

'You will do as I tell you, miss. You owe me for board and lodging over the last three weeks, while you have been lying in, and for the delivery of your child. And, since you were eating for two before it was born, there's money chalked to your account that I'll have now, thank you.' She folded her arms and stood over Molly with an expression of such menace that Molly shuddered.

With a sinking heart, she remembered how few coins her money purse, hidden beneath the floorboards, still held. She had calculated on it lasting until she could undertake her duties again but she doubted whether it contained anything like enough to satisfy Mrs Dobbs's demands.

'If you want to keep the child I can find a wet nurse for you, for which you must pay at least three shillings a week.

288

And she will want payment in advance.' Mrs Dobbs's expression made it clear that Molly need not expect her to lend her the money to do this.

'If you cannot afford this – and let me tell you, Molly, that you seem to have put little thought into your situation and how it could be managed once the baby was born – well, if you cannot afford a wet nurse then I suggest you approach the Foundling Hospital. They will provide a wet nurse and take good care of the child. You are at liberty to claim him back when you are in a settled situation and able to do so.'

Molly was only half listening. She had already decided she would borrow money from one of the girls – Kitty or Emma – and use this to pay her debts. Perhaps that would be enough and Mrs Dobbs would forget all about her plans. The thought of someone else feeding George, of spending time with him while Molly was deprived of him, was more than she could bear.

Mrs Dobbs bade Molly a frosty goodnight, advising her to think well on what she had proposed, and left the room. Molly tried to get to sleep, to take advantage of George being well settled, but the evening's conversation had left her too troubled to allow her to rest easy.

This was to be the start of a week of nights where sleep was in short supply. During conversations with Emma and Kitty, Molly found her requests to borrow money evaded and rejected. They had debts themselves, to their dressmakers or to Mrs Dobbs, or they had promised to send money home, they said. When she cast her net further afield and received much the same answers, she suspected that Mrs Dobbs had instructed the girls not to help her if asked.

By the end of the week, Molly was playing for time. She asked Mrs Dobbs to tell her more about the Foundling

Hospital, in an attempt to make her believe that she was coming around to her way of thinking. Mrs Dobbs stopped asking her when she was going to be repaid and instead concentrated on describing the hospital in glowing terms: what it did for women who found themselves with a baby they were unable to support and how that baby could be reclaimed once they were in a settled situation.

Clinging to this last fact was the only thing that gave Molly hope in the sleepless dark reaches of the night. Once it had become apparent that she could not borrow the money to repay her debts, her first thought had been to run away with George. But where could she go? They would end up sleeping on the streets for she didn't know anyone in London who might take her in. She'd briefly considered throwing herself on the mercy of Will and his family, then discounted it. His family might be scandalised, but even if they weren't, they were just around the corner from Half Moon Street. Mrs Dobbs would find her and insist on her return.

The only other people she knew in London were Martha and Daniel, in Bermondsey. But the house was too small for them to take her in, his parents no doubt still being there and, in any case, they believed her to have returned to Margate. She even thought about returning home, but without a doubt the welcome there would not be warm. There would be no room for her with a baby in her father's house, and her aunt and uncle would be horrified if they discovered she had borne Nicholas's son. She feared they would take George away from her and she would be no better off in that regard than she was now.

Sleeping on the streets was out of the question. It was the beginning of February, cold by day and even worse at night. George wouldn't survive. Molly wept bitter tears at

the thought. But neither could she tolerate the alternative –
working for Mrs Dobbs as she had proposed. Round and
round went Molly's thoughts, with no satisfactory solution in sight.

As another week began, Mrs Dobbs finally lost patience.
'Molly, I cannot carry on supporting you here. I need you to
pay me the money you owe me. I will give you until tomorrow to find it.'

Molly's hand was forced. She begged Mrs Dobbs for just
a few more days' grace, and promised she would take George
to the Foundling Hospital before the week was out. Then she
made her plans, but with a very heavy heart.

PART FIVE

JANUARY 1790–AUGUST 1791

Chapter Forty-Nine

It was still dark when Molly left Half Moon Street, George wrapped in his best blanket and clutched to her breast, within her shawl. Her heart was beating rapidly and her breath hung like frosted mist in the air, but she was too agitated to feel the cold. She followed the directions that Mrs Dobbs had given her, walking through the market – only just beginning to come to life at this early hour – then taking Princes Street and Duke Street before skirting Lincoln's Inn Fields. She had already journeyed beyond the small area surrounding Covent Garden that she knew. Turn north, Mrs Dobbs had said, and cross High Holborn, then look for Red Lion Street. Remembering that Molly wasn't the best at reading, she'd told her to keep an eye open for the inn sign on the corner, and there it was: a red lion glowering down at her as she passed beneath it, as if it knew what her business was in these parts. She walked on north until she reached what felt like the edge of the city.

Molly hesitated at the start of a road that appeared to lead away to nothing. Peering through the darkness, she could make out the dim bulk of a large building ahead of her. She set her face towards it and struck out, leaving the awakening city behind. As she drew closer, she could see that the building had an imposing height; a faint light behind some of the windows suggested candles were lit within and that residents were awake, despite the early hour.

She reached a gateway, uncertain all at once as to whether she should enter, but a watchman leant out of his hut and beckoned her through so she allowed her footsteps to carry her forward again. She faltered once more as she drew closer to the building: not only was this the first time she had been out since George's birth – and the walk had tired her – but she was also deeply reluctant to complete her mission. As she drew closer, she was surprised to see how many women were already there before her, waiting patiently on the steps. They all clutched bundles as she did, some of them mewling, but for the most part the women kept their eyes averted from each other.

Molly took her place in the line, aware, as time passed, of other mothers collecting on the steps behind her. She kept her head down, concentrating fiercely on George, who had been still and quiet throughout her journey. He was fast asleep, tucked into his warm wrappings and face turned away, but his features – the rosy cheeks and shock of dark blond hair, the dark eyes that seemed to regard her gravely – were already etched on her mind. She had no idea whether she was capable of going through with what lay ahead of her.

After some time, as the women began to move forwards, her feet carried her upwards and through the great entrance door. There they paused again in the hallway before shuffling into a room that was undoubtedly large but already full of people.

Molly became aware of a fashionably dressed group watching them from seats set along the wall. They were mostly ladies, but with one or two gentlemen in attendance. She felt her cheeks start to burn. Had they come to witness her shame, and that of her fellow mothers, all brought here out of necessity, out of a wish to give their babies the chance of a better life – indeed, of any life?

She flushed with embarrassment as she saw their eyes travel over her from head to toe, assessing her hair – flowing loose from beneath her bonnet but at least freshly brushed that morning – her drab clothing and her shabby footwear. Molly returned their gaze with a defiant stare until a man standing behind a desk at the side of the room called for the mothers' attention.

'I am the secretary of this institution. You have come here today because you are in the direst straits, finding yourselves in a situation where you cannot care for your babies. You have thrown yourselves on the mercy of the good ladies and gentlemen you see here.' He indicated the row of seated gentry who inclined their heads, unsmiling.

'It is through their good offices and generous donations that this institution is able to run, but even with their most welcome assistance we are unable to take all the babies brought to us.'

The secretary paused and looked meaningfully at the women before him. 'It is impossible to ascertain which of you is the most deserving. Therefore, when a great many of you attend, as you have done today, we operate a ballot. You must select a ball from this bag' – he held up a cloth bag so that they all might see it – 'and the colour of the ball will dictate whether or not your child will be accepted.'

The women before him gasped. For the first time, they looked at each other and Molly saw her own anguish reflected on the faces of those around her. No one had warned her of this cruel added humiliation. Had she come this far, and endured so much agony over her decision, only to be turned away? She looked down at George again. He was still asleep, eyes closed and lashes sweeping his cheeks, face calm, totally oblivious to the scene around him, to the fact that his fate was about to be sealed by the choice of a coloured ball.

The secretary held up his hand to quell the murmur of outrage swelling among the women in the room. 'Failure to gain admittance does not prevent you trying again in a month's time.'

Molly felt a wrench to her heart. Could she put herself through this again? Could she spend longer with her beautiful boy, only to have to resolve once more to give him up? In the split second after the secretary had told them of the ballot she had resolved that if it went against her she would take it as a sign: she would take George and somehow find a way to make a life with him.

'I want each of you to take a ball and I will tell you what the colour signifies.' The secretary was holding out the bag, its neck held too tightly for anyone to glimpse its contents.

Sweat prickled Molly's armpits and dampened her back as she stepped forward to take her turn. She looked to see what those ahead of her had picked. None had sought to hide what lay in their hand – a mixture of white and red balls, with one black. Molly reached in, clutching George tightly to her breast with her free hand. Her world hung dizzily on this one action. Her fingers closed around a ball and she pulled it out. She had a red ball clenched tightly in her grip. She stepped back, mute, and watched as the remaining women took their turn.

There was no need for the secretary to ask for silence. The women waited and watched until the last ball had been chosen. Was it for this moment the gentry had come? Did

298

they want to see which of these disgraced women would be further humiliated?

'Before I continue, I will remind you that if the ball you have chosen does not gain your infant admittance today, there is nothing to stop you making another attempt.' Was that a spark of compassion on the secretary's face? Did he dislike having to play the part of the judge in this way? Then he spoke again. 'White ball, instant admittance subject to health checks.'

A murmur passed through the waiting women.

'Black ball, no admittance on this occasion.'

Molly felt her knees weaken and she would have looked to the woman next to her for support, had she not been holding a black ball.

Molly barely took in his final words. 'Red ball, waiting list. A place will be allocated if an infant chosen for admittance fails the medical examination.'

All the women standing before the secretary were now weeping. If the gentry needed to be convinced that they weren't a feckless bunch, desperate to be rid of their inconvenient babies, surely this would suffice, Molly thought bitterly. Those who had picked white balls wept for the infants they would have to give up, those who had picked black wept because they were denied entry and faced destitution. And those who had picked red, like Molly, wept out of frustration and because their agony would now be prolonged.

The secretary spoke again. 'For those of you who are successful, we will take a history of you and your child. If you are of good character and your child is free of infection, we will take him or her. He or she will be baptised with a new name, then placed with one of our registered wet nurses in the city or country, before returning here at the age of four or five. You may leave a token with your child so that you can reclaim him or her when you are better placed to do so, but you will be expected to make reparation for the care your son or daughter has received during their time with us.'

The secretary sighed. Molly wondered how many of the women standing beside her would be in a position to fulfil the last condition. She had already vowed to herself that, if George were to be taken in, she would be one of them.

Now the unsuccessful applicants were ushered from the building, while the successful ones were taken through to another room, where admittance was processed. The possessors of the red balls, like Molly, were led out into the hallway and told to wait.

Molly felt herself start to tremble. George would wake soon and need to be fed and she was already wearied by the stress of the day. She was no further forward – in limbo between a future for her son and herself, or a denial of all help. She had just made the decision to leave, having convinced herself that their fate was the same as if she had picked the black ball, when a nurse appeared in the hallway and beckoned to the nearest mother to follow her.

Did this signify that a successful mother's child had failed the medical, meaning a place was now free? Molly gauged her position near the door. She was third nearest now – had the other mothers noticed what had just occurred? About ten of them remained. Was it possible that some would gain entrance after all?

The minutes ticked by on the great clock in the hallway and Molly's hopes began to dwindle as the long hand swept back towards the hour. There had been no further summonses and she began to fear that the odds were stacked against them. She sat on, wondering how long they would have to wait to hear their fate before she heard brisk steps along the corridor.

Molly expected it to be an announcement that there were no more places and they must all leave but the same nurse summoned two more mothers to follow her. All at once, the remaining mothers were alert, watchful. Molly was next in line and she shifted cautiously closer to the door, not wanting to make her actions too obvious but fearing that someone else would push ahead of her. She could hear mutterings of discontent from those on the other side of the room. 'It ain't fair. There should be another ballot among us lot waiting here.' The sound of footsteps in the corridor stilled the voice.

This time a different nurse entered by another door, taking the woman standing nearest to it away with her. Molly's heart, which had begun to beat rapidly at the thought that she would be next, slowed. Despondent once more, she wasn't sure how she could withstand such uncertainty.

Three hours had passed since they had been left in the hallway and the mothers had now sunk to the floor, leaning back against the panelled walls. Molly had managed to retain her place near the door. She had fed George and laid him in her skirts, his head resting on her raised knees as she sang quietly to him in an effort to soothe him. The volume of noise from the babies was high but the mothers passed very few remarks among themselves. They remained in competition with each other and couldn't afford to become friendly.

As yet another hour crept by, the despair in the hallway was evident. Sighs were the sound most commonly heard from the mothers, while the babies had gradually fallen asleep. Molly was beginning to drift into sleep herself, exhausted, when she became aware of the sound of brisk footsteps once more. She dragged herself back to full consciousness to find a nurse standing in the doorway next to her, looking from Molly to the mother seated on the floor opposite her.

Molly almost scrambled to her feet, then feared it would look too forward. She limited herself to looking at the nurse as respectfully and beseechingly as possible. Seconds ticked past while Molly's heartbeats hammered in her ears.

'You.' The nurse was pointing at Molly. 'Come with me.'

Using the wall behind her, Molly pushed herself upright while the nurse looked at the other expectant faces turned towards her.

'The rest of you will have to go. There'll be no more places offered today.'

Molly hurried along the corridor after the nurse as fast as she could. She didn't look back.

CHAPTER FIFTY

M olly followed the nurse into a small room, which, on first sight, appeared to be full of people. She struggled to take in what she saw: a large desk, with the secretary seated at its centre, a scribe on one side of him, another man and an older nurse in an imposing starched uniform on the other.

They wasted no time – it had been a long day for them as well as for Molly. The scribe was poised, ready to write on a fresh sheet of paper, as the secretary asked, somewhat wearily, 'Name?'

'Molly Goodchild, sir.'

'Name of infant?'

'George.'

'Where is the child's father?'

'At sea, sir. He doesn't care to acknowledge his child's existence.' Molly's voice shook a little.

'Your occupation?'

'I was a milkmaid, sir, for my uncle back in Margate. And a dairymaid for my father. But I've been in London a few weeks now, first working at Bermondsey Spa and then staying with … friends.' She hoped the hesitation wasn't noticeable.

'And can you return to your previous occupation?' The secretary was looking at her over the top of his spectacles.

Molly had a feeling that her answer would prove crucial. 'I'm not sure of the welcome I would get, sir.' A memory of her father's face, as she had last seen it, flashed before her. Normally calm, if careworn, it had been suffused with anger.

'Hmm. I see. And where are you living now?'

Molly paused. If she gave the Half Moon Street address, might it count against her? Was there a possibility that some-one involved with the institution would recognise it?

The secretary's eyebrows were raised and the scribe, who had been scratching away, paused to look up at her. Molly made a hasty decision.

'Will Turner, the artist, has been kind enough to help me find a place to stay in London, sir.' Seeing the sceptical expression on the secretary's face, Molly hastily added, 'He was a friend of mine when he was at school in Margate. His family lives in Maiden Lane. His father has promised to help me find work based on the outcome of today.' The lies tripped off her tongue and yet, until a moment before, she had had no thought of such a story.

'An artist, you say?' The secretary's interest was piqued.

'Yes, sir. He is at the Royal Academy.'

She was at pains to make him appear to be a respectable man, less keen that the secretary might discover he was only fifteen years old. Molly didn't know that her lie was a fortui-tous one. It was as the first public art gallery in London that the Foundling Hospital had attracted its wealthy patrons. Flocking to see exhibitions and musical performances there, they had been easily converted to benefactors of the charity to support the foundling children. The secretary had seen the glimmer of an opportunity to engage with a new artist who might grace their walls.

'And will Mr Turner vouch for your good character?'

'Oh, yes, sir.' Molly didn't suppose that one more half-truth would make a difference. Would they really follow it up?

'Matron, will you please examine the infant?'

The lady in the imposing uniform stood up and held out her arms for George.

Molly swallowed hard. 'Is … is this it?'

She was unprepared now that the moment had come. George gazed up at her, quite content in her arms. How could she bear to hand her beautiful, trusting boy to a stranger? Her eyes filled with tears. It was one thing to imagine herself doing this, quite another to break their bond now that the moment had come.

'He will be well looked after.' The matron spoke firmly, as if she had used the same words several times already that day.

Molly bent forward to kiss George's forehead, clutching him tightly as she did so. Tears were coursing down her cheeks and, if her limbs hadn't felt so heavy, as if drained of her life blood, she would have fled the room with her son. She had tried so many times to imagine this moment but now she knew she had failed. In desperation, she tried to drink in every feature of George's face even as she held him out to the matron, who nodded encouragingly.

'Now, we will examine George. If all is well, he will be baptised with a new name and sent to foster care. Have you a token to leave for him?'

The matron and nurse took George to one end of the desk. He began to wail as they removed the shawl swaddling him, and then his gown, protesting as the cool air reached his skin. Molly's tears flowed harder and her fingers shook as she reached into the pocket of her skirt.

She pulled out the two halves of a playing card, the King of Hearts, which she had cut in half, creating a scallop pattern. She didn't want anyone else to be able to replicate her token.

The secretary took one half of the playing card and handed it to the scribe, who placed it in an envelope.

'You must keep the other half safe,' the secretary warned her. 'Do you wish to leave anything else?'

Molly was stricken. She should have prepared herself better. Was it not enough that she was leaving a part of herself in that room?

The secretary took pity on her. 'Some mothers leave a scrap of cloth or a coin as an additional token, but it is quite all right to leave just the one.'

Her tears gave Molly a sudden inspiration. She had a handkerchief in her pocket, much laundered but unused so far today. It was embroidered in yellow thread with her initial 'M', surrounded by a circle of pale blue French knots to represent forget-me-nots. Hesitant, she held it out.

'We need just a scrap. The corner with the initial, perhaps.'

Molly nodded and the scribe ceased scratching his notes, laid down his quill and picked up a paper knife. He sliced the embroidered corner from the threadbare fabric and tucked it into the envelope. Then he handed the remainder of the handkerchief back to her, unsmiling.

'All is well. He can be admitted.' It was the matron's voice. The nurse was busy swaddling George, who was crying fiercely now, in a plain hospital blanket. Molly felt her milk begin to flow in response.

'Can I feed him one last time?' she whispered.

The secretary shook his head. 'I am sorry. It is better this way.'

The matron signalled to the nurse, and with swift foot-steps she removed George from the room. It took every ounce of Molly's remaining strength not to sink to the floor.

'Molly Goodchild, we will care for your infant until such time as you are in a position to return and claim him, by virtue of the tokens registered here with us. Should you do so, you will need to make reparations to the Foundling Hospital for the expenditure made on his care. If you are unable to return for him he will be looked after here until he is old enough to be apprenticed or to join the army. Make your mark here to signify your acceptance of these terms.'

Molly could barely see through the blur of her tears but she scrawled her name at the bottom of the registration document with the scribe's quill pen. The scribe began to collect his papers together as Molly stood on, unsure of what to do next.

The secretary spoke again. 'You have been given a second chance, Molly Goodchild, and we expect you to take that chance to live blamelessly and virtuously from now on. Please inform Mr Turner that we will approach him to vouch for your character. Now you may go.'

The nurse, who had returned to the room, held the door open for Molly and handed her George's knitted blanket. She tried to utter the thanks that she knew would be expected but no words would pass her lips, or perhaps her tongue was stilled for it felt to her that very little thanks were due for what had just occurred.

Molly stumbled a little as she walked along the corridor and had to hold onto the wall for support, aware as she did so of just how empty her arms now were. She had left very early that morning and it was now late afternoon. Not a morsel of food or drink had passed her lips in all that time. All that, though, paled into insignificance for surely she was the worst person in the world for what she had just done.

Chapter Fifty-One

Molly found her way back to the front door of the Foundling Hospital and she had just begun to cross the courtyard when a group of small children, walking two by two, crossed in front of her. She stepped back into the shelter of the porch and watched them. They were neat in their brown uniforms, the girls in dresses with white cotton aprons and the boys wearing white shirts with jackets and short trousers, their hair brushed and faces clean. Molly didn't have the energy to smile at them but, in any case, they looked neither right nor left. She was struck by how quiet they were. Apart from the sound of their boots on the yard, nothing else could be heard. They were following an adult, a teacher maybe, with another bringing up the rear. Perhaps they were moving between classes, Molly thought, or to the dining hall. She had lost all track of time but she could see now that dusk was falling so it must be late afternoon.

Molly watched them until they were out of sight, swallowed up by a building across the courtyard. She tried to imagine George among them, in a few years' time, then told herself she would claim him back before then. Wearily, she made her way towards the gate. The watchman stepped from his hut as she approached.

'Are you the last for today?' he asked.

Molly nodded.

'You look done in, love,' he said sympathetically. 'Have you far to go?'

Molly's thoughts spooled back through the morning's journey, now set to be performed in reverse as she made her way back into the city. She closed her eyes briefly. She wasn't sure where she would go or how she would manage.

'How about a cup of something hot to set you on your way?' the watchman asked cheerfully.

Molly hesitated, then shook her head, although she would have dearly loved one. The man had noticed her hesitation. 'Don't worry, love, I don't bite. I've got a daughter of about your age. I would hope that if she found herself in a pickle some kind soul would help her out. Why don't I make you some tea before you go on your way?'

He held the door of his little hut ajar. Molly realised that she wasn't going to get very far without any food or drink in her belly so she stepped in, offering a weak smile in gratitude. The watchman had rigged up a little stove, which kept the hut warm in the wintry weather. He set a smoke-blackened kettle on it and took a cup from the shelf.

'Here, you have a sit-down while I make this. Sugar?'

She shook her head.

He considered, looking at her, head on one side. 'Have you eaten today?'

She shook her head again, wordlessly.

'Well, I don't have anything to offer you, more's the pity, so a bit of sugar it will have to be. It will perk you up. And it's supposed to be good for shock and I'd say that's what you've had.'

Molly watched him as he made the tea. He was a solid little man, with a bit of a stoop, grey tufts of hair springing up around his otherwise bald head. As he moved, she noticed a limp.

'I'm lucky that my sister spares me a little of her tea, and her sugar. My bit of luxury, I call it. Here.' He was holding out a cup of steaming tea. She took it gratefully. It was too hot to drink but it warmed her hands. She felt chilled to the bone.

'I'd best introduce myself since you're to sit awhile,' the watchman said. 'Bartholomew. My friends call me Barty.'

Molly wondered whether to offer a false name for reasons that she couldn't entirely understand, then felt too exhausted to do so. 'Molly,' she said, in a small voice.

'Do you have somewhere to go tonight?' Bartholomew sounded concerned.

'Yes.' Molly's voice sounded strange to herself. 'I have friends who will put me up for a few days.'

This was untrue. She had nowhere. She had no intention of going back to Half Moon Street, and to disguise this she had left all her possessions behind when she left that morning, even the treasured picture that Will had painted for her. She had only George's blanket and tokens and, hidden beneath her skirts, her purse with its few remaining coins.

'And then?' Bartholomew persisted.

Molly wondered why he was taking such an interest in her. 'Why, then I expect I will go back to Kent,' she said, although she had no intention of doing any such thing.

'Aye, well, if you change your mind or something goes wrong you could do worse than see my sister, Hester,' Bartholomew said. 'She helps girls to get work as servants, and finds them somewhere to stay. London can be a danger-ous place otherwise for a girl on her own.'

Molly sat on, reluctant to leave the warmth of the hut even

310

though her tea was all but finished. The watchman let her be, not attempting to engage her in conversation, so she sat and stared at nothing, trying to blank out the events of that day. She was, though, all too aware of the absence of George: of his head nestled into her shoulder, the warmth of his tiny body as he slept pressed to her breast.

She realised she was being addressed and that Bartholomew was looking at her, head cocked as though waiting for an answer to a question.

'I'm sorry – I didn't hear what you said.' It was an effort to speak and she feared that it was going to be even more of an effort to move.

'It's foggy again.' Bartholomew, who had been outside to attend to a visitor, had drawn the door of the hut almost closed when he came back in. Fog had plagued London nearly every night over the last week, rising in chilly swirls off the river as dusk fell, then creeping through the city. 'The night watchman is due here any time now. No, it's all right.' He held up his hand as Molly, thinking he wanted her gone, made a move as if to rise. 'I'm not trying to drive you out. I think you should walk along with me and I'll take you to my sister's place. You can hear what she has to say and if it doesn't suit, well, no harm done. You can seek out your friends tomorrow, as you planned. But it looks to me as though you won't get far tonight, what with the fog and you looking so pale an' all.'

And so, when the night watchman appeared shortly afterwards, Bartholomew took Molly's arm and helped her up from the chair. Molly noticed that the new arrival didn't appear too surprised by her presence, or by Bartholomew's cheery 'We'll be off now, to my sister's.' She supposed he must be in the habit of helping some of the women who passed through the gates of the Foundling Hospital.

Bidding the night watchman 'A good night, and a quiet one, too,' Bartholomew guided Molly out of the door, where she shivered as the cold struck her once more. She was grateful for his arm as she stumbled wearily at his side, the fog now so thick that she was barely aware of the direction they took once they gained the city.

Bartholomew encouraged her as they went. 'Not far now. Just another few streets.' After he'd repeated this several times she suspected the journey was a good deal farther than he'd implied. It was impossible to judge, for the fog had obliterated any landmark she might have recognised. Just as she began to think she couldn't take another step, they came to a halt outside an inn. Molly was dimly aware of the smell of the river, familiar to her from her time in Half Moon Street. Then the door opened and Bartholomew drew her inside, into the warmth and the buzz of noise from the drinkers. She caught only a quick impression of a large, low-ceilinged room with a huge fireplace at one end, before he opened a door at the side of the bar and bade her follow him up the narrow stairway beyond.

Molly stepped off the upper landing into a parlour, lit by the glow of candles and by the fire burning in the black-leaded grate. Bartholomew was greeting a woman Molly presumed to be his sister, a woman whom Molly had imagined to be like Mrs Dobbs but who could hardly have been more different. She was small, like her brother, but wiry, with grey hair that she had attempted to dye red, with limited success.

Molly stood, swaying, as Bartholomew spoke to his sister in low tones. Then she came over to Molly, took both her hands, and spoke to her. 'My dear, you've had quite a day, Bartholomew tells me. I can see you're in no fit state to tell me much so I'm going to find you a bed here for the night and we will talk in the morning.'

Telling Molly that she was to call her Hester, Bartholomew's sister settled her brother by the hearth, then took Molly up another flight of steep stairs, opening a door at the end of the corridor to usher her into a small room, just large enough to hold a single bed with space enough to stand beside it.

'You get into that bed and I'll fetch you up something to eat.' And with that, Hester was gone, leaving Molly to strip down to her shift before slipping between the sheets, only to lie shivering. Hester reappeared shortly after, bearing a tray holding a bowl of stew and a hunk of bread. The aroma of the stew made Molly realise just how hungry she was and she could barely wait to begin spooning it up but, before she was halfway through the bowl, the memories of what had occurred that day came flooding back to her. She laid down the spoon. Her throat felt as though it would close up and tears poured down her cheeks.

'Now, now, don't take on so,' Hester said, patting her shoulder and lifting the tray away from Molly, who was in danger of letting it slide to the floor. 'It will all seem better in the morning.'

But it didn't. Molly stayed hunched in her bed for several days, barely able to lift her head to acknowledge Hester's visits when she appeared with food, three times a day. She slept a lot – deep, dreamless sleep that took her away from the agony of her waking hours when she remembered only too clearly and painfully what she had done.

When she was awake, she saw George's face over and over again and heard his wails as the nurse at the Foundling Hospital took him away. She was in physical pain at his loss, too. Hester brought her cloths soaked in cold water, which she instructed Molly to press against her breasts to ease the discomfort that the surplus milk, no longer required, was causing her. She thought of George at some other woman's breast and wept again. Did he feel her loss as deeply as she felt his, or had he forgotten her already in greedy, mindless suckling?

Once or twice her thoughts strayed to Mrs Dobbs. She wondered how she had reacted to her disappearance. She would be very angry, Molly supposed. She felt guilty about the money that Mrs Dobbs would have her believe she owed to her and Molly felt a pang that she wouldn't see James or the girls again, but she tried not to dwell on it. In her more lucid moments, Molly knew that if she was to get over the loss of George, she must shut down all feeling. She couldn't afford to care for anyone, ever again. What had loving someone ever done in her life but cause her pain?

After a week had passed, Molly felt she couldn't impose on Hester any longer. She had been extremely kind and patient but, mindful of the situation she had got herself into with Mrs Dobbs, Molly was fearful of being beholden. Yet she struggled to find the energy to move on, for where could she go? And so, when Hester said soothingly that she really didn't think Molly was well enough to go anywhere yet, she gave in readily enough. After a number of days – Molly really couldn't be sure of how many – Hester suggested that she might like to get up and sit with her that evening in her parlour. Molly made the effort to wash and dress herself, begging the loan of a hairbrush from Hester so that she might tidy her hair.

It felt strange to sit by the fireside but Hester made no effort to force the conversation, recounting something of the day's activity in the bar down below, but requiring nothing from Molly in return. Then Hester would lapse into a companionable silence, gazing into the fire, before relating another story. Before the evening was out, Molly had managed to engage enough with what she was saying to ask her one or two questions. Over the following week, Molly began to look forward to these evenings as an escape from her thoughts, until Hester said, as they neared the end of one such evening, 'I find myself short-handed. Do you have any experience of bar work, Molly? Or of handling money and customers?'

Molly had shared nothing of her past history until now but she found herself saying, 'Not bar work. But I sold milk on behalf of my father.' She paused, mindful of Hester's kindness towards her and said, 'Perhaps I could help out.'

Molly remembered Bartholomew, Hester's brother, mentioning that she found positions for girls as servants. She'd never mentioned it in all their conversations, speaking only of the inn, but perhaps, Molly thought, if Hester was pleased with the work she did, she might be able to raise it with her. It was time to move on, she felt.

CHAPTER FIFTY-TWO

At first, Molly found that the concentration her new work demanded was an effective way of blocking out her pain. She had to remember the orders and serve them in the right tankards or glasses, or risk the wrath of the customers. Then she needed to be quick with the change and watch out for those who hoped to cheat the newest barmaid by tipping coins into her palm and making off before she'd had chance to count them. The inn lay on a road running parallel to the river, not far from London Bridge, as Molly soon discovered. Its name, the Waterman's Arms, was indicative of the trade of the majority of its customers. They rowed the wherries for travellers passing short distances up and down the river and, for the most part, they were a rough bunch, but the inn was busy and the hours flew past. Hester was pleased with Molly's work, and after less than a week she offered her a bed in the large shared room upstairs, where most of the barmaids slept, except those who lived close by. She started paying her, too, although she said to Molly, almost apologetically, that she would have to deduct money over the first few weeks as a contribution to the board and lodging she'd already had.

'And you'll need more clothes than the ones you're standing up in if you're to be working here every day,' Hester said.

She cast a critical glance over Molly, then sent her out with instructions as to how to find the best fabric in the area and her own dressmaker. 'You can put the bills on my account and I'll deduct them, too,' she said.

It was only as Molly ventured out on her first shopping expedition in a long time that she realised how close she was to London Bridge. It came as a shock. She didn't wish to be reminded of the last time she had seen it, on her journey from Bermondsey to Covent Garden, or of anything that had occurred since then.

Once she had been provided with a couple of new dresses that she actually felt proud to wear – Hester had spoken the truth about the skills of her dressmaker – it wasn't long before she realised the trap she had fallen into. The offer of work was genuine enough – the inn employed several women and girls to work in the different rooms during the long hours that the inn was open – but Hester expected her barmaids to offer a service beyond merely serving drinks. It was explained to Molly that her duty was to keep the customers happy 'in every way', which at first had puzzled her. Then she noticed that when the other girls were clearing tables, there was a good deal of giggling and flirtatious behaviour with the customers. It wasn't long before Molly realised that they used the back alley behind the privy, known mockingly as Love Lane, to entertain their customers.

'Hester lets you keep nearly all the money,' Grace, one of the girls, confided in Molly even though she hadn't asked her. 'She don't want her customers going down the road to Mrs Fisher's house – she'd rather they spent their money on ale here. And we can set our own price.'

Molly had kept her head down at first and considered how best to avoid having to provide this additional service, but it sickened her to think there might be no way around it. The irony of having run away from Half Moon Street only to find herself in a much worse situation wasn't lost on her. She owed Hester for board and lodging already. Then there was the matter of the dressmaker's bills. Hester hadn't pushed Molly on this but she knew it was only a matter of time. She'd already had several customers grasp her wrist as she went about her work, asking, 'How much for Love Lane?'

After two weeks had passed, Hester said she needed a quiet word with Molly. She asked her upstairs to her parlour and this time kept her standing. There had been no more cosy evenings by the fire since Molly had begun work in the bar.

'I need you to take your job here seriously, Molly,' Hester said. 'I've given you a bit of time to get used to our ways because I know what you've been through. But the customers are asking after the new girl and I don't like to disappoint.'

Molly didn't argue with her, but went straight back to the shared dormitory, where the other girls who weren't at work were already fast asleep. She found Grace, just about to climb into bed after working since early that morning.

'You've been here the longest, Grace. I don't want to do the sort of work that Hester is expecting.' Molly bit her lip. 'Is there anything I can do to get out of it?'

Grace thought a moment. 'If you ask to work mornings you'll have to start at four every day but you won't get bothered so much that way. It's not until after noon that the men start to think about Love Lane. But it ain't so bad, you know. You get used to it.'

And so Molly, used to early rising for the milking back in Margate, in what felt like another lifetime, volunteered to swap with any of the other girls who found it a struggle to be at work so early in the day. After a week, though, Hester had got wise to Molly's ruse.

'The men are still asking,' she said sternly. 'Pleased though I am to have you working mornings, as you're a sight more awake at that hour than anyone else here, I need you to be nice to my afternoon and evening customers.'

Once more, Molly didn't acknowledge the landlady's words. She had been at pains to make herself indispensable at the inn, being efficient when serving the customers, and always on time to open the doors at first light for the water-men coming off the overnight shift, and those about to start for the day. She had watched the other girls at work and learnt from their easy flirtatiousness, all the time keeping an invisible barrier between herself and the customers.

Now she realised that if she continued to defy Hester, she might have to leave in a hurry. She had already begun to make plans. When she was first on early-morning duty, before anyone else was up, she had stepped into the great hearth in the bar and reached up on tiptoe, feeling about for a gap or a loose brick. Finding what she was looking for, she had slid out the brick and pushed the pouch that held her savings into the space behind it, then replaced the brick. She intended to add money to the pouch whenever she had the opportunity. It was to be her way out of this place.

Hester's insistence that she take on some of the evening shifts could no longer be denied so Molly complied, while still managing to dodge the men's demands for her company. One evening she noticed a young man, who looked to be her age or a little younger, following her every move, his eyes filled with such longing that, against her better judgement, she found herself wishing to tease him.

'And what's your name?' she asked, as she collected tank-ards from the table where he sat with a group of older men, one of whom was among Grace's regulars.

The men at the table laughed and catcalled at her words. 'Joshua, lad, aren't you honoured? Looks like you're going to be the first to get an invite to Love Lane.'

Joshua, who hadn't been to the Waterman's Arms before, looked puzzled, at the same time blushing scarlet to the roots of his blond hair on finding himself the centre of attention.

'Take no notice of them,' Molly said, having by now discovered that she could get away with speaking as she liked to the inn's patrons, as long as she added a wink or a toss of her hair. 'Are you new around here? I don't think I've seen you before.'

Joshua, overcome with shyness, managed to stammer, 'I'm not from these parts. I'm staying with my uncle,' he gestured at Grace's client, 'to do some work. I'm from Kent.'

'Oh, and what part of Kent?' Molly asked, without caring about the answer very much.

'Margate,' Joshua replied.

Several of the tankards slipped from Molly's grasp and fell to the flagged floor with a great clatter. The men jumped and cursed and the other customers looked around to see the cause of the commotion. Molly apologised, blushing. She cast a glance at Joshua as she picked up the scattered tankards but could see nothing to recognise in his features and no sign that he knew her, either.

Molly was in trouble with Hester.

'You'll be paying me for the dents in those tankards, my girl. What came over you? You're normally so careful.' Hester looked at her sharply but Molly was too upset to care. The thought of anyone from Margate finding her working in a place like this was more than she could bear.

The following evening Joshua, his uncle and some other

men were at the same table. Molly took care to stay away from that part of the room but she saw Joshua watching her and noticed that he was slaking his thirst with more ale than was good for him.

Late in the evening, no doubt egged on by his fellow drinkers, Joshua approached her. 'How much for Love Lane?' he asked her. He looked barely able to stand and his face was red, although this time Molly was sure it was from the drink rather than embarrassment.

'Have you done this before?' she asked.

Joshua was taken aback by the question. 'Yes … no …' he stammered. Then he blurted out, 'It's being paid for.'

Molly thought quickly. 'Why don't you come back another evening when you've had less to drink?' she suggested. 'You'll enjoy it more.'

With no intention of being around to fulfil her suggestion, she sent him back in the direction of his table while she pressed on with her work.

A few minutes later, Hester called her over. 'I've had a complaint about you,' she said curtly.

'Oh?' Molly tried to look as though she had no idea what she was talking about.

'Aye. It seems you turned down one of our customers.'

'He's young and he's had too much to drink,' Molly protested. 'It's his first time and I didn't want him to be disappointed. I suggested he came back another night.'

'That's not for you to decide,' Hester said. 'His friends are good customers here and they're paying. Now, get yourself out back and I'll send him to you. And you'll make sure he has a good time,' she added, by way of a parting shot.

'I'll not do it,' Molly said. The words were out of her mouth before she could stop them. She flinched, thinking that

Hester was about to strike her.

'Then you can get your things together and go. Now,' Hester said.

The drinkers in the area around where the two women stood, facing each other, had fallen quiet. Molly, cheeks flaming, turned on her heel and left the bar, climbing the steep stairs up to the dormitory in the attic. She didn't regret her refusal or fear what lay ahead. Whatever was to come, she would make it work. She felt a small twinge of excitement about the unknown possibilities and tried not to dwell on the fact that she had no idea where she would lay her head that night.

She waited until the inn was silent, apart from the snores coming from every bed, before she crept down the stairs and slid the loose brick out of the chimney. Then she took the pouch from its hiding place – the same pouch that Nicholas had given her back in Chatham – and took a few coins from it. She hesitated, then added a few more and left them on the bar. Someone would find them in the morning and once Hester knew she had gone, she would draw her own conclusions.

She tucked the pouch into her bundle and turned to leave, to find Hester barring her way to the door.

'Not so fast,' the landlady said. 'We have some things to discuss.'

CHAPTER FIFTY-THREE

Hester, it turned out, had had a change of heart. Molly had the regulars at the Waterman's Arms, as well as the other girls, to thank for that. The regulars, once Molly had left the bar, had wasted no time in telling Hester that she'd be a fool to let one of her best barmaids go.

'We know that we never have cause to check our change with Molly behind the bar,' one said. 'And she's always cheerful and ready with a friendly word, no matter how early the hour or how cold the day.'

'She's the best worker in the mornings,' the girls agreed. 'Why not let her stay, on the understanding that she works that shift every day?'

Their support for Molly wasn't untainted by self-interest: there'd be more work in Love Lane – and more money to be made – if Molly, with her striking looks and chestnut hair, was kept away from it. If she didn't care about the money, that was her problem, Grace reasoned.

Hester wasn't about to be swayed by any of their arguments. Molly had been told what she must do, and she'd been defiant. But once the inn had closed for the night and her annoyance had subsided, a plan had formed.

'I have a proposal for you,' Hester said, as she stood before Molly. 'One that would be of benefit to us both.'

Molly was wary. She had witnessed Hester's astuteness in all matters relating to the inn. She couldn't imagine how anything that Hester might suggest could benefit anyone other than Hester. But, with her exit barred, she had no option other than to listen.

'I'm ready to let you stay on and work as you choose, provided that you take the early-morning shift,' Hester said. 'I'll put no further pressure on you to entertain the men. In return …' Hester hesitated, as if unsure how to proceed '… I have a nephew working for the East India Company. Not Barty's son – I have an elder brother, too,' she added hastily. 'He's in need of a wife – a wife of good character. He'll be home on leave before long and, if all goes well, you could return to India with him as his bride.' She saw the expression on Molly's face and continued, 'You would do well to think on it. Remember your situation, Molly. You have a child in the Foundling Hospital, lost to you unless you can provide a respectable home. This is your chance to do just that.'

She took Molly's bundle from her hands and set it down on the bar, glancing at the money as she did so. Then, without a backward glance, she mounted the stairs from the bar to her room.

Molly was astonished at the proposal. Yet as she stood there, thinking, she could see some truth in Hester's words. A new life in a strange land, a life that would include George. It was something that had never crossed her mind, but now that she thought about it, the advantages of the scheme presented themselves to her. Until this moment she had been unable to consider leaving London in search of better prospects elsewhere because of George. She had already walked across town and along the road that led to the Foundling Hospital, her last connection with George, and stood there at a distance, waiting. She didn't think Bartholomew, the watchman and Hester's brother, would recognise her, but she didn't want to be seen, caught out in her desperation.

She had been able dimly to make out the foundling children as they crossed the courtyard from one building to the next – distant dots in a brown-and-white uniform. She knew that the foundling babies generally stayed with their wet nurses somewhere in the country until they were four or five years old, before returning to London to take up schooling until they were apprenticed. So there was no chance that George would be there, yet she intended to return when she could, to hold vigil.

She had let George down so badly and it felt like the only link she had with him now. She had already realised that, as time passed, her hopes of reclaiming George would fade. She would never save enough to repay his care, and the longer it took, the more money she would need. She had to work in order to save, but the nature of her current work would never find favour with the trustees of the Foundling Hospital, she felt sure. If she married, then as a respectable woman her prospect of reclaiming George would improve. But how would she explain about George to any future husband? And how well would such news be received? The two tokens that represented her hope of reclaiming her son, the cut playing card and the tattered remains of her handkerchief, never left her possession. Could Hester's proposal be the solution she needed?

A further consideration was that on her journey to the Foundling Hospital she been on the lookout, not wanting to run the risk of coming across Emma or Kitty, Cécile or any of the other girls in case they followed her and told Mrs Dobbs of her whereabouts. If she could start a new life, away from

London – indeed, in a new country – then all such worry would be removed.

Molly felt her spirits lift but, even as they did, her mind was urging caution. She had no knowledge of Hester's nephew, the man in question. While he might appear to be the answer to her problems, what if she was unable to tolerate him when she met him? What was wrong with him that he needed Hester to find him a wife? She tried to quell these doubts by telling herself she could bear anything to be reunited with George. Then, as the doubt threatened to grow, she told herself firmly that she would deal with it when the need arose. For now, she had a secure job for a bit longer and a chance to save. The rest of it could wait.

She scooped up the coins from the bar and put them back into the money pouch. Then she tucked it into its hiding place, picked up her bundle and went slowly back to the dormitory.

She had but a few hours' sleep remaining to her and, exhausted by the evening's events, she slept remarkably well, but when she woke, ready to open the inn for the early customers, again she felt swirling unease. Hester, though, was at pains to provide reassurance as soon as she took up her usual stance behind the bar at midday, her ill-humour of the previous evening apparently forgotten.

'I've given you my word about the nature of your employment here, Molly. There'll be no more talk of Love Lane. And I think you will find a new life with Matthew in India quite to your taste.'

Over the next few days, Hester delighted in regaling Molly with snippets from Matthew's past letters, painting a picture she seemed to believe Molly would find exciting but which only served to alarm her. There were tigers in the jungle not far from his residence, Hester said. He had heard them roar at night, and paw prints had been found in the compound. Seeing Molly's expression, she hastened to add that Matthew had many servants and there would be someone to keep an eye on little George at all times. She sounded wistful, Molly thought, as she described the wonders Matthew had seen. Speaking of the extreme heat of the country, she asked Molly to consider how pleasant it would be never to complain of feeling cold again. 'Imagine, not a flake of snow has ever fallen there!' Hester exclaimed.

Molly, looking out on a sunny spring day through the wide-open door of the Waterman's Arms, felt her spirits lift once more. But when she asked Hester what Matthew did for the East India Company, Hester became vague.

'I believe he works in one of their offices. He's a most well-educated young man,' Hester added hastily, in case a desk-bound occupation didn't match the exotic picture she had been trying to paint.

After a week or so, Hester's effusiveness about Matthew died away, although she told Molly she had written to tell him all about her.

'I've asked him to get his likeness done out there and to send it over for you to see,' she said, clearly proud of her action. She promised to share his letter with her when he wrote back. And any bad feeling over the Joshua incident had been quickly smoothed over, Hester explaining to all the gentlemen concerned on their next visit that Molly was 'spoken for' but that Sophy would be very happy to be of service.

Molly was glad of the return to what passed as normal at the Waterman's Arms, although it didn't last for long. The other girls, having felt they were getting the better deal by keeping Molly out of Love Lane, had begun to wonder out loud about Hester's preferential treatment of her.

Molly, embarrassed at first, decided to tackle it head on. 'Let's face it, there's bound to be a drawback,' she confided to Grace. 'Matthew is going to be hideously ugly or a hunchback. Hester doesn't make bargains that favour anyone other than herself. We must wait and see.'

As expected, Grace shared Molly's words with the other girls, and any lingering resentment of her gradually died away. The work was grindingly dull, and waking early every morning without fail was sometimes a struggle, but she focused on adding coins to her secret savings as the weeks turned into months while she waited for news of Matthew's arrival.

This had been further delayed by an outbreak of rioting in his district of India, which had developed into an uprising, and all leave had been cancelled. Summer had turned into autumn then winter, with the promise of him being in London by Christmas, but still he didn't appear. Now the first signs of spring were showing, time was passing and George was over a year old. Molly's initial anxiety at meeting Matthew and discovering some possibly unpleasant truths about him had been replaced by impatience to have it done with, so that she could move on to the next phase of her life.

She tried not to dwell too much on thoughts of George and where he might be living, comforting herself with the knowledge that it wouldn't be long before she would be reunited with him. Confined as she was for long hours indoors, she pined for fresh air so whenever she could escape at the end of her shift she took to walking the streets of the area. She soon tired of this: green spaces were few and far between and Molly found herself longing for proper open countryside. Grace had suggested that she should walk in the London parks but Molly hadn't found them to her taste. She missed fields and hedges and found the parks too much like the pleasure garden in Bermondsey – designed for promenading and to be seen, not somewhere to lose yourself in thought for an hour or so.

A memory returned to Molly, of a place Will Turner had mentioned to her when she had taken him to Margate Brooks. He'd said that they reminded him of the area around Brentford, a village outside London, where he'd lived for a while with his uncle. Now she got it into her head that this was where she must go to find the countryside she craved so she asked Hester where it was.

'Lord bless us!' Hester said. 'Whatever put that in your head? It's upriver, a few miles from here. No doubt you could get one of the watermen to take you although the distance will cost you dear. Why don't you try Chelsea first? It's a village, too, although much closer. I've no doubt you'll find what you crave there.'

Hester, aware of Molly's growing restlessness and fearful of her plan going awry, was disposed to be accommodating to her. The following afternoon, when Molly's work was done for the day, Hester called her over and told her she had engaged one of the watermen, Walter, to take her upriver.

'Meet him at Old Swan Stairs and he'll drop you at Chelsea, then pick you up two hours later on the turn of the tide. Make haste now. He's expecting you.'

Pausing only to utter her thanks and to fetch her shawl from the drawer in the dormitory, Molly half ran, half walked down to the river. Her spirits soared before she even reached its banks, for it was a beautiful day: sunny with a clear light and a crisp breeze that reminded her all at once of her days in Margate. The smell of the river was nothing like the salt tang of sea air but for the first time in many a long week, Molly was reminded of home.

She recognised Walter, waiting by the steps, as one of the older watermen. He was usually to be found in his favourite chair in the corner of the bar – closest to the fire in the winter – listening as the younger men complained about their passengers, the meagre tips, the eddying currents and the detritus on the water that made their job more difficult.

'There was a corpse today by Tower Stairs,' a man had said one evening. 'Bloated and stinking it were. Made me retch, but did my passengers bat an eyelid? Nay. Seemed surprised that I were even bothered by it.'

Walter took a draught of his ale and uttered one of his rare comments. 'Aye, if you'd been on the river in the summer of 1780, after the riots, the water were full of death. A corpse for every furlong, we used to say.'

Then he'd lapsed back into silence, brooding on his memories. If any of the younger watermen referred to him as Old Walter, he gave them short shrift. He was still sprightly, despite his stooped frame, his hair was white but thick and his blue eyes shrewd.

'I hear it's the countryside you seek?' he asked Molly, as she stepped nervously from the stone steps into his boat. She'd never been on the water before but she was determined not to show the fear she felt as the craft rocked alarmingly. She sat down hastily, heart beating fast, telling herself that the watermen plied the Thames every day and accidents were few and far between.

'We'll fair fly down,' Walter said, pulling on the oars so

that the boat nosed away from the steps and shot out into the broader reaches of water, much farther from the bank than Molly had imagined. Her knuckles were white as she gripped the boat's wooden sides and Walter chuckled. 'I'm thinking you're not in the habit of travelling by water,' he said.

'No,' Molly replied, aware that her voice was shaking. 'Hester keeps me busy behind the bar.'

'Aye, well, special treatment for you today,' Walter said. 'The boat to yourself. You'll be sharing the ride on the way back. Try to enjoy it now.'

Molly would have liked to close her eyes to try to blot everything out, but she breathed deeply and concentrated on the rhythmic dip of the oars, looking straight ahead even though Walter tried to interest her in the buildings they were passing along the bank.

'Here we are now,' he said, after what felt like a lifetime but could surely have been no more than half an hour. 'Bishop's Stairs. Wait for me here in two hours' time.'

He pulled the boat deftly to the side and handed Molly up onto the wooden platform, lapped by the water, at the base of Bishop's Stairs.

'Watch your step,' he called, as on shaky legs she climbed the slippery stone steps up to the road. She rested for a moment, watching as Walter loaded waiting passengers into the boat, then turned away as he pulled back into the river.

Where should she go? To the left lay a couple of rows of houses, close by the river. At the end of the road to the right there was a great wall, the tumble of vegetation over the top a sign that a garden lay within. Molly suspected it was the private garden of a grand house but she followed the wall anyway until she came to a gated entrance. She walked past and observed it from a distance. Hester's suggestion that she would find countryside in Chelsea looked to be at fault. Molly feared that she would have to walk a good distance to find it, and she was mindful that her time was limited. This wall, though, and the hint of the trees and vegetation within, reminded her of the walled garden at Prospect House. The pang that this memory caused her was enough to make her reach a decision. She watched until the man at the gate stepped out to talk to a carriage driver waiting at the road-side, the horse tossing its head and stamping impatiently as it waited for the occupants to return. While he was distracted, Molly slipped through the gate and quickly made a patrol of the grounds, trying to look as though she had a reason to be there. There didn't appear to be any other visitors, just men at work in the borders.

She followed the path unchallenged, for the gardeners were absorbed in what they were doing. It wasn't the countryside, but neither was it a park. It would do well enough, if she could remain there undetected. Wondering at her own boldness, Molly walked until she came to a secluded seat, out of view of the house that lay behind her. She could hear the slap of the Thames as it rolled past the long wall edging one side of the garden and she could sniff the familiar smell of it that seemed to come and go with the tide's ebb and flow. The sun's rays warmed her as she sat there, so she cast off her shawl and, listening to the birds singing from the surrounding trees, began to feel drowsy.

Unbidden, further memories returned of her time spent in the Prospect House gardens, with Charlie and Mr Fleming and, latterly, her sisters and Harriet. She tried to push them away but they were stubbornly persistent. She could hear her sisters' voices and see their faces, then Charlie came into view, a smile crossing his face as he picked up little Harriet and lifted her so that she could smell the fragrance from one of the roses tumbling over the wall. She squealed as she disturbed a bee and Molly laughed out loud, then opened her eyes with a start. She must have drifted into sleep – but for how long? She sat quietly for a moment, gathering her thoughts. The sun had barely changed position so she felt sure that little time had passed and it was safe to stay longer.

The memories had unsettled her. She had successfully blocked out all thoughts of her family, of Margate and Charlie. Now, reminded of Charlie's open, honest face, she felt a deep sense of shame. He had been a good friend to her in Margate. How could she have treated him in such a cavalier fashion when he had tried, in his halting way, to suggest they might have a future together? She buried her face in her hands as she remembered the expression on his face when she, impatient at what she saw as an inconvenient disturbance of her plan to marry Nicholas, had callously dismissed his attempt. She had brushed it away, under the spell of the great things she had imagined for herself, when she should have listened to him. How different would her life have been if she had accepted his offer?

Molly stood up suddenly. She couldn't afford to follow that line of thinking. It was all gone, lost to her, and she could only pursue the path that she was set on now. Becoming conscious of voices nearby and fearing discovery, she retraced her steps, finding as she did so that other people had now appeared in the garden. She walked slowly, stopping to look at the plants in the borders, and observed the visitors. They were not the sort she was familiar with from the parks. They didn't stroll the paths, chatting and admiring the occasional flower, or sit on the benches and gaze around. Instead, they got in among the plants, jotting notes in little books they carried with them. Some of them cut specimens, which they carried away to the grand building that sat beside the main gate.

Taking her cue from them, Molly walked briskly back to the main gate, nodded to the man standing there and went out into the road. She explored the streets immediately adjacent to the walled garden, finding a market nearby, a very small affair in comparison to the one in Covent Garden but it furnished her with an apple and a pastry, for she was hungry. Then she made her way back to Bishop's Stairs to look out for Walter, not wanting to miss him, but with plenty to muse on while she waited.

CHAPTER FIFTY-FIVE

Hester feared that the trip to Chelsea had dampened Molly's spirits rather than raised them, for she was quiet afterwards and not keen to relay what she had done. But the next day Hester had some news she couldn't wait to share.

'I've had a letter from Matthew.' She brandished the closely written single sheet. 'He says he will be on board ship by the time we read this. And he has enclosed his likeness.'

Hester held out a small card rectangle to Molly who took it, fingers suddenly trembling. The girls present in the bar crowded round Molly as she gazed at the portrait. The painted oval depicted a slim, fair-haired unsmiling young man with pale blue eyes. He wasn't ugly, Molly noted with relief, or fat – two characteristics she had thought inevitable in this strange arrangement. He wasn't unpleasing to the eye, but there was nothing to mark him out as engaging. The portraitist had failed to capture his character, she decided, but the girls were very taken with what they saw.

'Oh, Molly, how lucky you are!'

'How handsome he is!'

'When will we meet him?'

Hester wasn't sure of the answer to that. 'I don't know how far he follows behind the letter. I believe the journey can be anything from four to six months.' She looked again at the letter's date. 'So I suppose we should expect him anytime between now and September.'

Molly immediately began to calculate whether she might have sufficient money to pay as recompense for George's care. She wondered when she should go to the Foundling Hospital to tell them of her plans. They would need to send to the country for him and would surely require some notice.

Her thoughts were interrupted by Hester, who insisted on reading excerpts of her nephew's letter to the whole bar.

'*I hope that the girl you have found me will be obedient and not averse to hard work.*' Hester paused to assure Molly that she had given a very good account of her to Matthew. '*It is a shame that you haven't been able to furnish me with a likeness of her but I must curb my impatience until I can be with you. I can stay only a fortnight before we must journey back so the marriage must be contracted with some haste. I know, dear Aunt, that I can leave this in your capable hands.*'

Hester was beaming at the way her plans were coming so nicely to fruition, but Molly was struck by the prospect of the long sea voyage before she would see her new home. It wasn't something she welcomed but it must be endured for the sake of George's future.

As the weeks rolled by, Molly went about her daily routine in a mechanical fashion. She had tacked the portrait of Matthew to the wall beside her bed, in the hope that she would grow to look on his countenance with pleasure. She wished now that she had been able to write privately to him during the year that had passed since the question of marriage had arisen. Instead, she had to rely on whatever Hester chose to share with her from the letters between the two of them. Molly would have liked to discuss Matthew's plans for George with him, and to ask what kind of clothes she and her son would require for their new life in a different climate.

She'd been persuaded by Hester that it would be rash to approach the Foundling Hospital to arrange for George's return to her before Matthew arrived in London. 'He may be delayed on his journey and, in any case, they will not release George to you until they have proof of your marriage and changed circumstances.'

Molly had to concede that she was right. She forced herself to go through the motions of the daily routine at the Waterman's Arms and, to distract herself from nervous anticipation of Matthew's arrival, she continued to visit the gardens she had discovered in Chelsea whenever she could. She made her arrangements privately with Walter, and told herself that she was becoming more used to being on the river. Still, though, she felt herself too close to the water and, despite the obvious skill of her oarsman, she was always glad to gain dry land. A ship to India would be a different matter, she told herself firmly, although inwardly she quailed at the thought of weeks on end at sea.

Molly had discovered that she could enter the Chelsea garden unchallenged, by simply walking in as though she had every right to be there. The man on the gate greeted her with a nod and stepped aside, allowing her free passage. She took great joy in the garden, searching out her secluded seat and allowing herself to daydream of her life to come with George. It wasn't lost on her that Matthew, the pale ghost of her portrait, didn't figure in any of her imaginings. She told herself that this failure was solely because she had never met him.

Charlie, however, appeared to her every time she visited, although in memories only. She tried to blot out their last

338

unhappy encounter at Woodchurch Manor and to concentrate instead on happier times in the Prospect House gardens. She wondered where he was now, supposing he must still be working at Woodchurch Manor. She told herself that she hoped he had found a wife and was struck, for a moment, by the thought that he might have taken up with her sister Lizzie after she left. Then she pushed away the thought, impatient with herself. Matthew's arrival couldn't come quickly enough, for it would surely put an end to all the uncertainty in her life.

It turned out to be a long wait, which tested Molly to the limits of her patience. August had arrived before she was to meet her husband-to-be. The hot summer weather meant that she flung the doors of the Waterman's Arms wide open as soon as she began her morning's duties, to let in any lingering coolness from the night air. By midmorning, any benefit from a breeze was lost as the streets heated and a stench arose from the river, creeping into the bar to fill every corner. Despite the heat, the watermen took to rowing with neckerchiefs pulled up to cover their noses and mouths, and complained bitterly that they couldn't be rid of the smell 'even when we're trying to get away from it and have a sup of ale'.

Into this foetid soup on a particularly hot weekday morning came a stranger in a fitted jacket and breeches, looking most out of place among the watermen in their working garb. The bright sunlight behind him turned him into a silhouette as he stood at the bar, and, 'Can I help you?' came out of Molly's mouth – she thought he must have entered the inn by mistake – before recognition dawned.

Matthew, however, had little knowledge of his intended so Molly had the advantage of him, being able to observe him and garner some first impressions without being scrutinised in turn.

'I'm here to see my aunt, Hester Stanton.' The tone was sharp, impatient. Molly noted that he cast her barely a glance but was already drumming his fingers on the counter.

'It may be a little early for her but I'll see if she's awake,' Molly said, purposely avoiding the use of 'sir' when addressing him, although he surely expected it. She turned away from him, asking Sophy to keep an eye on the bar while she hastened up the stairs to wake Hester.

Once Hester had understood that Matthew had finally appeared, she could barely contain her excitement. 'Why didn't he send word?' she exclaimed, as she stood, indecisive, in her nightclothes in the middle of the bedchamber. 'Bring him up to my parlour at once. Have some coffee served to him. You must sit with him until I'm ready.'

'I'm not sure that would be right.' Molly had a sense that, as he was to be her betrothed, her first proper meeting with Matthew should be under the eye of a chaperone.

'Nonsense!' snapped Hester, thoroughly discomforted at being caught unprepared for his arrival. 'Go away and get on with it.'

So Molly returned to the bar where, seeing Matthew happily engaged in conversation with Sophy, she left them to it and prepared coffee from Hester's private stock, taking a tray up to the parlour before returning to collect Matthew.

'Your aunt will be with you shortly but she asked me to bring you up to her parlour to wait there for her.' Molly noted that Matthew seemed reluctant to part from Sophy but her insistence that the parlour was 'a more fitting place for a gentleman to wait,' appeared to please him, so he followed her up the stairs.

When he was seated and the coffee poured, she blurted out, 'I believe your aunt has told you a little about me. My name is Molly and I'm to be ...' She was at a loss as to how to go on.

An expression of disappointment crossed Matthew's face. 'Ah, *you're* Molly. I thought the girl downstairs ... But now I remember. *The girl with the chestnut hair.*'

Molly looked puzzled.

'That's how my aunt described you in her letter,' Matthew explained. 'So, Molly, are you equipped for a life in India, do you think? You will find it very different from anything you've known here.'

Molly had remained standing since pouring the coffee and Matthew hadn't invited her to sit. She felt as if she was being interviewed for a position she had believed to be already hers. This was not at all how she had imagined it. 'I'm afraid I do not know what to expect.' This time, she had to stop herself adding 'sir'. 'Perhaps you could enlighten me.'

Before Matthew could reply, Hester burst into the parlour, all fluster and effusiveness. 'My dear Matthew! It's so good to see you at last. How was the journey? Tiring, I'm sure. And you and Molly have already met, I see. There is so much to be done before both of you must return. But let's not talk of that yet, with you so newly arrived.'

Molly, hovering awkwardly, found herself ignored. She wasn't sure whether to stay or go but, deciding that Hester and her nephew must have some catching up to do, she slipped out of the room and back down to the bar, where she found Sophy, full of excitement.

'So he's here at last! What do you think? He's very nice, isn't he? How lucky you are!'

'I hardly know what to think.' Molly felt quite put out, then rallied. 'I'm sure once we've had chance to get to know

341

each other properly …' She tailed off, glad that an influx of customers put paid to any further conversation.

CHAPTER FIFTY-SIX

T he landlady didn't make her usual appearance to check on the bar but at the end of her shift Molly found herself summoned back to the parlour, where Hester and Matthew had already dined. Hester asked Molly to clear away the dishes, then to return. Feeling on the back foot once more, Molly did as she was told. Then, finally, she found herself seated at the table with Hester and Matthew.

'Matthew and I have discussed matters, Molly. We think the wedding should take place at the end of next week, and you can both be on board ship by Sunday, ready for the return journey. He cannot be spared from his post any longer.'

'But I'm not sure that will allow enough time to make the arrangements for George.' Molly's mind was in a whirl.

'Ah, George ...' Hester looked uncomfortable and Matthew hadn't yet spoken.

'Matthew isn't inclined to think that it will sit well with his employers if his new bride already has the encumbrance of a child.'

Molly stared at them both, uncomprehending.

'Matthew will be taking up a new position on his return. The accommodation will be entirely unsuitable for an infant,' Hester continued.

'The climate, you know. Not suited at all.' Matthew nodded.

'But,' Hester added hastily, 'Matthew has made a very generous suggestion. He will fund the child's care here, in London, by a suitable family under my supervision. So he will no longer be a foundling.'

Molly spoke at last. 'You mean that I will not be permitted to have George with me?'

'In short, no,' Matthew said.

Molly could barely hide her feelings of dislike for Matthew, feelings that were growing by the minute. His clipped way of speaking, the fussy way in which he fiddled with the frilled cuffs of his shirt, smoothing and rearranging them, had already irritated her, but his blatant disregard for her told her all she needed to know. The whole of the last year had been wasted. She had been tricked, for whatever reason, into believing that if she married this man she would be reunited with her son.

Living in another country, far away from George, would be worse than the position she was in at the moment. She wasn't even sure that she trusted Hester to do as she said with regard to George's welfare. But she held back what she wanted to say. She needed to work out what to do next.

Molly excused herself from Hester and Matthew's presence, citing tiredness at the end of her day's work, then hurriedly sought out Grace. She was in desperate need of someone else's opinion on the matter. But Grace had already spoken to Sophy.

'He sounds like a wonderful prospect,' Grace said. 'How lucky you are.'

When Molly told her that the wedding was now supposed to take place within the week and they would sail by the following weekend, Grace's face fell.

'So soon. We will miss you here, Molly.'

Even Molly's explanation of the new plan regarding George didn't dampen Grace's enthusiasm.

'Well, it's not to be quite as you hoped but surely it's still good news.'

Molly shook her head and tried to explain, but Grace cut her off and went to serve a customer. The memory of Hester's words stayed with Molly. *The encumbrance of a child.* It was not what she had hoped to hear from the man she was supposed to marry. Whatever was she going to do now?

That night, Molly went to bed early with a sick headache. There had been no further opportunity to spend time with Matthew, for he'd been closeted all day with Hester. She looked hard at his portrait before she climbed into bed, hoping to kindle some warm feelings towards him. It didn't work. The artist had been generous, she thought. Matthew's lips were thinner and his eyes even colder than in the portrait.

Molly awoke with a start in what felt like the middle of the night, shaken awake by Grace.

'You were right, Molly,' she said, in a fierce whisper. 'He's not a nice man. I fear you must tread very carefully.' She shook her head, tight-lipped, when Molly tried to question her and hurried away to her own bed. Molly was left to toss and turn and wonder whatever Grace could have meant. It was only as she rose, somewhat earlier than usual because it felt pointless to lie sleepless any longer, that she noticed Sophy's bed was empty.

A conviction gripped her that she found impossible to shake off. Barefoot, she crept out of the attic dormitory, down one flight of stairs and along the landing to the bedroom where she had first slept when she arrived at the Waterman's Arms.

Holding her breath, she gently turned the handle of the

door, hoping it was neither locked nor liable to creak. It swung open slightly, revealing two heads on the pale pillow-slips, one fair, the other with long, dark hair. Matthew and Sophy. Molly let the door close softly, then continued, in her nightdress and bare feet, to the bar. She stood on tiptoe in the fireplace, feeling the warmth still lingering on the flags under her feet, and found the loose brick with her fingertips. She eased it out and felt in the cavity for the money pouch. She would take it and go, before anyone else awoke. The long-awaited marriage would not now take place and she must start out again. The thought chilled her, but she was certain.

Her groping fingers found nothing. She felt around again, thinking the brick must have pushed the pouch too far back. Nothing. The pouch had gone. Hester must have watched her on the night she had prevented her leaving the inn. She must have allowed her to keep adding to the savings, biding her time. Yesterday, Hester must have realised how unhappy Molly was with the deal presented to her. She had known that Molly would seek out the money and leave, so she had taken it first.

Molly felt sick. She looked at the brick in her hand and a great rage filled her. Hester, Matthew, Sophy: they had all done her wrong. Hester had stolen her savings and the other two had stolen her future.

Chapter Fifty-Seven

Molly walked swiftly down to the Old Swan Stairs. She hoped Walter would still be at work there and that he would agree to her request. She clutched her bundle tightly to her. It held the two dresses Hester's dressmaker had made up for her when she was first employed at the Waterman's Arms, well-worn but still serviceable. And wrapped within a cream woollen blanket were the proofs of the tokens she had left at the Foundling Hospital – the cut playing card and the handkerchief with its corner missing.

She had little idea what to do next, other than to get as far away as possible from the inn. The Old Swan Stairs were just visible through the morning mist lying low across the river. She could make out old Walter hunched in his greatcoat in the boat and she quickened her steps. He didn't deserve to have his good nature taken advantage of, but she didn't know what else to do.

Walter grumbled, unwilling to make a trip upriver when he was thinking of his bed after working through the night, but Molly had pleaded. It was the eeriest journey she had ever undertaken on the river, the mist swirling around them as Walter pulled on the oars. One or two other boats loomed out of the mist and slid silently past, without the usual greetings between the boatmen. The water slapping against the sides of the craft and the bank echoed strangely and Molly shivered, wrapping her shawl more tightly around her.

The sun was rising higher in the sky as they pulled into Bishop's Stairs and the mist curled and lifted as the air began to warm.

'You'll have to take a ride back with some other boat today,' Walter said. He was still grumpy and the journey had been conducted in silence.

'That's all right, Walter. I'm not going back.'

The waterman's head, bent over the oars once more as he readied himself to return, snapped up.

'And, Walter, I'm very sorry but I have no money to give you. Please ask Grace to pay you what I owe. But don't mention to Hester, or anyone other than Grace, that you've seen me today. Will you do that for me?'

Walter's grumpy expression had softened. 'Aye, and I wish you good luck, Molly,' was all he said, as he pulled on the oars and guided the boat back towards the city.

Molly stood on the road and looked towards the gardens. It was too early for them to be open, she thought, but she would walk by, just in case.

'Morning, miss. You're early. I almost didn't recognise you with the curl in your hair.'

Molly had been planning to walk around the area until the gardens opened but the gatekeeper was just pulling back the heavy wooden door as she passed. She flushed at his words and her hand went up to her hair: the dampness of the mist had curled it into tendrils around her face.

'You'll not find it as quiet as usual. It's a public open day,' the man went on, as he looped a heavy chain through the door handle to hold it back. He waved her through. 'It'll be another hot one, once this mist has cleared. You go on in and enjoy it while it's nice and peaceful.'

Molly smiled her thanks and hurried past, half fearful that he might ask her more searching questions about her business there, since he had become so friendly, before she remembered that he had said it was a public open day. For the first time, she had as much right as anyone else to be there.

Her footsteps took her automatically in the direction of the secluded bench, but she stopped first to look at the pomegranate tree. She had noticed it on her second visit to the garden, but hadn't recognised it for what it was, drawn to it by the vivid orange-red flowers. It was only when these were replaced by fruit, which began to swell, that she wondered. These fruits were much smaller than the pomegranate she had seen in Mrs Dobbs's kitchen. Their shape and colour and the texture of the skin was right but they were less than a quarter of the size of the fruit she remembered. She had had no idea that the pomegranate, which seemed so exotic, might grow in England, and it gave her a jolt of surprise, like seeing an old friend when you least expected it. One by one, though, the fruits had withered and fallen, and today she could spot only one still hanging there.

Disappointed, Molly turned her steps towards the bench. She had kept her worries in check throughout the boat journey, hoping that things might become clearer once she had reached the peace of the garden. She could feel them now, though, lurking at the edge of her consciousness.

She reached the bench and sat down, placing the bundle beside her. The beautiful morning, the birdsong and the familiar slap of the river on the other side of the wall were lost in the tidal wave of rage and misery that came rolling in on her.

Her savings had been stolen from her, she had not a farthing to her name and all hope was lost of a reunion with George. She cared not a jot about Matthew or the promised life in India and she wondered why Hester had ever drawn her into that scheme. None of it made sense to Molly. Had Hester been trying to gain favour with Matthew's father, her elder brother? He had clearly done rather better for himself than his younger siblings, Bartholomew and Hester. Or did she have a secret wish that she herself might be invited to join Matthew and his new bride in India? She had certainly been very enthusiastic about everything Matthew had said of the country in his letters. Was it possible that Matthew had a past history that made him unmarriageable, either in India or at home, something that Hester could be certain Molly would be unaware of? After all, although it had been impressed on Molly that Matthew wanted a wife of good character, it had taken just a few hours in his aunt's inn to show that he was more careless of his own reputation.

And now, as if that wasn't enough, Hester had got her hands on Molly's savings. Molly had a feeling that if the marriage had gone ahead, Hester would have taken them anyway, citing wedding expenses or the need to pay towards George's care.

She had considered waking her that morning and demanding the return of her money, but feared that Hester would call for Matthew and, between the two of them, they would have kept her under lock and key until the wedding could take place. Molly felt her cheeks burn with rage. She should have acted on her first impulse, which was to dash out their brains. She could have taken her money then and she wouldn't be in this mess. But she had known in an instant that it was beyond her to do such a thing, no matter what they had done to her.

Tears started to her eyes as she thought about George and she gave in to the despair she had been holding at bay. She had so longed to be able to send for him and now all her plans were in ruins. All that time wasted, all her money gone and no stable home to persuade the Foundling Hospital to release him to her. She must start all over again. First, though, she must find work, and find it quickly, for she had nowhere to sleep that night.

In the back of her mind was the thought that, if all else failed, she could hide in the gardens and sleep there. When she had explored them during her earlier visits, she had spotted a spreading shrub, the height of the wall and as wide as it was high, close to the glasshouse where the gardeners often worked. Its branches touched the ground and, bending low, she'd peered in and seen how they formed a chamber within, lined with dry leaves. She'd thought at the time that children would enjoy playing in it, but now it offered her a sort of sanctuary.

Molly had come to the gardens in the hope that their peace would bring her clarity of mind and the idea that they might offer her shelter was an attractive one. She'd have to be careful not to be seen by the gardeners but she'd already become quite familiar with their movements around the garden, and the times they arrived and left. She would go now and leave her bundle underneath the shrub, she decided. Then she would ask at the local inns for work. If she was successful, she could return and collect it.

Chapter Fifty-Eight

Decision made, Molly's spirits lifted a little and she rose to make her way towards the glasshouse. She took a quick look around to check whether anyone was nearby, then slipped around the back of the shrub, ducking beneath its branches. She tucked her bundle behind the trunk, then crouched in the shade, listening for a moment, before backing out the way she had come. Molly paused once more, pressed up against the wall. Hearing neither voices nor footsteps, she edged out, brushing herself free of dry leaves.

She was keen to avoid being noticed by the gatekeeper as she left, but he was busy dealing with an influx of visitors and she slipped out unnoticed. Her spirits remained high as she walked along the road, staying close to the wall of the garden. It wouldn't do to get lost in the area and she must pay attention to where her search led her, but she had the river to guide her. As long as it remained nearby she felt sure that she could find her way back.

The first inn was situated only a little way along the road and, as Molly approached it, doubt crept in. She stood at the door, unsure whether to ask for work at the bar or go to the back entrance. Reasoning that it was still early and the bar wouldn't be busy, she pushed the door open and stepped inside. The contrast of the gloom of the interior with the brightness of the street meant it was a moment or two before she made out a solitary figure – a girl – wiping the wooden counter. The only other occupant of the room was an elderly man asleep in the corner, a mug of ale in front of him.

Molly approached the bar, aware all at once of how fast her heart was beating. She had never been in the position of asking for work before – it had found its way to her. Although it had not always been the best kind of work, she thought wryly.

The girl looked up, waiting for Molly's order.

'I'm looking for work,' Molly said. 'I have experience behind a bar, serving customers, handling money, opening up in the morning and closing …' She tailed off, conscious of the girl scrutinising her.

'We don't need no one, sorry,' the girl said, and carried on with her cleaning.

'Could I speak to the landlord? Or landlady?' Molly persisted.

The girl glared at her. 'We don't need no one,' she repeated. 'There's me and another girl. The potboy, too. And Mrs Beale, the landlady, and her daughter. They're both sleeping. You're wasting your time.'

She turned her back on Molly, who stood for a moment, irresolute, then left. From now on, she vowed, she would bypass the serving staff and ask for the landlord or landlady. This tactic proved successful at the next inn, but when the landlord asked who would vouch for her character, Molly was silent.

'Well?' he asked, bushy eyebrows drawn together in a frown.

'I worked at my last place for a long time – nearly two

years – but when I left I didn't think to ask for …' Molly halted, trying not to blush.

'Did you leave or were you thrown out?' the landlord asked. 'Dishonest, were you? If no one can give you a character there'll be no jobs to be had, my girl.' He stood and glared at her until she left.

Disheartened, Molly tried three or four other inns in the area, only to be met with the same response. Try as she might, she couldn't come up with a good enough reason as to why she lacked an account of her character. By then it was late afternoon and Molly found herself on the edge of the market where just a few fruit and vegetable stalls remained, now packing up for the day. Molly was hungry, but she had no money to buy anything. She bit her lip as tears sprang to her eyes. Her predicament was dawning on her. No work meant no money. No money meant no food, let alone a bed for the night.

As she hurried along, head bent, eager to get away from the place, an apple rolled almost to her feet. It had fallen from a basket being loaded on to a hand barrow. Darting a quick look around, Molly bent and picked it up, quickly hiding it in her hand. The stallholder hadn't noticed its loss and she reasoned that it would be bruised anyway, and worthless to him. Even as she tried to shake off the shame of having scavenged it, she was casting around to see whether she could spot anything else on the ground.

Her examination of the cobblestones provided some unexpected bounty, in the form of a couple of farthings glinting where the sun caught their edges. Molly had to scrabble to dislodge them from their resting places, for they had become firmly stuck by the passage of carts. Her prize was enough to buy her a small bread roll from the baker's and with this, and the apple, she made her way back to the garden gate.

The public open day had attracted a good many visitors, curious to see what lay beyond the high walls, and Molly found it easy enough to merge with a small group so that she could re-enter without causing the gatekeeper to remark on it. She strolled in the direction of the glasshouse, taking care to pause every now and then as if she was a regular visitor, all the while aware of the dull ache of hunger in her belly.

She loitered in the vicinity of the glasshouse until she was sure she wouldn't be observed, then slipped around the back of the shrub and into the safety of her leaf-carpeted chamber. She tucked herself away within it, staying as close to the back wall as possible and hoping there wouldn't be any inquisitive children among the visitors that afternoon. If her hiding place should be discovered, she didn't like to think of the consequences.

Despite her hunger, she ate the bread and apple surreptitiously, fearful of being heard from the path. As the afternoon wore on and it became clear to Molly that few visitors progressed to that part of the garden, she began to relax. She closed her eyes, weary after her broken night and, lulled by the distant snatches of conversation and laughter, drifted into sleep.

She awoke with a start some time later, instantly on the alert, wondering what had disturbed her. It turned out to be nothing more sinister than a blackbird, scuffling among the leaves. Only then did it dawn on Molly that the garden was silent – or, rather, quiet, for the only sound she could hear was birdsong. The visitors must have left, the garden now closed for the day. She was glad to venture out and stretch herself, for her quarters were a little cramped, but every rustle of the trees caused her to start anxiously and look around.

Once she was convinced that she was alone in the garden she made her way to the secluded bench. It was time to face up to her predicament. Leaving the Waterman's Arms as she had done had put her in a very difficult position. Yet what was her alternative if she had stayed? A rushed marriage to Matthew followed by exile to India, without George.

She was convinced that she had done the right thing, but now she found herself without work. And, with no proof of her good character, she could think of only one kind of work that might be open to her: work that she had already refused twice in her short life. The image of Mrs Dobbs and the house in Half Moon Street came at once, unbidden, to her mind. Molly stared at the ground, unable even to cry, for what good would it do?

The smell of the river and the slap of the water on the other side of the wall penetrated her consciousness. A boat must be passing, or the tide must be on the turn. It came to her then that she could cast herself into the river, letting it take her where it would. She wouldn't last long in the muddy swirl, weighted down by her sodden clothes. No one would miss her – she was no use to anyone. She had failed George: she would never be able to make up the money she had lost, never be able to get him back. He was better off never having known her.

Molly didn't know how long she sat there, her mind numb now that a solution had presented itself to her. Heavy drops of rain brought her out of her stupor and, looking up, she saw that dark clouds had driven the sun from the sky. She was trapped in the garden for now: she would have to wait until the morning to put her plan into action.

The night, spent huddled in the shelter of the huge shrub, was a long one. The thick foliage kept out the worst of the rain but lightning flashed across the garden and thunder rolled, terrifying Molly so that she shrank back and pressed herself closer to the ground. It was only as the storm receded that she fell into a fitful sleep, waking at dawn cold and cramped. Confident that no one would be around at such an early hour, she crawled out from beneath the shrub, impatient to stretch her limbs.

She crossed her arms and rubbed them vigorously in an attempt to get her blood flowing and chase the numbness from her body. The sun was rising but there was a damp chill in the air: the aftermath of the storm but also a sure sign that autumn was on its way. As feeling gradually returned to her limbs, Molly became aware of a desperate need to relieve herself. She glanced around, then chose another substantial shrub, as far away as possible from her hiding place. Squatting down, she lifted her skirts with a deep sense of shame. This was a public garden, not a midden.

She hastened to remove herself from the scene, her legs – still a little stiff from her overnight confinement – taking her in the direction of the pomegranate tree. She wondered whether the remaining fruit had survived the night. It was only when she saw the bare branch, the final fruit dashed to the ground by the rain, that she remembered the decision she had made last night.

Was this to be it, then? Her last day? And if it was, who would miss her? No one – not her family, for she had been lost to them for two years now. Not her darling George – he had no doubt already forgotten her and had a new mother to care for him. She had no one. Molly turned her steps back towards her hiding place, automatically seeking out her bundle. Despite her intentions, she would take it with her for it contained the only things she held dear, her only memories of George.

Her bundle safely retrieved, Molly knew it was time to leave her place of sanctuary. The gates would be open very soon. With the sun in her eyes, she almost didn't see that a man stood on the path before her and was looking right at her. She stopped and stared back at him, heart racing in shock. Even as she wondered what on earth she could say to him to excuse her presence she was also thinking that she had, finally, lost her mind. For wasn't this Charlie standing before her in the garden? Older and a little more filled out than when she had last seen him, but otherwise it was surely him. But he was in Kent, working at Woodchurch Manor. What business could he have here?

The man spoke, and it confirmed Molly's belief. The voice was deeper and the tone was harsher than she had ever heard him use but it was definitely Charlie.

'Who are you? What are you doing here?' he demanded.

Molly, taken aback, didn't know what to do. He hadn't recognised her, and she supposed she must be much changed. Eager to get away, she made to move past him towards the gate.

Charlie, seeing that she was poised to flee, spoke again, in a softer tone. 'I'm sorry,' he said, his eyes sweeping her up and down. 'I didn't mean to speak so rudely. You took me by surprise. I wasn't expecting to see anyone here at this early hour.'

He glanced in the direction of the gate. 'It must be later than I thought. Please forgive me.'

He nodded at her and made to step around her on the

path. Then he stopped, looked straight into her eyes and gasped. 'Molly!' he said. Then again, more hesitant, 'Molly?'

Part Six

August 1791–April 1792

CHAPTER FIFTY-NINE

C harlie's trips away from the garden at Woodchurch Manor had increased in frequency as his employer, Mr Henry Powell, had become interested in expanding the range of species that grew in the garden. He'd seen that this impressed his visitors from London and so, while his main interest lay in his art collection, he was increasingly to be found in the garden with Charlie and Mr Mawson discussing what else they might acquire.

With this end in view, Charlie had found himself travelling south to Cornwall and north to Yorkshire, examining gardens and collections, but of late he had been back and forth to the village of Chelsea, on the edge of London, to consult with John Fairbairn, the head gardener at the Apothecaries' Garden. He specialised in cultivating plants from around the world and he had been nurturing some specimens for Charlie, having taken a shine to the enthusiastic young man.

Charlie was lodging, as usual, at the Paradise Inn on Paradise Row, which ran alongside the Apothecaries' Garden. It meant he could spend long hours in the garden, from dawn until long after dusk had fallen. The landlady at the inn had a daughter, Isabel, and Charlie knew he received preferential treatment there because of it. Mrs Beale hoped he might be taken with her daughter and make an offer to wed her.

Charlie knew he could offer only disappointment. He had discovered himself in similar situations more than once during his journeys around the country, and occasionally he had been happy to partake of what was on offer, but love was never part of the bargain. His heart had felt as if encased in ice since that moment over two years earlier when Molly had turned him down in the first room he had ever been able to call his own, above the stables in Woodchurch Manor.

Since then, all his devotion had been poured into his work, to the benefit of Mr Powell's garden. Charlie knew that his employer and Mr Mawson had discussed trying to find a local girl who might catch his eye, for Mr Powell was worried that Charlie would leave, tempted by what the gardens elsewhere might have to offer. A wife and family would be an anchor, and to that end Mr Powell had also improved his accommodation: Charlie was now living in one of the very same houses that he had tried to tempt Molly with all those months ago. It felt too large for just one person, especially one who spent long hours in the garden, returning home only when he was in need of his bed. If truth be told, he would have preferred to remain in his old room, over the stables.

Despite his attempts to shut Molly from his mind, he sometimes awoke with a start from a dream in which she had appeared to him. Usually, it was a tangled web in which he could barely discern any meaning but he always woke at the same point: a vision of Molly, grown ever more beautiful, turning towards him.

He had arrived in the Apothecaries' Garden that morning rather too early for his appointment with John Fairbairn, impatient to discover whether the specimens that the gardener was nurturing for him were ready to be transported to Woodchurch Manor. He was on his way to view the pomegranate, Mr Fairbairn being the only man Charlie knew who had managed to grow a tree to maturity, when he was startled to discover someone who was quite clearly not one of the gardeners on the path in front of him. She carried a bundle and he wondered for an instant whether she had spent the night hidden somewhere in the garden.

He had spoken harshly, taken by surprise, and she had turned as if to flee. Something about her movement, and the colour of her hair, chestnut in the sun, struck a chord. It was only as he drew level with her, and looked into her face, that recognition dawned. The shock was so great that he could speak only her name – first as a statement, then as a question. Then he shot out his hand and caught her wrist. 'It's me – Charlie. Don't be afraid.' Had she recognised him? He wasn't sure. But he didn't have a moment's doubt that the woman he had once loved was there, caught in his grip, and he was desperate to prevent her leaving.

He had tried to shut Molly from his mind after she had turned him down at Woodchurch Manor, but he couldn't help enquiring after her when, by chance, he met her sister Lizzie on one of his infrequent visits to Margate. Lizzie's eyes had filled with tears as she'd told him that Molly had gone, no one knew where, vanished at dead of night. Some folks said she'd gone to Chatham, others to London, while a few spoke in hushed tones of her journeying to France. Lizzie had tried to get answers but neither her father nor her aunt and uncle had seemed able – or prepared – to furnish her with any.

Charlie had been shocked at the news. Why had Molly fled in that way? What had happened to her? Then, back at Woodchurch Manor and thinking on it as he'd worked in the gardens, he'd reasoned her disappearance must have been part of the plan she'd mentioned to him. *I don't intend*

365

to spend the rest of my life here. Wasn't that what she'd said? And so perhaps there was no great mystery involved in her disappearance after all, he thought. He'd tried hard to put her out of his mind but she was lodged firmly there, never away from him for more than a few days at a time.

And now she was before him, looking pale and tired, her eyes a little red as though she had been weeping. She was thinner than he remembered, he noticed, suddenly realising that he was still grasping her wrist, the bones fragile beneath his fingers. He let her go and stepped back, glancing at her bundle and wondering why she was carrying it. It was as if he had been her anchor, though, for even as his hand dropped to his side she began to sway, her face now alarmingly pale. His arm shot out again and this time he grasped her elbow and supported her back to the bench she had only recently left. She leant against his shoulder as they sat there and they remained so for some minutes, Molly still silent and Charlie's mind working furiously.

Finally, Charlie shifted slightly to look into her face. 'Molly, I don't know what's wrong but you don't need to say anything. I'm going to take you somewhere safe where you can rest and recover. It's nearby and I'll have to come back here to conduct some business but once that's done I will come to you. Now, let's see if you can stand.'

Charlie didn't bother to ask Molly whether this suited her. He wasn't sure that he would get an answer, in any case, and he feared losing her once more to the streets of London if he didn't take this action. He supported her to the discreet wooden door by the glasshouse that the gardeners used to come and go. Wordless, she walked at his side.

He was dimly aware of a few curious glances from passers-by as they made their way along Paradise Row but he was preoccupied, wondering how he was going to present her to his landlady, Mrs Beale, at the inn. In the end, he settled on a firm tone that brooked no argument.

'Mrs Beale,' he greeted her, as they walked in, 'I need you to find a room for this lady. She is a friend of mine from Margate whom I haven't seen for a long while and she is unwell.'

Mrs Beale's expression at the word 'lady' made it quite plain that she didn't agree with his description, but Molly's head was bent and she was gazing at her feet so the landlady's scorn passed unnoticed.

'I think Miss Goodchild ...' Charlie faltered slightly over her name, wondering whether it was still correct '... needs rest. I'm sure your establishment is the best place to provide it.'

Mrs Beale bridled at the flattery but still seemed a little reluctant. Charlie gave her no chance to object. 'You will, of course, be recompensed,' he said. 'I have to return to the gardens, but Molly – Miss Goodchild – and I will dine together tonight.' He looked thoughtfully at Molly. 'And perhaps you might find her something to eat now.'

Mrs Beale sighed noisily and called for the girl, Agnes. 'A cup of chocolate and some bread and butter for Mr Dawson's companion,' she said, when Agnes poked her head through from the kitchen. 'Then take her up to the room next to yours. It's the only one we have free so it will have to do,' she said by way of explanation to Charlie.

He nodded, paying no heed to his landlady's irritation, then turned his thoughts back to John Fairbairn. He would be waiting and wondering at Charlie's unusual tardiness.

'Molly, I will see you later. Please try to rest,' he said. Now that he had found her again he didn't want to leave her there, pale and silent, but he had no choice. He hurried out into the sunshine, for the first time ever impatient to have this much-anticipated visit to the Apothecaries' Garden over and done with.

CHAPTER SIXTY

Charlie's voice had come to Molly as though from a great distance as she stood in the garden, aware that he had grasped her wrist but unsure as to why. It was as though an immense cloud had filled her mind, so that there was no longer any room for sensible thoughts. For a moment, she thought herself back in Margate, in the gardens of Prospect House, and wondered whether they were playing a game. Was it hide-and-seek? Where were Lizzie and Mary? Then the colour had drained out of her surroundings, so that she saw the gardens in shades of grey, and heard a roaring in her ears, as if the river flowing outside the walls had turned into a rushing sea. She had a memory of Charlie helping her back to the bench, then walking with her through the streets to an inn, but all the time she felt so tired. All she wanted to do was lie down and sleep.

A girl called Agnes took her upstairs to a small room, simply furnished with a bed, a chest of drawers, a washstand and a chair, on which she placed Molly's bundle. If Molly had been more aware, she would have recognised Agnes as the first person she had approached, only the day before, about finding work. As it was, before the girl had even left the room, Molly lay down on the bed, fully clothed. She was dimly aware of the door closing, and a click that she knew meant the key had been turned in the lock, before sleep engulfed her.

Molly drifted in and out of sleep over the next few days. She woke once to find herself under the covers, wearing a nightgown, with no memory of how she had come to be there. She woke another time to find Agnes in the room, encouraging her to eat soup, which had appeared before her in a bowl on a tray. She woke in the dark reaches of the night, when the whole inn was abed, and thought to get up and see whether the door had been left unlocked, but fell asleep again before managing to do so. She woke on yet another occasion with a start and checked to see whether her bundle was still there. It was, in the same place on the chair. Another time, voices awoke her and she found three people in the room – the landlady, Charlie and a white-haired bespectacled gentleman. They were talking about her, she knew, but their words became enmeshed in her dreams and she fell asleep once more.

One morning Molly awoke and, for the first time in days, her eyes remained open and she felt no drowsiness. She turned her head to look out of the window, where white clouds were being blown swiftly across a pale blue sky. She turned to look the other way, where her dress hung from a peg on the wall. The sight of the wash jug and basin made her feel that she must make a move to get up. As she washed, she caught sight of herself in the mirror above the washstand. She barely recognised the gaunt face with hollow eyes and limp, lifeless hair.

The fogginess that had clouded her mind had lifted, though. Molly felt better than she had done since coming to this place and memories were returning to her. Memories of Charlie spotting her in what she now knew was the

Apothecaries' Garden, of a bowl of soup, of visitors in this room.

It was time to take up the threads of her life, Molly thought. But she had forgotten about the locked door. When she turned the handle, it wouldn't give. She sat down again on the bed and tried to piece together more of her thoughts.

She thought back to her days prior to seeing Charlie in the garden and found she could not recall them. She couldn't place herself in the garden – why had she been there? Was it by arrangement, to meet Charlie? And, if so, why? She remembered the bundle she had brought with her and jumped up to take it from the chair where it still sat. Would it hold some clues?

She undid the corners of the fabric and the bundle fell open to reveal a knitted blanket, a little grubby around the edges but made from the finest wool. Molly shook it out and saw that it was small – just a baby blanket – and that folded within it was a handkerchief, with one corner cut off, and half a playing card, cut in a complex fashion. She frowned. She knew this meant something but she wasn't sure what it was.

Then Agnes was at the door and when she saw Molly was up and dressed, she looked astonished, but said she would take her downstairs to see Charlie before he left for the Apothecaries' Garden.

'He'll be delighted,' she said. 'He's been fretting about you.'

When Charlie, at breakfast, saw Agnes shepherding Molly towards the table he, too, was astonished. He had been worrying about what to do for the best, fearing he must leave her in the care of Mrs Beale as the end of his week at the Apothecaries' Garden, and his return to Woodchurch

Manor, drew close. Molly had been ill – sleeping for so long that he had wondered whether she would ever wake again.

The doctor he had called in happily turned out to be a most sensible man. He had examined Molly, who had slept throughout the process, and said that it seemed likely she had suffered since Charlie had last seen her. The doctor's belief was that she had been living under some strain for a while and that being in a place of safety might well have caused her mind to shut down, out of a need to restore itself. He also mentioned to Charlie, albeit hesitantly, that there was evidence she had borne a child. He recommended bed rest, small regular meals and a great deal of understanding once she showed signs of recovery. Then the doctor departed, leaving Charlie greatly relieved by his modest bill and his reassuring attitude to what Charlie had feared to be a major collapse.

Charlie's circumstances had changed a great deal since he'd last seen Molly. Mr Powell, the owner of Woodchurch Manor, rewarded him well for his work in the gardens. Even so, the thought of a large bill for the doctor's fees and the prospect of paying for Molly's ongoing care and accommodation at the inn had been a worry to him. Now it appeared that he would be able to take her with him to Woodchurch Manor so he scribbled a hasty note to his employer to inform him that he would be returning not only with new plant specimens for the garden, as expected, but with a convalescing young lady, a friend, whom he had come across in difficult circumstances in Chelsea. He didn't feel the need to elaborate further and it was only when the note had been dispatched that it occurred to him that perhaps Molly would prefer to return to Margate, to her family.

While Agnes hovered nearby, Molly sat with Charlie as

he ate a hasty breakfast, but ate only a little herself. When Charlie revealed his plan to her, that he wished to take her back to Woodchurch Manor the next day – if she felt well enough to travel – so that she could continue to rest there, she was startled. But when he suggested she might think it more fitting to return to her family – her aunt and uncle, or her father – in Margate, she looked puzzled, then shook her head.

Charlie was surprised but didn't pursue it, bidding her to eat and rest well that day. He decided he would speak to her again that evening about returning with him to Woodchurch Manor, then departed for the Apothecaries' Garden, having first privately asked Mrs Beale and Agnes to keep an eye on her in case she should take it into her head to make off.

Mrs Beale was a little stiff with Charlie, feeling he had been neglectful of Isabel since he had appeared at the inn with Molly. Agnes was rather more sympathetic, having made up her mind that Molly was Charlie's long-lost love, whom he was intent on bearing home with him. Since the story hadn't come from a chapbook, however, she was more inclined to predict an unhappy ending but, seeing a handsome tip in it for her at the end of Charlie's stay, she saw no harm in being helpful and doing whatever he asked.

When Charlie returned late that evening, delayed by the need to supervise the packing of the specimens he was taking back to Woodchurch Manor, it was to find Molly waiting at the dinner table, toying with a piece of bread. He noticed that her eyes were red and a little swollen, as if she had been crying. He had barely taken his place opposite her when, to his great surprise, she spoke.

'Charlie, you have been very good to me. Much better than I deserve. But I can't return with you. I … I'm not the person you once knew. I've done things … and things have happened to me … I'm not a good person.' Her words came out in faltering, low tones so Charlie had to bend forwards to catch what she said.

The room was smoky and noisy, with customers calling greetings to each other as they arrived. Agnes bustled back and forth past their table with tankards of ale while Mrs Beale conducted a conversation at full volume with several people at once as she stood behind the bar. Charlie heard Molly's words with a sinking heart but they made no difference to his feelings. He didn't care what had happened in the past. He wanted to take her back with him and look after her for the rest of her life. If she'd have him.

CHAPTER SIXTY-ONE

Agnes had been as good as her word to Charlie and had kept a close eye on Molly that day, taking her out with her after breakfast to the local market where she had errands to run. Molly stayed at Agnes's side, smiling and nodding at the stallholders' banter but saying nothing.

'Paradise Row. It's a lovely name for a road, don't you think?' Agnes said, as they returned to the inn, although she had no expectation of an answer. She had become used to having one-sided conversations with Molly. 'Mrs Beale tells me it's because the inn was once famed far and wide for the ladies that worked there, entertaining the gentlemen. But I prefer to think that for someone it was where their little bit of paradise began.'

She looked wistful and Molly would have replied if her brain could have formulated the words, but they were already stepping into the kitchen and, within moments, Mrs Beale was quizzing Agnes about missing purchases, stirring a memory in Molly that she couldn't quite grasp. She slipped away, back to her room, and lay down on the bed, determined to uncover the memory and explore it further but falling into sleep before she could do so. When she awoke, dusk was falling and she roused herself, splashing her face with cold water and smoothing the creases in her dress. She would go downstairs to see whether Charlie had returned.

Turning to go, she caught sight of the items from her bundle once more: the blanket, the cut playing card and the fragment of cotton lawn. As she stared at them, it was as if a door opened in her mind and all the memories – good and bad, all suppressed – came tumbling out. She remembered Nicholas and Chatham, Bermondsey and Mr Keyse, Mrs Dobbs, Emma, Kitty and the other girls in Half Moon Street, Bartholomew and his sister Hester, the Waterman's Arms, Grace, Matthew and Sophy. At the centre of it all, though, was George. George, whose tiny face was fading from her memory. George, whom she had been so determined to reclaim, but knew now she never could. Molly broke down into sobs and covered her face.

She sobbed and sobbed, until no more tears would come. Then she got up and splashed her face with cold water over and over again, hoping it would ease the puffiness and redness. She would leave the inn, she resolved. But first she would go downstairs and thank Charlie for all his kindness to her. He didn't need to know what she had done but he deserved to know that she couldn't go with him.

She had to wait a while for Charlie at the dinner table, refusing all offers of food and drink other than a piece of bread. She didn't eat it, but employed her nervous fingers in rolling it into pellets while she waited. Her heart leapt when Charlie finally took his seat at the table, full of apologies for being away so long. But she hardened her heart to him. It was important to make him understand that she wasn't the girl he remembered. She was a woman now, one who had made bad decisions, decisions she would have to live with for the rest of her life. Matthew's words, passed on by Hester, had resurfaced. She had *the encumbrance of a child*, something that would clearly count against her for ever.

Her voice sounded strange to her ears as she told Charlie that she was no longer the person he thought he knew. It was an effort to continue but she knew she must, although she made no mention of George. Her heart would have broken if she had. She should have got up and left him as soon as she'd said what needed saying, but she didn't. She sat and listened to him tell her about the future that could be hers at Woodchurch Manor, and how he would take care of her. And all of this without him expecting anything from her, or so he said.

Then he ordered food for them as if they were an ordinary couple, just finished discussing some minor domestic problem, and she felt so tired and so secure that all thoughts of fleeing the inn left her and she found herself agreeing to the journey, to returning to Woodchurch Manor with him, to a different sort of future for herself.

That night, she slept a deep and dreamless sleep, and she went early down to breakfast the next morning to find Charlie already waiting. He made no comment as she set her bundle beside her on the chair, instead telling her of the journey that lay ahead, how they would travel by stage coach while the specimens for the garden followed by wagon.

She ate a hasty breakfast while he went to settle the bill with Mrs Beale. Agnes stopped at the table to say goodbye to her. 'I would like to know how your story ends, Molly. I hope one day you will come back to tell us.' Then, to Molly's surprise, she bent to kiss her cheek before hurrying away to the kitchen.

Molly dozed on and off throughout the journey and afterwards could not have told anyone anything about it, other than that they passed alongside and over the river and through parts of London that she wondered whether she recognised. They went on and on, past fields and cottages, with a stop to change horses and have food that she didn't really want. The road became bumpier, jolting the coach and its occupants. At one point, when she and Charlie were the only two people seated inside, she slid her hand into his. Although he looked surprised, he clasped it lightly and so they travelled on, as darkness fell and Molly dozed again. When she awoke, the coach was slowing to a halt and Charlie was looking out of the window. Two minutes later, they were standing at the side of the road in darkness, his bag at his feet while she clutched her bundle.

'Just along here,' Charlie said, sounding cheerful. And he took her hand this time, to guide her as she stumbled along, stiff from the long hours of sitting in the coach and apprehensive as to what lay ahead.

CHAPTER SIXTY-TWO

Winter was mild that year at Woodchurch Manor and Charlie had been hard at work in the garden almost every day. At first, Molly had appreciated the length of his absences for she continued to sleep for hours at a time in the cottage that Charlie now called home. It was set at one end of a terrace of small houses along a lane on the edge of the estate, with views over fields at the front. When they had first arrived there from London, the weather was wet and the drabness of the outlook oppressed Molly's spirits and made her unwilling to leave her bed. Her single room looked out into the woodland cradling the cottages at the back, and she would lie on her bed and gaze at the branches shifting in the wind against a grey sky, until her eyes closed. When she woke again, she was muzzy-headed and never quite sure whether it was day or night, other than from the meals that Charlie brought to her door, gently knocking to wake her.

As autumn gave way to winter and the last leaves fell from the trees, the skies cleared to reveal unbroken blue and Molly grew tired of being cooped up with her thoughts. She started to get up for breakfast with Charlie before he left for the gardens and she watched him set off down the lane, the overnight frost still crisping the grass until the rising sun lifted the temperature.

Molly began to walk out each day, at first avoiding times when she might be forced into contact with their neighbours in the terrace, but gradually progressing to nodding terms despite their curious glances. She supposed there would be gossip as to what she was doing there, a single woman staying in an unmarried man's cottage. She thought it best to ask Charlie what he had told others of her presence.

'I've told them nothing,' he said, and laughed. 'Mr Powell knows and it's of no consequence to him that you are staying here.' He looked at her troubled face and smiled. 'You can say that we're friends from childhood. It's the truth, after all.'

Molly began to make small changes within the cottage, moving the furniture around in the sitting room and rearranging the few plates, pots and pans in the kitchen. She insisted on taking over the cooking and they ate well, Charlie being provided with vegetables from the Woodchurch Manor store as well as the occasional gift of meat or wildfowl.

As December wore on, Charlie asked her – with some diffidence – whether she would like to accompany him to Margate. 'I have some purchases to make for the garden and I thought you might wish to buy fabric and see about having another dress made? And perhaps visit your family.'

Molly was silent. She disliked the memories that came with the only two dresses she had from her days at the Waterman's Arms. She would have loved to have something new to wear, but she had no money of her own. And she had no wish, yet, to see her family.

Finally, she spoke. 'I think perhaps I will join you when you next go into Canterbury. For now, I'm content to forgo a visit to Margate.'

Charlie didn't pursue the matter but he came back from Margate with a length of blue cloth, which he said the draper had advised would be sufficient to make a dress. Molly was deeply touched by his thoughtfulness but before she could respond he continued, 'Oh, and I have news of your family.'

Molly's new-found equilibrium seemed at risk. She both wanted to know, and feared what she would hear.

'I went to visit Mr Fleming, as I always do when I'm in Margate,' Charlie went on. 'He said your sisters still come to visit him in the garden.'

Molly was wistful – she would have dearly loved to see Lizzie and Mary, and Mr Fleming. Charlie misinterpreted her expression.

'I made no mention of your presence here,' he said quickly, in an effort to reassure her. 'Mr Fleming said your sisters are well, little Harriet too, and growing fast.' He looked sheepish. 'I did ask whether they had mentioned having news of you and he said no, that they still wondered over your disappearance and feared you lost for ever.' He paused. 'When you left, you were heard asking about how you might get to Chatham and your uncle asked his son, Nicholas, if there was news of you there. He said he had made enquiries but there was none.' Charlie paused again and looked at her.

She wondered how much he knew. Since her sisters had reported not knowing what had happened to her it seemed likely that her father and Hannah, the only people who knew about the baby, had kept their counsel. Could it do any good to tell all to Charlie now?

Before she could speak, Charlie pressed on. 'Mr Fleming had more news. I gather Nicholas has not brought the hoped-for glory on the family. Rumour in the town has it that he has deserted his ship – in the West Indies, I believe. Your uncle William is tight-lipped on the matter but a story came back with Nicholas's shipmates that a woman was involved. His wife, Sarah, has returned to her family.'

Charlie had turned away from Molly, busying himself removing his purchases from his bag as he spoke. She was glad, for her cheeks were burning.

She had tried very hard to put Nicholas out of her mind since their encounter in Chatham. She had come across many young men like him during her days in London, and she had the measure of him now. She would happily have forgotten about him for ever, if it wasn't for George. The sharp reminder of her lost son brought Molly to her feet and, making the excuse to Charlie of a sudden sick headache, she went up to her room. The troubled expression in Charlie's brown eyes, as he'd turned at her words, stayed with her as she lay down on the bed. She had imagined that, following Charlie's news, her thoughts would be of her family, of Nicholas and of George, but instead she found herself thinking only of Charlie. He had been so kind to her and so caring since he had found her in the Apothecaries' Garden. And she had been so thoughtless and cruel to him when they had parted at Woodchurch Manor well over two years earlier. Then, she had been so sure of her future. Now, she had no idea what it would bring.

She knew that Charlie cared deeply for her – he demonstrated it every day in the way he spoke to and behaved towards her. She had been content to accept it until now, for he appeared to expect nothing in return. His behaviour seemed natural, not calculated. But his expression just now had given him away.

She didn't know whether she could love anyone ever again. But if it would make Charlie happy to have her as his wife she was resolved to try. Hearing the news of her family today made her long to see her sisters, as well as her father, Aunt Jane and Uncle William. News of Nicholas's transgression somehow made that easier to countenance, although she would still need to provide them with a reason for her disappearance.

She looked at the bundle on the chair, set there when she had arrived in September and remaining ever since. She got down from the bed and went over to it. She untied the corners of the fabric and opened it, stroking the wool of the blanket, and sniffing it, breathing in deeply to see whether it held any traces of George's scent. Then she picked up the playing card and handkerchief fragments and kissed them. Tears ran down her cheeks as she retied the bundle, then stowed it carefully in the wall cupboard, on the top shelf.

She would never forget George. He would be two years old soon and she knew that, even if she found him tomorrow, he wouldn't know who she was, so much time had passed. She wondered whether it would be fair to reclaim him, if she was in a position to do so. She had failed him. He was better off without her. To imagine otherwise was unfair to him. However painful it was for her, she had to let him go, for his sake. It was the price she must pay for her own folly.

The thought brought her such physical pain that she doubled over and was forced to sit down again on the bed. Then, slowly, she straightened. Her real future, one she hadn't imagined for herself, needed to begin here.

CHAPTER SIXTY-THREE

Spring sunshine poured through the great glass lantern in the ceiling of the picture gallery. Molly paused in her dusting and looked around the room. The dark-red walls were hung with pictures in heavy gilt frames, portraits of family members and of naval battles to which she gave only a cursory glance. As usual, her eyes were drawn to two paintings, tiny by comparison, one above the other, that hung near the door. She always stopped in front of them as she left. The top image depicted a horseman, resplendent in a red jacket and a top hat, astride a prancing horse with hounds at his feet as he paused in front of the Dandelion, the old gateway on the road a distance out of Margate. The second picture, of a street in a coastal town, featured two young ladies who had just left a shop, parasols at the ready to be unfurled against the sun, despite the breeze that blew at their skirts and filled the sails of the ships visible in the harbour beyond.

Molly always smiled to herself at the thought that she had been the model for one of the young ladies in the second picture, painted by Will seven years before. And she had helped him to find the location for the Dandelion painting, too.

She had been in the picture gallery one day when Mr Powell had brought some house guests in to see his paintings. She'd made a move to leave as unobtrusively as possible but

Mr Powell had motioned her to stay. She'd carried on with her work and heard him say, 'It's these two paintings I'm most proud of. They're early works by the young William Turner, the one who's making such a name for himself, these days. They'll be worth something one day, I suppose.' Then they'd moved on to debate the merits of the depiction of one of the naval battles and Molly had slipped away. Would she ever see Will again? She thought regretfully of Will's Christmas gift to her, the painting she had been forced to leave behind when she'd fled Mrs Dobbs's house. Her old landlady would have been startled to learn that the picture had some value. If she ever troubled to find out, it would be more than recompense for the money she had said Molly owed her. Then she pushed the thought away. She didn't want to be reminded of her days in Covent Garden.

She'd been working at Woodchurch Manor since just before Christmas and she was very happy there. She'd heard the other servants talk of how Charlie was held in such high esteem by Mr Powell, which only added to her happiness. She had seen how much Charlie loved the gardens and only that Sunday, as they walked back from the tiny church on the estate, he had drawn her through the gate into the walled garden and taken her around it, pointing out all the renovations and changes for which he was responsible.

She'd thought, as they both stood looking at the pomegranate tree, newly unwrapped from the sacking that had been its winter protection since its journey from the Apothecaries' Garden, that he might kiss her. They had turned towards each other and their eyes had locked. It was the matter of a heartbeat or two, then the moment passed. But she'd wished for it, she realised afterwards.

Now, as she finished the dusting and stopped, as usual,

before Will's paintings, she knew what the summer would bring. She would visit her family at last. And there would be a wedding. Here, at the tiny church on the estate. She still feared there was a secret part of her that she could never share with Charlie. But she would make him a good wife. Of that, at least, she was sure.

Acknowledgements

Special thanks to my local writing group in Deal for their weekly support and encouragement, to my agent Kiran at Keane Kataria and my editor Eleanor Russell at Piatkus, to Hazel Orme and Sandra Ferguson for their eagle eyes and fine-tooth comb, and to all the rest of the team involved in helping me bring *The Margate Maid* to life.

HISTORICAL NOTE

This novel is a fictionalisation of a period in history and although every effort has been made to retain historical accuracy, some liberties have been taken with the setting and historical events of the time.

Jane Austen and JMW Turner were born in the same year (1775) and both had associations with east Kent. Turner studied at Thomas Coleman's school in Margate between 1785 and 1788 and three of his undated but early works of St John's Church, the High Street and Dandelion inspired scenes in the book. I was intrigued by the idea that as Jane Austen was also a regular visitor to Goodnestone, only a few miles from Margate, their paths might have crossed, although her documented visits took place a few years later.

The Shell Grotto in Margate exists and can be visited today. It was discovered in 1835, but no one is sure when it was created, or why: a Regency folly or a pagan temple are just two of the suggestions.

The Royal Naval Dockyard was established in Chatham in the mid-sixteenth century, but the Naval mooring at Admiralty Wharf is a figment of my imagination.

The Foundling Hospital's method of choosing infants to be admitted by the lottery of coloured balls was mostly discontinued by 1760 but recorded in use on occasion after that date.

The location of Woodchurch Manor and its estate is loosely based on that of Quex House, but otherwise everything about it is fictional.

Not ready to say goodbye to Molly?

Read on for a first look at the next book in
The Margate Maid series,

THE SECRET CHILD

Molly looked at her three daughters, each bent over her needlework, and bit her lip to suppress a smile. She felt quite sure that Catherine, the youngest and possessor of wild chestnut curls, would be the first to fling aside her embroidery with a wail. She would undoubtedly have pricked her finger, knotted her thread or discovered that she had run out of space to complete the word she was stitching.

Sally, the eldest and named after Molly's mother, had inherited her father Charlie's height and dark eyes and was guaranteed to carry on methodically until she was told to stop. If she was given a task, she liked to complete it, and it went without saying that the work would be neat, the stitches precise.

Agnes, aged almost ten, exactly fifteen months older than Catherine and fifteen months younger than Sally, had stopped to gaze out of the window. Molly guessed that she was wondering what creative touch she could add to her sampler. She'd already included an oak tree at the side of the grand building that represented Woodchurch Manor – just visible across the fields from the window of the kitchen where they were sitting. Sally had been shocked by this flight of fancy, while Catherine had been envious. Sparrows were squabbling in the cherry tree outside their own window as they stitched, and Molly had a feeling that they would find their likeness stitched into her middle daughter's work. Indeed, Molly noticed that Agnes had chosen some brown thread from the selection on the table and had bent over her work once more. The thread was almost the exact shade of Agnes's hair.

'Thank goodness there are only five of us, Ma,' Sally said. 'I've stitched your name, and Pa's, and there's just room enough for the three of us across the bottom.'

She held out her work for Molly to see. Under the neatly stitched mansion she had added 'Molly Dawson' and 'Charles Dawson' in tiny cross-stitches, either side of the year of their marriage, 1792. Below this, she was stitching the names of herself and her sisters, leaving just enough room next to her own name to add the current year, 1805.

Molly smiled to see the unusual formality of the name 'Charles' used for her husband, instead of Charlie. Then her lips began to tremble and her eyes filled with tears.

Sally's own smile faded and she looked down at her work, then back at her mother. 'Have I done something wrong?' she asked. She looked rather as though she might cry, too.

Agnes and Catherine had both laid down their samplers and were watching, worry creasing their brows.

'No, no, it's beautiful,' Molly was at pains to reassure her eldest daughter. 'You've put so much work into it. Why, you've all but finished.'

She glanced quickly at Agnes and Catherine. 'You've all worked really hard today. Just another half-hour and then we can put them away.'

Molly put down her own sewing and moved to the window to gaze out over the fields. She had been living in this cottage, one of a terrace tied to the Woodchurch Manor estate, for thirteen years now. Charlie was the head gardener and would be hard at work somewhere in the grounds, or perhaps in a meeting with Mr Powell, the owner of Woodchurch Manor, going over the latest plans.

Despite the passage of time she was still, every so often, floored by the terrible memory of the child who wasn't there, whose name wouldn't be stitched into the family sampler. Her darling boy, whom she had left at the Foundling Hospital in London, two years before her marriage. Left behind when he was but a few weeks old.

She had never told Charlie of his existence, although when she had given up her baby she had been determined to reclaim him at the first possible opportunity. Indeed, for the first two years she had scrimped and saved, hoping to find enough money to make reparation for his care. But she hadn't been able to make a respectable home for him, and when her savings were stolen, she had fallen into despair. As time passed she had tried to convince herself that, with a new name and undoubtedly no memory of her, he was better off without her. A small part of her knew, though, that this was no excuse.

How could she explain him to Charlie, to her own family and now, of course, to his half-sisters? She still had her portion of the tokens she had left behind with him at the Foundling Hospital, her unique mementoes that would allow her to reclaim him. She knew that Charlie would have given her the money needed to repay the hospital for her boy's care, but she had never asked for it. And she had never visited London in all the years since she had left it, although Charlie went frequently on Mr Powell's business. Molly rarely strayed far from the environs of Woodchurch Manor.

Now, in any case, it was too late. Her son was of an age at which he would have left the school at the Foundling Hospital. He would be apprenticed somewhere, or perhaps he had gone into the Navy. England was at war with France, which lay just a few miles distant over the sea from where they were sitting. Molly knew that many young men had volunteered for the Navy, and many of those who hadn't had been 'persuaded' that it was in their best interests. Would her son be among them? Would his life be at risk?

She had berated herself many times for leaving it too long to reclaim him. Now she feared that she would never know what had become of him. Sally's rejoicing that there were only five family names to stitch into her sampler had struck Molly hard. Her son's name – whatever it was now – would be missing for ever from this family record.

Molly gazed out of the window, gripping the edge of the sill as she fought to hold back the sobs that would frighten her daughters if she gave vent to them. It seemed impossible that so many years had passed. So many years since her girls' first tottering steps, first teeth, first words. And with every new milestone she'd been pierced through the heart that her son would have had these milestones, too, and she'd missed them all. Someone else had mopped his infant tears, held his hand and sung him to sleep. She hoped they had been kind.

Her heart turned over at the thought of him sent back to the Foundling Hospital at the age of five by his foster mother. His life would have changed again: he would have found himself sleeping in a dormitory, going to lessons in the Foundling School in that brown-and-white uniform she'd seen all the children wearing. He'd have had no one to comfort him if he fell over, to soothe him when he had a fever, to tell him that whatever ailed him would pass.

Why hadn't she gone to reclaim him? It puzzled her, even now. She'd tortured herself with memories, so faded that she couldn't even remember his face – just the horror of being parted from him. She hadn't fetched him, she thought, because once she was wed and with children of her own to care for they had been her priority. How would they manage with an older, bigger boy to feed?

But she knew that was nonsense: they would have managed perfectly well. She wondered now whether she had been frightened. Frightened that he would hate her for what she had done by leaving him for others to bring up. And then it had been too late. She'd persuaded herself that it was better they never met, never knew: that the past was buried.

Each year on his birthday, 7 January, she remembered how it had felt to have his small head nestled into her shoulder in those first weeks, his snuffling noises as he stirred, and she wept a few tears, alone. Then she went on and faced the day, and every day after that, but she didn't forget.

Behind her, Catherine flung down her sampler. 'Half an hour has gone by. Can we go and see Pa?'

Molly was ready to reprimand her youngest daughter for her impatience, but when she looked at the clock she saw that Catherine was right. 'It's a beautiful afternoon,' she said, moving away from the window. 'Tidy up your sewing and we'll walk along the lane. It's too early to disturb your pa at work but we can see what the spring sunshine has brought to the hedgerows.'

Catherine hastily rolled up her sampler and stuffed it into the workbox, then hurried in search of her shawl and bonnet before her mother changed her mind. Agnes had spread hers on the table to gaze at the effect, and Molly saw that birds were indeed fluttering from the tree, ready to land on the roof of Woodchurch Manor. Sally was reluctant to be dragged away – she had been intent on finishing her sampler that day.

'We must make the most of the weather,' Molly told her. 'It may be raining again by tomorrow. It's only April, although it looks more like summer out there today.'

She joined Catherine in the doorway, where she was ready and waiting with Molly's bonnet and shawl in her hands. As Catherine unlatched the door and opened it, a cool, fresh scent wafted in. Molly bent to tie the laces of her boots. It would be good to be outside in the fresh air, away from the memories crowding in on her. She told Catherine – already in the lane – to wait, and turned back to Sally and Agnes to chivvy them along. Then, picking their way around puddles left by the morning's rain, they set off for their walk. Molly, with the grim determination that had worked for her many times before, attempted to banish all thoughts of her lost son from her mind.